Blac...
Brides

Bound by more than just blackmail…

Three passionate novels!

*In November 2006 Mills & Boon bring
back two of their classic collections,
each featuring three favourite
romances by our bestselling authors...*

BLACKMAILED BRIDES

The Blackmailed Bride
by Kim Lawrence
Bride by Blackmail by Carole Mortimer
Blackmailed by the Boss
by Kathryn Ross

GIFT-WRAPPED LOVE

Christmas Knight by Meredith Webber
Christmas in Paris by Margaret Barker
Home by Christmas by Jennifer Taylor

Blackmailed Brides

THE BLACKMAILED BRIDE
by
Kim Lawrence

BRIDE BY BLACKMAIL
by
Carole Mortimer

BLACKMAILED BY
THE BOSS
by
Kathryn Ross

MILLS & BOON®

MILLS & BOON and MILLS & BOON with the Rose Device
are registered trademarks of the publisher.
Harlequin Mills & Boon Limited,
Eton House, 18-24 Paradise Road, Richmond, Surrey, TW9 1SR

BLACKMAILED BRIDES
© by Harlequin Enterprises II B.V., 2006

The Blackmailed Bride, Bride by Blackmail and *Blackmailed by the
Boss* were first published in Great Britain by Harlequin Mills &
Boon Limited in separate, single volumes.

The Blackmailed Bride © Kim Lawrence 2002
Bride by Blackmail © Carole Mortimer 2003
Blackmailed by the Boss © Kathryn Ross 2003

ISBN 10: 0 263 84972 4
ISBN 13: 978 0 263 84972 1

05-1106

*Printed and bound in Spain
by Litografia Rosés S.A., Barcelona*

THE BLACKMAILED BRIDE

by

Kim Lawrence

Kim Lawrence lives on a farm in rural Anglesey. She runs two miles daily and finds this an excellent opportunity to unwind and seek inspiration for her writing! It also helps her keep up with her husband, two active sons, and the various stray animals which have adopted them. Always a fanatical consumer of fiction, she is now equally enthusiastic about writing. She loves a happy ending!

CHAPTER ONE

JAVIER drove through the large ornate gates and up the long winding driveway lined with olive trees towards the distinctive Moorish tower that stood against the backdrop of the mountains. He pulled the Mercedes he was driving in a space beside a battered Beetle which stood out like a sore thumb amongst the other expensive models.

So, Serge still hadn't persuaded Sarah to part with her old car. An easy-going young woman who would, as a rule, do anything for her husband, Sarah did have a few blind spots.

Javier himself was unmarried, but did not lack female companionship. It had never required much, if any, effort on his part to have attractive women hanging on his every word, but no special woman had ever materialised from these adoring masses. The possibility that if and when he discovered her she wouldn't be interested had simply not crossed his mind!

Then he'd met Sarah.

Now he was thirty-two, didn't take *anything* for granted, and was, he liked to think, more discerning about women— *too* damned discerning, according to his grandfather, who wanted his chosen heir safely married.

Javier could have taken the easy option and chosen a suitable consort, a woman from a background similar to his own that would enable her to cope with the pressures of being a member of one of the wealthiest families in Europe, just as his father before him had. That was the problem, everytime he was tempted to take the easy way out Javier was confronted by the spectre of his parents' disastrous union.

Before he'd left the family estate in Andalucia to make the journey to Majorca the old man had finally issued an ultimatum.

'Marry before I die or I'll leave everything to Raul or one of the others!' Felipe Montero had warned his favourite grandson dramatically.

Javier's immediate reaction to this not very subtle blackmail had been anger; did his grandfather know him so little that he imagined he could be bought…?

He turned to Felipe with much of the pride and hauteur his grandfather was famed for etched on his own chiselled features. What he saw in the old man's lined face made him bite back the caustic response hovering on his tongue.

Javier had no illusions about what his grandfather was capable of. Felipe Montero was devious, he frequently bullied and connived, he routinely plotted and schemed—in short, when it came to getting his own way he was capable of acts of great ruthlessness. However he was never crude in his manipulations and, even more significantly, Javier had never seen his grandfather look frightened before!

'You'll live a long time yet…?'

Felipe smiled; Javier had never needed things spelled out. He was a sharp judge of character who read people almost as well as he read the financial markets.

'No, as a matter of fact I won't. The doctors give me six months at the outside.'

Javier didn't tell Felipe that this wasn't possible, he didn't scream, as people often did when they were confronted with the mortality of someone they couldn't imagine life without, that the doctors *must* be able to do something.

He wanted to, but he didn't.

Instead after a short pause he nodded, not insulting his grandfather by questioning the grim prognosis.

'What is it?'

'Cancer. The damned thing's spread from my lungs. So there's not much point packing these things in,' Felipe observed with a deep throaty chuckle as he inhaled deeply on his cheroot. 'And don't tell anyone else yet—*nobody*. If the news gets out millions will be wiped off the value of the company...' A flicker of revulsion appeared in the older man's eyes. 'And I don't doubt they'll all start treating me as if I'm in my dotage,' he added, a tremor in his deep voice. It wasn't dying but the manner of it that scared Felipe Montero.

'No one will do that.'

A silent promise was exchanged in the look that passed between the two men.

Felipe sighed, satisfied. 'Unfortunately this couldn't come at a worst time, of course, with the Brussels deal...'

An extremely disciplined man, it wasn't often that Javier's emotions got the better of him, but as he listened to his grandfather fret about the fate of the financial empire he'd expanded up over his lifetime something snapped.

'There is such a thing as a good time to die?' he gritted. 'To hell with the company!' His deep voice cracked. 'You're going to *die,* Grandfather.'

'We're all going to die,' came the careless response. 'If you really care,' Felipe goaded slyly, 'show it. Marry Aria...she loves you.'

A wry laugh was wrenched from Javier. 'You never give up, do you?'

If and when he did marry, Javier knew it wouldn't be to someone who loved him, someone he might hurt as his father had his mother. A fragile creature, his mother had never grasped the fact she was meant to turn a blind eye to her husband's mistresses; she was meant to look attractive, bring up their son and be the perfect hostess.

'This is no laughing matter, Javier,' the old man reproached sternly. 'Continuity, blood lines are important; you need sons.'

'I'm sorry, but I can't.'

The idea of losing his inheritance didn't frighten Javier.

He immediately recognised that there was part of him that might actually welcome the situation. A man who needed the constant buzz of physical and mental challenges, he could think of few things more exciting than the challenge of starting from scratch, and few things more satisfying than knowing at the end of the day that everything you'd achieved was down to your own efforts, nothing to do with being born into a wealthy dynasty.

Wealth brought its privileges, but Javier had been raised to believe it also carried responsibilities. His deeply ingrained sense of family duty would never allow him to do anything more than occasionally dream about the luxury of being a free agent.

Deep down, however, he was pretty sure it wouldn't come to that, his grandfather would never disinherit him for standing his ground. Nothing in his manner even hinted at this belief. He couldn't do much for his grandfather but he could at least let Felipe play the heartless tyrant he liked the world to see him as.

Felipe searched his grandson's unyielding face with growing frustration. 'This is about that silly blonde you let Serge snatch right from under your nose, I suppose... Don't look so stunned, boy.' He laughed. 'Do you think I'm blind? If you want my opinion, she'd have been a disastrous match for you...'

Javier swallowed his anger with difficulty.

'...Far too sweet and malleable. You need someone with a bit more fire...'

'Like *Aria*,' Javier cut in drily.

Felipe conceded this point with a grunt. 'Well, it doesn't *have* to be her…but if you want to be my heir you'll marry someone and soon…'

'We shouldn't be arguing…not now…'

'Why change the habit of a lifetime? If you start agreeing with me the family will know something's wrong straight away, and I won't be able to move for everyone being *nice* to me,' he observed with a shudder.

When two people who were congenitally incapable of compromise worked together there were bound to be some sparks. Javier's combustible relationship with his grandfather was not without its moments of conflict, often vocal conflict, at least on Felipe's side—Javier was more inclined to smouldering silences. Javier knew his rivals within the family frequently crossed their fingers and hoped he'd overstep the mark one day and alienate the old man totally. What they failed to understand was the deep mutual respect the warring parties felt for each other.

'I'm sorry.'

'You're a stubborn idiot!' the old man railed at his tall grandson's retreating back.

A man with extraordinary self-discipline, Javier pushed aside the personal issues that filled his mind as he stepped out of the air-conditioned luxury of his Mercedes. He barely registered the blast of baking heat which immediately hit him; Majorca had been experiencing one of its hottest Julys on record.

He consulted the discreet but expensive metallic banded watch on his wrist and nodded; he had a few minutes to spare. He couldn't abide poor time-keeping in others and always made a point of never abusing his position of power by keeping others waiting himself. To his mind punctuality was a matter of simple good manners.

As he made his way towards the rear entrance of the large mellow stone building even his well-known critical eye for detail could find no fault in the delightful terraced gardens and wide, well-tended sweeps of green tree-dotted parkland. The pool area, when he reached it, was almost deserted but for a few stalwart—or was it foolish?—tourists sunning themselves in the fiery Majorcan midday sun.

'Did you see who that was?' a female guest hissed excitedly as she clambered wetly out of the pool.

Her sleepy husband opened his eyes reluctantly as wet hands urgently grabbed his shoulder. 'Who…what…?'

'There, it's *Javier Montero!*' she hissed as the tall man in the exquisitely cut suit shook hands in a friendly manner with the elderly gardener before moving away.

'Sure, Javier Montero is on first name terms with all the casual labourers on the island…'

'There's no need to be sarcastic. I tell you, it was him. I mean, there can't be two men who look like him.'

'Don't drool, Jean. And think, woman, what would Javier be doing here?'

'Why wouldn't he be here?' she responded, with a gesture that encompassed the extensive grounds of the thirteenth-century Majorcan manor house with its distinctive Moorish tower. 'He owns the place.'

An army of local craftsmen had returned the once neglected building to its original splendour. Tucked away in the Sierra de Tramuntana the exclusive hotel now provided a hideaway for those people who liked their retreats to combine the most up to date modern conveniences with historic ambience, top-class Mediterranean cuisine and personal attention from helpful staff.

Naturally this combination was very costly, but no more so than the other two hotels the Monteros owned on the island. Each establishment was aimed to appeal to specific clientele. People who wanted the cosmopolitan sophistication of Palma would find everything they could want in the elegant surroundings of the hotel situated right in the middle of the medieval old town; and those who liked a resort that offered them the choice of six top-class restaurants on site, a spa and every sporting facility known to man, with top-class tuition thrown in, would adore the resort hotel on the beautiful undeveloped northern coast of the island.

'Sure, this hotel and God knows how many others around the world, and then there's the airline, the racehorses and the interests in property development. Is there any pie the Monteros don't have a finger in…?' he wondered enviously. 'I really doubt someone like Javier Montero involves himself in the day-to-day running of hotels,' he announced, settling himself back down to sleep.

'It was him.'

'If you say so,' her husband agreed, reapplying sunscreen to his peeling nose—it was too hot to fight.

He had been right on one count; though Javier was known to occasionally subject individual hotels to gruelling spot inspections, it wasn't part of his remit to involve himself in the day-to-day running of individual establishments. Javier's talents lay elsewhere.

Early on in his career he had displayed a remarkable ability for spotting untapped niches in the markets. This talent had been recognised and exploited, but he wasn't just an ideas man; when a project was beset by difficulties, be it labour disputes or legal wranglings, Javier was the person who could be relied upon to get things running.

The information that had brought him hot-foot to the island hardened the naturally severe cast of Javier's staggeringly handsome features as he knocked on the heavy oak-studded door of Serge's office.

Though of average height, due to his massively broad shoulders and deep barrel chest, the swarthy-skinned man behind the desk gave the impression of being much taller.

'Javier!' Serge rose to his feet with a welcoming smile and the two men clasped hands and hugged. 'It's been too long.'

'It has.' Javier responded with the sort of smile that would have shocked rigid those members of the press who had dubbed him Mr Deep Freeze. 'How are little Raul and…Sarah?' Nobody seeing him smile would have guessed that he experienced any difficulty saying this name. 'Where is she? I saw the car…'

'It broke down the last time she was here,' his friend admitted ruefully. 'You can laugh, Javier, but it isn't you that ends up pushing the cursed thing. Other than a stubborn, irrational affection for that old tin can on wheels, Sarah is fine—though your godson is keeping us both up nights.'

'Then I expect you could have done without me asking you to do some discreet digging for me…?'

Serge shook his head. 'Anything I can do, any time— you know this, Javier. I know you don't like me saying this, but if we live to be a hundred there still won't be enough time to pay you back what we owe you.'

'You owe me nothing, Serge.' Abruptly Javier changed the subject. 'About the other thing…' His dark angled eyebrows lifted and his eyes, startling blue in a face that was an even, deep gold, narrowed. 'You're sure about this, Serge?'

Serge sighed and looked grim. 'I'm afraid so. The reports you heard were right.'

'And you know who it is?'

'A waiter working at the resort, a Luis Gonzalez, youngish…about twenty five. He came to work there at the start of the season…'

Javier didn't make a note of the name but Serge knew that he would not forget the name or forgive the guilty party for the crime he had foolishly committed. Javier made a friend in a million but he was an implacable enemy.

'References?' Javier enquired, controlling his impatience; control was one of the things Javier prided himself on.

'Impeccable forgeries.'

'Nobody else is involved, nobody higher…?'

Serge Simeone shook his head.

Javier shrugged and squinted against the midday sun through the window, his expression inscrutable. 'Well, that's something.'

When it had come to his attention that a member of staff in the large resort hotel they owned down on the coast was using his position to deal drugs to guests, Javier, unsure as to how deep the rot was, had not risked involving any of the staff there; instead, he had gone to someone whose integrity he trusted totally.

'You haven't contacted the police yet?'

'You asked me to wait. What are you going to do, Javier?' His friend turned and for a moment Serge experienced a spasm of pity for the culprit. Javier's long, angular, aristocratic face had the texture of cold marble; his deep set eyes were equally chilling. Serge knew that Javier had precious little sympathy with recreational drug use and even less with those who peddled the stuff, after his younger sister had nearly lost her life to addiction.

'We're going to pay Luis a visit.'

Kate Anderson tried not to show her shock as she flicked through the pile of grainy, slightly out-of-focus photos her younger sister had silently handed her after she'd asked, 'Surely they can't be that bad…?' Now she knew they weren't talking a couple of topless shots on the beach which even their conservative parents could have laughed off.

'It could be anyone…?' she croaked, trying desperately to put a positive slant on a very negative situation as she handed them back to her sister, who tore the incriminating images into shreds and let them drop to the floor.

While the negatives were not in their possession, both sisters knew this defiance was just an empty gesture.

'It's not *anyone,* it's *me!* You've got to help me, Kate! You have to do *something,*' Susie added, her expression an accurate reflection of her total faith in her sister's ability to extract her from this present dilemma. After all, she'd been doing it successfully for the past twenty years. 'You can't let mum and dad find out…*I'd die…*'

Kate thought it was much more likely she'd have her generous allowance cut off, but then as far as Susie was concerned that probably amounted to much the same thing!

'That would be…awkward,' Kate admitted thinking of her parents' faces if confronted by semi-nude photos of their younger daughter. She didn't want to think about the consequences if they actually got into the hands of the press. She could think of several tabloids that would love to print compromising shots of a high court judge's daughter.

'What if he sends those photos to *Chris*…? He'll never believe I wasn't sleeping with Luis.'

'You weren't?'

Susie's wails got louder. 'See? Even you thought I was. Luis was someone to hang around with and go clubbing, he was fun… You don't believe me,' she accused. 'I can tell…'

'I believe you. Now hush, Susie, I'm thinking…' Kate pleaded as she concentrated on the problem facing them.

The frown line between her feathery brows, which like her lashes were dark in dramatic contrast to the silver-blonde hair colour both sisters had inherited from their

mother, deepened as she caught her lower lip between her
even white teeth.

Unlike her sister, Kate's features weren't *strictly* sym-
metrical; her mouth was too wide and full and her aquiline
nose had never inspired men to poetry. Her almond-shaped
brown eyes, without a doubt her best feature, were unfortunately more often than not concealed behind the round
lenses of her wire-framed spectacles.

With or without specs, the first impression people received of Kate Anderson was that she was a young woman
with a lively intelligence, sharp wit, and boundless reserves
of energy.

'Susie got my looks; Kate's the *sensible* one.' Kate had
lost count of the number of times she'd heard her mother
explain away her supposed deficiencies to people.

'What she lacks in looks she makes up for in personality,' was her father's kinder assessment.

Kate knew these were essentially accurate assessments,
and she hadn't done so badly out of the deal. *Sensible* had
given her a lifestyle she enjoyed; but just *occasionally,* especially when she saw the way men reacted when Susie
entered a room, she wished that she'd been standing a bit
closer to the front of the queue when they'd handed out the
sex appeal factor.

A spasm of sulky annoyance passed over Susie's pretty
face at this impatient dismissal; her tears in general evoked
a more sympathetic response.

Kate dropped down into the wicker chair and pulled her
knees up to her chin; her irritation bubbled to the surface.
'What on earth possessed you to get involved with the man
in the first place...? You're supposed to be engaged to
Chris... Are things all right between you and him, or are
you having second thoughts?'

'Don't start on about me being too young to settle down
again, Kate!' Susie scowled. 'I'm not like you; I don't want

a career and being engaged doesn't mean you can't have any fun,' she announced with a toss of her blonde head.

Kate didn't swallow this hard-nosed attitude for one minute, Susie was wilful but she was a long way from being as callous as she liked to pretend.

'*Fun!* Couldn't you have stuck to beach volley-ball?'

This evoked a watery smile. 'Well, if you had arrived last week, like you were meant to, I wouldn't have been so bored…' Susie stretched one long sun-tanned leg in front of her. The complacent contemplation of the smooth expanse of shapely golden flesh made the sulky line of her lips lift attractively.

Only Susie, Kate decided, could turn this thing around so that her sister had the ultimate responsibility—Susie really was totally impossible, Kate reflected with rueful affection.

'I had to work, you know that.'

'Work?' Susie snorted in disgust. 'It's all you ever think about. No wonder Seb dumped you.' She lifted her head, pushing a strand of long blonde hair from her eyes, and grimaced apologetically. 'Sorry, that was a bitchy thing to say,' she admitted. 'But,' she added swiftly in her own defence, 'this was the holiday from hell, even before Luis turned out to be a low-life, what with Mum and Dad spending every day traipsing around boring churches and things, wanting me to come along.' Her horrified expression was an accurate indicator that these pastimes weren't Susie's idea of pleasure. 'I always said a family holiday at our age was asking for trouble…'

'I thought you decided it wouldn't be so bad when you realised Dad was footing the bill,' Kate couldn't resist observing.

'I just thank God they didn't book that awful place in the mountains you fancied so much. There wasn't anything to do there but watch the grass grow.'

'There also wasn't a Luis.'

'Actually, Katie,' Susie began with an awkward rush, 'the photos…I think he might have spiked my drink when we were by the pool. I mean, I'm not one hundred per cent positive,' she added hurriedly, 'but I know a girl who had her drink spiked…'

Kate's horrified gasp went ignored as her sister, oblivious to the fact she'd said anything to send chills through Kate's blood, continued, 'Oh, she was all right. Fortunately a gang of us arrived as the stuff was kicking in and the guy in question made a quick exit. She collapsed in the loos and we had an awful job getting her back home,' she recalled. 'It's just B—*her* symptoms—' Susie corrected herself with a display of discretion that surprised Kate '—I felt a lot like that. I could hardly get back to my own room, I felt so woozy, and I'd only had a glass of white wine…'

'What a total sleaze!' Kate exclaimed in disgust. 'We should call the police.'

'Get serious, Kate!' Susie responded scornfully. 'I could kick myself. I'm normally really careful about things like that—I never leave my glass on a table, I carry it around with me. Of course, I *never* accept a drink from a man I don't know…'

'Of course,' Kate responded faintly.

As she had listened to Susie casually outlining the list of precautions which were obviously second nature to her, Kate wondered if she was herself extraordinarily trusting or just plain reckless, because even though she'd heard of such things happening since the advent of the so-called date rape drugs, she had never dreamt of taking any of these measures… But then she had never dated a stranger; her boyfriends such as they were had always been friends of friends or work colleagues.

'What really gets me, is that he didn't even *try* and touch

me… It was Dad's money he was interested in all along,
not me!'

'Well thank God for that!'

'I just feel such a fool. I was wondering how I was going
to let him down lightly; I thought he was potty about me.
God, Katie!' she wailed. 'What am I going to do…?'

Placing a comforting arm around the younger girl's shaking shoulders, Kate hugged her tight. She crossed her fingers. 'Don't worry, Suse, it'll be all right.' *I hope!*

'Then you'll lend me the money to pay him off…?'
Susie lifted her tear stained face eagerly.

'We're not giving him a penny,' Kate responded, her
tone outraged at the idea of giving into a blackmailer. 'I'll
get the photos and the negatives.'

'But how?'

'That,' admitted Kate frankly, 'I haven't worked out yet.'

'Listen, Kate, I don't think this is such a good idea. I
mean, Luis isn't going to hand them over, is he? And once
or twice I've seen him talking with some shifty-looking
types. Actually, I think he could be quite mean himself…'
She gave a shamefaced little grin. 'I suppose, if I'm honest,
that was half the attraction…the danger thing,' she sniffed.
'You know what I mean…' She looked at her elder sister
who pushed her specs up the bridge of her nose. 'I don't
suppose you do. I know you think I'm a selfish little cow
but even I might lose an hour or two's sleep if you got hurt
because of me.'

Kate pulled a tissue from the pocket of her shorts and
dabbed her sister's pink nose. 'Don't fret. I've no intention
of getting hurt, Suse.'

Kate had waited an hour in the darkness watching the staff
bungalow until she was satisfied there was nobody home.
The wait had taken its toll, by the time she tentatively tried
the door she felt physically sick with nerves and her heart

was pounding so loud, its frantic, echoey thud cut out all other sounds. She couldn't recall ever feeling this scared, not even the first time she'd made her court appearance as a newly qualified barrister.

She could hardly believe her luck when the door opened at the first try. Relieved she wouldn't have to put her admittedly hazy knowledge of lock picking—second hand, naturally—to the test, Kate slid the credit card she'd brought for the purpose into the back pocket of her dark jeans and adjusted the dark hood on her head so that it covered all her pale hair.

Shining her torch around the darkened room, she picked her way stealthily through the discarded garments littering the carpet. Her skin crawled and she stifled a scream as her foot got entangled in a shirt. This whole enterprise was making her feel grubby. *After this is over I'll need a stiff drink and a bath, not necessarily in that order* she thought as she carefully balanced the torch on top of the chest of drawers.

Her hands were shaking so much, it took her two goes to slide the top drawer open. *Concentrate, Kate* she told herself, taking a deep fortifying breath. *It's my lucky day* she decided as her fingers closed around an envelope—the shape of which felt very promising...

Her newly fortified wits fled gibbering in panic as the room was suddenly flooded with strong light from a powerful flashlight that dwarfed her own feeble beam. Before she even had a chance to turn around, a pair of strong arms snaked around her, pinning one arm to her chest as, arched backwards by the tight embrace, her feet were lifted off the ground.

Her rudimentary Spanish could not cope with the staccato burst of furious-sounding words which hissed like bullets in her ear. With Susie's warnings about this blackmailer and his shady friends ringing in her ears, she began to struggle wildly. With her free arm she flailed backwards, trying to inflict as much damage as possible, enough at least to make her captor loosen his grip. A chair and several sundry items, including her glasses, were casualties of her frenzied efforts to free herself.

Only this captor wasn't letting her go, not even when she brought her trainer-shod heel—stilettos would have produced much more satisfactory results—down viciously onto his instep, the way they'd taught her in self-defence class. She took small comfort from the fact it must have hurt like hell because he cursed—at least it sounded like a curse.

Kate wasn't a short woman and, though slim, she wasn't delicate—she kept herself fit, she ran and enjoyed playing sports—but it soon became clear to her that she was vastly outclassed. It was obvious that restraining her was not overly exerting her captor, who wasn't even breathing heavily. A pragmatist, she quickly accepted she couldn't fight her way out of this situation—that left talking her way out, and she was good at that...

'Please...let me go!' she panted, forcing her body to go limp.

'*English?*'

The startled exclamation across the room was the first indication to her that she wasn't only outclassed but outnumbered too.

'You're English?' The low, cultured voice close to her ear had only the faintest husky tinge of an attractive accent.

This must be one of the waiter's sinister friends, she reasoned, recalling Susie's comments on Luis's charming broken English—unless that too had been part of his scam.

'Of course I'm English!' she exclaimed at her most haughty.

'*A woman...?*' The voice from across the room exclaimed.

'I had noticed,' her captor replied drily before switching to rapid Spanish.

Probably issuing instructions about where to dispose of my body, Kate thought, as she struggled in vain to catch the gist of what was being said. Her mind was working furiously. How long will it be before anyone misses me…? Not until morning at the earliest, she realised with dismay.

She'd excused herself early from dinner with her parents, pleading a headache, and if Susie had carried on drinking wine at the rate she had been when Kate had left she would now either be dead to the world or dancing the night away in the nearest night-club.

'I'm going to put you down now. Do not try to escape.'

Kate nodded her head compliantly whilst privately vowing to do just the opposite should the opportunity arise.

Released from the iron grip and with her feet back on the ground, Kate's knees displayed the consistency of cotton wool. Fortunately her spirit was more resilient. Chin up—not too much: she didn't want to come across as bolshy, more an innocent victim of circumstance—she turned to face her aggressors.

'Will you take that thing out of my eyes?' she appealed, lifting a hand to shield her eyes from the glare of the torch.

After a moment someone responded to her request.

She could now see, though the loss of her specs meant the one standing some way away was nothing but a blurred outline suggestive of threatening bulk. The one who had held her was another matter! He was close enough for her to see quite well. Like herself, he was clad from head to toe in black. There the similarity ended!

The hard, lean, muscle-packed torso Kate already knew about from her struggles; the rest of the package reduced her to a stunned silence. She blinked several times as she assimilated the attributes of her assailant, who ironically turned out to be the most physically perfect specimen of manhood she'd ever come across. These numerous attributes included ridiculously broad shoulders, snaky slim hips and long legs, and then there was his face…!

And what a face! God I'm thinking in superlatives, some objective corner of her mind observed as she drank in the details of his long, arrestingly attractive, angular features. His was a starkly uncompromising face—a high intelligent forehead, an almost hawkish nose reminiscent of the strong Moorish inheritance she'd seen reflected in many parts of Spain, his beautifully sculpted slashing cheekbones stretched his even golden-toned skin taut and his mouth was an intriguing combination of control and passion. The jutting angles and sculpted planes married sweetly, giving their owner a countenance that could never be overlooked in a crowd, but combined with his incongruously blue eyes, fringed with extravagant lush lashes and slanted ebony brows, the exceptional became the extraordinary.

The deep-set, startling blue eyes narrowed as he subjected her to a scrutiny just as thorough as her own of him—he didn't appear overly impressed by what he saw. 'Now, *señorita,* where is Gonzalez?' he demanded impatiently.

CHAPTER TWO

MUTELY Kate shook her head.

He subjected her to another glare of biting derision before abruptly firing a quick sentence in Spanish at his companion who immediately extinguished the light.

For a moment there was total inky darkness. Kate, her brain working frantically, began to speculate on her chances of getting to the door before she was caught. It had to be evens or better? What did she have to lose? Quite a lot, actually, came the instant reply, and besides you haven't got the photos yet.

'Don't even think about it.'

She jumped as the wry voice emerged from the inky blackness, slicing through her frantic thoughts of escape.

The owner's powerful profile that matched the dark dangerous drawl was revealed as the second man pulled back the curtain, allowing the moonlight to filter into the room.

Kate blinked, dazzled, as the flashlight once more swept across her face; it moved past her and she saw the second man shake his head.

'Are you expecting him tonight?' The tall one, who had boss written all over him, recommended his interrogation.

'I've never met Gonzalez,' she rebutted honestly.

Kate suspected she might be in the middle of a falling out between villains; she didn't want to accidentally reveal anything that might make her position even more precarious.

Under the circumstances, playing dumb might not be so hard, she decided bitterly, because only someone spectacularly stupid would have blundered in here like this! They must, she reasoned—*now* I can reason!—have been lying in wait.

Her guileless response evoked no softening in the magnificently moody face of her sinister interrogator.

'You just wandered in here by accident...?' His eyes skimmed the outfit she'd chosen for her first foray into breaking and entering. 'Dressed like that?' A derisive snort emerged from between those fascinating lips—*cruel* lips, she thought, unable to control the fearful little shudder that chased along her spine.

'You're one to talk,' she retorted, peering myopically from one man to the other; both their muscular bodies were sheathed in close-fitting black outfits. We must look like a convention of cat burglars; her full lips twitched at the mental image of a social gathering of black-clad thieves.

'You find something funny about this?' he grated incredulously.

The second man had faded into the shadows, apparently content to let his partner in crime do all the talking—perhaps he was the muscle. Not that this guy looked like he needed any help in that area, she mused, as her eyes slid over his impressive torso—not an ounce of spare flesh anywhere that she could see. In fact, in that close-fitting top, if she squinted she could just about make out the slabs of individual muscle across... *Stop!* The warning voice inside her head shrieked.

Kate took a deep breath and pushed her fear and lustful speculation aside as she tried to view the situation objectively—or at least without gibbering fearfully or drooling lustfully. If she was going to get out of this, *he* was the one she had to talk round, she decided, weighing up her opposition objectively. What she saw was not wildly encouraging. She'd seen rock faces with more give than that chiselled jawline.

'Oh, yes, I'm just *wild* about being jumped on in the dark by some stupid big thug,' she was frustrated into com-

menting bitterly. She prodded her aching ribs tentatively.
'I'll probably be black and blue tomorrow, which isn't a
good look in a bikini...' she grumbled, even though she
favoured one-piece bathing suits. Talking, even if she was
talking rubbish, gave her time to think... At least, that was
the theory...

'If I'm such a vicious thug of limited intelligence,
shouldn't you be treating me with a little more respect...?'

The man had a point and, as for the intelligence part, if
those alert eyes were any indication at all he had a brain
like a steel trap.

'Is that a threat?'

'If I threaten you, you'll know about it.'

'I see not a threat, just a boast.' With dismay, she saw a
flicker of interest enter those laser-like eyes—she didn't
want his interest. Her release from this depended on him
considering her harmless and an air of stupidity wouldn't
do her case any harm either. Despite this conviction, she
couldn't stop herself adding, 'I'm normally prepared to give
anyone the benefit of the doubt, but in this instance I don't
think there's any *if* about it. You are a vicious thug and
yes, I probably should shut up, but when I'm nervous I
babble...always have done...'

'I don't think you're nervous,' he cut in smoothly. 'I
think that under that wide-eyed candour you're as hard as
nails. Did you arrange to meet Gonzalez here? Or did he
perhaps ask you to pick something up for him? Does he
know we're on to him? Well?'

'It won't do you any good to bully me.' She saw a flicker
of amazement chase across his strong-boned features and
wondered if she was being daring or just plain stupid to
antagonise him. The truth was, she couldn't help herself;
something about this man made her want to score points...

'I am not a bully!' he refuted in an irritated steely drawl.

She smiled in polite disbelief and heard what might have

been his even white teeth grinding. 'And it won't do you any good,' she elaborated. 'Because I've not the faintest idea what you're talking about.' She shook her head so emphatically that the hood of her sweat top slipped off her head.

One dark brow rose as her silver-blonde tresses tumbled free from the loose knot she'd hastily confined them in on her head. Her stomach lurched as, with studied insolence, those electric-blue eyes moved over her body pausing overly long in significant areas.

Kate's first instinct was to cover herself with her hands. She almost immediately saw how ludicrous and demeaning her response to the earthy sexual appraisal was, and let her hands fall away; in doing so she saw the strands of dark hair caught in her fist.

Unobtrusively she wriggled her fingers to dislodge them; it didn't seem wise to remind someone with such violent inclinations of the no doubt painful moment when her fingers had become blindly entangled in his hair—lush, silky hair, she recalled. Her fingertips tingled uncomfortably as her brain replayed the sensation. With a head of hair like that, she thought practically, he wasn't going to miss the little bit she had ripped out.

'Or maybe you knew he wasn't here... Maybe this is a bit of private enterprise...? You were taking advantage of his absence to help yourself?' He fired the fresh volley of questions at her like bullets without removing his unnerving gaze from her face for even a second. 'What was she about to take out of the drawer, Serge?'

It was spooky. This man it seemed didn't feel the need to blink—but then he probably had iced water running through his veins, not blood, she thought, rubbing her arms where a rash of goosebumps had broken out.

'It's true I didn't come here by accident exactly,' Kate admitted with discomfort as the silent second man, moving with surprising speed for one so large, headed towards the chest of drawers.

Apprehension made Kate's pulse rate soar, an acceptable thing to happen to the most cool-headed of individuals, given the circumstances; the problem was, Kate knew it was only part of the story—there was in fact a much more significant factor. The main reason for the state of near-collapse of her nervous system was—*that man!* She glared angrily up at the stranger's dark saturnine face and her insides tightened another painful notch.

The man projected raw sexuality like a force field; she'd never come across anything like it! However, now was no time to analyse her curiously strong reaction to her cold-eyed interrogator; she needed to be clear headed and focused.

Being clear-headed wasn't as easy as it sounded when you couldn't rid yourself of a nasty, nagging suspicion. What if Susie wasn't the only Anderson who was attracted by danger...? Especially when it came so spectacularly packaged. Oh, God, I'm so shallow! In the future she definitely wouldn't be making so free with her superior sniffs and pitying looks, Kate decided, swallowing a large dose of humility.

'I came here to retrieve something, but it doesn't belong to this Mr Gonzalez. It's...mine.' She kept her voice cool enough but she couldn't stop her eyes darting nervously in the direction of the bulky figure who was sifting through the contents of the drawer, which were now scattered on the ground.

A combination of nerves and the heat in the room made Kate's thin sweatshirt cling damply to her back; sweat pooled uncomfortably in the hollow between her breasts. Conscious of the constant presence of those piercing blue eyes drilling into her skull, she licked her lips nervously.

She'd studied enough guilty people to know she was displaying all the classic signs of guilt herself.

'She was holding this, I think, Javier.'

Kate couldn't stop herself from lunging wildly forwards for the parcel of photographs as they passed between the two men. 'They're mine!' she yelled.

For several stubborn seconds she resisted the compulsion of fingers like iron which closed mercilessly around her wrist before her stiffly clenched fingers unfurled. Tears of pain and frustration standing out in her eyes, she glared resentfully up at her persecutor.

'You've no right...' Her voice faded away as the one she now knew was called Javier slid one long finger under the sealed opening of the package. Paralysed by horror, she watched as he withdrew one glossy print and held it up.

Kate's face flamed as his clinical glance moved from the photo in his hand to her and back again before he slid it back in. He pulled out a strip of negatives and held it up to the light. His nostrils flared and his lips quivered faintly in an attitude of fastidious distaste as he briefly viewed the images revealed.

The other man shot him a question in Spanish which he replied to in the same language—the reply made the other man laugh in surprise. Kate's hands balled into fists as she gritted her teeth; every natural feeling in her rebelled at the idea of these two sniggering at her Susie's expense.

'Do you do this sort of thing for a living, or is it just a hobby?'

He thinks they're pictures of me! Kate's jaw dropped. In other circumstances she might have felt flattered to have her body confused with that of her lovely younger sister, but on this occasion it just made her flip. Where moments before she had felt embarrassed and defensively protective of Susie, now she experienced a flash of blazingly hot rage.

If her adversary hadn't possessed startlingly swift reactions, her closed-fisted blow would have made contact with his lean cheek. Kate, who had never felt the need to resort to anything as crude as brute force in her life experienced a moment of confusion and shock at her actions before the overpowering need to escape overwhelmed her.

'Let me go!' she shrieked, landing a kick on his shins before she subsided her eyes flashing, her breath coming in short gasps. Her nostrils quivered; underneath the light expensive male fragrance he wore she could smell the clean-washed, spicy, masculine scent that she'd noticed before she'd even laid eyes on him—it had bothered her then, and it bothered her more now.

'Now you show your true colours,' came the disdainful observation. 'Cool down, little cat. I have no interest in your sleazy snaps; you can have them…'

Kate felt so pathetically relieved by this contemptuous information that she could have wept. Trying to retain a semblance of dignity, still panting from her exertions, she looked pointedly at his dark fingers still encircling her wrist and did her best to ignore the languid contempt in his tone. She couldn't afford to lose her temper; he had the photos and for Susie's sake she had to get them, even if this involved a bit of humiliation.

With an unpleasant, sneery sort of smile that made Kate's fingers itch to remove it from his smug face, he released her hand and mockingly inclined his glossy head. '…When I have the information I require,' he completed the white crocodile smile fading completely.

Kate's shoulders slumped as her eyes stayed trained on the photos held tantalisingly out of reach. She was fast coming to the conclusion he was playing cat and mouse games with her and, the awful part was, there wasn't a thing she could do about it.

'I don't know anything.' She sighed wearily as she rubbed her tender wrist; the imprint of those strong brown fingers seemed to be branded into her flesh.

'Cut the innocent act. You obviously know him, unless you send pornographic pictures of yourself to total strangers…?' he sneered.

Pink spots of outrage appeared on her smooth cheeks. 'They are not pornographic, they're...they're *tasteful,*' she finished, unable to repress a weak grimace at the memory of the photos.

'Sure they're art,' he drawled insultingly. 'What's the connection? Is he your lover, or your supplier?'

'Supplier?' she exclaimed. Her eyes widened as her frown of incomprehension lifted. *'Drugs!'* Oh, God, what have I walked into? Had Luis Gonzalez tried to muscle in on the big boys? Were these men here to teach him a lesson, or worse...? 'This is a m-misunderstanding,' she stuttered. 'I know nothing about any drugs.'

'Of course you don't.'

Her eyes filled with tears of sheer frustration. She blinked hard to stop them spilling over. If she could weep like Susie—it was one of life's mysteries how Susie cried so picturesquely—tears might get her somewhere, but she couldn't see this man being touched by her own blotchy face and runny nose.

'Why won't you believe me? Do I look like a drug addict or something?'

'And what do they look like?' If he'd been so damned good at spotting the signs, Javier reflected bitterly, his sister would have been spared those agonising months of rehabilitation.

'You should know. It's your business, not mine.'

He went rigid. Not a muscle in his face moved, but his eyes blazed like twin points of fury. 'Women like you are incomprehensible! Why do you protect him?' he demanded. 'Is it fear, or some misplaced sense of loyalty? A man like that will pull you down to his level, and when you get there he'll leave you...'

Without any warning he grabbed her arm and, swiftly rolling up the sleeve of her top, ran one long finger softly over the blue-veined inner aspect of her left wrist and forearm. Under the light his accessory helpfully directed over the area, his keen eyes searched her fair blemishless skin for tell-tale marks.

Kate shivered helplessly as tingling arrows of electricity shot up her arm. Instinctively she started to pull back and then stopped as a strange heavy lethargy stole over her. Her leaden-lidded eyes were riveted on the image of his dark fingers on her skin; heat travelled like a flash-flood, bathing her entire body; the distant buzzing in her head got closer.

She only started breathing again when he released her.

'Satisfied now?' With dignity she rolled down her sleeve.

'Not quite.'

Her stomach muscles clenched as she saw his intention. Her angry dark eyes clashed with his emotionless gaze for several seconds before she conceded defeat.

'Let me,' she said sarcastically as she turned back the sleeve that covered her right arm. Chin lifted defiantly, she thrust out her arm in front of him.

She waited for him to look away, embarrassed, shocked or maybe repelled—she'd seen all the reactions which, to her mind, were wildly out of proportion to the small puckered area of skin, pinker than the rest of her skin, that lay along the inside of her arm, just above her elbow joint—there was another, smaller and less prominent area on her shoulderblade which the plastic surgery had not quite been able to conceal.

It was amazing how such a small blemish could throw some people and make them look at you differently. Kate had decided a long time ago that other people's squeamishness was their problem, not hers, and she didn't go out of her way to conceal or reveal the childhood scars she still bore from a domestic accident.

This man wasn't thrown. Neither did he fall into the category of those who politely pretended not to notice the marks. Seb had been one of those—Seb who, despite his protests that it really didn't matter to him, had never been able to bring himself to touch the scarred area.

This man had no such qualms. He took the arm she defiantly offered between his big hands and turned it slightly sideways, rubbing his thumb lightly over the shiny scar tissue as he did so. Kate shivered and the blue eyes lifted momentarily.

'A burn?' There was not a shred of pity in his expression and over the years Kate had become something of an expert at detecting it.

She cleared her throat, it felt raw and achey. 'Are you always this morbidly curious…?'

'You are not comfortable discussing it?'

Not just mad, bad and indisputably dangerous, he had to turn out to be into amateur psychology—this just got better and better! 'Not with homicidal maniacs.'

'Do you know many homicidal maniacs?'

Kate shook her head. 'Most murders are domestic,' she announced authoritatively. 'If you've seen enough…do you mind…?' she added, with a cool nod to her arm. It was hard to project cool when this man's touch made her shiver.

He straightened up and their eyes met again. Kate had the impression he saw through her bravado, saw right through to the insecure teenager she'd once been, still learning to cope with the occasional stare or rude comment. Disliking the feeling of vulnerability, she shook her head to dispel the scary illusion as she pulled the fabric back down over her arm.

'I hope,' he remonstrated severely, touching the stretchy cotton fabric of her top, 'you do not cover yourself all the time.'

This whole situation, she decided, was getting distinctly surreal. She was getting personal advice from someone who waited in dark rooms for blackmailing drug-dealers. Perhaps working with the criminals had given her a unique rapport with the fraternity; if her mother was to be believed, it had given her a twisted and cynical outlook on life.

'Only when I'm doing a spot of breaking and entering.'

She bit her lip. Irony was a luxury a person in her position could not afford. Then, emboldened by the unexpected gleam of amusement in his eyes, she nodded towards the photos. 'Listen,' she continued in her most persuasive tone—there was no point dismissing out of hand the slim possibility that he was human, after all. 'I honestly don't know your friend, so why don't I just leave and forget I ever saw you?'

'Friend? Por Dios...!'

Kate backed away from the lash of contemptuous fury in his voice and carried on backing nervously until the sound of the heavy-set second thug clearing his throat significantly brought her to an abrupt halt. She looked over her shoulder and discovered he was positioned, arms folded across his massive chest, in front of the only exit.

'I tell you, I don't know him. I'm just a guest here. I only arrived today...'

As she'd appealed to his partner, the second man sauntered up to join him—Kate had almost forgotten his silent presence. She turned her head as the flashlight he carried shone momentarily in her eyes. 'If we let her go, she could warn him we're on to him.'

The sinister significance of this observation was not lost on Kate, who paled with alarm. *'If,'* she exclaimed shrilly. 'What do you mean, if? You lay a finger or try and stop me leaving and I'll make so much noise...'

The one in command winced at her shrill tone. 'Make any more noise than you already are and a concerned guest or member of staff might call the police.'

The best news she'd heard all day—and a long, *long* day it had been. Had it only been this morning she'd boarded the flight to Palma...? Somehow this wasn't quite the Sangria and sunset sort of end to the day she'd anticipated.

'Let's cut out the middle man,' she suggested tartly, reaching for the phone and holding it out to him. Her scars might not have fazed him but Kate could tell her response had taken him aback, and maybe he was right. Maybe she was acting foolishly—somehow, though, she didn't think tears and pleas were going to get her very far.

'And I would naturally feel obligated to hand over these,' he tauntingly wafted the pack of photos in front of her nose.

'And they'd believe your story? I think I might have a little more credibility with the police than you,' she countered calling his bluff.

For some reason, this claim caused his companion to laugh, though he did sober up fast enough when he was on the receiving end of a silencing glare.

'You think so?'

He wasn't to her mind displaying the sort of dismay a shady character like him ought to when threatened with the forces of law. Perhaps he hid his illicit dealings behind a legitimate front, she speculated uneasily.

'I'm a very respectable person.'

'Now, I might be swayed by the throbbing note of conviction and the big brown eyes…but the police, they generally like more concrete proof…'

'You want proof…right.' With a triumphant smile of pure relief she remembered the card in her pocket. 'That's me, K. M. Anderson.' She shoved her credit card under his nose. 'I'm sharing one of the bungalows with my—with a friend…' No need, she decided, to involve Susie.

'You could have stolen it,' he replied glancing without interest at her gold card. 'In fact, under the circumstances, I'd say that's highly likely.'

Kate's chest swelled with indignation, a fact that didn't escape her tormentor's notice. Kate's eyes began to sparkle angrily as his eyes dropped with unabashed interest on the heaving contours. To her horror, she felt her nipples harden and peak.

Lecherous creep, she thought, her anger intensified by the treacherous reactions of her body and the accelerated rate of her heartbeat.

'One of the things I hate most in this world is men who can't keep their eyes on a woman's face when they're talking to her!' she announced with scornful defiance.

That refocused his attention all right; the astonished blue gaze instantly zoomed in on her face.

The startled gasp, followed by a low chuckle, didn't come from the man whose enigmatic scrutiny was making her wish like mad she'd kept quiet on the subject, but from his partner.

'As I was saying,' she began doggedly, 'I didn't steal the card. It's mine. I brought it along in case the door was...' She stopped abruptly, her eyes growing round in dismay as she bit back the incriminating explanation.

'Locked...?' The fascinating network of fine lines around his cerulean eyes deepened.

Kate felt her guilty blush deepen.

'What a resourceful woman you are.... You still haven't told me what you're doing here.'

'Why should I? You haven't told me why you're here and I'm pretty sure it's not by invitation,' she murmured stroppily.

'Hush!' he admonished, cutting her off with abrupt urgency before turning to his companion. 'Serge, did you hear that?'

The hot flare of anticipation Kate glimpsed in his blue eyes suggested to her that she was dealing with an adrenaline junkie, the type who got high on danger, she speculated. The sort that took risks and got a kick out of doing so. She'd often noted these two qualities, allied with a callous disregard for the law, in some of her clients—men who, had they channelled their talents into less anti-social endeavours, would probably have made very successful businessmen, or even for that matter lawyers like herself.

The other man nodded and replied softly. 'It could be Gonzalez?'

The light was suddenly doused and Kate's hopeful ears

were rewarded by the sound of footsteps on the paved area outside the window. She didn't care who it was, it was the chance she'd been waiting for. She opened her mouth to cry for help.

Before she had a chance to raise the alarm, a large hand clamped down hard over her parted lips whilst another twisted her arm behind her back. 'You want to warn your lover?' a cold, hateful voice rasped mockingly in her ear, Kate tried to turn her head, hating his contempt, hating the sensation of his warm breath on her neck, and fearing the confusing ripples of sensation it created. 'I don't think so…'

Biting his hand as hard as she could was not the most subtle response, but Kate was desperate by this point.

He didn't cry out, even though she felt the salty tang of blood on her tongue, but his grip did slacken—only slightly, but it was the moment Kate had been tensely waiting for. It was enough to allow her to break free. With a determined, sinuous wriggle, she twisted away from him and even before she was upright began to run. Head down, she hit the floor, running like a sprinter ducking desperately for the winning line.

CHAPTER THREE

KATE opened her eyes and moaned. She looked around groggily. This was new—waking up in a strange bed, in a strange bedroom. Not all new experiences were good ones and actually this was one she could well have lived without!

She couldn't have amnesia. She knew her name; she could even recite her pin number and other personal details. She just didn't recall the events that had culminated in her being in this bed—maybe this was an occurrence some girls could take in their stride, but not her. Don't panic, Kate, she told herself, there has to be a perfectly simple explanation for this.

The problem was, try as she might, she couldn't come up with it. She attacked the problem with her usual vigour and all she got for her troubles was a brain ache.

The last thing she remembered was getting on the flight for Palma; her memories of that were perfectly clear. She'd ended up holding a baby all the way for the harassed young mother travelling alone with two active toddlers and a fretful six-month-old. The mother had been grateful; the baby had expressed his gratitude by throwing up all over her cream linen designer suit.

The unthinkable suddenly occurred to her. What if she wasn't alone in the strange bed? Holding her breath, she reached behind her, a relieved sigh escaped her lips as the search came up empty.

Javier entered the room just as she was blindly patting the pillow, her eyes screwed tightly shut. He heard her hoarse sigh from the other side of the room. A spasm of amusement lightened the severity of his lean, dark features as he approached, a nightdress folded over one arm.

It wasn't too hard to interpret his guest's actions. Ms K. M. Anderson—it hadn't taken long to discover that they did indeed have a K. M. Anderson staying—was wondering if she'd woken up beside a stranger. From her reactions, it seemed safe to assume this wasn't an everyday occurrence for her.

Javier found himself idly wondering what her response would have been if her hand had encountered his own body instead of the pillow lying there beside her. For a brief moment he imagined her turning, arms outstretched, a smile of invitation on those full sexy lips. Reality intervened; it was much more likely, considering her reckless streak, she'd have picked up the nearest heavy blunt object and knocked him senseless with it. All the same, even his remarkable will power could not totally banish the lingering image of warm, welcoming arms.

Frowning, Kate rolled onto her back. The large fans swooshing silently overhead seemed in keeping with the tasteful and expensive Colonial-style furnishings in the room around her. Her parents' beachfront bungalow had similar furnishing, though it wasn't nearly as spacious.

Of course! She was on holiday. She was in bed at the hotel in the room she shared with Susie... Her relieved expression faded—this theory only worked to a point. This lavishly appointed space wasn't their much more modest bedroom with its twin beds, rattan furniture and a nice view of one of the pools from the dinky veranda.

'My head hurts,' she complained out loud.

'I'm not surprised.'

'*You!*' Kate shrieked in loathing.

She shot bolt upright, bristling with antipathy. The mystery of her brain blanking out the last few hours was a mystery no longer; it had merely been a protective reflex. Protecting her from the worst day of her life.

'How did I get here?' Not under her own steam, that much she knew, and where was 'here'? 'Kidnapping is a very serious offence.' It was in England, and she had no reason to believe the Spanish treated this offence any differently.

One slanted brow rose politely. 'So I believe.'

It was frustratingly apparent her stern warning hadn't had any effect on his bone-deep air of assurance—other than to infuse it with a slight edge of infuriating, indulgent amusement—but then why would it…? She was talking to a hardened, desperate criminal. There was every likelihood he had probably done a lot worse than kidnapping! Perhaps he still thought she was some junkie who nobody would miss?

'And there are people who will miss me…*lots* of people…' She broke off abruptly clutching her head as an arrow of agony shot through her temple.

Through a miasma of pain, Kate felt the mattress give as he came to sit on the edge; her nose quivered as she encountered the attractive male fragrance emanating from his warm body—any closer and she might feel the warmth too. Kate tensed at the thought. This was getting way too intimate for her liking! With a muffled cry of protest that hurt her head, she tried to shuffle blindly away, but a firm hand on her elbow prevented her.

'I won't hurt you.' Kate was mad with herself for instinctively believing him, despite all the evidence to the contrary. 'You should lie down; you took quite a knock.'

'You should know, you probably delivered it,' she retorted through gritted teeth.

'Actually you ran full pelt into the wardrobe—solid mahogany. Renewable sources of course; the owners have a very green policy…'

This information did actually correspond with Kate's

own hazy recollection of the incident. 'You make it sound as if I did it on purpose,' she muttered truculently. 'Actually, I had my eyes closed.' Like now.

Her blue-veined eyelids flickered as she felt the pad of one fingertip brush aside a strand of hair from her forehead. Her mind supplied a vivid lifelike image—possibly aided by the fact she could still smell his elusive male scent—to go with the action. The image of long, sensitive, tapering fingers, very dark in dramatic contrast to her fair creamy skin, lingered in her mind as her stomach muscles began to quiver uncomfortably.

Keeping her eyes closed, she told herself, had nothing to do with being afraid of seeing his raw sex appeal up close. The light hurt her eyes—that was all.

'From the look of your spectacle lenses, it wouldn't have made much difference if you'd had them open,' he murmured, his deep voice laced with disparaging amusement. 'Does the light hurt your eyes?'

'A little.' Kate was willing to ignore this insulting slur on her eyesight. He had her glasses—she needed them, and much as it went against the grain it was time for a bit of pleading. 'You've got my glasses? Give them to me.' She opened her eyes. '*Please,*' she added gruffly. 'Being without them is like…like being naked.' It was hard enough to explain the vulnerability of being short-sighted to anyone not similarly afflicted, but to someone as genetically perfect as this man it was probably a waste of breath.

His perfection was hard to miss this close too. She didn't need her specs to assimilate the dark, brooding magnificence of his strong-boned features—looking at them alarmingly intensified the dizziness she was experiencing.

'I'm afraid I stepped on them in the dark.'

'You did it deliberately!' she heard herself wail childishly.

'They say your other senses compensate…'

Kate watched with total fascination as his long fingers made a stroking sensation a hair's breath away from the pale skin of her forearm. As if those well manicured fingertips were electrified, the fine hairs on her skin became erect.

Was this the unnatural affinity she'd heard abductees developed with their kidnappers? she wondered hazily as her insides dissolved in the flood of scalding liquid heat which cascaded through her body. Like hell it is, Kate! Face facts! This is lust, sexual attraction—at least, on my side—plain and simple. His motivation for playing cat and mouse games were less immediately obvious.

'...when one sense is compromised,' the insidiously sexy drawl continued. 'In my experience, closing my eyes often enhances and heightens tactile sensations...'

Her shameless brain immediately provided several steamy images of situations where he might feel obliged to close his eyes. The situations revealed in those fragmented images uniformly necessitated him being naked, his golden skin gleaming beneath a layer of sweat. The hoarse groan of pleasure she imagined being ripped from his throat was so realistic that a swiftly subdued whimper emerged from her own throat—this was getting out of hand.

So the man was incredibly good-looking, sinfully sexy and packed more masculinity into his little finger than most men did in their entire bodies... That was no excuse to lose the plot, Kate told herself sternly.

'This might help that naked feeling you were talking about.'

Kate looked blankly from his enigmatic face to the creamy cotton scoop-necked nightdress he handed her. Her brain made the link between his words and the garment and she bit her lip. She wasn't—was she?

She hardly dared, but she forced herself to look downwards at her own body—it could have been worse, but not much. Her skin looked dramatically pale against the black of the simple bra she wore; she couldn't see them but she knew her matching pants would afford an equally stark contrast.

'You took my clothes off!' she choked, her voice shaking with outrage and suspicion. Was that all he'd done…?

'I did,' he confirmed, coolly unapologetic. 'It seemed the most sensible thing to do under the circumstances. You were burning up.'

If she hadn't been, she was now! With a fraught squawk of dismay, she belatedly slid beneath the duvet, leaving only her face and tousled ash-blonde hair peeking out.

One dark brow rose expressively. 'There is really no need for a display of false modesty; women on the beach wear less than you are.' One corner of his mouth lifted as a devilish gleam appeared in his eyes. 'Considerably less, actually,' he added drily. 'Or are you afraid you'll inflame my lust? Don't…I have strong control.'

In other words, he wasn't that desperate!

His languid drawl sent an extra-sharp stab of pain through Kate's pounding skull. Though she never normally envied Susie her looks, at that moment she wouldn't have minded having the equipment to make this man eat his contemptuous words.

'Oh, yes, you struck me right off as someone *oozing* strong moral fibre,' she sneered, oozing hostility. 'And as for women on the beach, *they* haven't been interfered with by a raving lunatic.'

'Do you always have such lurid fantasies?'

Kate's cheeks flamed. With one quirk of an eyebrow he'd managed to give the distinct impression he wouldn't touch her with a ten foot barge pole. 'None involving you!'

An honest girl, Kate knew she would in the future. It was inevitable; he was the sort of male that made the female unconscious run riot. She just hoped her fantasies would wait until she was safe in the bosom of her family—she refused to allow herself to contemplate *if*. She was going to get away from this man.

Javier saw her wince. 'You really should not shout or get agitated,' he remonstrated.

'Advice from you I can do without.'

He gave a shrug. 'I removed your clothes because you were dressed inappropriately for the weather conditions. Though ideally for a spot of larceny,' he added slyly.

'Are you calling me a thief?' she gritted.

'If the cap fits…?'

'Takes one to know one…' she countered childishly.

'Takes a thief to catch a thief,' he riposted without a pause.

'Gosh, your colloquial English is really very good.' I can't believe I just said that…! I've been knocked unconscious, kidnapped, I'm lying as good as naked in a strange bed in the company of an indisputably dangerous man who could do anything at any moment and all I can do is admire his grammar…!

His heavy lids drooped hiding the expression in his deep set eyes momentarily from Kate. 'The British, they're just priceless.'

'Pardon?'

Those lush dark lashes lifted off his cheekbones revealing cynical blue. 'Shades of the empire; you refuse to learn another language and delight in commenting on foreigners' *funny* accents.'

Kate, who was mortified by this interpretation of her unthinking observation, couldn't help but observe that his deep velvety drawl could be classified as many things, including dangerously seductive, but *funny* wasn't one of them!

'I didn't mean it like that!' she exclaimed, horrified to have him lump her together with an unpleasant, ignorant

minority she had nothing whatever in common with. 'Anyhow, it's an absurd generalisation, and I was *not* being patronising.' Why am I making such a fuss? she wondered
eyeing the good-looking cause of her discomfort resentfully. His good opinion is not something I'm going to lie
awake at nights thinking about—now his mouth, that was
another matter, her wilful thoughts added naughtily.

'You look feverish.'

Kate stiffened as a cool hand touched her perspiring forehead—she could hardly explain the likely reason for her
sweaty state. The hand lifted and she sighed.

'I'm prepared to give the benefit of the doubt,' he announced abruptly. Their eyes met and something indefin-
able passed between them that made Kate's breathing
quicken perceptibly. 'Actually, I went to school in
England,' he added casually.

Kate frowned. 'Boarding school?' That suggested a priv-
ileged background, as did his autocratic manner. Had he
chosen crime out of choice or had circumstances forced him
down that road? It seemed a wicked shame that someone
she sensed had so much potential should waste his talents.

'Do I detect a hint of disapproval?'

The edge of indulgent amusement in his voice made Kate
bristle. 'Well, if I had children I wouldn't ship them
away...' She encountered the interested glint in his eyes
and bit her lip. Like he's *really* interested in what you'd
do with your children, Kate... A sane person didn't enter
into a debate on private versus state education with her
abductor.

'It didn't do me any harm.'

Kate couldn't stop herself snorting derisively when he
wheeled out the tired old line.

'In fact...'

'It got you where you are today—which I'd say was looking at a kidnapping charge, at the very least.'

'Does that mean if I let you go you'll run straight to the police?'

Kate's face fell as she realised her smart tongue had got her into even more trouble. 'I'm in no position to go to the police without incriminating myself.' She waited, fingers crossed, for his response.

'You being such a hardened criminal...'

Kate unable to interpret the odd inflection in his tone frowned. 'Not *hardened,* exactly... You went to school in England—does that mean you're *not* Spanish?'

'A man could be forgiven for thinking you're trying to change the subject.'

'I'm curious, that's all...'

'About my ancestry?'

'About your eyes...' She cleared her throat and blushed hotly as the dangerous glint in his eyes intensified. 'I just happened to notice they're blue,' she explained carelessly. 'It's unusual for someone with your colouring,' she added defensively.

'Yes, it is. I have a Scottish grandmother.'

'It's never too late, you know...' she heard herself blurt out suddenly.

Much to her dismay, he eased himself farther onto the bed and folded his arms comfortably across his chest. Kate had his full, undivided attention and she didn't want it!

'For what is it never too late?'

Feeling deeply embarrassed by her earnest outburst Kate rubbed her nose against the duvet and surreptitiously shuffled as far across the big bed as she could without falling off. Why can't I leave well enough alone? she wondered in exasperation. Why do I always have to try and rehabilitate hopeless cases?

'Kate's problem is she doesn't know a lost cause when she sees it,' friends had frequently observed affectionately.

'To do something else,' she muttered awkwardly. 'Something…*legal*…'

'Are you trying to reform me?' An expression of amazement, tinged by something she couldn't interpret, chased across his sternly proud face.

'It's nothing to me if you end up rotting in prison!' she countered crossly. 'Now, if you give me back my clothes, I'll just be going…'

'Just out of curiosity, what would you do if I said you couldn't go?'

Kate's expression froze. The ambivalence of her response to this taunt was deeply troubling. A person who found anything attractive or exciting about being held captive by someone like him was a candidate for the funny farm! She gulped and her throat muscles locked down tight as her eyes welded with his shimmering blue gaze. It took her a few moments before the obstruction in her throat cleared.

'If I told you, I'd lose the element of surprise.' The truth, she reasoned, could not make matters much worse at this point. 'And, from where I'm lying, that's about the only thing I have going for me,' she added with feeling.

To her amazement he threw back his dark head and laughed; it was a warm uninhibited and incredibly attractive sound.

'You have a lot more going for you than that, K. M. Anderson,' he announced caressingly.

'What's with the charm offensive?' she asked suspiciously. And if I was a weaker, more gullible girl, it might just work—because a smile like that, she reflected bitterly, ought to carry health warnings.

'Do you think all men have a hidden agenda?'

'No, just you,' she declared without thinking.

He didn't appear offended by her reply. 'I've never met a woman with your brand of candour; it is most disarming.'

He didn't look disarmed, he looked worryingly thoughtful. 'Are you going to get me my clothes?'

'If the doctor says you can get dressed, yes.'

'Doctor? What doctor…?'

On cue, there was the sound of voices just outside the bedroom door.

'This doctor.'

A man entered the room but it wasn't a doctor, it was the heavy from earlier, looking a lot less sinister—unlike his partner in crime—in proper light. He smiled at Kate and she found herself smiling back, confused by this polite, totally unthreatening individual, a million miles away from her hazy mental image of him.

She turned back to the man ensconced beside her on the bed. 'You expect me to believe you've called a doctor?' she hissed in a contemptuous undertone.

His blue eyes swept over her flushed face. 'You will naturally believe what you think,' he returned haughtily. 'However, I have arranged medical assistance.'

'I suppose a dead body would be inconvenient, even for someone like you,' she spat back.

One brow lifted at her venomous tone but didn't respond as he rose to greet his friend. It didn't occur to Javier to ask whether Serge had managed to procure the services of a doctor; Serge wasn't the sort of man who didn't complete tasks.

'That was quick, Serge.'

'I didn't need to chase up the on-call doctor. Luckily they mentioned at reception that Dr Latimer was staying overnight after a party. I woke him up.'

'He did indeed, so I hope you'll excuse my appearance.'

Kate's confusion increased as a tall, grey-haired individual panting slightly and carrying a black case followed the younger man into the room. Despite his words, he looked casually but impeccably turned out to her.

'Javier!' The older man grasped the hand extended to him, his expression warm.

'Conrad!'

Kate's initial worry that an innocent doctor had been coerced into attending under threat of violence by her unscrupulous captor was fading fast, this respectable looking individual appeared to be no stranger.

'How good to see you,' the doctor continued warmly. The subtle degree of deference in his manner added to Kate's bewilderment. 'How is your grandfather? Thinking of retiring, I hear…'

Javier just smiled noncommittally.

'Hard for a man like that to take a back seat,' the doctor observed, blind to the air of tension which Kate had immediately detected in the younger man. 'Is he doing any of the things I suggested on our last meeting?'

'You mean, has he cut back on the cigars and brandy…is he taking regular exercise and watching his diet? Did you really expect him to?'

The respected medic, who was living in semi-retirement on the island, grinned ruefully. 'My wife tells me that I'm an eternal optimist.' He caught sight of Kate, who was lying there watching the proceedings, a frown on her face as she tried to make sense of their conversation—could she have got mixed up with a member of some notorious criminal family…? And why was this Javier uncomfortable discussing his grandparent? 'Is this my patient?'

'Yes this is Miss Anderson.' Taller than the other men, his every movement lithe and co-ordinated, the dark-clad figure walked back over to the bed and touched her shoulder. Somehow his body language and tone managed an easy intimacy which she wanted immediately to deny.

'Kate took a nasty knock on the head…didn't you, sweet-heart?'

If Kate blinked at this casual use of her name—she was pretty sure she hadn't revealed this detail—she almost choked over the endearment that followed.

'She lost consciousness?'

'She was out for several minutes,' he stated with the confidence of a man who didn't deal approximations. 'I don't know whether this is relevant, Conrad—' his magnificent shoulders lifted in an elegant, economic gesture—Kate, her eyes drawn against her will to the lean vital frame of the man beside her, shivered; she couldn't recall meeting anyone with such expressive body language. 'But she appears to have a temperature.'

'No, I haven't,' Kate intervened, hurriedly removing her glazed stare from the hard contours of his long, well-developed thighs. She judged it was about time she stopped lying there, meekly ogling, while they discussed her as if she wasn't there. 'And if anyone wants to know how I am, they can ask me,' she added pugnaciously.

The two men exchanged understanding glances that made Kate want to scream.

'Quite right, too,' the doctor agreed jovially, with that jarringly patronising manner his profession had perfected. He fished a pair of half-moon glasses to peer at her over from the breast pocket of his pristine shirt and she was almost amused to note that the picture of professional condescension was complete!

At least his irritating bedside manner reassured her of his authenticity; up to that point Kate had been harbouring suspicions about his identity. After all, she only had this Javier's word for it he was a doctor at all—and his word didn't inspire her trust.

'This is ludicrous. I don't need a doctor, I need—' she began, only to be smoothly interrupted.

'Don't get excited, Kate...'

Kate dragged herself higher in the bed, pinning the duvet under her chin. Under the circumstances, her restraint was nothing short of miraculous!

'You think this is excited...?' She gave a dry laugh. 'I think I've got a right to be *excited!*' she squeaked indignantly. 'And don't look at me like that,' she added shrilly.

Their eyes clashed combatively and Kate's chin went up; she considered it a matter of principle not to be the first to look away. 'I don't know what sort of women you're used to dealing with,' she began scornfully, 'but...'

The doctor cleared his throat tactfully and looked indulgently from one warring party to the other. 'Perhaps it would be better, Javier, if you left us to it?' he suggested tentatively.

The amused competitive blue eyes finally broke contact with hers.

'If you want anything, just call. We'll be...' The inclination of Javier's dark imperious head indicated the door.

Kate was suspicious of this unexpected capitulation; her frown was fielded by an improbably innocent smile.

'You must let me look at that wound on your hand afterwards, Javier. It looks as if it could do with dressing,' the doctor called after the departing men.

Kate's gaze shifted from Javier's provoking eyes to his hand at the same moment he raised it to his lips. She shifted uncomfortably and heat flooded her face as she recalled the moment she had bitten down hard. She chewed her lower lip in guilty agitation as their glances once more locked.

'I had an encounter with an angry cat,' he replied with a dismissive shrug.

'Perhaps,' Kate observed sourly, 'you provoked her...'

The doctor, oblivious to the undercurrents, commented

on the number of feral animals roaming free. 'I hope your tetanus shots are up to date, Javier,' he called as the other men began once more to withdraw.

A nod of confirmation and he was gone.

CHAPTER FOUR

THE sudden release of tension left Kate feeling limp; she couldn't believe her luck.

'Conrad Latimer,' the doctor formally introduced himself.

Kate ignored the introduction and, pushing back the duvet she swung her feet purposefully to the floor. The room began to tilt crazily. She clutched her spinning head and sprawled weakly backwards.

'I think perhaps I did that too quickly,' she murmured faintly.

'I think perhaps the fact you did it at all is the problem.'

'You don't understand I have to get out of here—*quickly!*' she fretted, frustrated that he wasn't appreciating the extreme urgency of the matter. Kate sighed. Whilst she would have preferred to appeal for help from a disinterested party, which this man obviously wasn't, she didn't have much choice. 'You're English?' she asked, in a desperate attempt to find some common ground.

'Yes. My wife and I spend most of the year in our villa on the island, since I retired; it's in a lovely spot just outside Pollensa. You must get Javier to fetch you to visit us, if he has time.'

Kate stared at him incredulously, presumably this depended on Javier having a gap in his busy schedule he could fit in this merry jaunt...somewhere between larceny and extortion, possibly? Just what sort of cosy relationship did he think she had with that wretched man? She'd never imagined herself as a gangster's moll before; it troubled her that she imagined it now.

'But enough of that, let's take a look at you.' He gently probed the tender lump on the side of her skull, Kate winced. 'I'm sorry. How did it happen?'

'Apparently I ran into a wardrobe.'

'An impetuous lady,' came the indulgent response.

'It wasn't my fault,' she began indignantly.

'No, these accidents happen—unlucky thing, certainly, but at least Javier was there—a good man in a crisis, Javier. None better…'

Kate almost choked at this unlikely description of her persecutor. 'He's very competent, certainly,' she replied grimly.

'The Monteros are all a pretty charismatic lot, but in my opinion Javier is the best of the bunch.' What bunch? Kate wanted to ask. *Javier Montero,* where had she heard that before? It definitely sounded familiar but her muzzy brain just wouldn't make the necessary connections. 'Have you known him long?' he asked, shining a penlight into her eyes.

'Not long,' she hedged. 'This might sound a bit strange, Doctor…'

'Any double vision, nausea?'

'No, but, Doctor…?'

'Yes, my dear?' He began to check her reflexes.

'Where am I?'

The doctor replaced his patella hammer in his case; he was too professional to display any overt alarm.

'Disorientation is not at all unusual after a knock like you've taken,' he soothed cautiously. 'Just what do you remember about the accident?'

'Too much,' she responded feelingly.

'And before?'

'There's nothing wrong with my memory. I just don't know where I am,' she gritted in frustration.

'You're the same place you were before the accident, I expect, my dear. The honeymoon suite at the…'

'*The what?*' Kate squawked, struggling upright.

'The honeymoon suite,' he repeated patiently. 'I'm sure you'll remember if you give yourself time.'

'I won't remember the honeymoon suite because I'm not staying in it. I'm not on my honeymoon… I'm in a nightmare!'

The doctor looked amused. 'Honeymoon! Well, that would make the headlines, wouldn't it?' he chuckled.

'It would…?'

Her bemused response made him laugh even more heartily, then abruptly the humour faded from his face. 'Don't think for a second that I'm prying. Why, I know how much Javier values his privacy, and I can see you feel the same way. Listen, your relationship with him is none of my business; you're his guest and my patient…and I can promise you that nobody will hear from me that you are staying here.'

Kate laughed at the irony of this reassurance. It was beyond her why he felt the need to make it, but then just about everything was beyond her at that moment.

'I do not have a relationship with this Javier Montero— why, I don't even—'

'Is she in there? Katie!' The sound of a familiar lilting voice stopped Kate mid-flow.

'*Mother?*' she gasped incredulously. Oh, my God, that knock on the head must have been worse than I thought, she decided as she frantically tried to come up with a reason for hearing her mother's voice beside insanity.

Not too keen to reveal she was hearing things, Kate broached the subject cautiously. 'Do you hear anyone?' she asked not particularly hopefully.

Her eyes widened as the door was pushed open and the

unmistakable figure of Elizabeth Anderson rushed in—if this was an hallucination, it was a very realistic one!

'My dearest child!'

Kate, enfolded in a fragrant maternal embrace, wouldn't have dreamt of contradicting her mother, but she knew her emotional statement was not strictly accurate. Whilst Elizabeth Anderson was undoubtedly fond of both her daughters, Susie, always the more demonstrably affectionate of the girls, was the indisputable apple of her eye.

'How did you know I was here, Mother?' she croaked bemusedly when the pressure on her ribs eased enough for her to breathe.

'Why, Javier came to get us, of course; what a lovely man he is. You naughty girl,' she remonstrated, wagging her finger with a playfulness that Kate couldn't make head nor tail of. 'Why didn't you tell us you were a…' She shot Kate a sly, knowing look from under her eyelashes that reminded Kate how similar physically Susie and their mother were. '*Friend* of Javier Montero. Why, I didn't even know you knew him!' she exclaimed with another girlish giggle that grated on Kate's frayed nerve-endings. 'I suppose that's why you left dinner early, to meet him…' She clicked her tongue in annoyance. 'Though why you should think all the subterfuge was necessary is beyond me… It's not as if we'd object, is it?' She laughed heartily at the notion. 'Not that you've ever worried about my feelings before.' A note of misuse entered in her voice.

'You're *pleased* I know him?' Kate echoed in a strangled voice.

'Katherine Mary Anderson, I wonder about you sometimes, child. The Monteros must be one of the wealthiest families in Europe!' she exclaimed in a scandalised tone.

'Oh, my God!' Kate breathed faintly as enlightenment dawned in blinding splendour. The mental leap required to transfer Javier from her mental file marked 'member of the shady underworld' to one marked 'member of a rich and powerful dynasty that could trace its origins back centuries' left her reeling.

'You always were a sly, secretive child.' She heard Elizabeth reflect in a long-suffering manner. 'You and your father, always so serious about something or other, but he swears he didn't know either... Is it true? Haven't you told him?'

'Told him what?'

Ignoring her daughter's shaky query, Elizabeth looked admiringly around the room. 'The *honeymoon suite,*' her mother exclaimed, in a voice loaded with significance.

Honeymoon suite—oh, God! Being familiar with the way her mother's mind worked, Kate could see where she was going. Marriage was the only career any woman needed, in her mother's eyes, and a woman who hadn't snagged her man by thirty was a failure. Much to Kate's relief, her frustrated parent had written her off before she'd reached that milestone and concentrated her efforts instead on her more malleable sibling.

'Mum, please don't read anything into that!' Kate pleaded. 'I had an accident; this was the most convenient place...'

With a display of selective deafness that was her forte, Elizabeth continued to examine the décor. 'Very impressive and extremely tasteful,' came her final verdict. 'And that Jacuzzi in the deck overlooking the sea, it's just like the one your father and I had when we were in Jamaica last year. Isn't it marvellous to lie there and listen to the waves?'

At that moment Kate could think of worse things than her hot, sticky body being immersed in cool water. She dwelt dreamily for a moment on an image of her naked body being caressed by the soft water, no sounds—especially not her mother's voice—but that of the sea. It was very soothing, until her fertile and wayward imagination added a disruptive element to the picture in the shape of… Perhaps it wasn't such a good idea to think about shapes, she decided, as images of long, glistening, lean limbs and taut masculine muscles floated around suggestively in her head. Suffice it to say, she wasn't alone in the tub! Her heart began to thud frantically against her ribcage as she shook her head to blank out the depraved activities her illusionary couple were indulging in.

Elizabeth turned, with a charming smile that could still dazzle, to the doctor. 'How is she, doctor?' she asked casting a critical eye over her glassy-eyed eldest born. 'She looks a bit strange to me…'

Strange! If this indeed wasn't some strange and bizarre nightmare from which she would awaken any moment, then the man she'd taken for a sinister crime lord was actually a prominent member of the legendary family whose business interests spanned the globe! A family whose marriages to equally newsworthy individuals made front page in newspapers from New York to Istanbul.

Naturally this put his presence in the blackmailer's room in an entirely different light; unlike her, he'd obviously been there legitimately. On top of all that, her mind was filled with steamy images of herself doing things she'd never even imagined before, and despite the suffocating heat her burning nipples were brazenly protruding through the flimsy fabric of her bra!

'It's awfully warm in here…' If she had ever felt this mortified or confused in her life before, Kate was pretty sure she'd have remembered!

'Actually, I was just wondering why the air conditioning is working full blast in here?'

Kate cast a startled look in the doctor's direction and was worried when his nod confirmed her mother's assessment.

'Miss Anderson has taken a nasty knock on the head,' he began to explain. 'I think peace, quiet and rest are the best things I can prescribe for that...'

Wearily, Kate shot him a pathetically grateful look; as much as she loved her mother, even at the best of times a conversation with her could be an exhausting experience...and her head did ache so...

'I'd like her to have an X-ray, just to be on the safe side. Javier will arrange that, no doubt. My main concern is the fever she's running...'

'I have a fever!' Kate exclaimed.

'You do indeed. Your throat is red and inflamed and your lymph nodes are enlarged, which is a sure sign of infection.'

Kate, who had been too occupied by foiling blackmailers and evading kidnappers to wonder about something as mundane as the feelings of general malaise afflicting her, felt beneath her jaw and encountered the tender area he was speaking of.

'It's probably a virus,' he continued. 'Maybe just the twenty-four hour variety...?'

Kate smiled back at him, approving his optimistic attitude.

'Have you been in contact with anyone with flu or anything of that nature?'

Elizabeth Anderson got up hurriedly from the bedside, regarding her daughter with reproachful horror.

'No, I don't think so...' Kate began; then she recalled the baby on the flight. 'There was this child on the flight over, I had him on my knee and he was a bit grizzly...you know, hot and snuffly.'

The doctor nodded. 'That could well be the explanation. The cramped conditions on planes make it a fertile breeding ground for bugs. On the other hand, it might be quite unrelated.'

'Really, Kate, that's so like you,' her mother complained, delicately examining her own neck. 'You never stop to think about how your actions affect others. This is your father's first break for months; how are you going to feel if he becomes ill because of your thoughtlessness?'

Kate accepted the strictures meekly. 'Sorry…'

'And I shall complain to the airline. You pay for a first class ticket—'

'Well, actually,' Kate admitted guiltily, 'I was travelling economy.'

Kate wasn't surprised when her mother looked appalled. Elizabeth was a terrible snob who went to great pains to disguise her own working-class roots. *'Economy!'*

'I didn't think Dad would mind if I traded in my ticket and put the money towards the deposit for my new flat,' she added defensively.

Kate, tired of flat-sharing and determined to enter the property market, had been economising wherever possible during the last year. She didn't know how people in less well-paid jobs than herself managed in the scarily pricey London property market.

'Are you decent? Can I come in?'

Kate welcomed the interruption as her father's round, cheery face peered cautiously around the door—Charles Anderson, with his cherubic countenance, did not look like most people's image of a sober judge. *'Dad!* Come in…*please!'* she added, with a harassed glance in her mother's direction.

After first assuring himself his daughter didn't look near death's door, Charles Anderson smiled. 'Well, what have you been up to, pumpkin?' he began heartily as he approached Kate's bedside, his arms extended.

Kate blinked, embarrassed by the way her eyes filled weakly with tears at the casual endearment; Dad hadn't called her that for years.

'Charles, don't go near her, she's infectious!' his wife shrieked in alarm.

'Nonsense, Lizzie, since when was a knock on the head infectious?' Charles Anderson returned, dismissing his wife's appeal.

Kate on the other hand, saw the good sense in what her mother was saying; she certainly had no desire to ruin everyone else's holiday.

'Actually, Dad…' she stopped, losing track of her train of thought as her attention was fatally distracted by the figure silently entering the room behind her father.

The younger man had to be at least six four or five to be able to dwarf Charles Anderson's burly figure. His autocratic air might make sense now but it didn't make it any less obnoxious to Kate.

As a man born to wield power, Javier Montero certainly fulfilled all the criteria. He was arrogant, overbearing and insufferably rude. An unashamed aristocrat, who smugly imagined an accident of birth gave him special rights and privileges, decided the woman who made a point of never judging people on appearances!

Mentally pulling his character to shreds gave her a temporary respite from examining in any depth the worrying fact she found his presence electrifying.

Kate wasn't the sort of person who normally had a problem laughing at herself or her mistakes when the circumstances warranted it, but there were limits! When she thought about how terrified she'd been, her blood boiled. No doubt he'd been having a laugh at her expense all night.

Amongst the things she'd said that made her squirm now, the recollection of the earnest advice she'd given him on reforming his criminal life stood out as particularly cringeworthy!

Kate constructively converted her embarrassment to anger as she glared with distrust and dislike at Javier's distinguished profile. Why the hell hadn't he just come out and explained who he was, like any normal person, instead of letting her blather on and on?

Javier wasn't surprised by the to-hell-with-you look in those velvety exotically slanted eyes as they met his—head on, of course. He'd already worked out that K. M. Anderson was an impetuous, head-on sort of female. This characteristic made her very different from most of the women he knew, women who often said what they imagined he wanted to hear. Though there was nothing remotely predatory about this Kate—in fact, if anything, she gave the impression of being unaware of her own attractiveness—she was undoubtedly intelligent and strong-willed.

As much as he admired these traits, Javier wasn't normally sexually attracted to women who possessed them. Perhaps the allure in this case had something to do with the fact these characteristics came wrapped in the sort of body he'd always admired—athletic without being muscular, curvaceous without being lush, he decided appreciatively as his eyes skimmed her recumbent form.

He acknowledged her antagonism with the very faintest of wry smiles that suggested to the seething Kate he was enjoying every second of her discomfort.

Childishly determined not to be the first to look away, she didn't know how long the silent eye-to-eye combat continued, but she was relieved and immensely grateful when Conrad Latimer's timely intervention gave her a legitimate excuse to look away.

'It seems likely that your daughter, Mr Anderson, has a viral infection of some sort to go with a mild concussion.'

'Caught no doubt from the horrid child she nursed all the way over in the plane,' Elizabeth clarified with a disapproving sniff.

'Always the soft touch, hey, Katie,' her father remarked fondly as, ignoring his wife's remonstrations, he hugged his daughter. 'Feeling pretty rotten...?' He straightened up and tugged one limp strand of blonde hair as he keenly surveyed his eldest daughter's pale face.

Now she wasn't looking at the elegant, tall figure oozing more vitality than seemed decent for one individual, Kate's breathing had almost settled to a normal rhythm.

'Not too bad, Dad.'

Javier, who had been conversing with the doctor in a soft undertone, stepped quietly forwards. It required no dramatic gestures to make his lean, dynamic figure the focus of attention; Kate found herself admiring his sheer presence even as she resented it.

She watched as he inclined his head courteously towards her mother, who looked bowled over by this old-fashioned display—though Kate suspected that her mother was so disgustingly impressed by his financial and social position it would take a lot to make her look upon him with anything but fawning approval! She watched his display with a cynical smile. Oh, no doubt about it, his company manners were second to none, she brooded, but having been on the receiving end of his anger she could have told them about another less pleasant side to his nature... Big bully!

'You'll wish to stay with your daughter no doubt, Mrs Anderson. I'm afraid for obvious reasons there is no second bedroom in this suite.' This comment elicited a flurry of smiles. 'But I'll arrange for a bed to be brought in here...or would you prefer it in the sitting room...?'

'Oh! Oh no, we couldn't possibly put you to so much trouble...'

Kate saw her mother's dilemma straight off; she also saw the cynical twist of Javier's lips as he listened politely to the older woman bluster.

If Elizabeth hadn't been so loath to appear anything but the caring mother in this man's eyes, she'd have recoiled in horror at the idea of playing nurse. Kate knew that anything to do with illness spooked her mother—especially the possibility she might become ill herself! Fortunately, other than her scald, both she and Susie had been extremely healthy children. But her burns had been bad and had left a lasting impact on Kate—and a dislike of hospitals.

'I'd much prefer to go back to my own room,' she put in hurriedly. 'I'm feeling much better.'

'Kate doesn't like to be fussed when she's ill,' her father explained to Javier. 'But do you think it's such a good idea going back to your own room, Kate? If Susie catches something, we'll all be…!' His bushy brows which met over the bridge of his nose arched expressively.

'*God, no!*' Kate exclaimed immediately. 'I can't do that.' Susie, like their mother, was not the most stoic of patients; she never suffered alone! 'And I don't want to pass this bug on to the other guests.'

'You will naturally stay here as long as necessary, Kate.'

The way he said her name made Kate's skin prickle— not a good sign. She just hoped it was antipathy and nothing more sinister that was responsible for this sensation! She longed to refuse the offer on more than one count— firstly all her instincts told her to disagree in principle with anything this wretched man said, secondly she desperately didn't want to be beholden with him, and last, but not least, she could sense her mother putting two and two together and coming up with an unhealthy five!

Kate tensed. If Mum starts dropping heavy hints of a matrimonial nature, I'll kill her, she vowed. Better that, though, she reflected worriedly, than seeing her blatant matchmaking mother annihilated by one of the cutting barbs she was sure Javier was more than capable of delivering!

'Now that's what I call a generous offer,' Charles Anderson said, looking mightily relieved. 'Isn't it, Kate?'

Kate smiled in a sickly way back at him and tried unsuccessfully to resist the mesmeric pull of mocking blue eyes—she failed miserably. Chin up, she glared, ignoring that sinking sensation low in her belly; whilst she was in no position to throw his offer back in his face, she could at least make sure he knew that's what she'd like to do!

'It's the least I can do, under the circumstances,' he responded smoothly.

'*You bet it is!*' Aware of the stares that her spiky retort had caused, Kate forced herself to smile. She gritted her teeth through the horridly bright grimace and fantasised about puncturing his ego—it was a healthier fantasy than others she'd indulged in recently.

'Yes, very kind,' she responded stiffly.

CHAPTER FIVE

IT SEEMED like hours to Kate before the room finally emptied and she was left alone. She waited until she heard the door click closed with a sound of promising finality before leaving her bed to search for the bathroom. Her need was fairly urgent and the search proved to be frustratingly slow.

'Never a loo when you need one,' she grumbled softly to herself as the first two doors she opened turned out to be walk-in wardrobes. She was about to try out the third when a voice at her shoulder almost made her leap out of her skin.

'You should not be out of bed.'

Hand pressed to her thundering heart, she spun around, an action which made her head spin as she tilted it back to look up at the tall man towering over her.

'You're gone…!'

Even before one dark brow rose, Kate was wincing at the inanity of this patently false observation, because he definitely was very much there!

Every lean, muscle-packed inch of Javier Montero was standing so close that, had she chosen to reach out, she could have touched him—touched his broad chest, his lean flat belly. In fact, had she wanted to touch him, like a child in a sweet shop she'd have been spoilt for choice!

Kate swallowed hard and averted her eyes before she was totally submerged by the wave of sensual inertia that washed over her. She might no longer fear for her life in his presence but she wasn't so sure about her sanity. This man's raw masculinity had roughly the same effect as a thousand volts of unearthed electricity on her nerves.

'I thought you were asleep.'

What would it be like, she found herself speculating, to wake up and find that face on the pillow beside you when you woke up? She swallowed convulsively, further unsettled by the alarming direction of her maverick thoughts. Aware that his heavy-lidded eyes were sliding thoughtfully over the length of her body, she folded her arms defensively over her chest and felt extremely glad she'd taken the time to exchange the slinky black undies for the pretty nightdress which was beautifully cool on her overheated body and, more importantly, given her present situation, covered her from neck to ankle.

It was doubtful she would have considered this a fortuitous exchange had she realised that, despite the demure design and sweet embroidered flowers around the scooped neckline, the borrowed nightdress was totally transparent beneath the electric light!

'So you just thought you'd, what…? Come and watch me?' Now there was a *very* unsettling thought. 'Have you been demoted to nursemaid, or has making money got boring?'

'If you'd agreed to be transferred to the clinic overnight, as the doctor suggested, I wouldn't need to…'

She may not have been in a position to explain to her parents and the doctor why Javier's hospitality was neither kind nor acceptable, but she was not willingly going to actively participate in the debate over her healthcare options. Once, however, she had realised that the possibility of her being transferred to some posh clinic or other—in her eyes, a hospital was a hospital!—was being mooted, Kate become animated for as long as it took her to make it abundantly clear to everyone that, short of hog-tying or sectioning her under the Majorcan equivalent of the Mental Health Act, there was no way she was going to any plush private clinic!

'And as for CT scans and skull X-rays, I won't have one!' she had explained firmly.

When she'd heard her father begin to apologetically explain away her unreasonable behaviour with a discreet reference to the numerous operations and skin grafts she'd bravely endured as a child, Kate had cut him short with a glare so ferocious he'd not attempted to continue. Her hospital phobia, well-known to those who knew her best, was not something she wanted revealing to a man like Javier Montero.

'Spend a night in hospital for a bump on the head…? *Nonsense!*' she contended stubbornly.

'*Bumps* on the head have been known to have serious consequences…and I do feel indirectly responsible for your injury…'

'With damn good reason—you are responsible!'

'The doctor told me to watch out for irrational behaviour. Help me out here… Is this the norm for you, or should I start worrying?'

'Very funny! You're a laugh a minute, not to mention a regular ray of sunshine!' she snorted. 'I suppose you're just hanging around in the hope I'll take a turn for the worse? Well, sorry to disappoint you; I'm feeling fine,' she lied.

Though he didn't respond as such to her childish retort, he still managed with just a look to make her feel petty and churlish. 'No, you're not. As I've already told you, I feel partially responsible for your injuries and, besides, who else was there? Your mother?'

'Leave my mother out of this… Not everyone makes a good nurse,' Kate defended hotly. 'And even if I needed one, which I don't, you wouldn't be it!'

'Possibly not, but as it happens I'm all you have, and fortunately I have an extremely robust immune system; I don't get ill…'

Listening to this complacent pronouncement, Kate

couldn't help but uncharitably wish he'd contract some-thing nasty, not dangerously so—she wasn't a malicious girl—but bad enough to turn that aristocratic nose red and make those glorious electric-blue eyes watery and red-rimmed.

'Pity!' It was deeply frustrating to discover her vicious comment merely seemed to amuse him. Beyond amusement there was a flicker of something else—something she couldn't quite identify, that moved behind his eyes and made her vaguely uneasy. 'I thought people like you clicked your fingers and minions came to do your bidding.'

One dark brow arched. 'People like me?'

'The disgustingly rich and idle.'

'Wealth is relative. Many would not think your upbring-ing impoverished; many more might even infer you would not have achieved the success you have if you hadn't had the—'

'What do you know about my achievements?' she flared angrily.

'Your parents are extremely proud of you...'

Kate's eyes widened with almost comic dismay. She could see it all, Dad rabbiting on in a besotted way about his clever daughter. God, how embarrassing...!

'My father is, you mean.' Kate instantly regretted she'd allowed him to goad her in to making this revealing ob-servation.

'No, your mother would prefer you to marry well, I think.'

Someone like you, she almost flung, before caution in-tervened. 'And I suppose *well,* to you, means someone with loads of money...'

'No I think that's what it means to your mother,' he returned, a shade of impatience entering his voice. 'It of-fends you to be judged on anything other than merit, doesn't it?'

Kate nodded. 'Of course it does!' She knew she'd had more advantages than many people, but she'd worked damned hard to get where she was and had never traded on her father's reputation, despite the fact it could have opened many doors for her.

'Yet you do not hesitate to judge me? You have a fine legal mind; do you not detect a certain inconsistency in your attitude…?'

Kate would have walked on hot coals before she'd have acknowledged the compelling justice of this stinging rebuke; she felt herself colour under his ironic gaze.

'Incidentally,' he drawled, 'I dislike inactivity; it bores me…'

Despite his languid tone, Kate could readily believe that; the man before her was not a relaxing person. It was impossible to imagine spending an evening curled up contentedly on a sofa beside him, watching an old film on telly, and not just because it was highly unlikely he'd ask someone like her; he exuded a restless vitality the like of which she'd never encountered before.

'I do beg your pardon,' she drawled crankily. 'Rich and active.'

'Aren't we rather losing track of the point here? Leaving my bank balance aside for one moment, the doctor did specifically say that you should stay in bed until the morning.'

'Slight problem there—I need the bathroom—*now!*' she revealed with malicious relish—such a statement was sure to dismay this fastidious individual. She was disappointed.

Head tilted slightly to one side, in a gesture she was starting to recognised as characteristic of him, Javier appeared to consider this blunt announcement calmly for a moment before he nodded his head in a manner Kate supposed was the equivalent hereabouts of gracious Royal approval.

'You might own the place,' she grouched, 'but I think

you'll find yourself on shaky legal ground when it comes to wandering uninvited into guests' bedrooms.' Perhaps this wasn't the most gracious response from someone who was occupying a swish suite, courtesy of the management, but Kate was too rattled by his presence to be polite about the intrusion.

'Perhaps we should discuss the legal definition of trespass after you have…erm…availed yourself of the facilities?' he suggested smoothly. 'Next door down,' he added, a sharp tilt of his head indicating the direction she needed to take.

Kate sniffed her disgruntled agreement. 'Everywhere I go he's there!' she grumbled darkly to herself in a voice just about loud enough for him to hear. 'Anyone would think you liked me…' *You wish…!*

His blue eyes dropped to the lush outline of her parted lips. 'Would that be so extraordinary?'

The husky rasp in his voice, combined with the scorching regard, had Kate diving through the door. She heard the sound of his husky amused laugh and her chin went up. Eyes narrowed, she poked her head out from behind the door.

'Yes!' she yelled succinctly before ducking back inside and slamming the door behind her.

Leaning heavily against the wall, waiting for her breathing to slow, she was alarmed to discover a silly grin on her face—anyone would think she enjoyed exchanging insults with the awful man.

A few minutes later, when she emerged from the bathroom, she discovered him lounging indolently in a leather easy chair he'd pulled up to the bedside. He got to his feet as she approached and poured a glass of iced water from the full jug that had appeared magically on her bedside table.

'Plenty of fluids, I believe the doctor said, and maybe

the robe is not such a good idea,' he murmured as she climbed back into bed, still muffled in the thick ankle-length robe she'd pulled on when she'd seen her reflection in the mirrored bathroom wall.

'You might have told me...' she hissed indignantly.

'Told you what?' he asked guilelessly.

As if he didn't know. 'That the damned thing was transparent!' she choked. Not coy about her body, it wasn't the fact that someone had accidentally got an eyeful...it was *who* had received it that had made her duck her head under the cold water tap until she could hold her breath no longer.

'I didn't look.'

The virtuous announcement wrenched a laugh from Kate's throat—so the man had a sense of humour after all. 'This is no laughing matter,' she retorted sternly.

'I wasn't laughing,' he reminded her gently.

Kate decided to anticipate his next inevitable observation. 'But I expect you saw enough to know it isn't me in the photos.' There was no way her trim but unremarkable figure could be mistaken for the celestial vision revealed in the grainy photos.

'Ah, the photographs.' He shrugged. 'The unusual hair colouring did mislead me initially.' His glance lingered on the freshly dampened strands that clung to her face and dripped wetly down her neck. 'But I had already come to the conclusion you were not the model.'

Of course, the figure in the photos didn't have any scars—how slow am I...? 'Pity you didn't catch on *before* you treated me like some sort of cheap tart!' The memory of his stinging contempt still rankled.

'I wasn't the only one guilty of jumping to the wrong conclusions,' he reminded her drily.

As if I could forget Kate thought, shifting uncomfortably as she reviewed with a mental shudder the whole humiliating incident.

'I only thought what you wanted me to?' she countered belligerently. 'It suited your purposes very well to have me scared stiff of you, didn't it?' she accused astutely.

'On occasion, a little bit of fear can expedite matters,' he agreed.

Kate wasn't surprised to see a total lack of remorse in his manner—the man was clearly without principles!

'However,' he continued seamlessly, 'it was obvious from the outset that you are a difficult person to intimidate…'

'An expert on intimidation, are you?'

Far from insulting him, her acid retort only made him look modestly smug. Kate gritted her teeth in frustration; if she hadn't experienced the frightening impact of his raw anger first-hand she wouldn't have believed it was possible to break through that urbane mask. Put him in the witness stand, she brooded darkly, and he'd be every lawyer's nightmare!

'It didn't take an expert at anything to figure out that you are not the sort of woman who would allow herself to be compromised in that way.'

Was that a backhanded compliment or an insult too subtle for her to figure out? Kate puzzled suspiciously. Her candid gaze, which had frequently in the past unnerved the boldest of adversaries, faltered; only by gathering all her mental resources did she maintain eye contact.

'I take it,' she replied finally, 'you still have them—the photos.'

'They are safe,' he confirmed with infuriating caution.

A frown marred the smooth sweep of her forehead as she fought to retain her shaky composure. 'They're mine.' She was unable to prevent the edge of desperation creeping into her belligerent claim.

His keen eyes scanned her tense, strained features. 'We'll discuss this in the morning when you are rested and hopefully feeling less feverish,' he announced, in the manner of someone who was accustomed to having his every suggestion treated as if it was inscribed in stone. 'I'll be in the sitting room, should you require anything; I have some paperwork to attend to. Do not hesitate—'

'We'll discuss it now!' Kate cut shrilly into his formal declaration; if she fell for this phoney concerned line she'd start forgetting who the enemy was.

Javier scanned her flushed agitated face thoughtfully. 'That is probably not a good idea.'

'As it happens, I don't give a damn what you consider a good idea,' she revealed. The biting scorn of her delivery was spoiled by the weak little wobble in her voice.

'As you wish,' he replied, resuming his seat beside the bed. 'I'm assuming you were acting as an agent for…whom exactly…when you broke into that room? The person in the photos? Your sister?'

Kate's tone became increasingly desperate as she sensed herself being pushed into a corner. 'I didn't break in; the door was open…' She might as well have saved her breath; brushed aside her feeble protest with a lofty gesture.

Javier took her lack of denial concerning the identity as confirmation of his suspicions. 'And she was being blackmailed by Gonzalez? He was her lover?'

Kate released a fractured gasp. 'He's not her lover,' she denied. 'He tricked her…maybe even—' She stopped, dismay washing over her as she realised her response had only confirmed Susie's identity. 'How did you…?' she began.

'It hardly required a giant leap to reach these conclusions. Listening to your parents' conversation, it was clear that your sister is somewhat indulged… The sort of person who would send someone else to do her dirty work.'

Kate would have given a lot to have denied this scarily accurate assessment.

'You know nothing about our family situation,' she protested gruffly.

'True,' he conceded, his eyes fixed on his own long interlaced fingers not her face. 'But sometimes families are not so very different.' The curtain of long dark lashes lifted and Kate briefly saw the shadow of something that looked like deep sorrow; it was there so briefly she couldn't decide if she had imagined it or not.

'Take the robe off,' he urged, revealing an unexpected smile of extraordinary charm which lightened his sombre, clean-cut features dramatically and left Kate's lungs fighting to replace the air she had expelled in one startled gasp. When he chose to display it, he had charisma that was off the scale. 'Before you spike a fever once more, for which I will no doubt be blamed.'

'I am a little tired,' she conceded reluctantly.

'Bruised, battered and bone-weary would be nearer the mark, I suspect.'

She should have found this concern coming from the very person she held accountable for her plight a theme for her scorn, but bizarrely she found his consideration and his accented deep tone oddly soothing. Frowning, Kate puzzled over her bizarre response as she slid her arms out of the robe beneath a modestly adjusted duvet.

Her own actions paled into insignificance beside the truly bizarre thing her suspicious sideways stare then revealed. The amazing sight of Javier Montero rearranging her pillows could safely be positioned in the extreme end of bizarre—just about where it started nudging surreal!

He seemed to perform the task most proficiently for a rich playboy.

'Comfortable?' he asked as she collapsed weakly back against them.

Kate nodded, her eyelids felt heavy and it was hard to focus on his dark face. 'If I told anyone you just did that they'd never believe me...' she observed, unable to stifle a jaw-cracking yawn. 'Don't worry, I'm not likely to do so...tell anyone, that is,' she added swiftly, in case he thought him shaking her pillows was something she might want to boast about in future.

His compelling gaze swept her face—Kate could only imagine what she looked like after the trauma of the evening.

'I'm not worried,' he revealed enigmatically before leaving.

A sleepily disarmed and confused Kate was just drifting off to sleep in the quiet of the bedroom when she realised that she still hadn't regained possession of the photographs for Susie.

'In the morning,' she promised herself out loud.

CHAPTER SIX

W<small>HEN</small> Kate awoke, the strands of golden light filtering through the wooden shutters had cast a dappled pattern over the wall beside the bed. For a while she lay there, watching the shifting pattern.

Arm curved above her head, her fingertips brushed across the carved headboard as she stretched languidly; the vast carved bed and fine linen were deliciously decadent. The enervating languor lasted approximately twenty seconds, right up to the point where her memories of the previous night came flooding back.

Why did it have to happen to me…?

Not a person inclined to wallow, she only indulged her self-pitying reflections for a few moments. By the time she turned her head towards the tantalising, nose-twitching smell and had discovered an attractively presented tray set beside the big bed, Kate was in a more pragmatic and positive frame of mind.

She was going to get Susie's photos back and then get on with the rest of her much-needed holiday, her encounter with Javier Montero completely forgotten. An image of his dark, devastatingly attractive features flashed through her head—well, perhaps not *completely,* but he would soon be a nasty memory.

To her surprise Kate discovered she was hungry—very hungry. This had to be a good sign, didn't it?

A few cautious stretches confirmed that most of the aches and pains from the previous night had gone, and when she rotated her head it thankfully no longer felt as though a miniature percussionist was pounding away inside her skull. Whatever bug had made her feel so awful seemed to have succumbed to her own immune system.

There was plenty to appease her healthy hunger and on reflection there didn't seem any danger of placing herself any deeper in Javier's debt by accepting this hospitality. As she surveyed the food she tried with only partial success not to wonder about who might have placed her breakfast there while she lay sleeping. Had Javier kept vigil the entire night or had he delegated the task? The latter seemed much more likely.

Trying to dispel the persistent image in her head of him watching her as she slept, Kate picked up a roll from the selection of breads; it was warm and just asking to be covered with lashings of the golden butter and honey that lay beside it. Her dry mouth watered at the sight of the pot of coffee set beside the comprehensive assortment of fresh fruit. Lifting the cover from the plate, she discovered a plate of fluffy scrambled eggs; with a fork she speared a sliver of smoked salmon from the mound and found it delicious.

Kate had showered, but was still dressing in the clothes she'd been amazed to discover folded neatly over the back of a chair in the bathroom, when she heard sounds coming from the adjoining room. The clothes fitted very well, but then they would; Kate had only purchased the pale green wrap around skirt and halter neck top the previous week.

She was sliding her feet into the soft leather open-toed mules—also new—when there was an extra loud rattle. Either someone was very noisy or they were tactfully letting her know she wasn't alone... She decided this ruled out Javier, who hadn't so far shown any sign of possessing either tact or delicacy!

Despite her conviction that it wasn't him, Kate couldn't help but wish, as she surveyed her pale face in the mirror, that her small make-up bag had been included with her other cosmetics. Not that, having been blessed with a creamy, flawless complexion and naturally dark lashes, she wore anything in the summer but a natural-looking lip-gloss and the occasional dusting of eyeshadow.

Kate would have strongly rebuffed any suggestion that this desire to don face-paint had anything to do with any underlying motive on her part to impress anyone—especially if the *anyone* in question was Javier Montero. This was about feeling confident and, call her shallow, but like most women a coat of lippy could make her feel more assured, and when dealing with an unknown quantity like Javier Montero she needed all the help she could get!

She caught sight of her femininely curved behind in the mirror and the defiant set of her shoulders relaxed as a rueful smile spread across her mobile features. Who am I kidding? Of course I'd like to knock him dead; who wouldn't?

It wasn't going to happen outside her dreams though because, truth told, unlike Susie and similarly blessed females, she simply wasn't endowed with the equipment to impress that way.

'I hope you didn't lock the bathroom door.'

Javier must have very acute hearing, she thought, because he had his back turned to her so couldn't have seen her cautiously entering the bedroom.

He sounded irritated. Not the most auspicious of beginnings, she thought in dismay. Still, if he was as fed up with her as his broad back suggested—what an extraordinarily expressive anatomy he had, she marvelled, momentarily diverted by the shape of his broad, splendidly muscled shoulders and strong straight spine.

Though this started off as an innocently innocuous line of thought, somewhere between his trim waist and snaky hips it took a sharp detour into a lot less virtuous territory, anatomically speaking!

Wrenching free from this downward mental spiral, Kate took a deep breath and began again—distracting anatomical observations strictly banned this time around!

He must be fed up with her; she'd been nothing but a nuisance to him. It stood to reason that he might feel inclined to hand over the photos without any fuss just to get shot of her.

The harsh scowl revealed on his lean, saturnine features as he turned around confirmed her assumption he was not in the best of moods. Standing there, gazing at her critically over long, steepled fingers, she discovered that the man looked much more remote than her overnight mental image of him, and, in a different way, even more threatening than the criminal she had once taken him for.

Whatever else he was, this man was spectacular, she conceded as her heart began to race so frantically it felt as if it might explode from her tight chest any moment. He also had more moods and faces than anyone she'd ever met!

Kate felt no desire to delve beneath the surface of this obviously complex man; superficial details were causing her enough problems, she decided, averting her gaze from the faint shadow of dark body hair she could see through the classic white shirt tucked into a pair of tailored pale linen trousers he wore this morning. Nothing about his vital, arresting figure suggested he hadn't had an uneventful eight hours sleep.

No doubt he was one of those tiresome types who could survive indefinitely on cat naps and coffee, whereas she needed her full eight hours to function at all.

His steely, sweeping scrutiny left her with the vague impression that he found her appearance in some way lacking.

A burst of antagonism made her skin prickle. *So what?* Since when did it matter to me, she challenged herself, that some man didn't like my outfit? It was plain daft to feel aggrieved; he was entitled to his opinion, just like she was entitled not to give a damn!

My appearance is probably a bit of a shock, she reflected contemptuously. He probably doesn't appreciate that it takes the glamorous types he wakes up next to ninety per cent of their time to look that way. These women dedicated to looking beautiful had almost certainly spoilt him for ordinary women like herself.

Fortunately she had never been attracted to the smouldering Southern Mediterranean type.

He could exploit his sexual magnetism for all it was worth; she wasn't going to be distracted. She had to stay focused! Think more about Susie and less about his stern, sensual mouth.

Her chin tilted to an aggressive angle that reflected her militant frame of mind she sauntered across the room.

'If you think this is bad, you should have seen me before the shower!' she snapped with a toss of her head.

Javier had.

He over the years had a number of lovers, but he was not in the habit of spending the entire night with them; perhaps that was why her face in repose had fascinated him so much. He judged it possibly wasn't a good idea, considering her overt hostility, to share these details with her.

'Have I done something to offend you?'

Other than look so damned superior? 'I didn't care for your tone.' Kate didn't care for the gleam of amusement in his eyes as he watched her progression across the room, either.

'You have something against Spanish accents?'

'No, just bossy men of any nationality.' She had no intention of revealing that she found his accent extremely attractive; the velvet rasp of his slightly foreign syllables sent forbidden little shivers down her spine.

'I didn't lock the door...'

She bent her head forwards and shook out her damp hair, teasing the knots in the silken threads with her fingers and showering his immaculate person with wet droplets. Throwing her head back she intercepted an expression in his eyes that almost made her lose her composure—imagined or real, the sensual heat of that fleeting look made her stomach collapse inwards.

'But if I'd known you were in here I definitely would have!' she boasted huskily.

One ebony brow arched expressively. He didn't appear impressed by this slightly desperate display of how unintimidated she was by him—but then it was hard to establish indifference when your voice quivered and shook.

'And if you'd collapsed?'

Well aware she didn't have a leg to stand on, she responded to this common-sense observation with a disdainful toss of her head.

'As you can see.' She held her arms wide and performed a graceful twirl for his benefit. 'I'm fit and well,' she finished triumphantly as her billowing skirts settled back around the long line of her thighs. 'Not a wobble in sight,' she lied cheerfully.

She'd have felt a lot more like smiling if the fact her head was spinning crazily had something to do with the manoeuvre or her weakened condition, but it didn't; it was breathing the same air as this wretched man that turned her into some sort of hormonal junkie!

'No headache, no ache and pains. In fact I'm absolutely fine.'

He picked up a peach from her breakfast tray and bit into the soft flesh.

A sigh snagged in Kate's throat; the fruit had left a faint film of moisture on the sensual outline of his lips, and her stomach muscles spasmed viciously.

'Before you cartwheel around the room...' Javier dwelt

indulgently for a split second on the image of her cart-wheeling around the room in that skirt, so demure, but in-clined, even when cartwheels were not involved, to expose intriguing glimpses of creamy thigh.

Kate intercepting the direction of his fixed stare glanced down, wondering if she had a blob of toothpaste or some-thing on her skirt that had offended his fastidious senses. She smoothed the fabric with her hand but couldn't see anything amiss. When she looked back up his gaze was now fixed on her face, his expression impassive, though there was a curious dark line of colour along the crests of his sharp sculpted cheekbones.

'...Or do fifty push-ups, possibly? I feel I should point out I am quite prepared to accept the fact you were suffer-ing from a twenty-four hour bug and concussion. Your mother—' he shook his dark head slowly from side to side. 'Now that might be a different story. I suspect she won't be satisfied by anything less than a medical certificate and a week's quarantine...and your sister, I got the impression earlier that she was quite happy to have you stay here.'

Kate's face fell as she was struck by the accuracy of his observation. Her mother was not the sort of person to ex-pose herself to the risk of infection, no matter how minus-cule that risk might be.

'You saw Susie?'

Javier had seen many *Susies* and this one had made as little lasting impression as the others. For his money, this sister was much more memorable. The sort of woman his grandfather would consider had fire; he was pleased to see that, true to her word, she didn't try and hide those insig-nificant scars, which to his mind only emphasised the creamy perfection of the rest of her smooth skin.

At a moment when Kate had rarely felt less composed, she would have been astonished to learn that he was ad-miring her confidence.

He inclined his head. 'A temperature of one hundred and two didn't keep you in bed, so I doubted if doctor's orders or myself would have better luck today. I thought you might like to wear your own things this morning. I must say, you look quite charming…'

Kate was dismayed to find herself shifting awkwardly from foot to foot and colouring up hotly like a schoolgirl at the unexpected but slick compliment.

'If it wasn't for the bruise…'

Kate forced herself not to retreat as he moved unexpectedly forwards and, lifting up her fringe, ran a fingertip gently over the discolorated area on her temple.

'You wouldn't know anything had happened. Sorry,' he apologised as she caught her breath sharply.

Kate nodded her head and smoothed her hair back down as his hand fell away. She wasn't about to reveal, not even if her life depended on it, that pain had had nothing to do with her response. The stab of sharp sexual awareness that had jolted through her body at his touch made further self-deception on her part futile.

She ran the tip of her tongue over her dry lips. 'It's bit tender, but don't worry—I'm not contemplating litigation.'

'Probably wise in the circumstances,' he observed drily. 'The truth would do your career more harm than mine.'

'I wasn't doing anything wrong!' she protested.

'Ah, but someone in your position not only needs to be above suspicion, but to *appear* to be above suspicion.'

'That's a horribly cynical thing to say.'

'But true…'

'We'll have to agree to differ.' She accompanied her words with a tight smile that didn't reach her wary eyes. 'Don't worry yourself about my accommodation arrangements, but,' she added casually, as if the idea had just occurred to her, 'before I leave, I might as well take those photos and be out of your hair…' Some perverse mental process immediately made her visualise sliding her fingers deep into that dark, glossy thatch.

'I'm sure we can come to a mutually agreeable arrangement…'

'I don't want to be agreeable!' she bellowed, stamping her foot. There was absolutely no point playing it softly, softly with someone like him. 'I want the photos—*now!*'

Shock flickered across Javier's face. He was not accustomed to receiving peremptory orders from anyone, least of all from a slip of girl like this!

'*Dios Mio,* what a temper you have!' he exclaimed. 'Calm yourself. I'm sure we can negotiate something.'

'Negotiate?' she parroted, brushing a section of damp hair impatiently behind her ear.

Javier's nostrils flared as the clean scent of the shampoo she had just used drifted towards him, the scent subtly mingled with a warm female fragrance. He felt his body react to the stimulus. The strength of the response startled him.

'Negotiation…I want something, you want something, we come to a mutually beneficial arrangement, possibly involving an acceptable degree of compromise,' he elucidated slowly in his rich dark chocolate drawl. 'I would have thought as a lawyer you were au fait with the way it works.'

Now, *compromise* worried her, but the idea of him wanting something she had worried her a lot more!

'What do I have that you want?' Kate quavered, wrapping her arms protectively across her chest. Though the droop of his heavy lids concealed the expression in his eyes, she could detect a worrying gleam through the lush screen.

'I need to get married.'

It was not a response she had expected.

'Congratulations,' Kate responded uncertainly. Trained to observe such things, she automatically noted the slight emphasis on *need* and the significant absence of want, both verbally and non-verbally.

'You have not asked me in what manner this concerns you?'

'I thought you'd get around to telling me…*eventually,*' she observed with an exaggerated sigh.

Her response made his lips quirk appreciatively.

'My grandfather is an old-fashioned man in many ways…' he began heavily.

'This might be quicker if I tell you what I already know. You're talking about Felipe Montero. The one with money, power and grasping relations all jockeying for position to replace him?' The financial pages were not Kate's choice of reading but she'd have needed to be living in a vacuum if she hadn't known something of the circumstances.

'The one with terminal cancer,' came the blunt response.

Kate's scornful smirk drooped. 'Oh, God! I'm so sorry,' she murmured, feeling a total, thoughtless cow. 'I didn't know.'

'That is not accidental; nobody does. If the financial markets learn of his illness, the bottom will drop out of Montero shares, wiping millions off the company's value overnight. To the world, my grandfather *is* Montero,' he outlined unemotionally. 'The obvious solution is for the mantle to pass smoothly to his successor before it becomes public knowledge.'

The cold-bloodedness of this analysis appalled Kate. Searching his face gave her no insight into his attitude towards his grandfather's illness. Did it really mean no more to him than figures on a balance sheet? Was he really that callous?

'You want to be his successor.'

'I am the logical choice. My uncle and cousins, whilst all are capable in their own way, lack leadership qualities.'

Kate marvelled at his astonishing arrogance. 'But you

have those qualities…?' She couldn't tell if he'd recognised the irony in her tone as he calmly conceded her point.

'I do, and I see no reason to deny the fact. I would have thought that you of all people would appreciate candour, but I was forgetting the British consider self-deprecation a virtue,' he drawled. 'Does that make me an arrogant Spaniard?'

His mockery made Kate flush angrily. 'I don't see your problem. Your grandfather needs an heir—you are it. What does it have to do with me?'

'My grandfather and I have not always seen eye to eye; he is not a flexible man…'

This classic demonstration of the pot calling the kettle black brought a grim smile to her lips; as amusing as this was she couldn't see where she came into it. 'Will you get to the damned point?' she pleaded tautly.

'He had let me know that I am his choice but—this is where his old-fashioned standards come into it—only if I am married. He has even gone to the trouble of providing me with a potential mate.'

'Doesn't he think you can find one of your own?' The mocking smile faded dramatically from her face as an extraordinary explanation for his grandfather's intervention presented itself to her. *'You're not…?'* Kate gasped. Another look revealed a tall figure oozing a staggering amount of aggressive masculinity; she smiled a little at her own stupidity and shook her head—*no way* was his sexual orientation in question! There had to be another explanation, but what?

'Not what?' Javier puzzled impatiently.

Kate's eyes dropped from his as she shook her head, extremely relieved she'd managed to put a brake on her impetuous tongue in time to stop her looking a total idiot and probably mortally offending him in the bargain. There were certain things you didn't ask a male and that went

double if he was a Spanish male! Questioning his masculinity definitely came into that category of questions and
the last thing she needed was a swaggering display of tes-
tosterone.

An incredulous exclamation suddenly burst from Javier's
lips as he watched the play of expression on her face.
Without warning, he reached out and cupped her chin in
his hand, raising her chin. Kate didn't offer any resistance,
she was too startled to do anything but stare up at him.

For an intensely uncomfortable moment which, for Kate,
seemed to last for an eternity he searched her face.

'*Madre mia!*' he breathed as an incredulous expression
spread across his face. 'That *is* what you meant, isn't it?'
he marvelled.

Guilty colour flooded Kate's cheeks as she jerked her
chin from his light grasp and dropped down into a convenient chair her knees shaking uncontrollably.

'I might be able to confirm or deny if I had the faintest
idea what you were talking about...' she prevaricated
stiffly.

'My sexual orientation is not something I've been called
upon to defend before,' he mused.

Kate covered her face and groaned. How could you argue
with someone who appeared to possess the ability to read
your mind?

'But,' he continued silkily, 'I've never been one to duck
a challenge...' Kate peeked through her parted fingers; she
didn't like the sound of that steely sentiment or the worrying gleam in his eyes. 'Let me reassure you I do *like*
women. *Exclusively,*' he added grinning wolfishly.

And I bet they like you right back.

'I'm happy for you,' she choked. 'It was only a passing
thought,' she added, trying to defuse the situation. 'No need
for any rash demonstrations; I'm totally prepared to believe
you're rampantly heterosexual.' The thought that any dem-

onstration might take the form of something crude—like a kiss—made it hard for her not to hyperventilate.

It would naturally be horrifying and appalling to be kissed under these circumstances. Part of her couldn't help but wonder if the price wouldn't be worth paying, just to satisfy her curiosity... What would it feel like to be kissed by Javier Montero?

'That makes me feel a great deal easier.'

Kate's eyes narrowed as she glared at him with resentful dislike. 'But I soon realised you weren't gay, just too immature to contemplate commitment.' A person had a right to think stupid things without being called upon to defend her thoughts. 'For one daft moment there I was actually worried about your fragile Spanish male ego coping with a perceived slur on your manhood.'

'It was a close thing for a minute...' he conceded drily.

'A force ten hurricane couldn't dent your ego!' Kate snorted.

'I'm sorry if I fail to comply with your stereotyping of Southern Mediterranean man, Kate. I'll walk around with my shirt open to the waist.' He flicked open a button at mid-chest level and revealed a section of deep golden flesh covered with a light sprinkling of dark hair. He contemplated the area with a lot more composure than she did. 'And wear a flashy gold medallion, maybe.' His head lifted. 'What do you think?' he appealed to her with searing sarcasm. 'Will a little tacky exhibitionism make you feel more secure? Or shall I pinch your bottom?'

Secure? Kate, the blood pounding heavily in her temples, dragged her glazed eyes from the section of tanned skin. While she was in the same country as this infuriating man who twisted everything she said, she wouldn't feel secure.

'I do not stereotype people,' she denied hotly. 'It's just you *are* single and not exactly in the first flush of youth...' Even to Kate's ears, this sounded a pretty feeble excuse.

'Not that you're old exactly…' Way to go, Kate—call him gay and decrepit and he's bound to hand over the photos.

'So all unmarried men in their thirties are gay. Let me see, have I got this right?' he pondered innocently. 'That's *not* stereotyping?'

'I didn't mean anything of the sort!' Kate closed her eyes and sent up a silent prayer for deliverance. She took a steadying breath and met his eyes with what she hoped was some degree of composure. 'It's not as if I could give two hoots one way or the other where, when or with whom you have sex. It's your aversion to arranged marriages we were discussing… What's wrong, is your grandfather's choice of prospective bride the problem? Is she a bit of a dog?' She'd never thought to hear herself use such a derisory term to describe one of her own sex which just showed what a corrupting influence this man had upon her.

'No; as a matter of fact, Aria is beautiful and accomplished and in love with me…'

He seemed to accept this adulation in his stride; it must have something to do with having been on the receiving end of adulation all of his adult life, she supposed.

'How nice for you.'

'I do not love her.'

'And that matters to you?' She couldn't hide her scepticism.

Did men like him marry for love? It surprised Kate that he even knew the meaning of the word!

But then who am I to talk? It's not as if I'm the expert, she thought gloomily reviewing her love life—it took all of ten seconds! Seb had been the only serious boyfriend she'd ever had, her first lover and sometimes she thought maybe her last! Not that she was pining; once the dust had settled she'd realised the only part of her hurt by the experience was her pride.

Maybe Seb had had a point when he'd said there was no point staying in a relationship that was going nowhere.

'I'll always come second to your career,' he'd accused. Well it hadn't taken him long to find a girl who put him first; they were expecting their first baby any time now.

'But I am fond of Aria, too fond to marry her. So what I need is a woman who will go through a ceremony with me; after a suitable interval we would part.'

Kate stiffened; the pupils of his eyes dilated dramatically as she stared up at him—he couldn't be suggesting…? *Could he?* She gave a wry smile and shook her head. Maybe that knock on the head had fused a few circuits, because nobody with a full complement of wits could imagine even briefly he'd come up with a plan like that!

'I wouldn't have thought you'd have a lot of trouble finding someone to oblige you, especially if the remuneration for the contract is generous,' she observed cynically. Actually, she could think of several women who would do it for free!

Even she could see the more obvious attractions of such a scheme.

'My grandfather is a highly intelligent man. He would not be deceived by some plausible gold-digger.' The furrows across his broad brow deepened as he re-examined the problem. 'I need someone *different*…preferably British and fair… Someone who will not be easily intimidated… Someone who at the end of the day will go back to her own life and leave me to mine.'

'Why British and fair?' Kate asked, intrigued despite herself by the reference that stood out in a truly bizarre speech as more puzzling than the rest.

'Because he knows that the woman I fell in love with is both.' Kate gasped but Javier continued, 'You find the notion of me loving someone so incredible?'

Actually she found the fact of some woman having the

good sense not to love him back incredible because, whatever else he was, he had sex appeal oozing out of every pore.

'Nice dental work, Kate,' he observed dryly, 'but the open-mouthed look is not a good one for you.'

Kate closed her mouth with an audible snap.

'Why don't you marry this woman?'

'That was my plan, although I doubt if she realised it, but that's irrelevant. She fell in love with someone else, someone who happens to be one of my best friends.'

Surely this was a man who wouldn't be constrained by the limits of polite society? Failure of any sort must be unpalatable in the extreme to a man of his disposition. It didn't matter how hard she tried to picture Javier as a rejected suitor, she couldn't! Her eyes drifted to the sensual outline of his mouth...why, even I would be *slightly* tempted in the unlikely scenario of him making a pass at me and I don't even like dark brooding types.

'And that puts her off limits?' It brought him down to a worryingly human level to discover he'd actually experienced rejection.

'This has nothing to do with morals; you cannot make someone love you.'

Undeterred by the repressive chill in his voice, she was unable to restrain herself from pushing it. For some reason she found his pragmatism depressing. She might accept her own fate with similar stoicism but, although she might personally prefer her men predictable with manageable-sized passions, the closet romantic in her wanted there to be men out there with souls of fire and passion, men who would fight with his dying breath to win over the woman he loved!

'Did you try?'

An unreadable expression, that might have been his equivalent of a violent emotional outburst, flickered across his taut features. 'What is this, a counselling session?'

'I see you did, but she wouldn't. Wow! I'd really like to meet her!' she responded incautiously.

'You shall. Sarah has agreed to be a witness at our wedding tomorrow.'

CHAPTER SEVEN

KATE blinked several times and waited until the room appeared the right way up once more before hoarsely responding. 'Come again…'

'*Come again…?* I am not familiar with the term.'

'My eye! The ignorance card isn't going to get you off this hook, mate!' Kate exploded. 'You must be out of your tiny mind if you think I'm going to agree to marry you so you can inherit the family store!'

Javier coughed; it took him several moments to adjust to hearing a multi-billion empire dismissively referred to as the 'family store.' 'It will cause you the minimum of inconvenience—a paper arrangement, no more.'

He was clearly unbalanced. 'I hope this Aria of yours is no relation, because I'm getting the strong impression here that there's already been a bit too much in-breeding in your family. Cousins marrying cousins, that sort of thing, if you get my drift…?'

'I thought you wanted the photos.'

A pained expression of regret crossed Kate's face, but perhaps it was best this way; maybe it was time Susie started taking responsibility for her own actions.

'I care for my sister.' Her eloquent sniff managed to intimate that he didn't know the meaning of the word. 'I'd do a great deal for her…'

His eyes touched the bruised area on her temple. 'Most people would say you already have.'

'But marrying a blackmailing lunatic is not one of them.'

'My grandfather will really like your candour.'

Kate threw up her hands. What I really need to do, she

decided, is take a deep breath and stand back from all this *weirdness*. Far enough away, this situation might even have a funny side…?

'Are you not listening to me?' Silly question—of course he wasn't; he obviously didn't listen to anyone. 'I'm not going to marry you!' she delivered firmly, drawing a shaky hand threw her damp hair. 'Not even if you send those photos to the newspapers, but you might like to reflect when you do it that when it comes down to it you're no better than that scumbag who drugged my sister and took them!' Bosom heaving, lip curled in contempt, she met his eyes.

What she saw on his face made her catch her breath and hold it. Maybe she'd gone too far, she reflected, as he visibly fought to control the rage that contorted his lean features… She watched as inch by inch he gained control until only the throbbing pulse beside his mouth was left to remind her of that blaze of consuming fury.

'They're yours.'

Kate stared at the packet he placed on her lap suspiciously. 'Is this some sort of trick?'

'I am not interested in shaming a family because of the mistake of one member and, as for Gonzalez, he will not escape justice.'

From any other man, Kate might have taken this as an idle boast but when Javier said it there was nothing idle or boastful about it—he was just stating fact, and she found herself accepting it as such.

She picked up the buff envelope and found her fingers were trembling—there had to be a catch. 'Isn't this your bargaining chip in the negotiation we were talking about? It hardly makes sense for you to give it away.'

'I am a tough negotiator, not a petty criminal,' he replied, the pride that had remained unruffled by her clumsy attack on his masculinity clearly offended by her opinion of his business acumen.

'Then I don't understand...' A small scornful smile curved her lips. 'Oh, you probably think everyone has their price...! Yes,' she mused letting her glance move over him from head to toe and back again, 'you would.'

The dark fan of lashes lifted from his cheek; his expression radiated confidence. 'It's just a matter of discovering what it is.'

The sinister implication that he had found hers made Kate shiver. She dismissed the idea as foolish; she had many sins but avarice was not one of them.

'You shouldn't judge everyone else by your own standards. You see, I don't want your money...' she revealed, injecting a note of pity into her tone that brought a satisfactory flare of annoyance to his eyes.

'Not for yourself, perhaps...'

Kate frowned. 'What do you mean...?'

'I was thinking about the project to provide an extension on the burns unit at the children's hospital you yourself were treated at, and the new accommodation facilities in the existing unit so that families of patients having long-term treatment can stay with their children...'

Kate surged to her feet, her body rigid with suspicion. Though it might be important to her and others involved, their fund-raising activities on behalf of the unit barely rated a mention in the local press, let alone any journal he might have read. Unless she talked in her sleep, there was no way he could know about them.

'What do you know about that?' she demanded, hardly able to hear herself past the alarm bells clanging in her head. 'H-how did you find out...? Did my parents tell you or...?'

'I have not seen your parents since last night.'

'Then how?'

'The how is irrelevant.' He dismissed her questions with a fluid gesture.

Kate's full lips compressed. 'Not to me it isn't.' She raised a hand to her spinning head and tried to think straight.

'It's not complicated. Information is easy to find at any time of the day if you know where to look, and who to ask.'

And he clearly did. What was obvious normal practice for him appalled her. *Implacable,* the word flashed into Kate's head as she met his impassive stare with one of incredulity.

'It's easy to invade someone's privacy, you mean,' she corrected, her distaste for his questionable tactics written clearly across pale, outraged features as she lifted her eyes to his.

'Someone in my position knows only too well how easy,' he agreed heavily. 'One learns the hard way how to protect oneself from intrusions.'

His hypocrisy was staggering! 'Clearly you don't believe in the principle of treating others as you would be treated yourself,' she observed contemptuously. 'What other questions did you ask about me when you were grubbing around in my life?'

'Only relevant ones.'

On anyone else, Kate would have been inclined to believe the slight flush along his cheekbones might have been a reflection of discomfort. 'Such as?'

'I know that you have no lover who might be an obstacle to our plan.'

As her knees sagged, Kate's hand closed over the nearest thing to hand, which happened to be Javier's forearm; it immediately stiffened to offer her extra support.

'*Our* plan…? *Your* plan!' she contradicted, wanting to disassociate herself with this absurd scheme straight off.

She stared at the image of her white-knuckled fingers digging into crisp cotton; she stared so hard everything else swam out of focus. Underneath the thin material she was conscious of the crisp texture of fine body hair, the heat of his skin and overlying everything else the sinewy iron strength. The stab of sexual energy that sizzled through her body was so unexpected, so shockingly intense, it took her breath away. Kate removed her hand as if burnt as her stomach took a great diving lurch downwards.

Head bent, hands braced on her thighs, she exhaled in a series of short panting breaths before she dared to lift her eyes to his. It was mortifying to discover she was so sexually receptive to someone she despised so completely, someone to whom she was no more than a tool to be callously manipulated for his own financial gain.

When she did angle a wary glance up at him, she was dismayed to see a flicker of something perilously close to sympathy in his eyes. That look seemed to say he understood her reactions better than she did herself. Not that that would be so damned hard, because at that moment Kate had never had less insight into what she was feeling or why!

Determined that, if nothing else, she would at least show him she was not another silly female who swooned at the sight of him, she returned the look with one of smouldering derision.

'What would you have done if I had had a boyfriend, Javier, arranged for him to have an *accident?*' she asked sarcastically. Her glance slid over his tall figure and hard, ruthless features and suddenly it didn't seem such a joke any more—he looked capable of *anything*.

'Now you are being hysterical,' he observed, his attitude that of someone getting bored with the entire discussion.

Kate gave a disbelieving laugh—was he for real…? 'No, but I'm getting there,' she told him grimly. 'And your in-

formation is wrong. I do have a boyfriend, Seb Leigh…'
She served a smug little smile. 'He's a QC and he's—'

'I'm sure his CV is as impressive as your own,' came
the cool contradiction. 'However, Mr Leigh *was* your lover,
isn't that so, Kate? Your second serious relationship, I believe…?' He appeared to interpret the choking sound that
emerged from Kate's throat as confirmation of this. 'But he
is out of the picture. You split up a year ago and he is now
married to someone else. Does that bother you?'

Kate stood there seething and feeling as foolish as anyone would caught pretending to have a relationship. What
made her angriest was the impression it gave that she felt
somehow inadequate and incomplete without a man, when
nothing could have been farther from the truth.

'You mean your sources didn't supply you with that information? How annoying.'

'It is not actually relevant,' he conceded. 'I was just wondering if you have any regrets… Of course, many women
like yourself delay marriage, concentrating their energies
on building their career, not a family.'

'I intend to have both one day.'

'Unlike many career-minded women you seem to have
retained an oddly naïve quality,' he observed thoughtfully.

'What's so naïve about thinking you can have both?' she
began aggressively.

Javier acted as though she hadn't spoken. 'It is not unattractive,' he revealed in his rough velvet drawl.

He held her startled gaze for long enough to see her
shock register on her face before allowing his gaze to drop.

This unexpected development ambushed Kate's wits. Her
pulses went haywire; she went hot, she went cold; for several seconds the only thing she could do was tremble and
admire the luxuriant sweep of his lashes as they brushed
against his high cheekbones.

And why? she asked herself.

Just because he's deigned to say you're not totally repulsive! How sad it is that? A bit of mild ego-boosting and you start thinking with your hormones, which can't be a bad thing from his point of view; someone smitten with lust is going to be a lot more pliable. The last thing she wanted to do was make Javier Montero's life easier!

'But not your type, obviously…' If an insult was pending, Kate made it her rule to get in first.

The iridescent blue gaze landed back on her face and stayed there.

Kate suffered a second searing jolt in as many minutes.

Being a sensible woman meant that she didn't read anything personal in the smouldering intensity she encountered when their eyes locked. Sensuality was innate to him; it was revealed in his slightest movement, the proud angle of his head, his voice… Another shiver snaked on her spine at the thought of his honeyed, husky drawl.

Her body either couldn't or didn't want to hear what she was telling it, because it responded brazenly to the glitter in his spectacular eyes. As she struggled to control the violent fluctuations of her breathing, she was acutely conscious of the burning sensitivity in her engorged nipples and the ache low in her belly.

'I wouldn't contemplate marrying anyone I found repulsive,' he revealed.

'Neither would I,' she retorted instantly. '*Normally*. What's so funny?' she demanded.

'You are a very bad liar.'

'No, I'm not!' she retorted indignantly. Amusement flared afresh in his eyes and Kate bit her lip. 'That is, I'm not lying.'

For what seemed like a long time he surveyed her with that air of inscrutable calm she found so exasperating; finally he shrugged. 'If you prefer for your own reasons to pretend you are totally unaware of the sexual chemistry that exists between us, I will naturally accept your wishes. These causes you espouse,' he continued seamlessly. 'They do require funds?'

There was a twenty-second time lag before his words made much sense to Kate, who had a lot more trouble than he appeared to have in shifting her turbulent thoughts from personal to business.

'We are raising money. The raft race, the sponsored—' she began numbly.

Sexual chemistry, he'd said. She swallowed hard as her eyes darted furtively towards his mouth. Oh, hell, Kate why did you deny it, act as if it was some big deal? Why didn't you just shrug it off? Maybe because you knew you couldn't?

He clicked his fingers. 'A drop in the ocean,' he responded dismissively.

'We'll get there.' Of course, an awful lot of sick kids would have grown up by then—the lucky ones anyway.

'You'll get there a lot faster if I make up the shortfall,' he interrupted casually.

Kate laughed shakily. 'Have you any idea how much that is? We're not talking hundreds or even thousands, we're talking—'

'Millions—yes, I know,' he interrupted calmly.

Kate's jaw dropped. 'And you'll pay for that?' She gulped—this man had taken moral blackmail to another level! What he was offering would mean so much to so many people. The injured children, the parents, the highly trained team of staff whose hard work and dedication could only partly compensate for a chronic lack of investment in the burns unit. How will I feel the next time a child is turned away because there is no spare bed, if I know that I could have made the difference…?

'If you agree to marry me I'll sign the cheque now… You fill in the amount.' He watched, arms folded across his chest, as the conflicting emotions tripped across her face.

Kate couldn't take her eyes from the cheque and pen he placed on the table. She touched her tongue to the beads of sweat across her upper lip.

'This money doesn't mean anything to you, does it? The children it could help, they mean nothing to you either? No more than I do?' He responded to her whispered accusation with a shrug—what did you expect? Him to dramatically reveal it's really you he wants, not control of the Montero empire?

Her trembling lips compressed into a mutinous line. 'What if I say I will, then I bank the money and back out at the last minute?' she asked, licking her dry lips.

His smiled thinly. 'I trust you, you are a woman of principle…' He made it sound like a vice. 'One who will put the welfare of others ahead of her own personal desires…'

Kate lifted her eyes an expression of loathing on her face. 'I'm not a martyr.'

'No,' he conceded. 'A martyr would marry me to save her family embarrassment. You will marry me to help thousands of children have better care in the future, because you care passionately about them.'

'Are you so sure of me?' she wondered, trying to hide her growing sense of despair.

'Yes, I am. We can argue for a while if you like—but your decision is inevitable and we both know it.'

Kate swallowed convulsively. 'I have a career.'

'I'm not asking you to give it up; a short sabbatical should suffice for our purposes.'

'I'll want everything in writing and you'll give the money to the unit up front?' I'm mad, quite mad…

'Naturally.'

'Including a clause that guarantees you don't lay a finger on me?'

'You can't legislate against passion between two people.' His glance moved over her body in a way that made her aware of it all over again in a very disturbing way. 'Will my word not suffice?'

Kate threw back her head and laughed to hide the fact she was still seriously spooked by his reference to passion. 'That's the funniest thing I've ever heard. I wouldn't take your word for it if you told me the sun is going to rise tomorrow.'

There was real loathing in her eyes as she glared up at him; Javier regretted her animosity but felt it was a small price to pay for letting his grandfather die a happy man—it was a pity, though. In other circumstances he suspected they could have been friends... Well, maybe not friends, not with the lust factor.

'And they say trust is the most important thing in a marriage,' he sighed.

CHAPTER EIGHT

JAVIER was sitting tapping his index finger impatiently against the steering wheel when the fair-headed figure finally appeared around the corner. As he watched she gave a quick furtive glance over one shoulder, then the other.

He half expected her to daub her face with camouflage paint and slither across the courtyard on her belly, commando-style, but as he watched she lifted her rounded little chin and took a deep breath; then, shoulders back walked purposefully towards the car as fast as the pair of ridiculously high-heeled strappy sandals she wore would allow. Clearly she was too proud to allow him to see her apprehension, Javier concluded with grudging admiration.

As Kate approached the long shiny car, the tinted window on the driver's side lowered. A supremely confident Javier, his lean body clad in a dark formal suit, was revealed at the wheel. Sometimes the drivers of classy cars were a bit of a let-down, but not in this case!

Kate stopped dead in her tracks as he slowly lowered the stylish dark shades he wore and looked at her over the top. She felt every muscle in her body grow tense and rigid as she endured his laser like scrutiny.

Elbow resting on the open window, his long fingers drummed against the shiny paintwork as he waited expectantly. 'Don't just stand there, get in!'

Kate flushed at the peremptory tone. 'I was just trying to decide whether what I'm doing could be termed elopement,' she replied, in an attempt to divert attention from the embarrassing fact she'd been staring at him with all the subtlety of a star-struck adolescent!

'Or if it's only elopement when star-crossed lovers are involved?' she finished, panting slightly as she took her place beside him in the passenger seat.

The mild exertion Javier noted had brought a very attractive flush to the smooth contours of her cheeks; he couldn't place the perfume but she also smelt rather good.

'You are late!' he rapped.

Kate, who had been about to apologise for her tardiness, closed her mouth with a snap. The sudden eye movement as she dealt him a cold look made her conscious of the irritating presence of the contact lenses she rarely wore—damned things.

'I had a visit from Susie; I had to wait until she'd gone, or would you prefer I'd brought her along…?'

She pushed a hank of fair hair from her face with her forearm and wondered if perhaps it might not have been better to put it up after all. Until Susie's comment about the length of her neck—there was too much of it, apparently—she had thought the loose chignon was not only cool but quite attractive.

Kate had been rather touched by Susie's unexpected visit to her sick bed until she realised that her sister had come to make sure that she had managed to retrieve the negatives before she'd been taken ill. Susie had been extremely relieved when Kate had handed over the envelope.

Once her own problems were solved, an elated Susie had moved on to the next thing on her agenda—Javier Montero and how did well Kate know him anyhow?

It had been insultingly easy for Kate to convince her sister that her own supposed friendship with the fabled Javier Montero was a big misunderstanding.

'I knew it was,' Susie had revealed smugly. 'I mean, no insult intended, Katie, but the likes of Javier Montero is hardly likely to date someone like you.' But not someone like me, her smug expression seemed to imply.

'True, but that's his loss,' Kate had replied grandly.

'That's right, Katie.' Susie patted her sister's shoulder in an encouraging manner. 'I do so admire your positive attitude. Tell me,' she added casually, 'is he seeing anyone at the moment?'

'Positive attitude nothing! If I had that man for a couple of weeks I might be able to teach him a bit of humility,' Kate boasted ambitiously. 'And that,' she declared, 'would be doing womankind a big favour!'

'But, Kate, when I saw him he was charming!'

'If you were wearing that outfit, I'm not surprised!' Kate retorted; the idea of Javier slobbering over her nubile baby sister was particularly unappealing.

Susie laughed and slid her hands complacently over her slim, evenly tanned hips.

'Stay away from him, Susie!' Kate advised abruptly.

Susie stared at her in astonishment.

'He'd eat you up and spit you out. He's a devious snake,' Kate had elaborated with so much vehemence that her sister had laughed nervously and remembered a previous engagement.

Just how she was going to explain away her comments when Susie discovered she'd married the snake she didn't know, but when she considered her other problems this one didn't rate priority treatment! No matter what spin you put on it, the bottom line was Javier had bought his bride, and she was it!

Despite her initial reluctance to keep her family in the dark, the encounter with Susie had made her think that Javier had a point when he had said that the fewer people that knew about this beforehand the better. There was certainly no way she was going to convince anyone who knew her that she was anything other than a very reluctant bride!

Javier gave her a veiled look. 'You would have preferred the support of your family today…?'

Rebellion simmering not far below the surface flared up as she eyed him resentfully.

'*Hardly!*' she responded scornfully. 'Marrying you is not an event I'd want anyone I know to witness; I've got a reputation as a rational human being to protect. Or did you mean it in a someone to hold while you're having a tooth pulled sort of way? Or maybe…'

The sound of his hissing exhalation brought her diatribe to an abrupt halt. She got the impression that he wanted to say quite a lot to her but he contented himself with, 'I'm prepared to put up with your sarcasm up to a point.'

Despite his level tone Kate was left with the impression that dismissal was implicit in his cool manner. Kate, who had felt nervous and anxious when she'd got into the car, felt her anger climb. She watched as he loosened a button of his exquisitely cut jacket before adjusting the driving mirror a fraction; it was obvious to her that he was a man to whom such minor details were important. He was also a man who she knew next to nothing about… So far, she'd kept her anxiety levels in check by not thinking too far ahead, but she wouldn't have that luxury soon, she'd be married!

Filled by pure panic, she launched immediately into a vitriolic attack.

'If you want people to believe this marriage is for real, you'll have to start talking to me as if I'm a human being, not a disobedient puppy being brought to heel…' Yes, mate, she thought as he turned his head, I can actually instigate a conversation without permission.

For a split second she thought he was going to explode, then a dangerous, contemplative expression slid across his grim features. She observed the transformation with deep foreboding.

'In what sense, *real?*'

Kate's head snapped back at this totally unexpected response. Heat flooded her face; the speculative gleam in his eyes made it impossible for her to mistake his meaning.

'Not that one!' she advised him darkly.

Aware his glance had wandered to her legs, neatly crossed at the ankle, she began smoothing down the skirt of her short cream shift dress, angry at herself for allowing him to discompose her so easily.

Her actions drew his gaze and inevitably his criticism— the girl he married for real was in for a rough ride, she decided sourly.

'You are wearing *that?*' If he were to be her husband in the real sense, the idea of other men lustfully ogling those long, extremely shapely legs would have disturbed him.

Kate drew herself up huffily. She may have to marry him; she wasn't going to let him criticise her dress sense into the bargain! Even if the dress in question had returned from the dry cleaners a good two inches shorter than it went there... This discovery had almost reduced her to tears, but there had been no time to change.

'I had this boyfriend once,' she explained, as she fixed him with a dangerously narrowed gaze. 'He thought I ought to wear winter colours, whatever they might be. He also wanted me to grow my hair and shorten my skirts... I have to tell you he lasted about five minutes, but I expect you've already learnt this from your in-depth dossier on my life and loves...' she observed sweetly.

'Your love life didn't take up much space, which surprises me for you are clearly a very sensual, passionate woman.' This frank observation was accompanied by a slow, sensual smile of the heart-stopping variety.

Kate felt her composure, already in pretty bad shape from sharing a confined space with him, shatter into a thousand fragments.

'Leave my love life out of this!'

'But you introduced the subject.'

'I wasn't introducing any subject; I was simply laying down a few ground rules,' Kate gritted.

'*You,* are laying down rules for *me!*' he responded with an air of startled incredulity.

Kate shrugged. 'You can like it or lump it.'

His eyes narrowed. 'I thought me *not* liking it was what this was about; you are determined to make the time we spend together as unpleasant as possible. Do you always feel the need to be in charge in a relationship?'

'We don't have a relationship.'

'Not of the conventional kind,' he conceded.

'Not of any kind.'

'We're going to be seeing quite a lot of one another, and life would be a lot more comfortable if rather than pick fights you tried to get along with me…'

'That's a big ask.'

'If you're nourishing some hope that I will find you so intolerable I will call off the wedding—don't. Incidentally, did the hospital receive the funds…?'

'Yes.' His smooth question threw her off balance.

David Fenner, the clinical director, had been euphoric. 'I don't know how to thank you,' he kept saying over and over. 'Please tell the anonymous donor how much this means to us, Kate. It's a marvellous thing he's doing for us.' It was at that moment Kate had realised that she'd burnt her boats big time!

'They were grateful.'

'I don't want their gratitude.' She felt him studying her face and lifted her head. 'I want you.'

Kate knew he didn't mean it that way, but all the same she felt the knot of sexual heat in her belly swell to bursting point. 'I have that effect on men.'

Her quip didn't make him laugh the way it was meant to. If anything, the tension between them increased.

'I won't have you dictate what I wear,' she heard herself

babble. 'I'm sorry I don't meet your high standards…' Her glare moved disparagingly over his tastefully clad figure— nothing to criticise there; everything about him shrieked good taste and money. 'Though some people might consider your orthodox style a bit on the well…on the *insipid* side,' she mused spitefully. 'But then I suppose not everyone has an individuality to reflect…' Her spite suddenly ran out of steam as a giant wave of despondency hit her. 'Oh, God!' she groaned. 'I wish I'd just worn the pink shorts suit and been done with it.' That childish act of rebellion would have at least shown him how totally unsuitable she was for the role he wanted her to play.

'And I'm sure you'd have looked charming in it,' he responded grimly.

A sudden giggle welled in Kate's throat; the sound as it escaped made him stare at her in a startled fashion. 'You wouldn't have said that if you'd seen me in it. My bottom looked like the size of a double-decker bus…' she elaborated.

A gleam of startled amusement appeared in his eyes. 'You are very frank and rather severe on yourself. I didn't actually say that I didn't like your dress…' he reminded her, his eyes sliding of their own volition to her legs.

Kate viewed this blatant attempt to steer the conversation away from the thorny subject of her bottom with a sour smile. Of course, if he'd been a total hypocrite he could simply have said, *It's a delicious bottom, just the right size,* but Kate recognised this was not the most likely of scenarios!

'I couldn't care less!' she sniffed childishly.

'Then why are you making such an issue of it? The fact is, I have no desire to act as some sort of fashion police. I was merely vexed that I hadn't taken into account the likelihood you would not have a suitable outfit with you. I know women care about such things as wedding outfits…'

'Your concern is touching, but quite unnecessary. You're confusing me with a real blushing bride again. I'm not going to be flicking through the wedding album all dewy-eyed and remembering how fantastic you looked in your wedding suit—at least one of us looks the part,' she inserted bitterly.

'My appearance seems to bother you.'

'Everything about you bothers me!' she countered with a frustrated groan. 'Listen, there's no point acting as if this is a society wedding.' Kate was horrified to hear the wistful note in her voice…which, considering she had never lusted after a big wedding and all the frills in her life, had no right to be there in the first place! It was too much to hope he hadn't detected it too?

'You are angry because I have cheated you out of your opportunity to float down the aisle in white on your father's arm.'

'I'm not bitter, and as far as I'm concerned the fewer things I have to remind me of today the better, so you see the fact that I can bin this dress is no bad thing.'

Javier was just about to deliver a biting response to this sneering retort when he saw a single tear slip down her cheek. As he watched she brushed it away with the back of her hand and blinked rapidly to prevent any more escaping.

'I expect Sarah will have something you can wear over your head. That will have to suffice.'

The mention of the other woman made Kate glance across at him; it was impossible to tell from his expression what he felt when he said her name, or even if he felt anything!

'My manner was a little terse when you arrived because I do not like to be kept waiting…' This conciliatory tack made Kate wary. 'I think it's quite useful for you to know little details like this; it builds up a picture of familiarity…intimacy.'

'*Intimacy…!*' She laughed, her scorn more fierce because the mental link of intimacy and Javier stirred up an unsettling mess of confusing feelings deep in her stomach. 'If you think I'm ever going to be able to act cosy with you, you're a deeply deluded man,' she observed pityingly.

'But you will try…' he replied, with a hint of steel in his voice.

'It was part of the agreement,' she conceded uneasily.

'Just so long as you don't forget it…'

'Don't you dare threaten or…'

'Or what…?' Javier immediately regretted that he'd allowed her to goad him into this taunt.

Kate felt her temper rise. They both knew the answer; she could do nothing. Flushing darkly she looked away.

'And while we're talking manners I think your own might need a little modification also…?' he suggested drily as he turned the ignition.

'What's wrong with my manner?'

'You are petulant, confrontational and cranky,' he enumerated calmly.

'Well, that's one of those *little details* you should know about me. I'm always *cranky* when I'm being coerced into marrying a loathsome man I deeply despise. A man who will stoop to any depths in his pathetic pursuit of power and money—'

'Enough!' Javier's savage exclamation sliced through her furious diatribe. '*Madre mia,*' he snarled, his air of faint indulgence vanishing as his patience snapped. 'You will not speak to me in that manner.'

'*Really!* I thought it helped build up a picture of intimacy?' she returned innocently.

'*Por Dios!*' he breathed.

Kate felt the beginning of a guilty backlash to her nastiness as she watched him lean back in his seat. Pressing his head into the head rest, he closed his eyes and, with an expression of frustration on his face, dragged a hand through his dark hair.

She sighed as her sense of fair play kicked in hard... You'll probably regret this, she told herself as she cleared her throat. 'I'm sorry.'

He looked up, startled, at the soft apology.

'I'm not being fair. I didn't have to agree to marry you...it was my decision.' She sniffed and searched for a non-existent tissue. 'Thank you,' she murmured as a freshly laundered handkerchief was pressed into her sweaty palm. 'You dangled a carrot and I went for it...' So, as nice as it was to blame him for everything and absolve herself from all responsibility, it just wasn't on.

'I exploited your weakness.' An expression she didn't understand flickered into his iridescent eyes as they swept over her face. 'If caring about other people is a weakness?' he added softly.

'You get something you want and I get something I want.' Quietly she outlined the bare bones of their contract. 'You've kept your end of the bargain, I'll keep mine,' she promised with a stoic little grimace. 'I just think you could have invested your money more wisely.' Just thinking about the sheer volume of money they were talking scared her; for that amount he could have employed an Oscar-winning actress! 'Nobody is going to believe you wanted to marry *me*.'

'That is because...?'

'I'm not exactly a supermodel...'

'Is this any supermodel in particular or...?'

Kate bristled at his smooth sarcastic tone. 'You know what I mean.'

'I do indeed,' he replied, fingering the leather steering wheel.

Kate eyed his steel-reinforced jaw with some misgivings; it seemed even when she went out of the way to avoid conflict she still managed to aggravate him.

'I have to tell you again that I don't consider the British habit of self-deprecation an attractive one... Neither do I care for someone assuming to know what I find attractive in a woman.'

This was too much for Kate, who laughed in disbelief...he was different from other men, but she refused to believe he was *that* different.

'It's not exactly a *big* assumption. I'd say that ninety-nine point nine per cent of men in the world fantasise about women like that. The only difference between you and them—' other than a perfect masculine physique, a strikingly handsome face made to haunt a girl's dreams, and an indecent quantity of rampant sex appeal '—is you're in a position to do something about it,' she finished breathlessly—her unwise contemplation of what he had going for him had played havoc with her breathing.

Her wariness increased as Javier absorbed her words in brooding silence.

'My money, you mean.'

'Well, that too,' she conceded dismissively. She was sure that even had he been dirt-poor Javier would never have lacked female attention. 'But it was thinking more about your...' Kate stopped, aghast at what she'd been about to say. You couldn't go around telling men they were incredibly beautiful.

'My...?' he prompted attentively as her cheeks grew pink.

Kate gave a sigh of defeat. 'Well, it's not as if you're exactly bad to look at, are you?' she observed crossly. 'And don't act as if you didn't know.'

'I'm flattered, Kate...'

His blue-eyed mockery was just too much.

'No you're not, you're…' Javier watched as she valiantly struggled to bite back a scathing retort. 'I'm trying,' she gritted. 'I'm *really* trying, but it's really hard to be pleasant to you. I was just attempting…I know you're rich, but even for you we're not talking small change here. I'm just worried I'm not going to be good value for money,' Kate observed before she subsided into red-cheeked silence.

'Actually, I consider you excellent value for money,' he revealed in a tone that made his exact meaning hard to define. 'And leave me to worry about my money. I'm considered by some to be quite astute, financially speaking. Incidentally, though I appreciate your restraint, Kate, on the whole I think I prefer your acid retorts to the wooden dummy look.'

She was so relieved to be given the green light to speak her mind that she was prepared to overlook this unflattering comparison.

'Don't you think it's possible that the thought of losing your inheritance has affected your judgement…?' she began tentatively.

Maybe she was right, though not in the way she thought. Perhaps wanting to make his grandfather happy had blinded him to the inherent flaws in his scheme? He was certainly acting more on instinct than objectivity, but that didn't bother him too much. Javier believed strongly in following his gut instincts.

'Even if that were so, I'd hardly admit it, would I?'

'You wouldn't…?'

'Are you forgetting you're talking to an arrogant, conceited Spanish male? We are never wrong,' he explained with an ironic glint in his eyes. 'If you remember that in future, we'll deal very well together.'

This particular Spanish male was disturbingly attractive when he revealed that under his macho exterior there lurked an unexpectedly dry sense of humour.

'Thanks for the tip,' she responded in a similarly ironic vein. 'Any more on offer?'

'Well, treating my every pronouncement as though it is a pearl of wisdom would probably not come amiss,' he admitted gravely. 'And laugh at my jokes.'

Kate couldn't repress the gurgle of responsive laughter that bubbled up.

Not a man she'd thought to be easily disconcerted, Javier appeared so now. 'You have the *most* remarkable laugh!' he breathed.

Their eyes meshed, Kate stopped laughing, his held a searching quality that threw her into total confusion.

She began to clumsily struggle with her seat belt. Her efforts were futile; her co-ordination seemed to be in an advanced state of decay!

The engine was almost silent but when Javier switched it off she noticed. Well, she hadn't actually seen him do so, but it seemed safe to assume this had happened; this wasn't the sort of vehicle that conked out or stalled.

'What's wrong? You know, I think there's something wrong with this seat-belt...' she observed, tinkering with the clip.

He brought his hands down with a thud on the steering column. 'You are right,' he observed, turning to face her.

'Now there's something I never expected to hear you say,' she observed drily.

'We do not give the appearance of two people who have intimate knowledge of each other,' he pronounced flatly.

Kate's expression brightened. Could it be he was finally seeing that this ridiculous charade was doomed to failure? Once she recognised the flip side to this scenario, her hopeful expression faded. If he changed his mind about marriage she'd have to hand back the money, and she couldn't do that—not now, when they were already planning how to spend it! Perhaps she'd presented her arguments for the prosecution a little *too* successfully.

'You shy away from me when I touch you.'

Kate's plan had been not to look at him but the magnetic pull of his eyes proved greater than her willpower. 'That's because I don't like you touching me. I do *not!*' she added fiercely, in the face of his glittering scepticism. 'But,' she added, taking a deep breath, 'I expect I could get used to it.' An occasional hug and a bit of hand-holding was not a big price to pay for what he had given in return.

'That's extraordinarily generous of you.'

'The least I can do…'

'It's traditional for the groom to kiss the bride, Kate…' As he spoke his smoky eyes lingered suggestively on her mouth.

Kate was ashamed of the small bleating sound that emerged from her lips. 'If you're thinking of kissing me…?' she mumbled apprehensively.

It came as something of a shock to Javier to realise how much he'd been thinking about it, almost since the first moment he'd laid eyes on her. Now, of course, he had a perfectly legitimate reason to do so.

'There's something…'

'You should warn me about…?' he suggested helpfully.

Kate frowned at this frivolous interruption—what was Javier doing being frivolous, anyhow…? 'I've forgotten what I was going to say now!'

'Then don't say anything,' he suggested.

Kate's nervous system simply closed down as he took her face between his hands and drew her towards him.

Her eyes half closed as she swayed towards him. This wasn't the body language of rejection and Kate was painfully aware of the fact, but she felt curiously unwilling to do anything to correct the false impression she was giving.

This close to his masculinity was totally overwhelming.

Breathing in his male scent reminded her of the time she'd downed two glasses of champagne in quick succession at Seb's wedding reception, only this time she was *much* dizzier.

Shock, a knowledgeable voice in her head observed.

'No…!' Kate began, recovering control of her voice but little else.

She felt the feather-light touch of his fingertips sliding across her jaw and shivered. His burning gaze watched her soft, succulent lips as they parted slightly beneath the gentle pressure of his thumbs.

If you don't say something he will kiss you, the voice in her head warned—he might even think you want to. He might even be right!

There eyes met and Kate's insides seemed to melt. His olive skin was pulled taut over his slashing cheekbones and his masterful nose was covered by the faintest sheen of sweat. His warm breath, coming almost as fast as her own, fanned out over her cheek as their noses almost grazed. Kate half closed her eyes and inhaled the scent of his warm male body like an addict.

'You can tell a lot about a person from the way they kiss,' he explained thickly.

This didn't sound very scientific to Kate. 'A kiss is a kiss,' she protested huskily.

'Kissing also requires split-second timing,' he contradicted confidently.

'I knew that…' she whispered as he nipped gently at her full lower lip—could that be classified as a kiss? she puzzled as his fingers began to stroke her throat in light, feathery motions.

'It's extremely risky to let our first kiss be a public one—at the altar, even.'

He had a valid point. 'I hadn't thought of that.'

'These things need thinking about.'

His dark head lowered and her treacherous senses went wild in anticipation. His mouth covered hers, and there was nothing hard or invasive about the pressure as he kissed her gently.

Anticlimax.

Kate was dismayed to discover the almost chaste, teasing salute left her feeling cheated.

'That wasn't too bad,' she admitted hoarsely as his mouth lifted fractionally from hers. She prayed that none of her irrational pique showed in her face.

They were still so close she could see the individual gold flecks in the drowning sapphire of his eyes. Her breath snagged painfully in her throat as she witnessed his pupils dilating until the drowning blue was almost swallowed up by the inky blackness.

'A little bit of bad can be quite good,' he promised in a sexy rasp that made goose bumps break out all over her hot skin, just before he reasserted his authority over her mouth.

This time there was nothing even vaguely chaste about the deep, probing kiss. The erotic stabbing incursions of his tongue made her moan and wind her arms around his neck.

Later, she would try and convince herself that this had been a calculated—callous, even—attack on her senses, by a man who'd been the centre of female attention since he could smile, but at that moment nothing much mattered but the wave after incredible wave of scalding sensation that washed over her as he sank deeper into the warm recesses of her mouth.

When he lifted his mouth from hers, Kate's fingers were tangled in the dark hair on his nape and she was panting frantically. It was several sweaty seconds before she could prise her eyelids, which felt as though they were weighed down with lead, apart.

The combustible heat from his blue-eyed gaze, besides

making the sensitive muscles of her stomach cramp viciously alerted her to the way her body was pressed closely to his virile torso—second skin wouldn't have been pressing the point!

She drew back with a sharp gasp and fell back, her head against the padded restraint as she panted for Britain. She was vaguely aware that his actions had roughly followed the same pattern.

Almost in unison they turned their heads. Where Kate had expected smugness, perhaps a hint of gloating, she saw a look that on anyone else she'd have described as disconcerted.

'Good practice session,' she managed, between gasps. 'But quite honestly I don't think you need it.'

Credit where credit was due. Whatever else Javier Montero was he was a quite spectacularly good kisser—this didn't automatically mean he was a spectacular lover too, but the odds were definitely stacked in his favour!

Not that she was ever likely to put the theory to the test.

His eyes dropped to her lush lips. 'Neither do you.'

Kate shifted in her seat; perhaps some explanation for her enthusiastic response was called for. Obviously this was what happened when you became a slave to your work and ignored your more *basic* needs. She could hardly tell him this without making herself sound like a sad, sexually deprived loser.

'Well, I think we might be able to muddle through at the ceremony now,' she heard herself claim brightly.

'I think a modified version might be appropriate for that occasion.'

Dots of feverish colour appeared on her smooth cheeks. 'I think I might be able to restrain myself from ripping off your clothes.' Though it won't be easy, she thought, averting her covetous gaze from his arresting profile. 'About the wedding…' she began tentatively.

'You are nervous?'

'Would that be so surprising?' she charged, resenting his careless attitude. 'I've never been married before, and I'm not as practised at deception as you obviously are. I'd feel slightly more comfortable…if that is the right word,' she mused wryly, 'if there weren't too many surprises.'

'There will be no surprises, just the padre and Sarah and her husband as witnesses.'

'What's Sarah like?' Kate blushed as the impetuous words escaped, but rather to her surprise he didn't comment on her tasteless display of curiosity.

'She is gentle and sweet, and not nearly as robust, emotionally speaking, as you.'

Kate was less than flattered to discover that he clearly thought of her as some emotional Amazon.

She gritted her teeth. 'Sensitive qualities can be such a handicap.' Not that he was ever likely to suffer on that count, he had the sensitivity of a brick.

'I have offended you.'

'Not in the least, we emotionally robust types are by definition pretty tough.'

'It was not intended as an insult, quite the opposite. You are resourceful and independent; not all women have your confidence and natural resources. Sarah is a…*fragile* person, who is less well equipped than yourself to cope with the demands of modern life.'

'You mean if you'd accused her of being in cahoots with some sleazy drug-dealer she'd—'

'There was no way I would have made that mistake…' Javier interposed quickly.

'I should recognise her straight off, then; she's the one *without* the natural criminal tendencies I exude.'

'There is no need to be facetious.'

Kate, who thought there was every need, maintained a restrained silence.

'I met Sarah when my sister was in a drug rehabilitation programme in England; she was a fellow patient being treated for an eating disorder.'

Kate's cynical expression faded, as did her detachment; despite his opinion she had a soft, vulnerable heart. 'Your sister was…?'

'Addicted to drugs. Yes, she was.' Despite his remote expression, Kate could sense that his sister's dependence had deeply affected him. She took him to be the type of man who shouldered the mantle of responsibility for all those close to him. Kate sighed; his sister's sad history explained away the puzzle of his personal involvement when he had discovered someone was dealing drugs at the hotel.

'She became friends with Sarah during their stay and late that year my sister invited her to join us on the island.'

'And you fell in love with her?'

He stiffened. 'That was something I mentioned in confidence…'

'As if I'm going to blab about it.'

'I've offended you again.' He seemed intrigued by this discovery.

'Forget it; it's like water off a duck's back with us emotionally robust types. You're not hoping to make this Sarah of yours jealous with me, are you?'

'She is not my Sarah,' he retorted with frigid disapproval.

'Fair enough. Your sister, is she all right now…?'

Javier searched her face and instead of the prurient curiosity he'd expected he discovered a genuine concern. 'Thank you, yes, she is. She is studying modern history at Oxford.'

Kate beamed with disingenuous pleasure.

'That's good. You know,' she told him, reaching across and squeezing his hand lightly, 'you shouldn't blame yourself. These thing happen. The important thing is you were there for your sister when she needed you.' Seeing the direction of his disconcerted gaze, Kate removed her hand and, blushing deeply, sat on it.

'How do you know I was there for her?' With an expression she found impossible to interpret, his interest focused on her hot face.

'Well, I just assumed…' She stopped and gave an exasperated sigh—what was the point in beating about the bush? 'Well, if you must know,' she informed him frankly, 'you come across as the sort of person who would be there…' This admission surprised her as much as it seemed to him. 'But then,' she admitted with a wry grin, 'I always was a terrible judge of character!'

There was a short, tense silence before he began to smile, the transformation of his grim features was nothing short of miraculous.

Wow! she thought exhaling gustily as he fired the engine into life. It might not be such a good idea to laugh too often!

CHAPTER NINE

'THERE'S very little space to park beside the church,' Javier explained as he slowed the car to let an elderly woman dressed from head to toe in black cross the narrow street. 'We'll park the car here and walk up if that's all right with you?'

'Fine,' she replied, surprised to be consulted on the minor detail. Her agreement might not have been quite so swift if she'd realised that the village was literally cut into the side of a mountain.

Actually, as far as she was concerned there was very little space here too, so little in fact that she held her breath as he reversed the big car with what seemed like impetuous haste to her into the small space between two stone houses. Like most of those in this quaint village, they both had attractive wrought-iron balconies and so many flowers crammed in window boxes that you hardly noticed the peeling paintwork.

'Perhaps this wasn't such a good idea,' Javier observed a few minutes later as he paused once more to let her catch up with him.

'You should have left me at base camp,' she puffed.

'There is a step there; be careful…'

Kate ignored his guiding hand. 'It's all right, I can see, I'm wearing my contact lenses. I didn't bring a spare pair of glasses.'

'You have beautiful eyes.'

Kate tripped.

'It's not that far now.'

Kate decided it was preferable to shift the blame for her

123

stumble on her footwear than let him suspect that a casual compliment from him could make her fall flat on her face. Balancing on one leg, she extended her ankle towards him. 'If you were wearing these you wouldn't say that.'

'What possessed you to wear anything so impractical for a wedding?'

'How was I to know marriage meant a two-mile hike?' she asked indignantly. Her frivolous shoes with the pretty jewelled clip and the high spindly heels were ornamental and not suited to climbing mountains, even cobbled ones. 'If I'd known, I'd have brought my trainers.'

'You're going to injure yourself in those things,' he observed showing scant appreciation of the delicate footwear. 'Perhaps I should carry you.'

She wasn't small, but she knew his arms were more than capable of coping with the task of carrying her. Her stomach flipped over as she thought of those hard, muscular arms; it flipped some more when she thought of them holding her. She ruthlessly smothered the hot flames of excitement before they could take hold.

Taking control of herself, Kate swallowed past the constriction in her throat. 'I've got a much better idea,' she trilled brightly.

'Which is…?'

'This,' she said stepping out of the shoes. Always conscious of his superior height, suddenly slipping down to his shoulder level intensified the dramatic height differential.

He looked down at narrow feet on the dusty ground. 'You can't walk barefoot to your wedding.'

'Why not?'

'Because it's inappropriate.'

Kate laughed. 'It's a bit late for a man who'd bought a bride to start worrying about convention.'

His dark brows drew together in a disapproving line. 'I haven't bought you!' he denied harshly.

'No, just a short-term lease; I keep the freehold.'

'And no doubt you would place a very hefty price on that.'

Her eyes slewed evasively from his. 'No, actually I'd give it away free to the right man.'

Embarrassed by her own contribution to this strange exchange, Kate bent over abruptly to pick up her shoes, one in each hand, and ran a little ahead of him. 'Don't be such a stick in the mud. Go on, live a little!' she urged as she twirled around and waved the shoes at him.

A lazy smile appeared on his face as he watched her antics. Their eyes met and his smile faded, leaving a brooding, restless expression that made Kate's tummy muscles quiver. There was no knowing how long the silence that grew between them might have lasted, had not a small boy perched on a bicycle that looked way too large for him chosen that moment to race past them at a breakneck speed. Javier had to push Kate to one side to avoid a head-on collision.

He called out angrily in Spanish after the figure.

'Are you all right?'

Kate looked up into his concerned eyes and nodded, very conscious of his hands resting lightly on her shoulders.

'I'm fine, but your lovely suit is covered in dust,' she cried in dismay.

Javier glanced down at the damage. 'No matter,' he said dusting half-heartedly at the sleeve of his jacket.

Kate clicked her tongue. 'Stand still!' she instructed, examining the damage. 'It should come off,' she announced.

'Do not trouble yourself...' He stopped as Kate began to vigorously brush at the powdery layer of dust across his lapel.

Javier stood a curious smile playing about his lips. *Lovely suit?* I thought my clothes were insipid and lacking in individuality?' One dark brow lifted. 'Have I got it right?'

Kate stopped and grimaced. 'Pretty well,' she admitted. 'If you must know, it's pretty tiresome being around someone that looks so damned perfect all the time!'

Javier looked amazed at the accusation. He looked down at himself. 'Well, I am not perfect now. Does that make me a little less *tiresome…?*'

Kate pursed her lips as she considered the matter. 'The jury's still out on that one.' Liking him could be a complication.

Javier took a second look at her pink-painted toenails and nodded. 'Go barefoot if you must, but I want one thing understood—don't expect me to take off my shoes.'

Kate grinned. 'Don't worry. Taking off your shoes is only for the advanced class. You need to start with loosening your tie…just a little.'

'You like to show me how much?' Javier asked, touching the tasteful grey silk.

Shaking her head, Kate backed off. 'No way!' If she got that close she didn't think she'd be able to resist the temptation to touch his lean jaw where already a faint shadow was just visible.

Javier accepted the rejection with a philosophical shrug; clearly he was never likely to lack candidates eager to loosen his tie. In fact, Kate found it extraordinarily easy to imagine his tie being ripped off by eager hands; in this imaginary scene his tie was closely followed by his shirt.

They walked along in silence and without Kate's heels to contend with it wasn't long before they reached the crest of the hill and the small church came into view.

'How pretty!' she exclaimed.

Javier looked pleased by her appreciation. 'Yes, isn't it? It's very old. My grandfather and grandmother were married here. They met in Madrid after the war; her parents were diplomats and she was engaged to a junior consul. There was an enormous scandal when they ran away.'

'And they ended up here?'

'Yes, she always had a soft spot for the island after that.'

There was no particular reason why this information should make her feel even worse than she already did about what they were doing, but somehow it did. Kate had been uneasy from the beginning about a church ceremony but Javier had been firm, explaining that in his grandfather's eyes a civil ceremony was not worth the paper it was printed on.

'That's why you brought me here, to impress him…?'

'My grandfather is not a man easily impressed. I just thought that this would be a nice place to be married with little fuss, but now you mention it the continuity will please the old man.'

It sounded as though Javier's grandfather was big on tradition and continuity.

'So you picked this place so that nobody you know would see us and ask awkward questions?' she concluded dully. A perfectly logical thing for him to do under the circumstances, so why did it bother her so much…?

Kate was taken by surprise when Javier caught her hands; she winced as his fingers closed tightly around her wrists, immediately he let her go.

'Did I hurt you?'

Kate didn't know what he was talking about until she saw his eyes were fixed on her wrists. 'I'll live,' she replied, rubbing her wrists.

'I do not run away and hide,' he replied clearly outraged at the suggestion. 'If anyone asks me questions I don't want to answer, I don't reply.'

'I get the picture. If bullets were whistling past your head it would be beneath your dignity to get down in the dirt with everyone else.'

'I think you'll find I have a pretty well-developed sense of self-preservation.'

'But not common sense. I see now that the idea of you keeping a low profile was a pretty daft one. You're too pigheaded.'

'If you've quite finished calling me names, come sit here.'

Kate could cope pretty well with his I'm-in-charge manner—he probably didn't even know he was doing it—but the sight of his long, tapering brown fingers curled, gently this time, around her smaller paler hands... That was another matter entirely. Kate's coping mechanisms were not built to deal with that! Such a silly thing, but she fell to pieces inside.

She didn't resist as he drew her to the side of the road, where he indicated she should sit down on a large, smooth rock. This weak capitulation was outweighed by her success in resisting the strong impulse to rub her cheek against his hand.

'Look, someone's left flowers,' she said pointing at the pretty nosegay propped up beneath a crude but beautiful statue of the Madonna.

She watched puzzled as Javier went over to the place. Careful not to disturb the flowers, he squatted down beside a small bubble of water that gurgled out of the ground into a small pool. Her covetous gaze clung with helpless fascination to the supple lines of his back; it was turning out that there was barely any part of his anatomy her fertile imagination could not spin erotic fantasies around.

'This spring is meant to have magical powers,' he explained as he cupped his hands and let them fill with the fresh water.

'What sort of magical powers?' she asked as he walked towards her, shiny drops of water falling like bright jewels from between his cupped fingers onto the parched ground below.

Javier knelt at her feet.

Finally seeing his intention, an astonished Kate drew back her feet. 'You can't...' she protested.

'I'm not marrying a woman with dirty feet.'

'I didn't think Monteros performed menial tasks.' It wasn't the menial nature of the task that bothered her, it was the uncomfortable intimacy.

'Don't provoke, Kate, just give me your damned foot.'

His tone was exasperated, nothing very lover-like about that, which ought to make her feel better...*ought!*

Reluctantly, she extended her foot.

Javier looked so long at the her slim calf and slender ankle that Kate finally cleared her throat noisily.

When he lifted his head jerkily at the sound, there was an odd, unfocused expression on his face.

The water he trickled slowly over her hot, dusty extremity was so icily cold that she gasped.

He grinned at her reaction. 'I forgot to warn you, it's cold.'

The eyes that rested on her face were not cold, they were warm. She looked hurriedly away as one of the little jolts of sexual awareness she was coming to recognise so well knifed through her body.

'Now he tells me,' she grumbled, angling her arm as casually as she could across her chest to hide the brazen thrust of her nipples. This was sexual craving of a type she'd never experienced in her life before; having come to terms with her apparent low sex drive, this transformation was hard to get her head around.

She sat there passively while he repeated the process with the other foot; it seemed to take him an eternity. If anyone had suggested this morning that having a man pour cold water over your hot feet could be a deeply erotic experience, she would have thought they were mildly deviant.

'Those magical powers you were talking about,' she asked, more from a desperate need to distract herself from the dangerous frissons of pleasure his lightest touch evoked than any genuine desire for an explanation, 'what are they?'

Javier shook his hands free of the moisture clinging to them and rose lithely to his feet, mockery danced in his eyes. 'Fertility.'

'*Oh!*'

The amused lines radiating from his eyes deepened as she blushed.

'Local folklore has it that women wanting to conceive who drink from here will bear a son,' he explained solemnly.

Kate looked at the innocent trickle of water and laughed nervously. 'Do people still believe things like that?' she joked.

Javier didn't smile back.

'Well, I'd say from the floral offering that someone does…wouldn't you…?'

'But you don't?' Kate flashed him an incredulous look at his lean, guarded features. 'Do you…?' She shook her head unable to reconcile the notion of this sophisticated man believing in a superstitious myth.

He shrugged. 'I'm not superstitious, but I respect other people's beliefs, and I do believe that we are in danger of losing many things of value by turning our backs on our roots.'

Kate was astonished; Javier was the last person in the world she would ever have imagined voicing such opinions.

'Personally, I'm quite happy to leave the fear, bigotry and superstition in the past,' she told him with a shudder.

'Are you sure it isn't your own fear that bothers

you…fear of things that you can't explain away with twenty-first century science…?' he challenged.

'Rubbish!' she denied. 'I'm just not going to campaign for a return of witch-burning.'

'Maybe you have a personal interest there.'

'Are you calling me a witch?' Kate demanded indignantly.

For a moment he stood there, looking down at the bare-footed figure at his feet, hair spread like a bright nimbus around a delicately flushed face. 'I can't think of any other explanation,' he replied sardonically. 'Put your shoes on,' he added tersely, before Kate had time to puzzle over his cryptic response or even the peculiar expression on his saturnine features. 'The wedding can't start without us.'

Kate's stomach muscles quivered at the reminder. 'You're an extremely bossy man,' she remarked, staring indecisively at his outstretched hand.

A satisfied expression slid into Javier's eyes as her slim hand was placed cautiously within his, even if the manner of it getting there did remind him of a child daring to explore forbidden territory.

At the outset of this reckless enterprise all Javier had wanted was her co-operation; now gaining her trust seemed to occupy his thoughts almost as much as the attractions of her body did. He had to constantly remind himself that possessing that body would create all kinds of complications; his own body didn't always listen to these warnings.

'But I have many redeeming qualities,' he assured her as he heaved her to her feet with a grunt.

Kate dusted down her dress and sent him a wry look from under her lashes. 'I bet a female told you that.'

'More than one actually.'

'Smug, conceited, bossy *and* superstitious,' she observed with a superior expression.

'Everyone is superstitious, to some extent, be it the footballer with his lucky pair of socks or the banker who flicks salt over his shoulder,' Javier contended.

'Not me.'

'You sure about that?'

'Absolutely,' she told him with an emphatic little tilt of her chin.

'Prove it,' he challenged softly.

'*What…?*' Kate shook her head and laughed uneasily. 'There's no way I can prove it.'

'There is. Drink some water from the spring.'

'I'm not thirsty.'

A dark brow lifted. 'Like I said,' he drawled. 'Everyone is superstitious.'

Kate gritted her teeth, unable to stomach his triumphal air a second longer. 'If it's contaminated, I'll know who to blame,' she grumbled as she picked her way over the uneven ground. She extended her hand beneath the ice-cool drops and then, with a defiant glare in his direction, raised it to her mouth—the water was sweet and icy cold.

'Well…?' she challenged him, wiping the excess moisture from her lips with the back of her hand.

His darkened glance dwelt on the full, moist outline; when he spoke his voice had a husky strained quality. 'I'm impressed.'

Despite his immediate capitulation Kate was left with the uneasy feeling that somehow she'd done exactly what he wanted.

They were only a few feet away from the church, which Kate found was even prettier close to, when a stone bench built into the wall, which had previously been hidden from view by the overhanging lemon trees, came into sight.

A couple were sitting in the shade talking in quiet voices; their whole manner to one another made it clear they were not strangers. Kate felt a sudden unexpected stab of envy.

It was Kate's cry as her heel caught on a stray stone in the road that made both turn.

The woman immediately sprang to her feet, an expression of uncomplicated delight on her face; the man beside her with the dark-haired baby in his arms did so more sedately.

'*Javier!* You're here...*finally!*' The petite figure cried as she rushed forward. 'This is so exciting, I can't believe it! Marriage...!'

Beside her Kate felt Javier tense; she heard the sibilant hiss of his shocked intake of breath. Without stopping to analyse the impulse that drove her to do so, Kate caught his hand and squeezed hard.

Javier's head turned sharply he looked from Kate's concerned face, dominated by a pair of wide troubled eyes desperately trying to telegraph comfort, to their tightly clasped hands and back again. The restive glint slowly faded from his eyes and he smiled.

It was no ordinary smile. Kate caught her breath; every instinct told her this was one of those special moments. The sight of lemon trees, the scent of jasmine on a warm afternoon, would always hold a special meaning for her in future; they'd unlock this memory. She could almost hear the sound of something deep inside—maybe her reserve snapping?—as the warmth of his eyes caressed her before he turned to the other woman. There was no hint of any underlying trauma in his manner as he responded to her greeting.

'Sarah!'

Now she had time to look properly, Kate was stunned to discover the love of Javier's life, far from being the supermodel material she'd expected, was a tiny creature with big blue eyes, a cute button nose complete with freckles and an extraordinarily sweet smile. She was extremely feminine, the sort of woman that brought out the chivalrous instincts in men—they evidently had done in Javier. Kate, who had never in her life wanted to be protected by a man, experienced an irrational pang of envy.

'This is Kate,' Javier said, drawing her forwards.

You had to hand it to him, Kate conceded as she smiled stiltedly. Nobody watching him operate would guess the proprietorial pride was not the genuine article—so long as *you* remember it isn't, Katie, the spoilsport voice of common sense in her head inserted wryly.

'Kate, this is Sarah, and of course you already know Serge, and the little one is Raul. *Madre mia,* but he's grown since I saw him last,' he observed, reaching out to tentatively touch the head of the sleeping baby.

'That's because you don't come and see us nearly often enough,' the baby's mother returned reproachfully. She turned to Kate. 'Perhaps now you'll be able to make him come see us once in a while,' she appealed.

'I'll do my best.' Well, she could hardly admit her influence was nil, because it was abundantly clear that this woman thought the marriage she was about to witness was for real.

'Miss Anderson...' The swarthy-skinned man who had witnessed the worst indignities of her life nodded diffidently as their eyes met.

Kate felt an embarrassed tide of colour wash over her skin. Now here was someone who didn't, who *couldn't*, think the marriage was for real!

'Kate,' she corrected stiltedly. 'Very nice to see you again...' she lied fluently. 'And quite a surprise,' she added, throwing Javier an acid look of reproach which the rat pretended not to see, but as Sarah was nestling affectionately up to him maybe he didn't, she thought, experiencing a nasty stab of something that felt scarily like jealousy.

Her smile was bright and ever so slightly desperate as she hurriedly turned her attention back to the thick-set figure beside her. Though he didn't come right out and call her a liar, she could tell from his expression that Serge didn't believe in her delight at renewing their acquaintance.

Or maybe paranoia was setting in! The way today was going it seemed best to assume the worst.

She watched as he carefully adjusted the sunhat on the tiny head of the baby, who continued to cling limpet-like to his massive chest. She sighed. Forget flashy cars, and as far as she was concerned there were fewer sights more guaranteed to thaw a woman's heart than the sight of a big, brawny man with a tiny baby.

Javier could at least have warned her about who one of their witnesses was to be.

The embarrassment she could cope with if she had to, but being pitched headlong into the middle of a situation that had all the ingredients of a Greek tragedy was another matter!

Javier loved Serge's wife, but did Serge know…? Did Sarah know…if so, all that touchy feely stuff with Javier was a bit below the belt!

Talk about love triangles!

As she looked back to the previous occasions she'd seen the two men together, acting very much as a team, Kate couldn't recall witnessing any tension or underlying hostile currents between them. That of course didn't necessarily mean there was none…

'What a lovely baby.' In her experience, admiring their offspring was always a good way to please parents, but in this case her observations were nothing but the truth; the sleeping child was quite beautiful.

'Well, don't I rate a hug with you these days, big guy…?' she heard Sarah chide.

From the corner of her eye she was aware that an enthusiastic embrace was being exchanged. Worriedly she looked at Serge and saw he was already watching them; to her relief he seemed to view the proceedings with an air of faint indulgence.

Indulgence wasn't the first emotion she experienced when she got her first proper look at the hug-fest. She was a big fan of spontaneity and definitely no prude, but to Kate's way of thinking this was way over the top!

For someone so fragile-looking, Sarah had managed to get a pretty firm grip around Javier's neck and was pressing some vigorous kisses to his lean cheeks and mouth. If she did know of Javier's feelings for her, Sarah's actions could only be termed callous and uncaring, Kate decided indignantly. She looked away as Javier placed the fairy-like figure back on the floor, troubled by her ambivalent reaction to the spectacle.

Seeing the sparkle of tears in the other woman's eyes. Kate found it impossible to hold on to her antipathy.

'I didn't know if you'd have time so I picked these from our garden…I hope you don't mind…?' She thrust out a bunch of flowers tied together with a blue velvet ribbon and then a small package towards Kate.

'Thank you!' Kate exclaimed feeling horribly guilty about her uncharitable thoughts towards this woman who exuded a wide-eyed sweet sincerity—not qualities she'd have imagined would have attracted Javier, but then men were strange, unpredictable creatures.

'We're just so happy that Javier has found someone to make him happy.'

Kate felt increasingly uncomfortable as Serge produced a tissue for his tearful wife.

'He's the sweetest man in the world, but then why am I telling you?' she sniffed emotionally. 'You already know that…'

I know nothing!

Javier didn't respond to her flustered look of appeal in quite the way she'd anticipated.

'Kate thinks I'm bossy and arrogant, don't you, *querida?*' he drawled.

Thanks for nothing, Javier! She allowed her resentful glare to linger pointedly on his incredibly handsome, mocking face. 'Amongst other things.'

You'd have thought it was in his best interest to ensure I don't put my foot in it, but if that's the way he wants to play it, fine!

'You've known him longer than me,' Kate appealed to the other woman. 'Has he always fancied himself as an authority figure?'

Once Sarah recovered from the shock of hearing anyone speak to Javier so daringly, she let out an appreciative chuckle.

'Kate's definitely got your number, Javier,' she told him.

His brilliant eyes flashed. '*Now* you're scaring me,' he asserted sardonically.

No, I'm not, Kate thought tearing her eyes free from the hypnotic glow of his, but she was scaring herself badly!

She had no legitimate reason to wonder what it would be like to play this part for real, to conjecture on what it might feel like to actually be the loved, cherished bride Sarah thought she was. Besides, being loved by a man like Javier would be a nightmare.

A girl would have a heck of job retaining any individual identity; he would be an overwhelming and demanding lover who would not be content to fit himself in around her busy career. It would be quite a dilemma for an independent career girl to find herself in love with a man like that...luckily for her, her contractual obligation stopped short of that requirement!

She congratulated herself on her impregnable heart and felt queasy.

'Now, Kate, come and tell me everything,' Sarah suggested in a deeply alarming, cosy-girls-together sort of voice as she tried to draw Kate slightly apart from the men folk—a manoeuvre which Kate resisted stubbornly. 'Serge's been about as informative as a rock,' she continued, shooting her husband a look of affectionate exasperation. 'So how long have you two actually known one another?'

'Not long.'

Kate's evasive reply seemed to seemed to appeal to the other woman's deeply sentimental nature; her round kittenish eyes softened.

'Time's not a factor when you meet the right person, is it?' she sighed soulfully. 'Where are you going to live? Don't worry about the language thing, Kate... I couldn't speak Spanish when I came here, but I'm fluent now... aren't I, Serge?'

'You are indeed, *querida*,' he agreed smoothly. 'I hate to interrupt, but the padre will be waiting...'

'All right, I can take a hint.'

'Only when it's broad,' Kate was amazed to hear her sober-looking mate drily quip.

'Very funny... So I talk a lot,' Sarah admitted. 'But at least let her open the parcel. No, it's for you, not him,' Sarah insisted with a secretive smile when Kate went to hand the parcel to Javier 'Open it now,' she coaxed.

Kate shrugged and handed Javier her sweet-smelling bouquet instead. If she hadn't been so distracted she'd have laughed at the sight of him standing there staring at the flowers as if they were about to bite him.

'I can't accept this!' She gasped when a cobwebby lace mantilla was finally revealed; it was exquisite and clearly very old. Shaking her head she pushed it towards the other girl who held up her hands.

'It's not really mine.' She glanced towards Javier. 'I was just borrowing it. Javier let me use it on my wedding day. It was his mother's; you should wear it, Kate.'

'I...' How to explain to a hopeless romantic who was clearly under the impression she was witnessing a love match, that she was the last person in the world Javier would want to see wearing a family heirloom?

Javier solved her dilemma by taking the lace veil from her hands. He tilted her chin up towards him and arranged the delicate folds carefully over her bright hair.

'She looks so beautiful!' said Sarah. Her enthusiastic clapping stilled abruptly as she remembered the sleeping baby. An anxious look revealed he was still soundly sleeping.

'Very beautiful,' Javier agreed softly, putting the flowers back into her trembling hands.

Kate's lashes lifted as, lips parted slightly, she looked directly into his eyes—major mistake! Even knowing his performance was for Sarah's sake, she couldn't halt the rippling progress of the spasm that contracted all the fine muscles across her abdomen. She snatched her eyes away, her breathing all askew.

Oh, help! she thought, trying to smother the prickles of sexual excitement that coursed through her sensitised body as she saw the church door swing open. *I can't do this!*

Against all expectation a sense of deep calm descended on Kate as she entered the tiny church. Perhaps she was affected by the atmosphere of cool and quiet? Perhaps she had accepted her fate? But whatever the reason, when the time came she made her responses in a clear composed voice interrupted only by the fretful whimpers of Raul. Kate was hardly aware of the off stage distractions so totally focused was she on the ceremony and the man beside her. If anything it was Javier who looked unexpectedly tense, perhaps he was worried that she'd wimp out at the last minute?

She'd expected to feel as if she was taking part in travesty, a cruel parody of what should be one of the most important events in a woman's life, but when Javier lifted her veil it felt natural and *right* to kiss him back.

Back out in the sunshine, on the arm of her husband—*husband!*—the reality of her situation kicked in and her head literally spun.

She found it almost impossible to concentrate when an embarrassed Sarah apologised profusely for Raul. 'He needs to be fed, don't you darling?' she cooed, taking the baby from her husband. 'Does anyone mind if I find a quiet corner…?'

Her husband looked at her anxiously. 'You can manage, *mi esposa?*' he asked.

'You can do many things quite beautifully, darling, but produce milk isn't one of them.'

At any other time the sight of big beefy Serge blushing would have afforded Kate considerable amusement, but at that moment all her efforts were concentrated on putting one foot in front of the other. The physical and emotional demands of the last two days were finally catching up with her.

'I think I need to sit down!' she gasped faintly.

Javier took one look at her ghostly pallor and immediately scooped her up into his arms as if she were a child. *'Por Dios!'* he exclaimed as Kate's head fell limply against his shoulder.

Javier cursed quietly under his breath. A man famed for his legendary cool, he wasn't accustomed to finding his wits flying out the window in moments of crisis, but for several seconds his mind was a total blank. What if this was some sort of delayed reaction to the head injury…? Much more likely it was a reaction to being forced into a marriage that was repugnant to her, he thought grimly.

'This is so stupid.'

Javier watched as her blue-veined eyelids fluttered, as if it took all her effort to lift them.

'Perhaps I should have eaten breakfast,' she murmured vaguely.

'There's no *perhaps* about it!' he thundered, relieved that the blue tinge around her lips had lessened. 'I hope you are not one those foolish women who starve themselves,' he added suspiciously.

Lifting her head from its resting place on his shoulder took all her effort. 'Do I look like one?' she asked, gloomily contrasting her own generous proportions with Sarah's delicate ethereal build.

'You look...' he began in a goaded voice, only to break off abruptly, his expression that of a man who'd just suffered a body blow. 'Like a ghost,' he finished hoarsely.

'Take her to the house, Javier. A lie-down in the cool will help. Sarah has prepared a small supper; we thought you might like...'

'I'm not sure, but thank you, Serge. If only I'd tried to get the car all the way up here.'

'Leave her with me, Javier, while you get the car,' Serge urged after thoughtfully scrutinising his friend's tense, strained expression.

Javier was extremely reluctant, but he was finally persuaded to relinquish his burden who by now was proclaiming herself quite capable of walking to the car under her own steam.

'You will stay with her, Serge?'

'I won't let her out of my sight for a second,' his friend soothed.

'This is silly!' Kate protested as she was placed beside Serge on the stone bench. 'I was light-headed for a minute, that's all.'

'You will do as I ask!' Javier announced imperiously.

'Dream on,' Kate muttered under her breath.

His brows arched. 'You said something, *querida?*'

'Nothing you'd like.'

'I never doubted it,' he gritted back with a glittering smile before he strode off. Kate watched until he disappeared from view; when he did a long tremulous sigh escaped her lips.

'*You care for him…?*'

Kate jumped at the amazed accusation voiced by the man beside her. 'Pardon?'

Serge calmly repeated his observation.

Kate, furiously ducking and diving from the truth, found it hard to meet his level dark gaze. 'I don't know him; how can I care for him?' She laughed at the absurdity of the notion. 'Javier married me so that he can take control of the company. And if you didn't know that, I'm in big trouble. He'll probably accuse me of industrial espionage, this time!' she predicted wryly.

'Is that what he told you…? That he was worried about his inheritance.' Serge shook his head and looked amused. 'I take it you've never met Felipe.'

'We don't exactly move in the same circles.' Kate was puzzled by Serge's peculiar reaction to her shocking explanation.

'If you'd ever seen Felipe with Javier you would know that he'd *never* disinherit him; it just isn't an option,' he stated positively.

'They've argued,' Kate explained. 'He wants Javier to marry some girl…'

Serge dismissed this with a shrug. 'Sure, they clash occasionally, it's inevitable. They are both strong-willed, but Felipe adores Javier. Did you know he brought him up after his mother's death?'

Something in his tone caught Kate's attention; she was good at picking up the things people *didn't* say. 'How did she die?'

'She took an overdose, Javier was only ten at the time, he found her.'

'How awful!' Kate gasped, sickened by the horrifying thought of a ten-year-old child carrying that image around in his head for the rest of his life. Her tender heart ached; poor Javier. 'Is his father dead, too?'

Serge shook his head. 'No. He was overcome with guilt after his wife's death; she adored him you see, but...he was a womaniser and not a very discreet one. He drifted for some years. I believe he lives on a ranch the family owns in Venezuela these days, but he keeps a very low profile. He left Javier with Felipe; to all intents and purposes Felipe is the only father he remembers.'

'But I don't u-understand...' Kate stammered, absorbing the implications of Javier's tragic family history. 'Why would he marry me if what you say is true? If he knows his grandfather won't disinherit him?'

'I'm sure he had his reasons.'

This clearly was enough for him, but not for Kate, whose head was spinning.

'He lied to me!' she wailed.

'Maybe, but I think he...cares for you.'

Good God, the man had clearly been infected by his wife's terminal sentimentality. 'Cares for me? Are you mad? You know how we met—all of forty-eight hours ago. He doesn't even like me!' she cried.

Serge responded with an infuriatingly enigmatic smile. 'I loved Sarah the moment I saw her.'

'So did Javier, and much good it did him!' Kate retorted recklessly. 'Oh, God!' she gasped, clapping her hand over her mouth. 'I didn't mean...I'm s-so sorry...' she stammered.

'It's all right, you are not telling me anything I didn't already know.'

Good God, had they discussed it? Now that was a mind-boggling proposition.

'*And you don't mind…?*'

This man had to be a very unusual Spanish male if he didn't mind another man lusting after his wife, and to Kate he appeared to have the full complement of possessive traits.

'It doesn't worry you?' No matter how much you trusted a friend, wouldn't there always be a nagging doubt?

'What should I worry about, Kate?'

Kate shook her head; she could hardly ask him if he wasn't worried that, despite his lofty ideals, one day Javier might succumb to temptation and make a move; having experienced Javier's skills on the kissing front, Kate could imagine that even a happily married woman might be hard put to resist.

'Sarah has always been unaware of the strength of Javier's feelings and I'd like to stay that way. I know he will never mention it to her…' He looked at Kate expectantly.

'I won't say a word,' she promised.

'Good. Let me tell you a story, and perhaps you'll understand why Javier will always be welcome in my house. When Sarah was young she contracted a disease, a pelvic inflammatory condition she contracted from a lover.'

'Chlamydia.'

'You have heard of it; I hadn't when she told me,' he admitted. 'It left her unable to conceive naturally, you see, and she was afraid that I would reject her,' he recalled with an incredulous smile that wrung Kate's heart. To her way of thinking, Sarah was an extremely fortunate individual to inspire that sort of love—in not just one man but two!

'I am not a wealthy man,' Serge continued.

Which begged the question of how he became a close friend of Javier.

'And IVF treatment is not cheap. We scraped together enough money,' he explained. 'But our expectations were frankly unrealistic and when we were not successful it hit Sarah hard; she became very depressed.' Kate could see that thinking of these dark days clearly affected him deeply.

'But you have Raul now.'

His dark eyes flashed. 'Yes, we have Raul—*thanks to Javier.*'

Kate swallowed her impatience and a desire to shake the information out of him as he lapsed once more into a reflective silence.

Finally she was unable to contain her curiosity.

'Javier helped somehow…?' she prompted.

He nodded. 'Javier arranged for us to spend some time with her family in England, and after Sarah was feeling better he arranged for us to see one of the leading infertility experts in England. The doctor was frank about our chances. Because of Sarah's previous eating disorder as well, the odds were not on our side. After much soul-searching we decided to go ahead with the treatment; it helped enormously that Sarah had the support of her family this time, and Raul was the result.'

Kate was stunned by this extraordinary tale of altruism, made all the more so by the fact that if Javier had wanted Sarah all he'd needed to do was stand by and do nothing while her marriage had disintegrated under the strain.

God, what a frustratingly complex person he was. Clearly there was a hell of a lot more to Javier Montero than your average macho male. Knowing all this didn't alter the fact that her main qualification as a prospective wife had been the fact she didn't love him! It was something she had better remember the next time she felt inclined to argue with him.

It was just as well there was very little traffic because Javier had effectively blocked the road with his car, Kate was in the middle of pointing out the inconsiderate nature of such behaviour when Sarah appeared breathlessly at their side.

'Oh, Kate, are you all right?' she cried.

'I'm totally fine,' Kate responded. 'Don't let the fact I'm being hauled about like a sack of potatoes fool you; Javier wouldn't let me walk,' she explained, treating him to an exasperated scowl.

'Are you sure? Serge said you fainted.' A flash of inspiration flickered across her face. 'Gosh, you're not pregnant, are you?'

'P-pregnant…? *No,* I'm definitely not!' she returned, not daring to look at Javier.

The petite blonde's face fell. 'That's a pity. It would be nice if there wasn't too big a gap between Raul and your first baby.'

Kate could hardly believe it when Javier added in a provocative husky undertone that made her tummy muscles quiver, 'Not yet, anyway, but she did take a drink from the spring on the way here, didn't you, *querida*?'

Kate shot him a look that she hoped made clear he'd better quit all that sexy *querida* nonsense, or else. 'It was hot and dusty,' she defended.

Sarah looked sympathetic. 'Don't tease, Javier, can't you see you're embarrassing the girl?' she remonstrated. 'I hope I haven't offended you, Kate,' she worried. 'It was just you had the quiet ceremony, and I thought maybe…?'

'We *had* to get married?' Kate responded bluntly. 'Well, we didn't, but…' No matter how hard she racked her brains she couldn't think of a single halfway plausible explanation for the hole in a corner nature of the ceremony.

Unexpectedly Javier came to her rescue.

'My grandfather is not well, Sarah. It wouldn't have been fair to put him through the strain of an elaborate wedding, but we couldn't wait,' he explained, giving a very authentic impression of an eager lover. 'Could we, *querida*?' he purred.

On the receiving end of a caressing look that reduced her to a quivering wreck, Kate nodded numbly.

'Oh I'm so sorry about your grandfather, Javier. I didn't know.'

Javier brushed aside her embarrassed apologies. 'I'm sorry Kate's not well enough to come to supper...a rain check?'

'Definitely,' Sarah beamed.

CHAPTER TEN

UNLIKE the suite at the resort, this one had two very large bedrooms. Kate didn't have any possessions to put in the one allocated to her, but she soon discovered that Javier had anticipated this. A comprehensive array of clothes in her size, all with expensive designer labels she coveted, were hanging up in the walk-in wardrobe and more were neatly folded on the shelves. As she fingered the fine silk of a matching set of bra and minuscule pants, she tried not to think about how he knew her bra size!

Still a bit sleepy-eyed and grouchy after her nap in the car, she entered the sitting room carrying a bar of soap which was the same herbal-scented brand she preferred to use—no coincidence, she was sure.

'How did you know...?'

'Meticulous research,' Javier explained languidly as he took a sip from the glass of whisky he was nursing. The ice chinked as he saluted her with it. 'A shower might refresh you...' His eyes slid over her cream dress and ended up on her bare toes before making the return journey to her face. 'Or would you like some food brought up?'

In other words, I look like a dish rag!

'A bar of soap I can live with,' she gritted unsmilingly. 'But I can't accept clothes from you.'

'Millions of pounds you can accept but a few clothes you can't? I'm sure there's some logic in there somewhere, but I must admit it escapes me momentarily.'

'That's not the same thing and you know it!'

'You do need to dress for the part; as my wife you will be expected to project a certain image.'

'I'm sorry if you don't like my clothes sense but I'm not about to be made over into some plastic bimbo clone!' she announced, planting her hands firmly on her hips as she glared belligerently across at him. 'So you can cancel the hair appointments and the image consultant,' she told him quiveringly. 'That wasn't part of the deal. You can't say you weren't warned—I told you I was poor value for money—but you went ahead and married me anyway. So if you're ashamed of me in front of your posh friends and family, *too bad!*'

Her piece said, Kate experienced a sudden and strong desire to burst into tears…as if it mattered what he thought of her?

Javier examined the antagonistic glitter in her eyes and let out a long, slow whistle. Sitting forward in his chair he placed his glass on the gleaming surface of an antique metal banded oak chest beside him.

'I knew you couldn't bring luggage with you without causing comment, so it seemed sensible to arrange for some clothes in your sizes brought here,' he told her quietly. 'I merely asked for them to be classic, simple and understated, like the things I have seen you wear,' he revealed with what seemed genuine admiration.

'*Oh!*' Looking down at her crumpled linen shift Kate could only wonder at his taste.

'If I'd wanted to play Svengali,' he added drily, 'I would not have chosen you as a subject; you are probably the *least* malleable person I have ever known. It is true however that we will attend functions where people will be expensively dressed. You may wear chain-store clothes if that is what you wish.' His broad shoulders lifted in a negligent shrug. 'But I did think you might find it less of an ordeal if you blended in. I see no reason for you to suffer financially to that end.' Having shot down in flames just about every aspect of her complaint and made her feel petty and ungrateful in the bargain, he picked up his drink.

As he raised the glass to his lips, he continued to study her unblinkingly over the rim. 'Incidentally, I like your hair.'

His eyes held a possessive gleam as he examined the silvery tumble of soft waves that had unexpectedly excited his admiration.

'I shall take the risk of you rushing out to cut it off, or dye it purple to establish your total disdain for my opinion, and admit I would not like it at all if you changed anything about it,' he told her softly.

Kate gulped and regrouped. 'Maybe I was a bit hasty about the clothes, but you should have told me we'd be coming here.' She pushed her fringe from her eyes; it felt lank and floppy, which made his reaction to it all the more amazing in her eyes. The picture of a glowing bride she was not!

Despite the fact he had discarded his jacket and his tie was loosened, Javier still looked as fresh and vital as ever.

'My parents will be worried...' God, she still had to tell them. That should be fun; what'll I say...? *Mum and Dad, I got married yesterday, but don't worry, it's not going to change my life...* Only it already had, she realised as her eyes were drawn to the sleek figure slouched in the chair.

Javier had to be the only man in the universe who could slouch elegantly!

'I left a message for them explaining that you were feeling much better and I was taking you to visit friends and we'd probably be staying overnight.'

'A lie for every occasion.'

'No lie; Serge is a friend and he is manager here.'

'Oh, is that how you know him?'

'My grandparents had a villa about a mile from here; we

would spend summers here.' His soft reflective smile suggested these were happy memories.

Kate found she was fiercely glad about that. After what Serge had told her about the tragedies in his childhood she was glad that Javier had some good memories. She swallowed as an image of a small, lonely boy materialised in her head—a boy with golden skin and blue eyes; the image made her heart ache.

'Serge's mother was their housekeeper,' he explained. 'We used to run wild together. This very spot was one of our favourite places; it was just a ruin at the time, and probably dangerous into the bargain, but you don't want to hear about my childhood.'

Actually, she did. Kate was horrified to discover that she was in fact interested in everything about him! She ate up the details like an addict.

'You are happy about the arrangements I made…?'

'You seem to have anticipated everything…'

'Not everything. I thought I had…' he mused contemplating the bottom of his glass through narrowed eyes. His long lashes suddenly lifted. 'But I was wrong.'

Being the sudden focus of his curiously intense blue gaze unsettled Kate, who was already incredibly jumpy. Unable to bear his scrutiny any longer, she turned her back on him and pretended a great interest in the fine examples of local art hanging on the wall, when all the time all she was actually conscious of was Javier.

All her senses were finely tuned to his smallest gesture, the slightest inflection in his voice; in fact, she was so hyper-focused there was a strong possibility that she was seeing and hearing things that weren't there.

'You're not happy that I left the message?'

'It's not that, it's just… Well, I'm used to doing things for myself. It feels strange to have someone else speak on my behalf.'

'Ah, yes, the independent career woman.'

Kate spun around angrily. 'Don't you dare patronise me…or…'

'If you're going to threaten, Kate,' he advised her smoothly, 'it's always more effective if you decide beforehand with what or how you're going to intimidate your victim. With married people I believe the withdrawal of your sexual favours is a popular method. Of course,' he mused silkily, 'you have to grant them first…'

Was the hint of a question in his voice or a figment of her fertile and overheated imagination? The remotest possibility that he was actually suggesting they consummate their union had her heart beating like a drum.

She sharply veered her thoughts from the dangerous direction they were taking. 'I'm just saying…' Damned if I know what I was saying! She exhaled and started again. 'It would just have been nice to be consulted. I might have felt less…'

'Less what?'

Her hand went to the base of her throat as their eyes met, she could feel the heavy throb of a pulse there. 'Manipulated,' she ground out.

'Is that how I make you feel?'

Out of control, sexually depraved…*needy*…? The list went on and on!

She shrugged and tucked a stray strand of hair behind her ear. 'Forget it; I was just shocked to wake up and find myself here.'

She hadn't been shocked at first, he recalled; that had come a few moments later when the wary light in her eyes had resurfaced.

In those very first moments after he'd gently shaken her awake there had been no concealing caution, her velvety eyes had been filled with sleepy, sensual invitation that had taken his breath clear away. In that brief, unguarded moment she'd looked up at him, all softness and warmth, glowing as if lit from within.

The recollection of it made his body respond as it had done at the time, when all he'd wanted to do was pull her beneath him and kiss her senseless in a prelude to removing every stitch of clothing from her delicious soft body, then he'd taste every inch of that too. He wouldn't allow himself to satisfy his hunger completely, though, not until she was begging him to...drawing out the pleasure until it hurt.

When she had reached out and touched his cheek, her fingertips light and delicate as they ran over the stubble on his jaw, Javier had been forced to reassess the timescale of his plans. Javier understood the power of sex, but the hunger that gripped him at that moment was more urgent than any he could recall.

A small pucker had appeared between her feathery brows as her hand fell away. 'You're not a dream,' she breathed in the moment before she realised where she was, and who he was.

Javier, not a man given to wishing, was left wishing hard that he was the man she had taken him for. A man whose existence he discovered he deeply resented.

Kate stepped backwards as Javier suddenly levered himself up from the chair in one lithe, fluid motion. She watched as he began to move around the room, his whole manner radiating restless energy... Perhaps he was feeling the confines of this paper marriage already?

Perhaps regret was responsible for the brooding expression on his face she speculated as she watched him push open the double doors that led out onto a flower-decked wrought-iron balcony. As he turned back to face her, Kate's breath caught; standing there with the light breeze ruffling the smooth glossy outline of his dark hair, drawing the fabric of his shirt tightly over his torso, he made a simply magnificent figure.

The frown line deepened above his classical nose as his eyes skimmed her motionless figure. 'I thought you would welcome an opportunity to…adjust to our…arrangements before you face your family.' A wry expression drifted across his face. 'I know I do. Surely you didn't think we'd be going back there tonight? That you would be sharing a room with your sister?'

'Well, actually, I was so busy wondering how I was going to get through the wedding itself,' she revealed ingenuously, 'that I hadn't thought as far as the honeymoon.'

In fact, Kate, you haven't thought much at all! With a sigh she slumped despondently into a tapestry-covered easy chair.

'Have I said something funny…?' she asked as he smiled one of those lop-sided numbers that she found not only wildly attractive but impossible to interpret. 'I'm not speaking honeymoon in the literal sense, of course,' she hastily clarified.

'You know it will do my over-inflated ego a power of good to be in your company…' If he hadn't had to fend off some determined candidates, Javier might have been forced to reconsider the widely held belief amongst his envious contemporaries that there were any number of women who might not consider marriage to him was something to be *endured!*

'Have you any idea how long we might have to…'

'Cohabit?'

'I was going to say pretend to be married,' she corrected tartly—cohabit had an uncomfortably intimate sound to it.

'We *are* married and I have the papers to prove it.'

'Not properly!' she countered crossly.

'I had noticed.'

Kate took the gutless route and acted as if she was oblivious to the challenge in his eyes. 'This is a very nice hotel,' she observed, sweeping past him onto the balcony which looked out onto a sunny courtyard and the mountains beyond. Hands on the wrought-iron scroll work, she leaned over to get a better look at the fountain beneath. The only sound was the trickle of the water and the distant hum of bees going about their business; it was a lazy, relaxing sound.

'When we were trawling through the holiday brochures, I wanted to stay here, but I was overruled.' Eyes closed, she lifted her face to the sun.

It didn't take a genius to figure out by whom; as far as Javier could see the little sister with her charming manner and shallow smile seemed to get exactly what she wanted. Worse still, Kate seemed to be quite resigned to taking second place. As far as he was concerned, if there was ever a woman who ought to take first place it was Katherine M. Anderson.

Kate didn't realise that he'd followed her until she felt his breath against her neck.

'Coward...' he whispered softly.

Kate started so violently that for a moment she lost her balance and tipped too far forwards until only her toes were still on terra firma.

'Por Dios!' Javier cried harshly as he hauled her bodily back from the balustrade. He turned her roughly around to face him.

The hand he planted in the small of her back brought her hard up against his body; the one twisted into her hair tilted her face up to his. Every point of contact between them was an exquisite kind of torture as her receptive nerve-endings came to life. As far as Kate was concerned, colliding head-on with his blazing blue eyes was a far more terrifying experience than nearly falling fifty feet onto cobbles.

Held this close, she was aware not only of his amazing strength, but the waves of fury vibrating through his lean, hard body too. In his heightened emotional state he unconsciously slipped back into his mother tongue. Kate stood there in a blank condition of shock while a hot tide of furious Spanish washed over her.

His perfect mouth twisted. 'Are you trying to kill yourself?' he demanded thickly, apparently unaware that she hadn't understood a word of his tirade to that point.

'Why, are you offering to do it for me?'

She saw straight off—it was hard not to!—that her defensive flippancy had not gone down well. Javier drew a sharp breath that made his muscled torso strain hard against the fabric of his shirt.

'Do not tempt me!' The irony of this advice brought a self derisive twist to his lips… *Temptation.* His eyes moved hungrily over her face. He had always prided himself on his self-control but her mere presence was temptation.

The crackling sexual tension between them was suddenly like a physical presence in the room. Without warning, Kate's legs turned to rubber; if he released her now she'd certainly slide gracelessly to the floor, but he showed no sign of releasing her. If anything, his grip tightened. She felt as though an invisible hand was inside her chest, squeezing her heart; the pressure made it hard to breathe.

'It was your fault,' she contended belligerently. 'You shouldn't have crept up on me like that.'

Javier's nostrils flared as he inhaled sharply. 'You are the most infuriating woman!' he exploded, lowering his dark face down towards hers.

His burning glance dropped to her mouth and stayed there. The fingers in her hair tightened as his rapid respirations grew slower and slower…until he didn't seem to be breathing at all.

She ran her tongue nervously over her dry lips and a shocking groan of pain was wrenched from Javier's throat.

'S…sorry.' Without being precisely aware of how, Kate

knew that she was in some way responsible for his apparent agony.

It was her turn to moan when he suddenly touched his thumb to her mouth and slowly traced the still moist outline of her tender lips. Kate shivered as hot desire drenched her like a cloud burst.

'*Please…*' she whispered brokenly just before his mouth came crashing down on hers.

Kate opened her mouth, wanting the taste of him in her mouth, wanting to feel his hard, vital body against hers, in fact just *wanting* him! There was an element of desperation and driving urgency in his whisky-flavoured kiss that excited her beyond bearing.

She twisted her fingers deep into the dark hair on his nape, drawing herself upwards so that her hips were sealed to his, so that her heavy aching breasts were flattened against his chest, so that his hard arousal ground into her belly.

Eyes squeezed shut, she moved restlessly as his lips moved in her hair, over her eyelids, her neck, across her collar bone, before he returned his attention to her mouth. He kissed her as though he would drain her.

When he finally drew back, 'You are so beautiful,' she gasped reverently as she began to press her lips to the brown column of his neck. Her fingers plucked feverishly at the buttons of his shirt. It was a clumsy hit-and-miss process, her hands were shaking so hard, but even so in a matter of seconds there was a gap big enough for her to slide her fingers through. She gave a sigh of relief as her flattened palms slid across his skin; it was satiny and firm, just the way she had imagined it, only better!

She bent her head and pressed her lips to the exposed area of firm, golden flesh.

There were feverish streaks of dull colour across his cheekbones and his smile was fierce and predatory as he urgently took her face between his two hands and looked with a rapt expression deep into her passion glazed eyes.

'I want you,' he gritted.

'Then what are you waiting for?' she sobbed. 'A written invitation? *Touch me!*'

'Where?'

'Anywhere…everywhere…!'

A smile of male triumph spread over his taut features. 'Like this…?' His hands left a trail of white heat as they moved over her skin.

'Exactly like that,' she sighed voluptuously. Eyes closed, lips parted, Kate's head fell back; the intensity of the feelings coursing through her was like wild white fire in her veins.

His eyes didn't leave her aroused face as he slid the long zip of her dress all the way down. Kate's eyelids lifted as she felt the fabric slip over her shoulders. Gathering momentum, the fabric pooled around her feet. Beneath it she wore a lacy bra and pants.

'My arm…' she began, revealing a vulnerability she didn't even admit to herself. Of course he'd say the scars were irrelevant, they were part of her, but deep down did his stomach tighten with disgust…?

'Don't worry,' he soothed with a smouldering smile. 'I will get around to your little scars, too. I intend to kiss every inch of you…' he elaborated, in reply to her confused expression. Kate shivered as erotic images flashed across her consciousness. His dark head poised above her quivering body, her pink engorged nipples disappearing into his mouth…

He drew a light line between her straining breasts with the tip of his finger.

'I like a man with ambitious goals.'

Her shivers became full-blown febrile shudders when he dropped down onto his knees before her.

Kate stood there gazing in disbelief at the top of his dark head as he licked his way across the soft curve of her stomach; muscles she didn't know she had started quivering. The softness inside her grew more aggressive, more demanding, as his caresses drove her to the edge of reason for the first time in her life.

When he wrenched down the stretchy lace that sheathed her breasts so that the soft, warm, coral-tipped mounds of flesh spilled out, Kate gave an aching needy cry as his big hands curved greedily over the quivering peaks, drawing them into his mouth.

At first, neither of them noticed the ringing of the phone above their own needy murmurs. When they did, by unspoken mutual agreement they ignored it, but finally the constant shrill chime just couldn't be ignored.

Javier swore in his native tongue and ran a frustrated hand over his sweat slick forehead. His shirt hung open to the waist, exposing his finely muscled torso.

'I will be back,' he promised, levering himself upright.

Believing that was the only thing that made the brief separation bearable for Kate, who sank weakly down to her knees.

'If you don't, I'll come after you,' she promised, watching him cross the room, taking incredible pleasure from something as simple as the way he moved, the sheer animal grace of his stride, the delicious quiver of finely toned muscle beneath firm flesh... The combination sent a stab of intense sexual longing through her aching body.

Seeing the grim expression on his dark, hard-edged features as he lifted the phone to his ear, Kate felt a fleeting sympathy for the person the other end of the line—only fleeting, she was too conscious of the empty ache inside her to empathise for long with the person responsible for this untimely interruption.

Even though the conversation was conducted totally in

Spanish Javier hadn't been speaking for long before she knew that something was wrong—*seriously* wrong.

By the time he put the phone down Kate was seated on the edge of the sofa, her hands folded primly in her lap. As he approached she was glad she'd haphazardly pulled on her clothes. She knew her instincts had been right; the window of opportunity had passed her by. Javier wasn't about to become her lover.

'My grandfather has died.' He sounded chillingly matter-of-fact.

Kate gasped. 'But I thought he had…'

'It wasn't the cancer,' he interposed swiftly. 'His plane crashed. Somewhat ironic?'

'I'm so sorry, Javier.' If anything, her sympathy seemed to make him retreat farther from her. Looking at his remote profile, it was hard to believe that this was the same warm, passionate man who only moments before had introduced her to a sensual world she hadn't even known existed. It looked as if he wouldn't be taking her there any time soon…if ever!

Maybe ignorance wasn't such a bad thing. At least then she wouldn't have any idea what she was missing.

'I'm needed.'

'Of course you are.' But who do *you* need her heart cried, as she he stood there self-contained and in control. Who comforts you?

'The private jet, the *other* private jet,' he corrected himself with a display of dark irony. 'Is coming to pick me up. I'll be leaving first thing in the morning.'

Kate's normally sharp brain was slow to make the connections…I am leaving, not we are leaving, but of course everything had changed he no longer had any reason to pretend.

And that leaves me where…? Redundant, no longer

needed. He doesn't need a wife now; he doesn't need me. An image of his strong face driven by desire materialised in her head; his need had not been in question at that moment!

'You must be pretty gutted that you married me. If only you'd waited a day longer…'

His mouth twisted. 'One of life's little ironies,' he agreed unsmilingly.

'Why did you marry me, Javier? Serge said there was no way your grandfather would have disinherited you…'

'That's true,' he conceded. 'I pretended to take his threats seriously; it required very little effort on my part. Playing the heartless despot was one his pleasures in life.'

His expression as he spoke of his grandfather brought tears to her eyes. 'Then why…?'

'I wanted to make his last days happy ones,' he explained simply.

'So what happens now…to me…?'

A deep silence grew around her hasty question—one that Javier showed no inclination to break. The longer it lasted, the more deeply embarrassed Kate felt. *He's just learnt his grandfather has died and all I'm bothered about is where it leaves me—how selfish does that sound, Kate…?*

'I know you've got a lot of other things to think about, but I was just wondering…'

His hard voice sliced through her stumbling explanation. 'What do you want to happen, Kate?'

The abrupt question shook her. '*Me…?* Her slender shoulders shrugged and a small frown appeared between her eyebrows. 'I suppose I want things to go back to the way they were…?' *Suppose…?* Where had the suppose come from? She smiled staunchly and tried to put a bit of conviction into her tone. 'I mean, it's not even as if anybody need ever know what happened.' *Only I will.*

Suddenly Kate knew without question that things could

never go back to the way they were because she had been altered by events of the last couple of days, and most of all by her contact with this man.

A possibility she'd been doing her best to avoid needed facing. She might have fallen a little bit in love with him...was it possible to be a little bit in love? No, came the bleak reply, at least not if Javier was the man in question! *Oh, God...!*

'As you wish.' He shrugged in an offhand manner that drove home painfully to Kate that his lovemaking had been nothing more than an opportunist response to the signals she'd been broadcasting. 'I will arrange transport for you back to your hotel.'

'Thank you.'

His eyes lifted to her face and the pain she saw in his eyes was so profound that she raised her hand towards him in an unthinking gesture of comfort.

It was a gesture that he seemed to view with disdain, if not distaste. Under the cold regard of his eyes her hand fell away.

'If you'll excuse me, I have to ring my sister. She doesn't know yet and I'd like to be the one to tell her. It will be hard for her.'

Kate had lain for hours in her room, her body rigid and tense as she listened to the sound of Javier pacing up and down in his own room. Her empathy with his pain was like a knife in her chest, and her inability to do anything about it twisted the blade.

She genuinely thought no feeling in the world could be worse until the pacing stopped and there was ominous silence. That was when her imagination kicked in. Javier was a strong man, but strong men were notoriously bad when it came to expressing emotion. When those emotions finally escaped people could behave in ways quite out of character.

After half an hour of imagining his silent suffering she could bear it no longer.

If he was asleep, fine, she could just slip away and he would never know she'd been there; if not…well, she'd work out the what's if and when she came to them. She'd know he was all right and that was what she needed.

He wasn't asleep.

When Kate pushed open the door Javier was sitting on the bed, still fully clothed, his head in his hands. Suddenly being here didn't seem a good idea; she backed up and was actually reaching for the door handle when he revealed he was aware of her presence.

'You should be asleep.'

'I…I could hear you moving around.' He looked so haggard it hurt. She wanted to rush to him and throw her arms around him, but the hostility he was radiating stopped her.

'I'm sorry I disturbed you. I will be quiet…'

'I don't care about that!' she ground out in frustration. He was broadcasting so much pain she wanted to cry, Let me take it away for a little while. This approach would almost certainly have been rejected so Kate had to rethink her strategy.

'Then what do you care about? Ah, I see, my *agony*— you feel pity.' His lip curled derisively. 'You wish to comfort me. By offering me the comfort of your lovely body, perhaps…?' A muscle in his lean cheek jerked as his bold glance roved with insulting familiarity over her lightly clad body.

Kate's chin went up. 'You won't get rid of me that easily,' she declared coolly.

Inside she wasn't nearly so confident; inside she was a mass of painful insecurity. Throwing yourself at the man you loved when you knew that your feelings were not reciprocated was not a light-hearted step to take!

She saw Javier's eyes widen. He flattened his palms

against his thighs and, leaning forwards heavily, shook his head. 'What do you think you're doing?'

'What does it look like?' she replied as she eased the shoe-string straps of her nightgown over her shoulders. Taking a deep breath, she released her grip and let the fabric fall into a silken pool around her feet.

Javier released a long shuddering hiss.

A defiant glint in her eyes she stepped away from the fabric.

His burning gaze held all the distinguishing hallmarks of compulsion as it roamed over her slim pale flesh. '*Dios mio,*' he breathed in a shaken tone. 'I do not require a sacrifice.'

'Actually, Javier, I'm not thinking about what *you* want, but what I want…what I *need*,' she added in a driven, quivering voice. 'You started something earlier…' God, what are you doing, Kate? a horrified voice in her head asked— *this isn't you!*

But it is me, she realised, smiling. I have never been more *me!* Relief and a fresh flood of confidence surged through her.

'I have not forgotten,' Javier choked, seeing her lovely face through a shimmering haze of heat. His eyes dropped. '*Madre mia,* but you are perfect!' he exclaimed with husky, gloating appreciation.

'Perfect, no, but I am here and I'm getting cold,' she revealed from between chattering teeth—a condition that had nothing to do with the temperature and a lot to do with the trauma of throwing herself at the most gorgeous man in the world with no upfront guarantee he wouldn't laugh in her face.

'I think I can do something about that.' Off the bed in one lithe bound, he picked her up as though she were a size eight and not a size twelve going on fourteen, and carried her over to the bed.

She closed her eyes, feeling his mouth touch the pulse spot at the base of her throat. She let out a deep sigh as his big, clever hands moved over her heavy, aching breasts then across her stomach. One stayed there, resting softly on the feminine curve of her belly, while the other boldly moved lower, sliding between her legs. For a moment Kate's body stiffened in resistance but then her instincts kicked in and she relaxed, opening herself joyfully to his exploratory caresses.

'Do you like that?' Kate moaned and pushed against his hand. 'And that...?' he persisted, reaching deeper inside her.

Kate gasped, eyelids lifted to reveal her dark passion-glazed stare. 'I don't *like* anything you do,' she told him. 'I *love* it! I love the way you look, I love the way you sound, I love your smell and most of all I love what you do to me!' she cried.

He kissed her then with a deep, drowning desperation that fired her blood. Lips still attached to his, Kate began to rip at his clothes with feverish haste as she looped one long leg across his thigh.

'Did I mention that you're absolutely the most beautiful thing I've ever seen?' she gasped as he stopped kissing her—*which was bad*—to assist her frantic efforts to undress him—*which was good!* 'The bits that I've seen, anyhow.'

Javier laughed, a low husky sound that sent shivers of hot anticipation curling down her spine.

When she got to see the rest, Kate got a lot less vocal. She felt weak with lust and longing as she hungrily absorbed the rippling strength of his long, lean, tightly muscled body as he knelt between her legs. She knew the mind-blowingly erotic image of his golden body, with its strategic drifts of dark body hair, glistening with need for her, would never fade from her mind.

'What's the verdict?'

Kate dragged her eyes upwards. He had room to sound confident; he really was nothing short of spectacular!

'Don't talk,' she begged, her voice thickening emotionally as she reached for him.

Javier's eyes darkened dramatically as he came down to her, brushing the rosy tips of her trembling breasts with his tongue before sliding down lower over her body.

Back arched, Kate cried out and pushed up towards him, moaning his name, her fingers tangled in his dark hair.

He licked his way back up to her face, reducing Kate to a mindless, mass of inarticulate craving somewhere along the way.

Eyes closed tight, she felt him kiss her paper-thin fluttering lids. A long soundless gasp of anticipation escaped her lips as he parted her legs.

His tongue plunged into her mouth at the same moment he plunged into her body, sheathing himself deeply in her tight, hot wetness.

'You hold me so tight,' he whispered against her ear.

Her body clenched around him. 'Oh, God, Javier!' she gasped brokenly, nipping frantically at his neck and shoulders with her teeth. His face above her was a mask of dark, primitive need that fuelled the raw urgency coursing through her blood.

'Please,' she breathed into his mouth and he thrust carefully into her. *'Harder…!'*

Her ragged plea had an electrifying effect upon him.

Later, as she lay there, her body throbbing with contentment, Kate recalled with a bemused smile the moment something inside her had recognised and instinctively responded to the savagery in his wild possession.

While the sweat cooled on their bodies, she lay there in the darkness, stroking Javier's dark head as it lay nestled between her breasts. She was still awake when he awoke hours later and turned once more to her.

His lovemaking was less urgent but no less sweet the second time and if anything her release, because he delayed it so long, was even more shattering. Afterwards she did sleep and when she awoke it was light and she was alone.

She didn't cry; crying would have been some sort of release and Kate couldn't find that. She doubted she ever would.

CHAPTER ELEVEN

THE head of Chambers, a normally morose character, was quite animated when he came across to their table to personally congratulate Kate on the way she'd handled the Benton case.

Kate smiled uncomfortably as she listened to the glowing comments he made about the combination of inspiration and dedication embodied in her attitude that was making her such an extremely valuable member of the team.

'Another bottle of bubbly, I think,' her date for the night cried as the older man returned to his own table. He lifted his glass to Kate, unable to prevent a shade of jealousy creeping into his bright toast. 'Who's a clever girl, then? Quite the teacher's pet.'

'It was a bit over the top, wasn't it? I expect he's had a bit too much to drink.' She smiled, trying to play down the incident. She was well aware that Ian's competitive nature resented her recent successes.

In truth she felt a bit of a fake, receiving the praise; it was not dedication or a desire to outshine her contemporaries that had made her throw herself body and soul into her work, but a need to fill the hours.

In theory, since she arrived at the office long before everyone else and left her desk long after everyone else, usually piled high with briefs, she shouldn't have been left with any time to think. Unfortunately the great yawning gap between theory and practice meant that no matter how hard she worked or how exhausted she was when she fell into bed, Javier was never very far from her thoughts at any time.

168

The most ridiculous things reminded her of him. She'd never noticed before how many unusually tall men there were in London; as for Spanish accents, she couldn't catch a bus or the Tube without hearing one…! Not that any of them had possessed Javier's incredible velvet drawl.

When one of the secretaries had returned from her holiday in Majorca, waxing lyrical about her experiences there, it had taken Kate half an hour locked in the ladies' room to compose herself…and night time was definitely the worst. Then the memories crowded in, leaving her to toss and turn restlessly all night.

Fortunately her red eyes that afternoon had gone unnoticed, as did the fact she had returned from Majorca a different person to the one who had left. Kate felt sure the very deep differences she felt inside must be mirrored on her face, but amazingly the only thing anyone had commented on was the fact she'd begun to wear her contact lenses almost full time.

'No, can't blame it on the booze,' her date contradicted. 'Sampson's a Quaker, teetotal.'

'Not for me, thanks, Ian.' Kate smiled, quickly placing her hand over her half-full glass.

Though normally an undemanding and entertaining companion, when he had had too much to drink, as he had now, Ian tended to become loud and sulky; neither quality endeared him to Kate. Ian was a barrister, as were most of the other people at the glittering charity gathering organised by the Law Society. It was late and there was an atmosphere of general jollity. They'd been fed well, they'd endured the inevitable speeches from luminaries; now they were all eager to party and Ian was more eager than most.

'Don't be a wet blanket, Katie,' he slurred. 'You haven't had a drop all night.'

Sandy, sitting opposite Kate threw her friend a sympathetic look. Though she hadn't said anything, Kate thought maybe Sandy had her own suspicions about why she was avoiding alcohol.

'I'll have some of that, thanks, Ian,' she cried cheerfully, pushing her own glass towards him. 'I think old Sampson must be worried about you being headhunted, Kate.'

Though Sandy's actions achieved the desired purpose of distracting Ian from his determination to fill Kate's glass, they didn't improve his disposition.

'Then the rumours are true, you have had an offer from Hargreaves and St John!' he exclaimed with a scowl. 'Must be a big help to climb the greasy pole when Daddy's there to put a word or two in the right ear,' he reflected bitterly.

'Out of order, Ian, old boy,' the man beside him said quietly. 'Kate is a damned good advocate and you know it.'

The sound of the placid old Etonian drawl acted like a red rag to a bull on Ian in his present ugly mood. 'Shove it, Toby, *old boy!*' he snarled, his complexion deepening to an unattractive red.

Kate was relieved by the fresh distraction afforded when the two women who'd been missing from the table retook their seats. They both looked animated.

'You'll never guess who we've just seen…!' one cried.

'I'm only guessing if you narrow the odds,' Kate responded. 'Give us a clue—actress, politician, royalty…?'

'Not a *she,* a *he.*'

'The sort of man you'd find in the ladies' loo…?' Kate pretended to think hard. 'That doesn't narrow the odds much,' she complained and everyone laughed.

'We didn't see him in the loo, he was just coming in with the minister of…you know, the politician that wrote that thriller.'

'Now that narrows the odds even less,' Toby reflected drily. 'Your lack of political awareness is staggering, dar-

ling,' he continued smoothly drawing his pretty partner to
her feet and dragging her towards the dance floor.

'Go on,' Sandy urged the remaining talebearer, once the
couple were gone, 'tell us who this exciting person is before
you implode. My money's on let me see…Brad Pitt…' she
decided with a lascivious smile.

'Optimist,' Kate chuckled.

'Much better than that,' came the smug response. 'Oh,
God, I don't believe it…' she gasped suddenly, her face
going pale. 'Don't look now, but I think…yes,' she hissed,
'he's coming over here!'

'Dance with me, Kate,' Ian, who had been watching with
a scowl as Toby smooched across the floor gracefully with
his pretty girlfriend, said abruptly. 'That idiot really loves
himself, doesn't he?' he brooded irritably to nobody in particular.

'Thanks, Ian, but I'm not really in the mood…' Not anxious to inflame the situation, Kate softened her refusal with
a smile.

His eyes still on Toby, Ian rose unsteadily from his chair.
'I'll get you in the mood,' he boasted aggressively, grab-
bing Kate's wrist.

'I really don't want to dance, Ian,' Kate insisted, trying
to pull her hand free from his grip.

Being breathed on by someone whose breath was forty
per cent proof was not her idea of fun, and she wouldn't
have put it past Ian in his present mood to pick a fight with
Toby on the dance floor. She was deeply regretting accepting his invitation, if 'we might as well go together'
could be termed as such. These occasions could be awkward if you went solo.

'Of course you do…'

A voice of steel and ice from behind Kate softly contradicted this sulky claim.

'The lady does not wish to dance with you.'

Kate froze, all the colour rushing from her face, only to be replaced seconds later by a flood of colour. Her heart was pounding so hard she could hardly hear her own jumbled thoughts.

An irritated snarl on his face, Ian spun around. Under normal circumstances, his sense of self-preservation would have been immediately activated by the size and character of his adversary, but the alcohol in his veins made him reluctant to back down. Drunk or not, though, he couldn't hold that scornful shimmering blue gaze for more than a nanosecond.

'What's it to you…?'

Kate deliberately didn't make the same mistake as Ian and look at the intruder. Choice didn't enter into the decision; she simply didn't trust her body not to betray her in some weak shameful way if she permitted it a glimpse of what it had been too long starved of. His voice, the faint familiar scent of his cologne that made her nostrils flare was already doing some very alarming things to her nervous system. Any second now someone was going to notice she was shaking like a leaf. What unkind twist of fate had brought him here tonight…?

'Ian, leave it,' Kate breathed urgently. In considerable agitation she rose unsteadily to her feet. She forced her lips to smile and clutched the table with her free hand for support. 'Leave it alone; I'll dance with you.'

Still she didn't look at him. She was desperately trying to compose her traumatised thoughts.

Think…think… As tempting as the idea was, she couldn't follow her first impulse and hide under the table—up and coming barristers in slinky strapless ball gowns did not scrabble about on the floor without exciting unwanted attention. No, somehow she had to deal with the fact this wasn't one of her fantasies; Javier really was here in the flesh… *Don't think flesh, Katie!*

Her resolve weakened and she couldn't resist the over-powering desire to turn her head and risked a furtive peek from under her lashes—the pit of her stomach vanished into a black hole. Caution and self-respect forgotten, she stared hungrily.

He looked exactly how she remembered, only *more…!*

Six feet four inches of mouthwateringly delicious, rampant masculinity. Moreover, he looked perfectly at home in his surroundings and supremely, shockingly sexy in a dark, well-cut evening jacket.

Kate hardly wondered at the awed, open-mouthed silence around the table or the intense level of interest his presence was arousing. A tall, elegant, outrageously *male* figure projecting an effortless air of cool command that was at sharp variance to the younger man's truculent aggression, Javier was always going to attract buckets of attention.

As if he felt her scrutiny, his sapphire gaze suddenly swivelled towards her. The room and everyone in it disappeared as his eyes moved over her face, as if he was memorising every curve. At some subconscious level she registered the ripple as his throat muscles moved convulsively, a deep sigh that juddered through his tense frame.

'You will not dance with this man, Kate,' he stated emphatically.

As if her obedience was something he took for granted—some things didn't change—he immediately switched his attention back to the younger man. His narrowed eyes moved to the hand still curved around her wrist. 'Let her go,' he purred softly.

'*Says who…?*'

Kate, who had seen the menacing expression in Javier's eyes, decided Ian was a lot more stupid than he looked!

In reply, Javier's hand closed around Ian's own wrist and the younger man paled as his fingers opened in response to the steely pressure. He swore.

'You will dance with me!' Javier decreed autocratically.

Kate's jaw dropped, even for Javier this was over the top! 'Your wish is my command and all that...' she breathed shakily.

A humiliated Ian jumped in before Javier could respond to her caustic jibe. 'Who the hell do you think you are, waltzing in here trying to pinch my girlfriend?'

The danger lurking just beneath the elegant façade of Javier's silken smile, the barely suppressed fury in his expression, finally penetrated even Ian's drunken bravado. The younger man instinctively drew back.

'Boyfriend?' One dark brow rose to an incredulous angle. 'I suppose we are all permitted errors of judgement occasionally,' he acknowledged directing a glance of dismissive scorn towards Ian. 'As for who I am...' he began forcefully...

Kate gave a horrified gasp, suddenly sure this explanation wasn't going to stop at his name.

'You're Javier Montero!' Toby, who chose that moment to wander back to the table with his girlfriend, exclaimed. 'Worth a bundle,' he elaborated to a pale-looking Ian. 'Several bundles, actually. If you ever need a good legal brain...? The name's Toby Challoner,' he grinned, pumping Javier's hand with friendly fervour.

A flicker of amusement crossed Javier's taut features. 'I'll keep that in mind,' he promised, before turning his attention to Kate, who was experiencing the bizarre sensation of her two separate worlds colliding.

She looked at his hand, stretched out towards her, and was seized by an overwhelming compulsion to meet it halfway. Not one to submit without a struggle to inevitability, she tucked her tingling fingertips behind her back.

'I don't care who he is. He can't dance with you, Kate.'

'For God's sake, Ian, shut up!' she flared, exasperated by his feeble chest-beating. In fact, she was tired full stop of being told what to do by men! 'I'll dance with whoever I want to.'

'And you want to dance with me, Kate?' Javier suggested, tilting her chin with one finger. 'I can't believe we have never danced together, *querida*.'

The gasp around the table was audible.

'And I can't believe you're here doing this to me, Javier,' she responded hoarsely.

And, other than the fact he enjoyed any opportunity to throw his weight around, she couldn't see *why* he was here now...unless...? Did he want a divorce...? she wondered despondently.

'He knows our Katie!' Toby boomed good-naturedly. 'Kept that quiet, sweet girl.'

'Sort of,' Kate replied vaguely as she felt the pressure of Javier's strong fingers close about her own.

Javier, his dark head imperiously high, drew her to his side. '*Sort of* as in Kate is my wife,' he announced, bestowing a hawkish smile of blinding brilliance upon his stunned audience.

The image left in Kate's mind as she was dragged off was Ian's sickly pale expression of shock.

'*Oh, my God!*' she groaned over and over as he drew her inexorably towards the crowded dance floor. 'What are you trying to do?'

'Avoid your toes. Listen to the music, *querida*.'

'What are you doing here, Javier? Were you just in town and you thought, what the hell, I've nothing better to do, I'll go and ruin Kate's life...that should be good for a laugh!'

'I am not laughing.'

Indeed he wasn't; his eyes were fixed with uncompromising solemnity on her flushed, upturned features.

'If you're after a quickie divorce, you couldn't have chosen a worse way to ensure my co-operation,' she warned him grimly. 'A simple letter from your solicitor would have done. Right now, I'm feeling particularly vicious!'

His sombre expression momentarily softened. 'You haven't got a malicious or vindictive bone in your body.'

Kate found his confidence was deeply frustrating.

'Don't you understand? Now everyone will *know!*' She lifted her horrified eyes to his dark face as her body began to respond automatically to the gentle rhythm and Javier's light, guiding touch. They flowed together like honey, moving as one fluid unit.

A stab of sexual longing of paralysing intensity lanced through her body. Helpless to control what was happening to her, Kate felt her starved senses react with pathetic predictability to his closeness; they drank in eagerly the unique fragrance of him and revelled in the hard-muscled male angularity of his lean body.

A judicious application of pressure from his fingers played across the hollow at the base of her spine brought her in close contact with his thighs; the resulting flicker of shock in her wide eyes as she felt his unashamed arousal made him smile with bold brilliance down at her.

'I can see it might limit your social life somewhat,' he admitted with a thin-lipped smile. 'A certain type of man is attracted by the forbidden pleasures a married woman's bed offers but I don't think your admirer is one of them. He looked a little unwell, I thought...'

This display of smug hypocrisy made Kate momentarily loose her footing. She doubted very much if Javier had been broadcasting his unavailability amongst the eligible high-born Spanish lovelies who had been no doubt falling over each other in their eagerness to offer him comfort. The thought of it made her feel physically sick.

'Even if Ian was my boyfriend, which he isn't, it wouldn't be any of your business.'

'I'm making it my business,' he revealed calmly. His scrutiny was unbearably penetrating as he scanned her face hungrily. 'You look very beautiful tonight, *querida,*' he continued seamlessly as Kate blinked back up at him in stunned disbelief.

'So do you,' she admitted wistfully, without thinking. 'What do you mean, *your business?*' she puzzled in a troubled whisper.

'I mean that marrying in haste…'

'And for all the wrong reasons.'

'As you say,' he conceded impatiently. 'It doesn't make the pledges we made any less binding.'

'Since when?' A dark shadow of anguish crossed her face. 'You're the one who walked away from me.' An experience Kate knew she could only bear once in a lifetime.

'You have no idea how hard that was for me, but I thought it was what you wanted. I thought you wanted your life I had stolen back.'

'It is what I want,' she replied in small defiant voice.

'I was a fool!' He appeared oblivious to the curious looks his loud, bitter pronouncement had drawn.

'Did you come here about the divorce…?'

His laugh almost hurt to hear.

With no warning Javier stopped dead in the middle of the dancing couples who diverted curiously around the motionless pair. He closed his eyes and his head fell back. Kate watched with growing bewilderment as the muscles in his brown throat worked convulsively.

'I missed you.'

Kate firmly doused the flare of hope that fluttered in her breast and shook her head stubbornly. 'I don't believe you.' She *couldn't,* not knowing how much being wrong would hurt.

His head jerked upright, the fan of dark lashes lifted from his cheekbones revealing an expression of implacable determination. His powerful chest expanded and his shoulders firmed as if he was marshalling all his not inconsiderable authority.

'Let me convince you.'

For the first time Kate noticed the tell-tale signs of quivering tension in his body. The nerve throbbing in his lean cheek. The extra sharp edge to the jutting angularity of his facial bones.

'You've lost weight,' she observed in a distracted, worried manner.

His body, always greyhound lean, had an even more spare look to it. This lean, hungry look was probably connected to the combustible, dangerous aura he was exuding. He looked like someone who had been sustained on adrenaline and will power alone for too long.

Probably the stress of his grandfather's death, and the extra responsibilities that had fallen on his broad shoulders were responsible for these changes. Plus making sure that Luis Gonzalez finally got his comeuppance. Kate felt indignant that nobody close to him had had the good sense to see he needed taking care of. She contemplated the pleasure it would give her to give them a piece of her mind, were she really his wife and in a position to do so.

A wistful expression made her soft mouth quiver.

Of course, if she had been his wife in a real sense, there wouldn't be any need for anyone else to make sure he didn't push himself too hard; she could have done that herself.

He gave a dismissive shrug, displaying an infuriatingly cavalier attitude to his health.

'Everyone has their limits, Javier, even you,' she remonstrated.

He gave an odd laugh. 'If I didn't know that, the past six weeks taught me that and many things I didn't know before.'

Her eyes darkened. 'Has it been very bad…?' Her concern increased as she noted the faint sheen of perspiration gleaming on his vibrant, golden skin. Kate, who had seen him appear cool and collected on occasions when the temperature had reached the high thirties, knew that Javier was totally impervious to the heat.

'*Hell!*' came the succinct response. 'Are you seeing anyone?' The words emerged from between clenched white teeth.

Her round chin firmed. 'And if I was?' some perverse imp impelled her to respond.

A white line appeared around his compressed lips. Kate had never seen the veneer of sophistication that covered his passionate nature thinner. Only pride prevented her from revealing how shaken she felt by the raw emotions spilling from him.

'*Por Dios,* do not trifle with me, Kate. I am not *safe!*' he confided, breathing hard as he fought to retain his shredded self-control.

Shaken to the core by his raw pronouncement, Kate had no intention of testing the authenticity of this claim.

She cleared her bone-dry throat.

'No, I'm not seeing anyone, Javier. I think,' she hypothesised, exposing her inner soul to him with a rush of relief, 'that it's likely you've spoilt me for any other man.'

When Kate finally worked up the courage to look at him, her bruised, aching heart stilled and then soared at the expression of tender triumph she encountered on his devastatingly handsome face. Even at that moment she hardly dared trust her interpretation of his expression.

'That is as it should be, *mi esposa,* for there is no doubt that you have spoilt me for any other woman. I think I fell in love with you that very first moment I saw you. I didn't realise it until you fainted outside the church. I was overwhelmed by my selfishness; I was sure you must despise me. Like a fool I let you go…I was too afraid of rejection to ask you to stay with me, but now as you see my pride is in tatters.'

'Not so as you'd notice,' Kate breathed with a delirious laugh as she gazed transfixed into his stunningly handsome face. Wonderingly, she lifted her small hand to his bronzed cheek; Javier murmured her name as he turned his head and pressed a fervent kiss to her open palm.

Kate's tummy muscles quivered violently as she gazed at his dark glossy head.

'I don't believe this is real.' She bit her lip, struggling to hold back the emotional tears. If she started crying, she feared she wouldn't be able to stop. 'I've dreamed so often about this moment, but I never thought it would happen…'

Javier gazed with fierce pride into her luminous eyes. 'I think I might just know a way of convincing you.'

Kate responded body and soul to the demands of his burning kiss which only ended when they both registered the polite 'Wouldn't disturb you for the world!'

'Toby, isn't it…?' Javier responded with only slightly less cool assurance than usual.

'Thing is, I thought you might like to know the music stopped playing about five minutes ago, and not to put too fine a point on it,' he glanced sympathetically at Kate's fiery cheeks and cleared his throat, 'you are the floor show.'

'Oh, God…!' Kate moaned, suddenly conscious they were standing quite alone in the middle of the large dance floor, the focus of several hundred pairs of curious eyes.

'There is no shame involved in kissing your husband, *mi esposa*,' Javier reproached, surveying the room with a staggering display of supreme indifference which Kate deeply envied.

'Blame it on my British inhibitions,' she gritted cringing at the thought of the spectacle she must have presented.

A gleam appeared in his fabulous densely lashed eyes. 'I had not noticed you had any.'

Kate choked and shot a glance towards Toby, who was tactfully examining his fingernails. 'For God's sake, Javier!' she reproached, a laugh quivering in her throat.

Javier smiled complacently down into her deliciously flushed face before turning politely to the young lawyer.

'We are indebted to you, Toby,' he said smoothly as he inclined his head towards the loose-limbed younger man. 'Do you speak Spanish?' he asked abruptly.

The other man looked startled. 'Pretty well; appalling accent though,' he admitted with a self-deprecating grin.

'Well, if you were serious about work, ring this number,' he said in an off-hand manner as he handed the startled young man a card.

'*Are you serious…?*'

'Always where business is concerned,' Javier responded with a wolfish grin. 'Now, if you'll excuse us, Kate and I were just leaving.'

'Good of you to tell me,' she murmured as he drew her to his side.

One dark eyebrow rose to a satanic angle. 'You prefer we continue our conversation here?'

'We weren't talking.'

'That is why I thought it would be wiser to adjourn to somewhere less public. I have an overwhelming desire to make love to my wife, you see,' he explained, with a contemplative smile that sent a sharp thrill of sexual desire through her.

'In that case,' she responded huskily, 'lead the way.'

Kate gave a sigh of relief as they finally reached the porticoed exit. She had tried to emulate her husband's splendid indifference to the stares and whispers that had dogged their progress, but it hadn't been easy. As for Javier, he hadn't been much help; his reserves of tolerance had quickly worn thin when people with the slightest claim to his acquaintance repeatedly approached them. Towards the end, his methods of ridding himself of those unwise enough to impede their progress were brutally abrupt enough to make Kate cringe.

'Being rich and important is no excuse for bad manners.'

He immediately accepted culpability. 'I know, but I am desperate to make love to you, *mi esposa.*'

Kate was quick to recognise that these were extenuating circumstances.

'You think I'm a pushover, don't you?' she accused as she happily allowed him to draw her into his arms.

'I think you are the sweetest, most enchanting little witch in the world,' he told her throatily.

'Well, I suppose you have your good points; you were pretty nice to Toby,' she admitted.

'No, I was not *nice* to Toby. I rely on first impressions and my first impression of him tells me he is loyal but not afraid of speaking his mind. People like that are surprisingly rare.'

'So your first impressions are always right, are they?' She widened her eyes innocently. 'What about your first impressions of me?' She looked up at him, her eyes dancing with bright laughing expectancy.

'Oh, my first impressions of you were one hundred per cent correct,' he assured her.

Recalling some of his less than flattering accusations at the time, Kate's eyes widened indignantly.

'I knew you were trouble, even then.'

Trouble…? Kate liked the sound of that; it made her feel bold and dangerous, a real femme fatale.

'You'd better believe it,' she purred, giving a provocative little wriggle.

Delighted to see his eyes darken responsively to the light-hearted provocation, Kate was winding her arms around his neck when she was blinded by a series of bright camera flashes. Javier immediately moved to block her from the view of the opportunist photographer.

He moved swiftly but even when she was in the back of the chauffeur-driven limousine which had pulled up in front of the building the photographer, his camera pressed up against the glass, was still popping away.

Javier, white-faced with anger, gave his instructions to the driver before pressing the button that brought down the smoked glass screen between them.

'Does that happen to you often?' Kate asked, sinking back into the luxurious upholstery with a sigh.

'I'm afraid it does.' He regarded her pale, distressed features with concern. 'I'm sorry, *querida,* for exposing you to that, but someone inside must have contacted the press about our rather public display. I should have anticipated it.' He frowned.

'It wasn't very nice,' she admitted candidly. 'And I expect seeing myself looking like some cross-eyed sheep in some scummy paper tomorrow won't be nice either, but I suppose I'd better get used to it,' she returned with a philosophical shrug. 'That is, if you're serious about wanting this marriage to be for real…?'

Javier's tense anxious look was replaced by one of wondering appreciation. 'You know something, you are quite incredible. You do realise that as my wife you won't have the luxury of anonymity any longer?'

'To be your wife,' she admitted shyly, 'I'm willing to put up with a good deal.'

A look of fierce joy flared in his eyes as, with a sharp intake of breath, he gathered her soft yielding body close. 'I am the luckiest man on earth.'

Kate emerged breathless and dishevelled from the crushing embrace.

Javier leaned back in his seat and loosened his tie. 'Combining your career and marriage will not be easy,' he observed, watching her face carefully as he smoothed down his own rumpled hair. 'You will often have to deal with conflicting demands upon your time.'

Was he asking her to give up her career, was that what the wife of a Montero was expected to do…? Perhaps she had been naïve not to see this coming.

'Are you asking me to choose between you and my job?' she asked him bluntly.

'What do you take me for?' he demanded in a tone of deep affront. 'You think that I respect what you have achieved so little, I would ask to throw it away, so that you can be at my beck and call?' He reached out for her and curving his hand over the back of her head drew her face to within an inch of his.

Kate's head spun dizzily.

'I would not try and destroy all the things that make you the woman I love.' His electric blue eyes swept over her face. 'You are courageous, often terrifyingly so…' he mused darkly. 'And funny, of course,' he added, sliding his fingers through her silky hair. 'Bright, infuriating and stubborn. You think you know better than me and say so, which I admit is good for me…'

'I'm going to remind you that you said that,' Kate promised huskily.

'I used to think I wanted a woman who needed me to shelter her from the harsh things in life…'

'Sarah…'

Javier nodded ruefully. 'That would have been a total disaster,' he confessed, shaking his head. 'Her vulnerability, it touched me deeply. Please do not laugh,' he added, an uncomfortable slash of embarrassed colour appearing along his cheekbones. 'I think I saw myself as some sort of gallant white knight. She didn't need a knight or a social worker, just a man who loved her, and she was wise enough to recognise him straight away.'

Kate felt a lot happier with the nagging Sarah question disposed of—there was now only one unresolved issue…and how he was going to take that she didn't know.

'I might need saving occasionally, and if not I've heard that role-playing can be very stimulating,' she observed cheekily.

Javier's rich laughter rang out. 'Meeting you has taught me that it is very much more exciting to have a mate who can constantly surprise me. Of course you must continue your work,' he insisted. 'It will require some adjustments…' he continued absently as he began to nuzzle her sensitive earlobe. 'You have no idea how much I've missed you…' he rasped throatily. 'So many times something happened and I thought, I must tell Kate, only to remember you were hundreds of miles away. I picked up the phone so many times, when desperate to hear your voice…it was only stubborn pride that stopped me dialling your number…'

Despite the delicious shivers chasing up and down her spine and the desire coursing sweetly through her blood, Kate gently pulled away. It wasn't easy; she was so sensitive to him, all he had to do was look at her and she melted.

She had to tell him now.

She cleared her throat; Javier was looking at her warily. Her love for him was like an aching knot behind her breast bone. She wondered how he was going to be looking at her in a few minutes.

'Actually, Javier…'

'Mi esposa…?' He cupped her chin in his hand and studied her troubled face. 'What is worrying you?'

'Those adjustments you were talking about, it might require a few more than you think,' she admitted apologetically.

'How so…?'

'Well, you know how I wasn't superstitious…'

The colour drained dramatically from his face. He shook his head. 'You don't mean…?' he gasped.

Kate nodded. 'Yup!' she breezed with a levity she was far from feeling. 'I did two tests just in case I was wrong, but yes, I'm definitely pregnant.'

Worryingly, his expression didn't alter at all.

'And you feel…?'

'Sick as a dog in this morning,' she admitted. 'And I can't stand the smell of coffee, but other than that…'

'I mean, how do you *feel?*'

'Well, I've never actually fancied myself as the maternal type…' Looking down at her flat belly with an expression of wonder, she didn't see the flicker of despair cross his face. 'But once the shock wore off I danced around the bedroom like an idiot,' she revealed, pressing a protective hand across her tummy. 'I'm tickled pink, over the moon and prone to violent tearful outbursts, one of which I feel coming on now,' she confessed. 'Of course, I don't expect you to feel the same way…'

'Feel the same way?' he exclaimed, running his hands down her bare arms before taking both her hands in his. He lifted them to his lips. 'There was never any question of how *I* feel. How could I not be delighted that the woman I love is carrying my child?' he asked her incredulously. 'It was your feelings that I was worried about. I thought you might resent having motherhood thrust upon you because of my carelessness.' His stern frown held self-reproach. 'It was criminally irresponsible.'

'Hey, I was there too, remember! I don't recall fighting you off with a stick. I enjoyed making this baby…'

Her defiance brought an amused glitter to his eyes. 'I

think someone in the outer Hebrides might not have heard that, *querida*.' His eyes softened tenderly. 'I enjoyed making him too.'

'As far as I'm concerned, Javier, this is a very wanted pregnancy. In fact, there's only one more thing worrying me...'

'What is that?'

A little encouragement, she decided, looking lovingly into the face of her husband, would not go amiss. 'When are you going to get criminally irresponsible again?'

'I am yours to command,' he told her with a smile.

Now that opened up all sorts of interesting possibilities. 'Are you sure you know what you're letting yourself in for...?'

'Forty years of being under your delicious thumb?' he suggested hopefully as he drew the digit under discussion into his mouth.

'I wouldn't mind too terribly if you were on top occasionally,' she admitted, darting him a sultry look from under the shade of her lashes.

'Well, variety, so I hear, is the spice of life.'

Kate, giving herself up wholeheartedly to his kiss, was smugly confident she'd have plenty of that with Javier!

BRIDE BY
BLACKMAIL

by

Carole Mortimer

Carole Mortimer was born in England, the youngest of three children. She began writing in 1978, and has now written over ninety books for Harlequin Mills & Boon. Carole has four sons, Matthew, Joshua, Timothy and Peter, and a bearded collie called Merlyn. She says, 'I'm happily married to Peter senior; we're best friends as well as lovers, which is probably the best recipe for a successful relationship. We live on the Isle of Man.'

June,
a very good friend as well as
mother-in-law. We all miss you.

CHAPTER ONE

'YOU didn't mention that your parents had other guests staying this weekend,' Georgie remarked interestedly as they drove down the driveway. She could see that not only had Sukie, Andrew's older sister—by the presence of her sporty little red car—decided to pay one of her rare visits, but that there was also another car parked on the driveway next to Gerald Lawson's serviceable Range Rover. A gunmetal-grey Jaguar sports car. Very nice!

Although it was only big enough for two people, Georgie decided, which perhaps meant there wouldn't be too many other guests this weekend. Georgie had only recently become acquainted with her future in-laws—Andrew's parents and only sister—and they were quite enough to cope with for the moment: Sir Gerald and Lady Annabelle Lawson—Sir Gerald had been knighted two years ago, on his active retirement, at fifty, from politics—and Suzanna Lawson, Sukie to family and friends alike, a model.

'I wasn't aware of it myself,' Andrew answered apologetically in reply to her query. 'Could just be a—a friend of Sukie's, I suppose,' he added disparagingly. There was no love lost between brother and sister. Sukie's career as a model didn't sit too well with Andrew's more serious role as a successful lawyer. Sukie's bohemian friends didn't go down too well with him, either!

5

But, after the battles that had gone on in her own family over the years, Georgie considered the Lawsons quite normal by comparison!

'A successful one, by the look of the car,' Andrew continued with appreciation as he parked his black BMW next to the Jaguar. 'That will make a nice change,' he added dryly.

Georgie chuckled as she got out of the car, the gravel crunching beneath her shoes—flattish brown court, to complement the brown knee-length dress she was wearing because their time of arrival coincided with dinner.

Tall and slender, Georgie wore her red hair in a short boyishly gamine style, with wispy tendrils on her forehead and at her temples softening the severity of the style. She had clear green eyes slanted beneath auburn brows, and her nose was small and snub, with a dusting of the freckles that often accompanied such fair colouring. A peach lip-gloss softened the fullness of her mouth, and her pointed chin hinted at the determined nature beneath her smile. Stubborn contrariness, her grandfather had once called it…

Her smile faded slightly to be replaced by a perplexed frown, some of the warmth disappearing from the summer evening because of the unwelcome intrusion of thoughts about her grandfather. Though otherwise hers was a contented life.

How could she not feel contented? She had Andrew, dear, sweet, kind, *predictable* Andrew. Her first children's book was in print and doing very nicely, thank you. Her apartment was decorated and furnished to her own taste. In fact, almost everything in her life was perfectly sunny at the moment.

Which was usually the time, Georgie knew from experience, when someone decided it was time to send in a rain cloud!

'Okay, darling?' Andrew had collected their weekend bags from the boot of the car and was waiting at the bottom of the stone steps that led up to the huge front door for Georgie to join him.

'Perfect,' Georgie instantly assured him, very firmly shaking off the momentary cloud that thoughts of her grandfather had evoked. She smiled warmly at Andrew before tucking her hand into the crook of his arm.

At twenty-seven—four years older than Georgie— Andrew was six feet tall, with blond hair that occasionally fell endearingly over his brow and eyes of warm blue in a youthfully pleasant face. A couple of games of badminton a week at the gym that he frequented after work was over for the day maintained his fitness. He owed his successful career as a junior partner in a London law firm completely to the fact that he was good at his job, and not to the fact that he was Sir Gerald Lawson's son.

Andrew was everything that Georgie wanted in her future husband: pleasant-mannered, considerate, caring, and most of all even-tempered. Completely unlike—

Stop!

Unwelcome thoughts of her grandfather had been quite enough for one evening, without thinking about *him* too!

'Your parents and Miss Sukie are in the drawing room, Mr Andrew,' the butler answered in reply to Andrew's query, at the same time relieving Andrew of their luggage.

'The drawing room, no less. Not the family sitting room,' Andrew murmured ruefully as he and Georgie walked arm in arm through the wide hallway towards the formal drawing room. 'Definitely not one of Sukie's less-than-respectable friends, then,' he teased.

'Andrew!' Lady Annabelle greeted him warmly as they entered the room, standing up to rush over and hug her son. She was tiny and blonde, and still very beautiful despite being in her early fifties. Her plain black dress was a perfect foil for her delicate build and fair colouring.

Sir Gerald Lawson had risen at their entrance too, moving forward to kiss Georgie lightly on the cheek before shaking his son warmly by the hand.

An older version of Andrew, Georgie had found Gerald easy to get on with from the first. Annabelle, she was a little less sure of, she acknowledged, even as she stepped forward to accept the other woman's cool kiss on her cheek.

Although Annabelle was outwardly friendly, Georgie nevertheless sensed there was a certain reserve in her manner towards her. But, to be fair, Andrew was her only son, as well as the 'baby' of the family, and Annabelle obviously wanted the best for him. It was up to Georgie to convince the other woman that was what she was!

'Isn't it a beautiful evening?' Gerald enthused as he poured them both a pre-dinner glass of sherry. 'Almost warm enough to eat outside.'

'Don't be provincial, Gerald,' Annabelle rebuked gently. 'Besides, we have guests for dinner,' she reminded him archly.

Speaking of whom…?

What had become patently obvious to Georgie in the last few minutes was that the older Lawsons were alone in the drawing room. Which begged the question— where were Sukie and the mystery guests?

Andrew gave Georgie a conspiratorial wink before turning back to his mother. 'I noticed Sukie's car outside; where's she hiding herself?'

'Taking my name in vain again, little brother?' the recognisable voice of his sister queried as she came through from the conservatory that sided this sunlit room.

A younger version of her mother to look at, but with her father's height, Sukie was another member of the family that Georgie wasn't too sure of yet. Only a year older than Andrew, Sukie had a brittle hardness that was reflected in her cool blue eyes. The short blue dress she was wearing this evening showed off the slenderness of her figure and a long expanse of slender bare legs.

'I had no idea you were interested in flowers, Sukie,' Andrew taunted his older sister as she strolled into the room to kiss him on the cheek.

'Only the type delivered by the florist, darling,' Sukie answered him with cool dismissal. 'I was actually just showing our guest around.'

Guest, not guests. Which probably meant *she* was the other guest, Georgie realised ruefully. Oh, well, only time could change Annabelle's opinion of her. She—

Georgie gasped as the guest stepped into the room behind Sukie, the smile becoming fixed on her lips, her expression like a mask as she simply froze. Even her breathing seemed to stop momentarily as she simply stared at the man. This wasn't a rain cloud—it was a hurricane!

Named Jed Lord!

Cool, fathomless grey eyes looked across the room at her as he registered her shocked recognition. A shock that wasn't reflected in his own demeanour. Which could only mean that he had already known the two of them were to meet this evening...

Aged in his mid-thirties, he was well over six feet tall. The tailoring of his well-cut suit did nothing to hide the powerful physique beneath. He had hair as dark as night, though it was the sheer power in the hardness of his face that dominated: his grey eyes scrutinised the scene from beneath jutting black brows, and above a straight, un-compromising nose; his sculptured lips, although curved into a humourless smile at the moment, hinted at the hardness that was such an integral part of his character, and his jaw was square and determined.

Georgie, who had thought—hoped!—she'd never see him again, was completely thrown by the unexpected-ness of this meeting. A fact of which Jed, so supremely self-confident as he strolled further into the room, was obviously well aware.

Damn him!

What was he *doing* here? Was he Annabelle and Gerald's guest, or had he, as Andrew and she had thought earlier when they'd arrived, come here with Sukie? The latter, Georgie noticed, was certainly looking at him like a cat about to lap up the cream!

But hadn't women always looked at Jed in that way? Hadn't *she* once? Once, perhaps, but certainly not now!

'Jed, do let me introduce you to the rest of the family.'

Gerald encouraged the other man to join them, drawing him into the circle. 'Jed Lord: my son, Andrew, and his fiancée, Georgina Jones. Although we all call her Georgie,' Gerald added warmly.

'Andrew.' Jed moved forward to shake the younger man's hand.

Georgie found she was holding her breath as he slowly turned towards her, having no idea what was going to happen in the next few minutes. Would Jed acknowledge that the two of them already knew each other? Or would he greet her as if she were a complete stranger to him?

Although hadn't she always been so, even when they should have been at their closest…?

Either way, Jed's being here, in the home of Andrew's parents, was completely disastrous to her peace of mind!

'Georgina,' Jed greeted her throatily as he stepped close to her.

She stared down at the hand he held out to her, a long tapered hand with a masculine beauty that totally belied its strength. How could she possibly shake it when she didn't even want to touch him? It was—

'Or may I call you Georgie…?' he prompted huskily, that grey gaze intent on the paleness of her face as she still made no effort to take the hand he held out to her.

Almost like a peace offering. Except there could never be any sort of peace between Jed and herself!

'Of course,' Georgie accepted vaguely, forcing herself to brush her fingers lightly against his, a shiver running icily down her spine even as she snatched her hand away before his fingers could curl around hers. Just that brief touch had been enough to tell her that she still couldn't bear to be anywhere near this man!

'Dinner is served, Sir Gerald,' the butler announced politely.

'Thank you, Bancroft,' his employer rejoined cheerfully. 'Shall we go through to the dining room?' he suggested lightly.

Dinner. There was no way that Georgie could eat. No way she could possibly sit down at the same dinner table as Jed Lord!

Except... What choice did she have? Like her, Jed had given no indication that the two of them already knew each other. She knew her own reasons for not doing so, but she had no idea what Jed's were for the lack of disclosure on his part. But one thing she did know about Jed, though—they would be his own reasons, and no one else's. Because Jed never did anything that wasn't to his own liking.

'May I?' Gerald held out his arm to escort her in to dinner.

Well, at least she wasn't expected to go through to dinner as Jed's partner; that would have been more than she could stand. In fact, she wasn't sure how she was still standing at all after the shock she had received!

'Thank you.' She took Gerald's arm, noting that Sukie had laid a firm claim on Jed, her long red-painted nails on his hand as she moved in close to him, while Andrew was left to escort his mother.

But Georgie was completely aware of Jed walking behind her as they went through to the dining room, could feel the heat of his gaze on her back. That enigmatic grey gaze that could freeze with coldness or burn with desire…!

But more often freeze with coldness, she reminded herself hollowly.

She had been so looking forward to this weekend in the Hampshire countryside with Andrew; the Lawson family home edged the New Forest. But with Jed here it had turned into a nightmare from which she couldn't seem to wake!

To make matters worse, Jed sat opposite her at the oval dining table. Although it would have been even more unbearable if he had sat next to her. The simple truth was he shouldn't be there at all!

She looked at him from beneath lowered auburn lashes as their first course was served to them. He looked much the same as when she had last seen him a year ago, although there were perhaps more lines beside his eyes and mouth, and a faint dusting of grey amongst the black hair at his temples. Although that, she acknowledged disgustedly, only made him look more devilishly attractive!

'Is the smoked salmon not to your liking, Georgie?' Jed remarked mildly. 'You aren't eating,' he pointed out as she gave him a startled look.

She could feel the colour warm her cheeks at having attention drawn to her in this way. Deliberately so, she was sure. One look at the mocking amusement in Jed's eyes was enough to tell her he was enjoying himself. At her expense.

What else? Jed had been laughing at her most of her life, it seemed to her. But it was time it stopped!

She gave him a brightly false smile. 'You know, Mr

Lord, I love smoked salmon.' She picked up her knife and fork and began to eat.

'Please, do call me Jed,' he invited dryly, grey gaze assessing.

'Such an unusual name,' Annabelle remarked lightly.

'Isn't it?' Georgie agreed, turning back to Jed, the light of challenge in her own gaze now. 'Surely it must be the diminutive of something else…?' She looked at Jed expectantly.

His gaze hardened and his mouth twisted into a grimace. 'Jeremiah,' he supplied tersely.

'Goodness me!' Georgie laughed softly, easily holding his warning grey stare with her own clear green eyes. 'No wonder you prefer Jed.'

'That's a little unkind to our guest, Georgie.' Annabelle Lawson shot her a reproving glance.

'As it happens, Annabelle,' Jed turned to his hostess, smiling wryly, 'I wholeheartedly agree with Georgie!'

That must be a first, Georgie acknowledged ruefully. Still, at least she had proved—to herself, if no one else!—that this evening didn't have to go all Jed's way!

'I wasn't meaning to be rude, Mr Lord,' she assured him, although she was sure Jed, at least, didn't miss the edge of derision in her tone. 'It was just a comment on the names some parents expect their children to live with!'

'Your own, for example,' Jed came back softly.

'Touché.' She gave an acknowledging inclination of her head; she should have known she wouldn't have the last word! She never had where Jed was concerned. 'I was named for my grandfather,' she said determinedly.

Jed raised dark brows. 'You have a grandfather called Georgina?'

'I—' Georgie broke off her sharp response as Sukie, seated beside Jed, gave a shout of laughter.

Really—Jed's joke hadn't been *that* funny, Georgie decided irritably as Sukie continued to chuckle.

'I think you rather asked for that one, darling.' Andrew, seated on Georgie's left, lightly covered Georgie's hand with his own as he smiled at her indulgently.

Possibly, she inwardly conceded. But it really hadn't been that funny. She could—

Jed was looking at Andrew's hand, which still rested on Georgie's, his forehead furrowed over hard eyes.

What on earth—?

'The emerald of your engagement ring is the same colour as your eyes,' Jed bit out unexpectedly.

That was exactly what Andrew had said to her the day they had visited a jewellers to choose it!

But she didn't for a moment think that Jed meant it in the romantic way that Andrew had that day. She could clearly hear the accusation in Jed's tone, even if no one else could.

'When is the wedding?' Jed's icy gaze moved from the ring to Georgie's face, although his closed expression gave away none of his thoughts.

Had it ever? Georgie acknowledged disgustedly before answering him tersely, 'Next Easter.'

His mouth quirked wryly. 'Such a long time away...' he remarked enigmatically.

Georgie gave him a sharp glance. Exactly what did he mean by that? Impossible to tell; his expression exactly matched his tone of voice. But he had meant something. She had known Jed long enough to know he was a man of few words, and the ones he did choose to say always had meaning.

'We have our hearts set on an Easter wedding.' Andrew was the one to answer Jed, squeezing Georgie's hand reassuringly as he did so. 'Are you a married man yourself, Jed?' he asked interestedly.

Georgie suddenly found she was holding her breath as she waited for Jed's reply.

His mouth tightened. 'Not any more,' he finally answered slowly. 'I recently entered the statistics of divorced men,' he added with humour.

'How sad,' Annabelle put in sympathetically.

Jed turned to smile at the older woman. 'Thank you, Annabelle, but I doubt my ex-wife thinks so! She was the one to divorce me,' he enlarged bitterly.

'What a very silly woman,' Sukie put in throatily, her blue eyes full of invitation as she looked flirtatiously at Jed from beneath lowered lashes.

'Not at all,' Jed dismissed, picking up his glass to sip the white wine that had been poured to accompany their salmon. 'The grounds for divorce were typical—my wife understood me!' he drawled sardonically.

'Shouldn't that be, 'My wife *didn't* understand me'?' prompted a perplexed Annabelle, obviously not at all happy with the slant the conversation had suddenly taken at her dinner table.

Which wasn't surprising, Georgie acknowledged impatiently. Jed Lord's divorce—for whatever reason!— was hardly appropriate dinner conversation anywhere!

'No, Annabelle, I do believe I had it right the first time,' Jed replied meaningfully.

'How absolutely priceless!' Sukie was the one to answer now as she chuckled throatily. 'Were you a very naughty boy, Jed?' she prompted with amusement.

He shrugged broad shoulders. 'My wife obviously thought so, otherwise she wouldn't have divorced me.'

'Do eat some more of your salmon, Jed,' Annabelle encouraged nervously. 'I believe you've recently spent some time in America, do tell us about it?'

Which was Annabelle's way of firmly saying that was the end of that particular subject.

Which was probably as well, Georgie thought as she determinedly focused her attention again on her plate of smoked salmon. The murmur of voices around the table were now passing her by completely. If Jed had said one more word about the wife who had divorced him because she understood him, she might not have been able to stop herself from standing up and hitting him!

Because, until six months ago, *she* had been his wife!

CHAPTER TWO

'YOU were very quiet during dinner, darling; are you feeling all right?' Andrew asked concernedly once the party had moved back into the drawing room after their meal, to enjoy coffee and liqueurs.

Georgie moved closer to him as he sat down beside her on the sofa, studiously avoiding looking across the room to where Jed and Sukie stood talking together softly. 'I'm feeling fine,' she assured Andrew. 'A slight headache, that's all. I'll be fine after a good night's sleep.'

Although she wasn't sure, with Jed in the same house, that she would be able to get the latter at all! But just to be away from his oppressive company would be something!

'What do you think of Jed Lord?' Andrew prompted, seeming to pick up on at least the subject of her thoughts, and glancing consideringly across the room at the other man.

If she were to tell Andrew, here and now, exactly what she thought of Jed Lord then he would probably be extremely shocked. But she accepted that after tonight she would have to talk to Andrew about Jed at some time in the near future.

So far in their five-month relationship she had put off telling Andrew that, at only twenty-three, she had already been married and divorced. At first it hadn't seemed the sort of thing you just confided to a relative stranger, and then as they'd got to know each other, to love each other, it still hadn't been something she felt she could just baldly state as a fact.

But with Jed's appearance in the Lawson home she realised she wouldn't be able to put it off for much longer. In fact, she was surprised that the troublemaking Jed Lord she had known of old hadn't already just blurted out that she was the ex-wife about whom he had been talking over dinner. If only to watch her squirm!

But he hadn't. Which meant he must have his own reasons for not doing so...

No wonder she had a headache!

'Think of him?' she answered Andrew brightly. 'In what way?'

'In any way,' Andrew replied. 'Sukie certainly seems to find him fascinating—and my big sister isn't easily impressed!'

No, she wasn't. But then Sukie didn't know Jed in the way that Georgie knew him, and obviously found his dark, brooding good-looks and arrogant self-assurance extremely attractive. So had Georgie once...

'I doubt she would have brought him here with her if she wasn't.' Georgie evaded answering Andrew's question directly.

'Oh, Jed Lord didn't come down with Sukie. My father told me over dinner that he's a business acquaintance of his,' Andrew confided.

Georgie looked frowningly at Jed. Gerald Lawson, since his retirement from politics, had returned to his earlier business interests. But as far as she was aware

they didn't include hotels, which she knew was where
Jed's family business concerns lay.

'Really?' she murmured contemplatively. 'In that
case, Sukie is certainly a fast worker,' she added dryly
as Andrew's sister all but draped herself across Jed as
they talked.

Andrew gave a disgusted snort. 'She's wasting her
time with a man like Jed Lord.'

Georgie gave him a quizzical frown. 'What do you
mean…?'

'From what's been said, the man has only just escaped
from one disastrous relationship—I seriously doubt he
intends embarking on another. And he's experienced
enough to realise my big sister is trouble with a capital
T!' Andrew dismissed scornfully.

Georgie gave a wry shake of her head. 'He doesn't
give the impression that he's a man who runs away from
trouble.' In fact, she knew he wasn't! 'Besides,
Andrew—' she turned to him teasingly, deciding they
had talked about Jed Lord quite enough for one evening
'—when did you become so knowledgeable about experienced men?' She gave him a mischievous smile.

Andrew smiled. 'I'm twenty-seven, Georgie, not
seven!' he returned.

This was what she liked about being with Andrew:
the complete freedom to do and say whatever she liked
without fear of offending or angering him. Andrew was
so easy-going she was totally relaxed in his company.

Something she had never been in Jed's!

She frowned as she remembered her response earlier
to the brief brush of Jed's hand against hers when they
were introduced. She had thought she was completely

over him, that the finality of their divorce six months previously had severed all emotional ties to him. But, to her chagrin, she had felt more than just loathing earlier at his touch...

'Hey, I was only joking, Georgie,' Andrew chided softly, misunderstanding the reason for her frown. 'I've never pretended to be an innocent, but neither am I a man of experience myself.' He gave a rueful shake of his head. 'I've been too busy making a successful career for myself to have too much time for that sort of thing.'

'You don't mind that the wedding isn't until next Easter?' she said concernedly, knowing that it had been her decision that they wait; she hadn't told Andrew so, but she wanted time to make sure she didn't make yet another mistake in her life. Although she was already pretty sure that Andrew would never let her down. Unlike— 'I just thought an Easter wedding would be nice,' she added warmly. Especially as her wedding to Jed had taken place at Christmas!

She still cringed at how young and naïve she had been then. How trusting. How utterly, utterly stupid!

'And it will be.' Andrew hugged her reassuringly. 'We—'

'I hope you don't mind if we interrupt you two love-birds?' interrupted a sarcastic, familiar voice.

Georgie stiffened at the sound of Jed's voice, glancing up reluctantly to see that he and Sukie were beside the sofa. Sukie looked no more pleased than Georgie. Obviously it had been Jed's decision to come over...

Georgie looked up at him challengingly, his sarcasm not lost on her even if it was on Andrew and Sukie. Hard grey eyes returned her interest, that sculptured face set into uncompromising lines. It wasn't hard to guess, after his reference to 'love-birds', just why he was looking so grim.

But it was no longer any of Jed's business who she showed her affection to. If it ever had been! Besides, Andrew was her fiancé, the man she was going to marry.

'Please do,' she answered smoothly, at the same time deciding to stand up; she did not intend giving Jed any sort of advantage over her!

Petty, perhaps, but that was the level to which their relationship had deteriorated before that final big blow-up.

Andrew stood at her side, his arm moving lightly about the slenderness of her waist. 'My father tells me that your family are in hotels, Jed,' he prompted with polite interest.

'Yes,' Jed answered the other man abruptly while his eyes continued to rest on Georgie.

Georgie, who was becoming more and more uncomfortable by the second, was aware that Jed, a man who had never particularly cared for the social niceties before, was now behaving very rudely by continuing to stare at her. In the same way that their brief conversation at dinner hadn't been socially polite either. If he didn't start behaving in a more circumspect way someone in the Lawson family—probably the more astute Sukie—was going to guess that they weren't complete strangers after all.

'That must be very interesting,' she put in lightly, her expression warning as Jed looked at her.

'It can be.' His answer was maddeningly unforthcoming.

Like getting blood out of a stone!

Like trying to find a heart somewhere in that stone...

'You're an author, I believe, Georgie.' He spoke mildly.

'Yes,' she confirmed warily.

'Will I have seen one of your books in the shops?' He continued his line of questioning.

Her mouth tightened. 'Not unless your taste runs to children's books, no,' she bit out tautly, wondering exactly where this conversation was going. Or if, indeed, it was going anywhere!

One thing she did know just from looking at Jed's face: he had already known what her answer was going to be—if not quite prepared for the way in which she gave it!

So he already knew that she had written and had published a book for children...

How had he known that? There had been no personal contact of any kind between the two of them for over a year now, all correspondence concerning their divorce having passed between their two lawyers. And Georgie had deliberately avoided seeing anyone who might have contact with Jed.

But, nevertheless, she had no doubt that Jed already knew everything there was to know about the book she had written...

Jed's mouth quirked. 'I'm afraid not. Still, it's an—unusual career,' he added softly.

'What's unusual about it?' Georgie prompted sharply, on the defensive as she glared at him.

He shrugged broad shoulders. 'Perhaps it's only that I've never met an author before.'

That wasn't what he'd meant at all—and they both knew it. Even if no one else in the room did...

'Yes, I'm very proud of Georgie.' Andrew spoke warmly, giving her waist a reassuring squeeze as he smiled down at her.

'And what about you, Georgie?' Jed spoke hardly. 'Are you proud of your achievement?'

'Of course,' she answered him stiffly.

He gave an acknowledging inclination of his head. 'Is it something you've always wanted to do? Or—?'

'Would you care for another brandy, Jed?' Sukie cut in firmly, obviously intending to change the subject, not at all happy that the conversation was focused on Georgie.

Which was perfectly okay with Georgie—she wasn't happy about it either!

'No, thanks.' Jed answered Sukie dismissively, not even glancing her way as he did so. 'Have you always known you wanted to be an author, Georgie?'

Her eyes narrowed on him warningly. He knew damn well she hadn't always wanted to be an author, that until two years ago her only ambition had been to be his wife, to spend the rest of her life with him.

Which, in retrospect, was no ambition at all!

'I've always known I wanted to be something,' she replied with firm dismissal. 'It seems I've been lucky enough to find a career that I not only like but which one publisher at least thinks I'm good at.' That knowledge still gave her an inner warm glow.

'How do you feel about having a working wife, Andrew?' Jed looked at the younger man mockingly.

'I feel absolutely fine about it,' Andrew came back,

sounding perplexed. 'Most women want a career of their own nowadays—to be more than just some man's wife.'

'Do they?' Jed murmured softly.

'Of course we do.' Sukie was the one to answer lightly, linking her arm with Jed's. 'Maybe that's where you went wrong, Jed,' she added teasingly.

Jed continued to look at Georgie for several long minutes, before he straightened and turned to Sukie, his smile wry. 'Maybe it was,' he murmured in agreement. 'Although, listening to my wife, I would be hard pushed to find anything I did right!'

'Ex-wife,' Georgie heard herself correct, heated colour entering her cheeks when she realised—as Sukie and Andrew had no idea of her past relationship with Jed! To them she probably sounded as if she was being rude again.

'I stand corrected.' Jed gave an acknowledging nod of his head, lips curved into a humourless smile as he dared her to add to that admission.

It was a challenge she had no intention of taking him up on—they had talked about Jed Lord and his defunct marriage far too much already this evening as far as she was concerned!

'Are you staying the whole weekend, Mr—Jed?' She corrected herself before he could do it for her. 'It's a beautiful area. I'm sure Sukie would love to show you some of the surrounding countryside.' She received a grateful smile from her future sister-in-law at this suggestion.

'You're right; it is a beautiful area,' Jed drawled dryly. 'Unfortunately, I'm leaving in the morning.'

Unfortunate for whom? Georgie's raised eyebrows

conveyed her amusement. Certainly not for her; she couldn't wait to see the back of him!

Also, she couldn't believe he was enjoying this encounter any more than she was; the two of them had made their opinions of each other more than plain the last time they had spoken at length together.

'What a pity,' she answered, completely disingenuous.

'Isn't it?' he came back, with the same insincerity, laughter crinkling the lines around his eyes as he met her gaze.

Georgie drew in a sharp breath, knowing that the two of them weren't behaving very well. They really were going to arouse suspicion if they didn't stop this verbal fencing—right now!

She turned to Andrew, her hand resting lightly on his arm. 'Shall we go and make our excuses to your parents now, darling?' she suggested. 'We've both had a busy week, and I'm sure you must be tired after driving down here.'

Andrew brightened at her obvious concern, making Georgie feel doubly guilty. Firstly, because she knew her desire to escape to the privacy of her bedroom had nothing to do with concern for Andrew, and secondly, because she knew how upset and confused Andrew would feel if he knew it had everything to do with getting away from Jed Lord!

'I hope you'll excuse us, Jed?' Andrew said politely. 'It's been a great pleasure meeting you,' he added warmly, shaking the other man's hand before putting his arm firmly about Georgie's waist to steer her across the room to where his parents sat, softly conversing together.

'"A great pleasure" meeting him?' she muttered to Andrew sceptically.

He gave her waist a light squeeze. 'I'll explain later,' he promised.

Having made her excuses to Andrew's parents, Georgie could once again feel Jed's piercing grey gaze burning into her back as she walked to the door, knowing her movements lacked their normal graceful fluidity, but unable to do anything about it. She wouldn't be able to relax again completely until she was safely away from Jed. Make that until Jed was far, far away from the Lawson home!

Although she did breathe a little easier once she and Andrew were outside in the hallway.

She was grateful for the fact that Jed hadn't given away their previous connection, but at the same time she questioned why he hadn't. It certainly couldn't have been to save any embarrassment on her part; Jed just didn't work that way.

'You didn't enjoy this evening, did you?' Andrew enquired ruefully, his head tilted as he looked down at her questioningly.

Georgie looked up at him quizzically. 'Whatever makes you think that?' she delayed.

Had she and Jed given themselves away after all? It wouldn't be so surprising if they had; they certainly hadn't spoken to each other like people who had just been introduced...

Andrew laughed softly. 'I know, from personal experience, that my family is enough to cope with without someone like Jed Lord thrown in for good measure!'

She frowned. 'I had the impression a few minutes ago that you actually liked the man.'

Andrew grinned. 'That was the impression I intended giving.'

Georgie still frowned, not altogether sure she was happy with this explanation. She hadn't believed Andrew capable of subterfuge, but his explanation now gave a different impression completely...

'But why?' Her expression showed complete confusion.

Andrew elaborated as they continued to make their way up the stairs. 'My father owns some land that the L & J Group is interested in purchasing for yet another of their luxury hotels. You've heard of the L & J Group, haven't you?'

Heard of them—she had once been part of them!

'Hasn't everyone?' she dismissed dryly.

'Hmm,' Andrew sighed. 'Anyway, Dad's playing hard-to-get with this piece of land,' he explained.

'Good for him!' Georgie came back vehemently. A little too vehemently, she realised, as Andrew looked at her in surprise. 'Sorry.' She grimaced. 'But even on such short acquaintance I got the impression that Mr Jeremiah Lord is a little too fond of having his own way.'

Andrew nodded slowly. 'He does give that impression, doesn't he? Makes you almost feel sorry for his ex-wife, doesn't it?'

Once again Georgie gave him a frowning look. 'Only almost...?'

'Well—he isn't my type, you understand,' Andrew replied, 'but I got the distinct impression from Sukie's behaviour towards him that Jed Lord is rather attractive to women.'

It would have been impossible to miss Sukie's interest in Jed! 'I didn't find him in the least attractive!' Georgie exclaimed forcefully.

'I know,' Andrew agreed. 'Actually, darling, it might have been a little more politically correct—for the sake of father's business deal, you understand?—if you hadn't shown your dislike of the man quite so openly.'

Her eyes widened at the unexpected rebuke. 'I can't be less than I am, Andrew,' she responded. 'And being pleasant to a man I dislike is not—'

'Don't take it all so seriously, Georgie!' Andrew cut in teasingly, obviously realising he had gone too far. 'I love you just the way you are.'

Georgie looked up at him uncertainly in the dimmed lighting of the hallway. 'I love you too, Andrew,' she told him uncertainly.

'That's all that matters, then, isn't it?' he murmured, before kissing her.

For a brief moment Georgie froze, still thrown by Andrew's sycophantic attitude towards Jed a few minutes ago. Not only that, Andrew had actually criticised her for her behaviour towards the man!

But as Andrew continued to kiss her the anger she felt towards him began to evaporate, and she kissed him back with a fierceness that bordered on desperation, knowing that the last thing she needed at this moment was to feel less than sure of the feelings she and Andrew had for each other.

'Wow!' he murmured a few minutes later as they broke their embrace, his forehead resting lightly on hers as he looked at her. 'Perhaps we shouldn't wait until next Easter to get married, after all?' he urged huskily.

No! Yes! Georgie was no longer sure about anything at this moment... Part of her wanted to marry Andrew tomorrow. But another part of her knew that, no matter how she might try to shut it out, Andrew's attitude towards Jed, even if it was purely a business manouevre, still bothered her. For a start, it didn't seem characteristic of the Andrew she'd thought she knew...

She was also aware that it was seeing Jed Lord again that was making her have doubts about waiting until Easter to marry Andrew...

'If it takes you this long to think about it...'

Georgie's frown deepened. Andrew sounded almost sulky...

'I was only joking, Georgie,' Andrew assured her as he saw the consternation on her face. 'An Easter wedding is fine with me. Which reminds me. We really should start doing something towards making plans in that direction. My mother tells me that it takes months to arrange a wedding.'

Maybe it did, to arrange a church wedding, with hundreds of guests invited and a huge reception afterwards at a fashionable venue. But, as a divorced woman, Georgie knew that wasn't the sort of wedding she and Andrew were likely to have. Something else she really needed to discuss with him...

But not now. She needed to get this weekend over with first, then she and Andrew could sit down and talk about their future together. Including what sort of wedding they were going to have and who the wedding guests were likely to be. The fact that she didn't want to invite one single member of her family was definitely going to be cause for discussion!

Oh, Andrew knew that both her parents were dead, and that she had been brought up by her grandfather. But he wasn't a subject she had discussed in any great detail either. Andrew had seemed to accept her reticence, but Georgie wasn't as sure Annabelle Lawson was going to be so agreeable about it. Especially when the other woman learned exactly who Georgie's grandfather was!

'If you're really sure about waiting, we still have plenty of time for all that,' she soothed.

Andrew looked at her searchingly. 'All this discussion about divorce hasn't put you off, has it?' he asked.

In all honesty, it wasn't talk of divorce that had suddenly made her feel less than certain about her wedding to Andrew; it was this other side of her fiancé that she had never seen before.

Nevertheless, her mouth firmed as she recalled exactly whose divorce had been discussed this evening. 'Not in the least,' she answered. 'You are absolutely nothing like Jed Lord,' she added with certainty. That was one thing she was sure of; she wouldn't be attracted to Andrew if he were anything like Jed Lord! 'I can all too easily imagine why his wife wanted to get away from him!'

Andrew looked concerned. 'You really didn't like him, did you?'

'No,' she confirmed with an inward shudder. Jed wasn't a man who was easy to like; you either loved him or hated him. And Georgie knew which emotion she felt towards him!

'Oh, well, with any luck you may not have to meet him again,' Andrew said. 'I don't think my father will keep him waiting too much longer for an answer on that land.'

Georgie looked at him searchingly. 'Is everything all right? With your father, I mean?' If it wasn't, maybe that would explain the difference she had sensed in Andrew's manner earlier?

Of course,' Andrew dismissed. 'Now, it's time we both went to bed, young lady; I for one am absolutely bushed.' His words were followed by an involuntary yawn. 'See.'

Georgie shook off her earlier mood of uncertainty as she smiled at him; it was probably seeing Jed again that had given her these misgivings! 'I'll see you in the morning, then.'

Andrew nodded. 'But let's not make it too early, hmm?' he ventured, sounding tired.

'As late as you like,' Georgie assured him.

With any luck Jed would already have left the next morning by the time she put in an appearance.

She could always hope!

CHAPTER THREE

'LAWSON has absolutely no idea you were once married to me, does he?'

Georgie froze in the doorway of the bathroom that adjoined her bedroom, staring across to where Jed reclined on the bed—her bed!—still dressed in the dark suit and white shirt he had worn for dinner, his head resting back on the raised pillows as he calmly returned her startled gaze.

Georgie could feel the anger building within her, was absolutely furious at finding him here, incredulous that he could have dared—have dared—

But why should she be surprised by anything Jed chose to do—hadn't he always done exactly as he pleased?

Of course he had. And he would see no problem now in invading the privacy of the bedroom allotted to her by Annabelle Lawson if that was what he chose to do. Georgie should have known she had escaped too easily earlier!

Georgie stepped further into the room, relieved she had put on her nightgown and robe after taking her shower. Although she doubted that if she had been stark naked it would have bothered Jed unduly. After all, he had seen it all before, hadn't he.

'Get out,' she told him in a coldly even tone.

Being Jed, he didn't move. 'Exactly when are you

33

going to tell Lawson about me?' he demanded scornfully. 'Before the wedding, one hopes,' he added mockingly.

'I don't happen to think that is any of your business,' Georgie responded icily.

'No?'

'No!' she confirmed shortly. 'I believe I told you to get out,' she then reminded him forcefully, all too aware of how alone they were in the privacy of her bedroom.

'I believe you did,' Jed confirmed, still making no effort to move. 'Expecting Lawson, are you?' he continued scathingly, eyeing the pale peach-coloured silk robe and nightgown she wore.

Georgie drew in a sharp breath, her body feeling suddenly warm under the onslaught of that assessing gaze. 'Again, I don't happen to think that is any of your business,' she snapped.

Jed shrugged, sitting up to swing his legs over the side of the bed, his sheer size suddenly dominating the room. 'Maybe you don't,' he conceded hardly. 'But I do.'

Her eyes widened. 'You—'

'You're looking good, Georgie.' Jed cut in huskily on her angry rebuke, grey eyes moving slowly over her, from the top of her fiery head to her size four feet. 'Very good,' he amended appreciatively.

Georgie's cheeks were as fiery red as her hair by the time that caressing grey gaze returned to her face.

How did he manage to do that? To make her completely aware, not only of the forceful attraction of his body but also her own body's response to it? Her skin seemed to burn beneath the silk material, her nipples were taut and pouting, and there was a warm glow at her thighs.

'*You* look awful,' she returned bluntly.

If not exactly truthfully. Jed did look older, there were lines beside his nose and mouth that hadn't been there a year ago, and now there were flecks of grey threaded into his almost black hair, too. But none of those things detracted from the fact that he was extremely attractive—he'd always been!

And probably always would be, she conceded wearily. Jed was not only a very handsome man, his hard features seeming as if they were carved from granite, his body lithe and fit, but he also exuded a strength, an arrogance, that would always be attractive to women, no matter what his age.

Some women, Georgie amended forcefully. She—thank goodness!—had been irrevocably cured of her own attraction towards him!

His mouth twisted ruefully at her deliberate insult. 'I see you're still as truthfully honest as ever,' he drawled. 'At least as far as I'm concerned,' he continued pointedly.

Back to the subject of her honesty with Andrew about her previous marriage…!

'And you, I see, are still as dogmatic as ever,' she returned scathingly, not rising to his challenge. 'What do you want, Jed?' she prompted sharply.

He shook his head slowly. 'I'm not sure you want to hear that,' he murmured softly.

Georgie's head snapped up. His eyes were now a deep gunmetal-grey, and a nerve was pulsing in his squarely set jaw. What—?

She took an involuntary step backwards as Jed stood up, her eyes blazing deeply green as she saw his look of speculation at her obvious response.

'Not as self-possessed as you would like me to believe, are you?' he observed with lazy satisfaction.

'Even a fox knows when to be frightened of the hound!' Georgie shot back insultingly.

Angry colour darkened his cheeks. 'Frightened?' he echoed harshly. 'You've made it more than obvious— on several occasions!—that you hate me, Georgie. But fear…?'

'Wary, then,' she amended wearily. 'Jed, it's late, and I—'

'Frightened was the word you used,' he persisted hardly.

Maybe because frightened was the right word! Five years ago, as an inexperienced eighteen-year-old, she had been frightened of the intensity of her own feelings towards this man—had sometimes felt that she couldn't breathe for loving him. Becoming his wife had only intensified those feelings, until at times she'd felt as if she was being totally consumed by him, that her own personality was becoming totally melded with his…!

'So it was,' she acknowledged lightly. 'But, as I said, it's late, and perhaps I used the word unwisely.' She sighed heavily. 'It was—a shock, finding you here this evening, Jed. Perhaps if I had known—'

'You would have found an excuse not to be here!' Jed finished for her, laughing softly as he saw more guilty colour enter her cheeks. 'Don't try to deny it, Georgie, I know you too well to be fooled by the lie. Or did you think I didn't know exactly how you would react if you had known I was to be a guest at the Lawson home this evening?'

Her eyes widened. 'So you *did* know I was going to be here?' she said slowly. She hadn't been wrong, then, in her feeling earlier that Jed had been in no way as surprised to see her this evening as she had to see him?

Jed seemed unconcerned. 'You're a very difficult woman to track down.'

Georgie was taken aback. His words had been 'track her down'. But why? What possible reason could he have for—?

'My grandfather sent you, didn't he?' she realised quickly, her spine stiffening in instinctive defence.

Jed eyed her coldly. 'Nobody sent me, Georgie,' he rasped harshly.

Of course not; Jed wouldn't allow himself to be any-one's errand boy!

'Asked you to find me, then,' she corrected impa-tiently. 'But it amounts to the same thing, doesn't it?'

Jed's eyes were narrowed to icy slits. 'Your grand-father has no idea that I intended seeing you this week-end,' he bit out coldly.

That didn't exactly answer her accusation, did it…?

She shrugged, turning away to toy absently with a china shepherdess that adorned the dressing table. 'In what way was I difficult to track down?' she asked.

But she already knew the answer to that. She lived in a secure apartment building, where the doorman had firm instructions not to allow any of the Lord or Jones family admittance; her telephone number was ex-directory, and as she worked from home there was no office where she could be contacted either. But she had arranged her life in that way for a purpose.

A purpose that had been rendered completely null and void by Jed's unexpected presence at the Lawson home this weekend!

'I'm sure you already know the answer to that, Georgie,' Jed replied. 'It was only the announcement of your engagement last month in *The Times* newspaper that gave us any idea of your present whereabouts,' he explained grimly.

An announcement that had been put in the newspaper by Annabelle Lawson, the other woman having firmly assured Georgie that it was social etiquette for her son's engagement to be publicly announced in this way.

'You didn't waste much time after the divorce, did you?' Jed accused.

Georgie looked at him sharply. 'I don't think my personal life is any of your business, Jed—'

'Until six months ago your personal life was completely my business!' he came back angrily, that nerve once again pulsating in his jaw.

'And now it isn't,' Georgie reminded him. 'Just say what you want to say, Jed, and then leave, hmm?' she prompted bluntly. 'It's been a long week.' And an even longer evening! 'I would like to get some sleep now.'

He stepped back from the bed. 'Don't let me stop you,' he said.

She sighed her impatience. 'You and I both know that I have no intention of getting into bed until you are out of my bedroom!'

'Why not?' he queried softly.

Her cheeks coloured hotly at his deliberate probing. 'You know why not!'

'Because you and I once shared a bed as husband and wife?' Jed's face had hardened angrily. 'You're a beautiful woman, Georgie, perhaps even more so now than you were a year ago. But I'm really not so desperate for a female to share my bed that I need to force my attentions on a woman who has claimed—more than once!—to hate me!'

'Especially when there's one just down the hallway who so obviously doesn't feel the same way!' she came back heatedly.

Jed became very still, his expression unreadable now. 'You're referring to Sukie Lawson?' he said slowly.

'Of course,' Georgie snapped. 'Although Annabelle doesn't seem impervious to your charms either,' she commented scathingly as she remembered the way the older woman had lightly flirted with Jed during dinner.

He shook his head. 'That's your future mother-in-law you're talking about.'

'She's still a woman, isn't she?' Georgie scorned. 'And you—' She broke off, completely dazed as she realised she was resorting to the sort of arguments that had peppered their three year marriage.

'Georgie—'

'Forget I said that, Jed,' she cut in quickly, disgusted with herself—and Jed!—for allowing the conversation to deteriorate in this way. 'As I said, it's been a shock seeing you here this evening,' she said in a calmer voice. 'But that's no reason for me to be insulting.'

'My, my, you have grown up,' he mocked.

Georgie ignored the taunt. 'You said earlier, or im-

plied—' she corrected ruefully '—that you've been trying to contact me… I've had the final decree through for
our divorce, so it can't be anything to do with that.' And
those papers, signed, sealed, and legally verified, were
very securely locked away in the safe at her apartment.

'No, it's nothing to do with the divorce,' Jed conceded. 'As you say, that is definitely final. But there is
a problem. A family problem,' he went on.

Georgie froze, her hands clenching into fists at her
sides as she tensed. 'My grandfather—?'

'No, not your grandfather,' Jed interrupted her
harshly. 'I have no idea what the rift that exists between
the two of you is about, but he, it seems, knows better
than to ask you for anything!' he concluded disgustedly.

Georgie was well aware that his disgust was levelled
at her…

And maybe on the face of it that feeling was justified.
Her grandfather had brought her up after her parents, his
only son and his daughter-in-law, had both been killed
in a skiing accident when Georgie was only five.

At sixty years of age, George might have been thought
to be well past the age of wanting to be bothered by
such a responsibility, and might quite easily have paid
for a full-time nanny for the little girl, followed by
boarding-school when she was old enough. But George
had done neither of those things. He had taken Georgie
into his home, becoming father as well as mother to her,
and taking her with him on his business travels whenever
she didn't have to be at school.

As a young child Georgie had absolutely adored him,
knowing that behind the forbidding façade he presented
to the world in general there was a softer, more caring

man. Whatever love he'd had, he'd generously given to her.

She could have had no idea then that she was just part of a grand plan...!

She scowled. 'Then what makes you think you could possibly succeed where my grandfather wouldn't even try?' she challenged Jed.

'Because, no matter what your differences were with your grandfather, I know you have always loved my grandmother,' he answered.

Georgie frowned. 'Grandie? What does she have to do with this?' Whatever 'this' was!

'Everything,' Jed answered flatly, his expression grim. 'She had a heart attack three weeks ago—'

'Grandie did?' Georgie echoed sharply, feeling a sinking feeling in her stomach that had nothing to do with her loss of appetite earlier. 'Why didn't anyone let me know? What—?'

'You've refused to see any of us except in the presence of a lawyer, remember?' Jed replied bitterly.

Her cheeks coloured at the rebuke. 'Yes, but—'

'No buts, Georgie,' Jed rasped harshly. 'You can't have it all your own way, you know. You've made it more than obvious that you want nothing more to do with the family. More to the point that you want them to have nothing more to do with you.'

Georgie couldn't quite meet that icily accusing grey gaze, knowing that what he said was true. But she had her own reasons for making that decision. Reasons that hadn't allowed for the illness of the one person in the family that she still adored...

'How is Grandie now? Is she all right?' Georgie asked agitatedly.

'Do you care?' Jed scoffed.

Her eyes flashed deeply green. 'Of course I care!' she responded angrily.

Jed gave a brief nod of his head. 'That's something, I suppose,' he allowed. 'Grandie is— She's—changed,' he finally said reluctantly. 'She wants to see you.'

Again this was typical Jed. No 'will you?', no 'could you?', no 'would you?'. Just that single bald statement.

Georgie moistened dry lips. 'When?'

'Well, not tonight, obviously,' he drawled with a sweepingly appraising glance over her night attire.

'Obviously,' she echoed, hoping that none of her inner panic at the mere thought of what was being asked of her was apparent on her face.

Her break with the family two years ago had been irrevocable, final; the thought of walking back—voluntarily!—into that lions' den made her feel weak inside!

Jed nodded abruptly. 'Tomorrow will do.'

'Tomorrow...?' Her eyes widened. 'But—is Grandie *that* ill?'

'Your concern is a little late in coming, but no doubt Grandie will be too pleased to see you to care too much about that!' It was obvious from his own tone that he didn't share the sentiment!

Georgie's hands clenched so tightly into fists that she could feel her fingernails biting into her palms. 'Is she?' she persisted tautly.

Jed shrugged. 'I think I'll leave you to be the judge of that for yourself.' He straightened. 'I've said all I wanted to say—'

'And that's it, is it?' Georgie attacked incredulously. 'You come here completely unexpectedly, take advantage of your host's hospitality by invading the bedroom of one of his guests. Then you tell me that Grandie is ill and wants to see me, and refuse to say anything else?' She was breathing hard by the end of her outburst, her eyes blazing, her cheeks fiery in her outrage.

'That's it exactly,' Jed answered with complete calm.

Yes, that was it, wasn't it? Jed had always said exactly what he wanted to say, and no more. And, as she knew from the past, no amount of questioning, wheedling, asking, would make him say any more if he chose not to do so.

As he chose not to now...

'Tomorrow could be a little—difficult,' she said slowly.

'What's difficult about it?' Jed replied. 'I'm sure that if you explained to the Lawsons that you have to leave in order to deal with a family problem they would understand. Or is it Andrew Lawson you're worried about?' he added shrewdly. 'Tell me, Georgie, how can you be engaged to marry a man, and yet that same man knows absolutely nothing about you that matters?' he demanded.

'All Andrew needs to know about me is that I love him!' she returned, her cheeks flushed red with anger.

'I thought I knew that you loved me once, too,' Jed shot back harshly. 'For all the good it did me!'

Georgie drew in a deeply controlling breath, knowing that to allow this conversation to—once again!—deteriorate into a slanging match would achieve nothing.

'I'll see what I can do about going to see Grandie tomorrow,' she told him evenly.

Jed's mouth thinned. 'I should try to do more than see what you can do, if I were you,' he advised.

Georgie stiffened at his tone of voice. 'Or what...?' she prompted warily.

'I wasn't aware that I had said there was an "or what",' he denied, moving towards the bedroom door.

Her chin rose defensively. 'I know from experience that there usually is where you're concerned!'

Jed turned before opening the door. 'Isn't it time you got over this childish belief that I'm some sort of monster?'

She had thought she had! Until faced with Jed once again...

She sighed, giving a self-disgusted shake of her head. 'What time is best for visiting Grandie?' That's it, Georgie, stick to the point. That way there was less chance for this verbal fencing she and Jed seemed to fall into whenever they did happen to meet—by chance or design!

'What you really mean is what time would be best not to find your grandfather at home?' Jed derided knowingly. 'Tomorrow is Saturday, Georgie; even your grandfather doesn't work at the weekend!'

'There was a time when he did,' she defended.

'He's seventy-eight years old, for goodness' sake,' Jed responded. 'Even he recognises that it's time he slowed down. Besides,' he added heavily, 'Grandie's heart attack has been a shock to him.'

Georgie could understand that. Estelle Lord, Jed's grandmother, and George Jones, Georgie's grandfather, had met and fallen in love fifteen years ago, marrying only months later. Both of them were aware that they had found this second-time-around love rather late in their lives and had been determined to enjoy together the years they had left.

Georgie knew that her grandfather would be devastated now by his wife's sudden illness.

'So, to answer your question, Georgie,' Jed continued firmly, 'in view of the fact that neither my grandmother nor your grandfather has set eyes on you in two years— any time is probably a good time to go and see them! In fact, I would say it's past time!'

Georgie's mouth tightened at the rebuke. 'You—'

'You know, Georgie, I still can't believe you did that,' Jed opined. 'You decided you no longer wanted to be married to me—fine. But to include your grandfather and Grandie in your desertion—'

'I didn't desert anyone,' she defended heatedly.

'No?' Jed raised dark brows. 'That's not the way I remember it.'

She shook her head, knowing she couldn't stand much more of this. 'Think what you like, Jed,' she said wearily. 'You usually do anyway— Forget I said that!' She winced as she instantly realised she was lapsing into childishness once again.

'Thank you for letting me know about Grandie. I'll go and see her some time tomorrow.' When she had built up her courage for the inevitable meeting with her grandfather such a visit would incur.

'Very politely put,' Jed said. 'Make sure that you do.'

'I—'

'You know, Georgie, I was wrong earlier. When I

claimed that my wife divorced me because she understood me,' he explained huskily at her puzzled expression. 'You don't understand me at all, do you? I don't
think you ever did,' he added heavily. 'For instance,' he
continued softly as Georgie would have spoken, 'what
do you think I would like to do at this precise moment?'

'You should have made it something more difficult
than that, Jed! Strangulation comes to mind,' she suggested ruefully.

He shook his head slowly. 'What I would most like
to do at this moment is lie down on that bed with you
and make love to you all night. But as I know that is
never going to happen…'

Georgie could only stare at him as he left the bedroom
as abruptly as he had first appeared in it.

She sank down gratefully onto the side of the bed, her
breath leaving her in a ragged sigh of exhaustion. Had
Jed been serious about that last claim? Could he really,
even after all this time, want to make love with her?

She didn't know—wasn't sure of anything any more.
Anything to do with Jed always left her feeling confused.

And she didn't think her meeting with her grandfather,
a man almost as forceful and arrogant as Jed, was going
to be any easier…!

CHAPTER FOUR

SHE didn't feel much better the following day as she hesitated outside her grandfather's Belgravia home. She was so nervous her legs were shaking and her palms felt damp. Almost as if she had never been to the house before. Which was ridiculous; she had lived here with her grandfather until she was eighteen years old. Before she married Jed...

Her resolve deepened as she thought of him. Of their marriage. Of the reason for it.

She had no reason to feel in the least nervous about this visit; if anyone should feel uncomfortable about it then it should be her grandfather!

'Miss Georgie!' the butler's pleasure in seeing her as he opened the door was unmistakable. He was an elderly man of unguessable years, although he had certainly been working for her grandfather for as long as Georgie had lived here.

Well, at least one person was pleased to see her! 'Good afternoon, Brooke.' She smiled in response to his greeting. 'I'm here to see Grandie,' she explained, less confidently; after all, there was no guarantee that her grandfather would agree to her doing that. After the way they had parted two years ago, he might not even let her inside the house!

'Of course.' Brooke stood back to allow her entrance. 'We've been expecting you,' he added warmly.

Georgie paused as she stepped inside, giving him a startled look. 'You have...?'

'We have,' remarked an all-too-familiar voice. Georgie turned in time to see Jed strolling into the large hallway from the family sitting room, his brows rising mockingly as he saw the surprised look on her face. 'Thanks, Brooke. I can handle things from here,' he dismissed the elderly butler.

'It's wonderful to see you again, Miss Georgie,' Brooke told her before disappearing down the stairs that led into the realms of the Victorian kitchen.

Georgie eyed Jed uncertainly. What was he doing here? He had already left the Lawson house by the time she'd gone down to breakfast late this morning, but he hadn't mentioned anything last night about being at her grandfather's house today...

'Grandie is looking forward to seeing you.' Jed broke into her thoughts. 'I have no idea how your grandfather feels about it.'

As if he had known exactly what her next question was going to be! And perhaps he did. She had never been a complicated person to understand!

Jed grinned. 'He made no comment when I told him you would be coming to see Grandie today. Nor has he made one since.'

When he had told her grandfather she *would* be coming to see Grandie today... He had been so sure, then, that she *would* come?

'Is Grandie upstairs in her bedroom?' Georgie wasn't sure how ill Estelle was, whether or not she had been moved to a ground-floor room so that she didn't have the bother of climbing the stairs.

'She is,' Jed confirmed grimly. 'Georgie, there's something I have to tell you before you see Grandie—'

'You came, then,' rasped a harshly critical voice.

Georgie turned sharply, to see her grandfather standing in the hallway that led to his private study. He was a tall, autocratic man, his hair iron-grey and his face was deeply lined but still showed signs of how handsome he had been in his youth. At the moment his deep green eyes, so like Georgie's own, were as hard as the jewels they resembled!

No forgiveness there, then. Perhaps as well, because there was no forgiveness on her part either!

She swallowed hard. 'Grandfather,' she greeted him tersely.

'Georgina,' he returned curtly. 'It's nice to see you still have enough sensitivity of feeling left to come and visit Estelle.' His voice softened with tenderness as he spoke of his beloved wife.

It was a love-match. The marriage of George Jones and Estelle Lord might have combined their two hotel chains into the forceful L & J Group, but Georgie had never doubted that George and Estelle loved each other deeply. She had come to doubt many other things about her grandfather, but never that!

Her chin rose challengingly. 'If I had known of Grandie's illness earlier I would have come before,' she confirmed.

Her grandfather gave a scornful snort. 'You could hardly be informed of anything when you chose not to tell even your own husband where you are!'

'Ex-husband,' Georgie corrected sharply.

'I'm sure you are well aware of my feelings concerning divorce, Georgina,' her grandfather countered.

Oh, yes, she was well aware of them. In other words, he refused to recognise that she and Jed were divorced!

She gave a dismissive shrug. 'Fortunately, it's unimportant what you think—'

'Shall we go up and see Estelle now?' Jed put in, shooting Georgie a warning glance as she turned to glare at him. 'She's refused to take her afternoon nap until after she's seen you,' he went on to say.

As if Georgie should have already known that!

Really, these two men had been screwing her life into knots for far too long; the quicker she got this visit to Estelle over with, the sooner she would be able to get away from both these arrogant men.

'I'm ready whenever you are,' she assured Jed as she turned abruptly away from her grandfather.

Just looking at him, remembering their closeness in the past, was enough to break her heart. Actually having to feel the force of his displeasure towards her was almost more than she could stand.

They had always been so close in the past. Even George's marriage to Estelle fifteen years ago had not broken the bond that had arisen between them after the death of Georgie's parents. Seeing her grandfather again in these awkward circumstances was almost unbearable.

Jed was glowering heavily, and Georgie was able to feel the vibrations of his displeasure as they walked up the wide staircase together.

But instead of turning left at the top of the stairs, in the direction of the bedroom Estelle shared with Georgie's grandfather, Jed turned suddenly to the right.

Georgie came to a halt. 'Where are you going?' she demanded, well aware of the bedrooms that lay in this direction.

Jed's gaze was flinty grey as he paused to look at her. 'I need to talk to you before you see Grandie,' he said seriously.

She eyed him warily. 'Why?'

'There are some things you need to—be made aware of before you see her.'

Georgie gave him an impatient glance. 'I'm not a child, Jed. I do know what illness looks like!'

'I'm sure you do, but—'

'But nothing, Jed.' She cut across him, turning determinedly in the direction of Estelle's bedroom. 'Are you coming with me or not?'

He struggled to hide his irritation with her. 'I'm coming with you,' he confirmed tersely, his hand lightly clasping the top of her arm as he walked down the hallway beside her. 'Just remember, I did try to explain the situation to you,' he said enigmatically.

Georgie gave herself a mental shake; Jed could be as mysterious as he pleased, but she refused to become embroiled in any of his games.

'I'll remember,' she assured him reluctantly.

To say that she wasn't dismayed by the changes she could see in Estelle would have been to tell a lie. The older woman had always been tiny and delicate to look at, but that delicacy had been teamed with a seemingly boundless vitality. Now Estelle merely looked frail as she sat in a chair looking out over the garden at the back of the house. There was not an ounce of superfluous flesh on her tiny frame, and her hands were almost clawlike as they rested on top of the rug that covered her legs. Her face was still beautiful, but obviously ravaged by the illness that had struck so suddenly.

But the deep lines of illness were dispelled as her face lit up with pleasure, blue eyes bright with emotion at the sight of Georgie. 'Georgie!' she breathed excitedly, holding out her hands in welcome.

'Grandie!' Georgie went to her unhesitatingly, clasping the slender hands in both of hers as she went down on her knees beside Estelle's chair. 'Oh, Grandie,' she repeated emotionally, holding the iciness of one of those waif-like hands against the warmth of her own cheek.

'Jed said he would bring you, but I— Oh, my dear, it's so good to have you back,' Estelle assured her emotionally, tears of happiness welling in her deep blue eyes.

As if Georgie needed any such assurance; the older woman's pleasure in seeing her was enough to bring tears into her own eyes. Along with a certain feeling of guilt. How could she have cut herself off so irrevocably from this lady who had shown her nothing but kindness from the moment the two of them met, who had sheltered and nurtured her as if she were the daughter Estelle had lost so long ago?

'Almost the return of the Prodigal,' Jed drawled from somewhere behind her.

Reminding Georgie all too forcefully that he was the main reason she had behaved in the way that she had the last two years. Jed. And her grandfather.

She sat back on her haunches, giving Jed a censorious glare before turning back to smile gently at Estelle. 'It's good to be back,' she said firmly.

'Mmm, pretty.' Estelle touched Georgie's hair. 'Your grandfather will be so pleased to see you!'

'Yes,' Georgie confirmed vaguely, sure that 'pleased' wasn't the best word to describe how her grandfather had looked when he had seen her a few minutes ago!

Estelle's expression became compassionate. 'He's missed you so much, Georgie,' she confided. 'We all have.' She squeezed Georgie's hand encouragingly.

Georgie deliberately didn't look at Jed after this last statement, sure that he didn't share his grandmother's feelings. 'I would have come before, Grandie, if I had known you weren't well—'

'I know you would, my dear,' Estelle accepted warmly. 'Such a silly argument, wasn't it?' she said sadly. 'But it's all over now, isn't it?' She brightened.

Georgie hesitated. Was it 'all over'…? Neither Jed nor her grandfather had given her that impression earlier…

'Now we can just get back to being a happy family again,' Estelle continued with satisfaction. 'And we were a happy family, weren't we, Georgie?'

They had been, yes. Briefly. But—

'I think we've stayed long enough for now, Grandie.' Jed was the one to excuse them gently, stepping forward to draw Georgie back onto her feet at his side, retaining that hold on Georgie's arm as they stood together looking down at Estelle. 'We'll come back after your nap,' he assured his grandmother as she would have protested.

Estelle relaxed back in her chair. 'Of course you will,' she accepted with a happy sigh. 'We have all the time in the world now, don't we?'

Georgie was alerted. 'What—?'

'Come along, darling,' Jed cut in, his hand firm on

her arm as he turned her towards the doorway. 'Grandie needs to rest now,' he insisted.

Georgie was totally bewildered by Estelle's remarks—so bewildered that she allowed herself to be determinedly guided from Estelle's bedroom, Jed's hand still tightly gripping her arm.

But only for as long as it took him to close the bedroom door behind them. Georgie instantly pulled out of his grasp. Although, no doubt, she would have bruises on her arm later to show for her bid for independence!

'Exactly what is going on?' she demanded of Jed. 'Estelle seemed under the impression—'

'Let's go somewhere less—public,' Jed replied as one of the maids passed through the lower hallway.

'But—'

'That wasn't a request, Georgie,' Jed grated between clenched teeth. 'I'm not in the habit of discussing private family matters where anyone can overhear!' he added, before striding off in the direction of the hallway opposite.

The hallway Georgie had veered away from so determinedly earlier on. The hallway where the bedroom she had once shared with Jed was situated…!

'No, Jed.' She stood her ground, her chin raised defensively as he stopped to turn and look at her with narrowed eyes.

His mouth twisted derisively. 'I want to talk to you, Georgie—not make love to you!' he announced insultingly.

'Love!' she repeated scathingly. 'I don't remember there being too much love in our relationship!' Except on her side… She had once loved Jed to distraction.

With blindness where his own motives for their marriage were concerned!

She had been so besotted with him five years ago, so much in love with him, that when he'd asked her to marry him she hadn't even noticed that there were no words of love forthcoming on his side. That realisation had come later. Much later.

Jed sighed, shaking his head impatiently. 'If this isn't the place to discuss Estelle's—condition, then it certainly isn't the place to discuss our marriage!' he snapped coldly, before resuming his progress down the carpeted hallway.

To Georgie's surprise he went straight past the doorway of the bedroom that had once been her own, and then later the bedroom the two of them shared as husband and wife, only stopping when he reached the room that he had occupied in the past whenever he'd come to stay with Estelle and George.

He turned as he opened the door. 'Satisfied?' he said.

Not exactly, but she supposed it would have to do. After all, she had no wish to discuss family matters where any of the household staff could overhear either.

His chilling grey gaze moved over her mockingly as she swept past Jed into the bedroom. 'That's the first sensible thing you've done since we met again last night!' he derided as he followed her into the room and closed the door behind him.

Georgie was far from sure about having that bedroom door closed. She felt distinctly uncomfortable in the intimacy of the room where Jed had stayed immediately after Estelle and Georgie were married and, later, on the occasions when he'd come to visit after he had moved into his own apartment at twenty-one.

On the surface of it, she and Jed had very similar backgrounds: both had been brought up by their respective grandparents from a very young age, although the necessity for Jed to live with Estelle had been vastly different from the death of Georgie's parents.

Jed's father, as far as Georgie could ascertain, had been a complete mystery—might have been any one of a number of lovers his mother had had in her life at that particular time.

His mother had been someone Estelle had even refused to have mentioned in Georgie's hearing, disgusted that her daughter could have just abandoned her baby son of four years old in order to go to live in France with yet another lover.

Jed had never talked of his mother, and because Estelle had refused to even have her name mentioned Georgie had never really got to know anything about the other woman. It had worried her a little when she and Jed were married, wondering how she was going to explain the situation to any children they might have had. But obviously *that* situation was no longer even a possibility…

Georgie shook her head, deliberately hardening her heart to the signs of Jed's earlier occupancy of the room; the worn paperback books on the bookcase beside the single bed, the masculine wallpaper and bed linen, a rugby ball he had used at university, the trophies and cups he had won for both rugby and rowing.

She looked across at Jed unflinchingly. 'Would you

like to tell me what's going on?' she demanded, refusing to rise to his deliberate insult of a few minutes ago.

'I would ask you to sit down, but as the only available space seems to be the bed…' He trailed off.

She could feel the heat that entered her cheeks even as she drew in a sharply controlling breath. Jed had been deliberately goading her, in one way or another, since the two of them met again the previous evening, and she wasn't going to give him the satisfaction of rising to those insults.

'Jed, you asked me to come here today, and at considerable awkwardness to myself I've done so, but—'

'What did you tell Lawson about that, by the way?' he interrupted her mildly. 'Not the truth, I'm sure,' he added dryly.

Her mouth firmed. 'My relationship with Andrew is none of your business—'

'The hell it isn't!' Jed responded.

Georgie's frown turned to one of puzzlement. 'Jed, we've been divorced for six months now—'

'I know exactly how long it's been, Georgie,' he returned swiftly, a nerve pulsing in his tightly clenched jaw.

'Well, then,' she muttered, no longer quite meeting his gaze.

He could have no idea of the strength it had taken to leave him in the first place, let alone actually go through with the divorce. But, having done those things, she wasn't going to back down now. And she certainly wasn't going to be fooled into thinking Jed actually cared that she had divorced him!

'Well, then,' he repeated. 'You've grown up a lot in

the last two years, Georgie,' he opined, changing the subject.

She looked up at him, eyeing him warily. 'Maybe I have,' she conceded, 'but I'm obviously still not in your league when it comes to getting my own way.' After all, no matter how she felt about it personally, she was here, wasn't she?

His mouth firmed. 'I asked you to come here for Grandie's sake, not mine,' he replied.

'Believe me, that's the only reason I came!' she assured him.

'Nice to know you still care about one member of this family,' Jed replied, with more than a hint of sarcasm.

Her eyes flashed deeply green. 'Grandie, as far as I'm aware, has never used or deceived me!'

'What the hell does that mean?' Jed exclaimed, taking a step towards her.

A step Georgie took exception to, her expression glacial now, the look in her eyes warning him not to come any closer. 'Grandie seems...under the impression that we're all friends again now...' she said slowly.

'Friends!' Jed repeated scornfully. 'Were the two of us ever friends?'

Georgie flinched, at the same time furious with herself as she felt the sting of tears behind her lids, angry with herself that this man could still manage to hurt her.

Because, yes, the two of them had been friends. Maybe that friendship had always been a little one-sided—eight-year-old Georgie following Jed about adoringly whenever he was at home, and as an infatuated teenager gazing at him in the same way as she grew older. But Jed had seemed to be kind to her then, gentle—two things she could never accuse him of being now!

'Maybe not,' she accepted dully. 'Tell me about Grandie,' she prompted abruptly.

He drew in a sharp breath. 'I told you she had a heart attack three weeks ago. Would you like to cast your mind back to what other event took place three weeks ago?' He furrowed dark brows.

Three weeks ago…? What on earth—?

Her eyes widened incredulously. 'You aren't trying to tell me that my engagement—the announcement of my engagement to Andrew—had anything to do with it?' That would just be pushing things too far! Although it was exactly three weeks yesterday since that announcement had appeared in *The Times*…

Jed's mouth thinned at her obvious scepticism. 'I'm not trying to tell you anything—because I already know it had everything to do with it!'

'But—'

'George went up to have coffee with her as usual that morning, and found her slumped over the newspaper,' Jed explained. 'He discovered later—once the doctor had come, and Grandie had been rushed to hospital— that the newspaper was open on the page containing the announcement of your engagement to Andrew Lawson!'

Georgie stared at him. He couldn't be serious? He didn't really think—? Her grandfather didn't believe—?

But she could see from Jed's accusing expression that he did think that. Not only did he think that, but he totally believed it. Which had to mean her grandfather believed it too…

But what did they want her to do about it? What *could*

she do about it? She loved Andrew. The two of them were going to be married. So what—?

Her gaze sharpened suspiciously as she remembered something. 'Grandie said something earlier about us all being a happy family again…?'

Jed agreed. 'Because that's what she thinks we are.'

'What?' Georgie stared at him, incredulous.

He gave a confirming inclination of his head. 'Grandie believes us to have reconciled our differences. That your engagement was a mistake. That the two of us are back together.'

Georgie's eyes had got wider and wider as Jed spoke. 'How on earth—? Why—? Who could have told her such a thing—? You!' she instantly guessed, staring at Jed accusingly as she recognised that challenging tightening of his jaw. 'You told Grandie—gave her the impression that the two of us— How could you?' she gasped disbelievingly. 'How *could* you?' she repeated, dazed.

'What choice did I have?' Jed returned vehemently, hands clenched into fists at his sides.

'What choice?' Georgie repeated incredulously.

'Grandie was very ill—could have died. I—I decided that if it was seeing the announcement of your engagement in the newspaper that had made her ill, then the best way to help her get better was to tell her it had all been a mistake, that the two of us were back together!'

'*You* decided?' Georgie questioned forcefully, so angry she was shaking. 'What right did you have to decide any such thing? *Who* gave you the right?' she amended furiously.

Jed's expression was icy cold now as he met her accusing gaze unflinchingly. 'My love for my grandmother gave me that right,' he told her. 'Tell me you wouldn't you have done the same thing if it had been your grandfather's life that hung in the balance,' he added hardly.

Georgie's anger left her so quickly she felt like a deflated balloon.

Would she have done what Jed had if it had meant safeguarding her grandfather's life? Would she have lied in the way he had to achieve that end?

She and her grandfather had had their differences, there was no doubting that, but— Yes, Georgie knew without a doubt that she would have done exactly what Jed had if it would have brought her grandfather back from the jaws of death!

But now that Jed *had* done it, exactly where did that leave them?

More to the point, where did that leave her and Andrew?

CHAPTER FIVE

'REMEMBER, Georgie, I did try to warn you earlier—'

'You didn't try hard enough!' she bit out fiercely, glaring across the bedroom at Jed, knowing that he *had* tried to warn her; but how could she possibly have guessed the enormity of what he was trying to tell her?

Jed thrust his hands into the pockets of his black denims, unwittingly drawing Georgie's reluctant attention to his lean muscularity, the width of his shoulders, tapered waist and the long length of his legs.

She didn't want to be here, Georgie realised with panic. Didn't want to get drawn back into this family. Certainly didn't want to get drawn back into close proximity with Jed!

'Okay, so you did try to warn me,' she conceded impatiently, unaware that she was now pacing the room.

'That's something, I suppose,' Jed accepted dryly, watching her anxious movements. 'But the real question is, do you accept the reasons why I did what I did?'

The honest answer to that was—yes, she did understand. But honesty on her part wouldn't change the unacceptable position into which Jed's lie had now put her. Or the anger she felt towards him for doing so!

She looked at him crossly. 'How well is Grandie now?'

'Not as well as she thinks she is—and certainly not as well as you would like her to be!'

Georgie stiffened at his taunt, knowing that Jed was aware of exactly how she felt about this situation. A situation she didn't intend letting continue for a moment longer than was absolutely necessary. The question was; how long was necessary…?

'The months following a first heart attack are the most dangerous,' Jed told her frankly. 'Because a second one, quickly afterwards, could prove fatal.'

How did he do that? How did he manage to read her mind now, enough to be able to answer questions before she had even asked them, when for the three years of their marriage he hadn't seemed to know how she felt about anything!

Georgie stopped her pacing to look at him hard. 'So where does that leave us? Me,' she added. Because she really wasn't interested in Jed, or the life he now led, was she?

Jed raised dark brows. 'As far as Grandie is concerned? No longer engaged to Lawson. But not yet remarried to me.'

'This is—this is intolerable!' Georgie burst out. 'You had no right, Jed. No right at all!' She resumed pacing the room, her movements those of a trapped animal.

'For goodness' sake stand still, Georgie,' Jed snapped irritably. 'You're making me dizzy!'

'I'm making you—!' She shook her head disgustedly. 'Grandie has to be told the truth, Jed,' she told him firmly. 'She has to know that—'

'And are you going to take responsibility for what comes next?' Jed cut in. 'Are you?' he pressed.

She had been shocked by the changes she had found in Estelle, deeply disturbed by the older woman's frailty.

She certainly didn't want to be the cause of further distress. But the price she would have to pay for Estelle's continuing health—having to keep up some sort of pretence of a reconciliation with Jed, in front of Estelle at least—could be her own sanity!

Besides, how could she ever explain any of this to Andrew…?

'Tell you what, Georgie.' Jed broke into her troubled thoughts. 'You do this for Grandie and I'll double the offer I've made Gerald Lawson for his land.'

'Don't be ridiculous, Jed,' she responded distractedly. 'I'm not in the least interested in your business dealings with Gerald.'

'But he is,' Jed assured her softly.

'I don't understand…' Georgie looked at him frowningly, completely puzzled by the strange turn this conversation had taken. What on earth did her future father-in-law have to do with any of this?

Jed looked grim. 'Gerald Lawson is in trouble, Georgie. Financial trouble.'

She hadn't known that—had always assumed, from the way they lived, that the Lawson family were extremely wealthy. Not that it made any difference to her if they weren't; it was Andrew she was marrying, not his family. Although it did explain that slight feeling of something being left unsaid she had experienced the evening before, when Andrew had mentioned the proposed business deal between his father and Jed.

'An injection of a few million would certainly go a long way to easing the situation,' Jed continued.

Georgie had no idea why he was persisting with this. Gerald was Andrew's father, and she felt for him, and the family, if he was in financial difficulty. But it would make no difference to her feelings for Andrew if Gerald were to lose all his money tomorrow.

'I told you,' she persisted, 'that is nothing to do with me—'

'No?' Jed challenged. 'I suppose you know that Annabelle Lawson had a nice wealthy Lady Someone-or-other picked out as the wife of her only son? Before he produced you, of course,' Jed added dryly.

'What are you talking about?' Georgie exclaimed exasperatedly, having no idea what any of this had to do with Grandie's condition.

Although, if what he said about Annabelle was true, that might explain the other woman's reticence towards her as a prospective daughter-in-law...

Jed seemed unmoved by the emotion in her voice. 'Sukie mentioned her mother's hopes concerning Andrew yesterday evening. It appears that as far as the Lawson family is concerned you're a bit of a dark horse, Georgie,' he said. 'No family of your own—or so it appears to them. A first-time author of a children's book. Not quite what Mummy was hoping for as the wife of her only son and heir!' he concluded.

Not that it was any of Jed's business, but she was already well aware of that fact. She had just hoped that, with time, when Annabelle saw that Andrew was happy with Georgie, she would come to accept her and the situation.

'I'm not marrying Andrew's mother!' she stated firmly.

'I doubt that Gerald would marry her either, given his time over again,' Jed drawled. 'She's most of the reason he's in such a financial mess,' he explained at Georgie's questioning look. 'She likes to live the life of the Lady to the full. House in London, country estate, apartment in New York, private education for both her children. The right friends. The right social gatherings.' He paused, then went on. 'And to think, when she and Gerald first met, he was just a graduate with a vague interest in politics, and Annabelle was the daughter of a postman!'

'I happen to like Gerald very much,' Georgie told him defensively.

'So do I,' Jed agreed. 'He was a good politician. Did you ever wonder why it was he retired two years ago, at only fifty?'

'No,' Georgie sighed. 'But I'm sure you're going to tell me,' she added wearily.

She still had no idea where this conversation was going, but Jed's words were hypnotic.

'He got out before the whole castle he'd built on sand came crashing down around his ears and caused a public scandal.' Jed grimaced.

'How do you know these things, Jed?' Georgie looked at him uncomprehendingly.

He shrugged. 'I made it my business to find out.'

'Why?' But she was afraid she already knew the answer to that question. Oh, not that she thought it had anything to do with Jed actually minding that she was engaged to marry someone else. He needed something from her. And he wasn't a man who liked to ask for anything…

He gave her a half-smile. 'I'm sure you've already worked that one out for yourself.'

Oh, yes, she had worked it out. But she was no nearer knowing what he expected her to do about it.

'You see, Georgie,' Jed continued evenly, 'Gerald needs either a large inflow of money to pay off the accumulation of debts, or for his son to marry a woman with money. And as the last time I spoke to your grandfather on the subject you had told him exactly what he could do with your inheritance, you don't appear to be that woman!'

Georgie *had* received a large sum of money, that had been left in trust to her by her parents, when she was twenty-one. But it was money she had used to buy her own apartment after she and Jed separated—money she had used to live on while writing her book. She had received an advance payment on her book, but any royalties would take some time to materialize. And as she was determined not to accept anything from her grandfather...!

'Andrew isn't in the least interested in money,' she said defiantly, although even she could hear a certain amount of defensiveness in her tone.

'No one is—until it's no longer there,' Jed drawled knowingly. 'Come on, Georgie, be honest; didn't you find it a little hard after you had left—once you had distanced yourself from the family? Learning to live within a budget, knowing there were certain things you could no longer afford to do?'

Yes, never having had to do that before, having first lived with her grandfather and then married Jed, it had been hard to suddenly be on her own, to manage the money her parents had left her. But there had been benefits too—and no longer being answerable to her grandfather—or Jed—had definitely been one of them! Although that situation didn't exactly apply where the Lawson family were concerned, did it…?

She shook her head dismissively. 'Andrew lives perfectly well on the salary he earns as a junior partner—'

'The rent on his apartment is paid for by his parents. His car was also bought by them. As was—'

'How do you *know* these things?' Georgie demanded; he knew more about Andrew's financial situation than she did!

'Just take it that I know, okay,' Jed replied. 'You—'

'No, I won't "take" any such thing,' she cut in accusingly. 'What does it matter about Andrew's apartment. We can both live in mine after we're married. As for his car—'

'Georgie, I think you're missing the point,' Jed interrupted softly, grey gaze enigmatic.

She glared at him frustratedly. 'That point being?'

He gave a humourless smile. 'Without that large cash inflow I spoke of earlier materialising during the next few months, Andrew Lawson's father is going to have to declare himself bankrupt.'

Georgie became very still as she looked across at him, very conscious of the way in which Jed had phrased that statement; not just that Gerald Lawson would have to declare himself bankrupt, but that *Andrew's father* would have to do so…

Because although it might not bother her whether Andrew's family were as rich and influential as they gave the impression of being—in fact, it might be easier for her if they weren't!—it would assuredly bother Andrew if his family were put in that position. And not only because he would be deeply upset to see that happen to his parents, but because it might—just might—affect his chances of rising any further in the law firm he was associated with.

A fact Jed was well aware of, if his satisfied expression was anything to go by!

She gave a disgusted shake of her head. 'If Gerald's piece of land is that valuable, then I'm sure he could find another buyer for it,' she surmised.

'Not for the inflated price the L & J Group is willing to pay for it,' Jed assured her.

Georgie looked at him intently. 'How inflated?'

'Enough to settle Gerald's outstanding debts and leave him a million or so over with which to start again.'

Georgie wasn't even going to ask how he knew all that about Gerald Lawson's private business. She knew Jed well enough to know he wouldn't be saying this at all if he weren't absolutely sure of his facts. It was his reason for bothering to find out those things that was of more interest to her...

'Would you like to get to the bottom line here, Jed?' she said slowly.

He gave a rueful grin. 'Since when did you become a "bottom line" person?'

'Since the beginning of this conversation,' she returned unhesitantly.

Jed smiled widely, his eyes a deep smoky grey now. 'You know, Georgie, you're really rather beautiful in this mood,' he said appreciatively.

She sighed her impatience. 'If that's meant to be some sort of compliment, Jed—don't bother! I stopped looking for any sort of approval from you long ago.'

His expression tightened speculatively. 'Did you now?' he murmured.

'Yes! I—' Georgie's words were choked off as she found herself being pulled determinedly into Jed's arms, his face mere inches away from hers as he looked down at her. 'Let me go, Jed!' she ground out from between gritted teeth, standing absolutely rigid and unresponsive within the circle of his arms.

Not that she felt completely unresponsive inside. Part of her wanted to scream and shout at him to release her. But another part of her—the part that needed to be heard!—was burning with a remembered desire.

'And if I don't?' Jed finally returned mildly—when Georgie had got to the point when she thought she would have to scream and shout for her release after all!

She looked up at him unflinchingly. 'Then I'll be forced to stamp on your toes!'

Jed's eyes widened incredulously for a few brief seconds, then he immediately gave another smile, that quickly turned to open laughter.

Much to Georgie's amazement. Oh, not that she particularly liked the fact that he was apparently laughing at her. But to see Jed laughing at all was a complete surprise to her. It had been so long since she had seen him smile, let alone laughing like this, she realised with affection.

Finally, as his laughter ceased, Jed looked down at her, his hold having loosened about her waist, although he didn't completely release her. 'I'll have you know I'm wearing hand-made Italian shoes,' he informed her.

'In that case, in a few moments they're going to be crushed handmade Italian shoes,' Georgie told him lightly, not absolutely sure what had actually happened between them just now, but nevertheless knowing that a moment of danger had passed.

Danger…?

Yes—danger. Because she had no doubt in her mind that Jed had been about to kiss her before she made him laugh instead. And, in all honesty, she wasn't sure how she would have reacted to that kiss…

Jed stepped back, his arms falling lightly back against his sides. 'Perhaps not,' he accepted.

Georgie felt as if she could finally breathe again, although she could still feel the imprint of Jed's arms about her waist—still felt a sensitive tingling against her skin where he had touched her.

She gave a pained frown at the realisation. She had thought she was completely over Jed, that their disastrous marriage had cured her of any feelings she had for him. But that tingling of her skin just at his touch told a completely different story…

What a fool, she admonished herself inwardly. What an idiot. This man had never loved her, had married her for one reason only. And it had nothing whatsoever to do with loving her.

She drew in a harsh breath before looking across at him with hard green eyes. 'The bottom line?' she reminded him.

'Ah, yes…' he recalled, his own gaze narrowing guardedly as he straightened. 'Well, obviously, for the moment Grandie has to be kept free from stress or worry of any kind. Which is going to require a little co-operation from you—'

'Co-operation?' Georgie echoed. 'After the lies

you've told her about the two of us I think it's going to require a little more than that!'

Jed could barely conceal his irritation. 'At the time I was more interested in the immediate problem of keeping my grandmother alive than I was in any long-term repercussions that might result from those "lies", as you call them.'

'Well, Grandie lived—I'm happy to say,' she added before he could possibly turn any of this around on her—which she knew he was quite capable of doing, if he felt so inclined. 'But we, it seems, have been left with the problem of what to do now.'

Jed's irritation had turned to a scowl. 'I'm sure I've made myself more than plain on that subject, Georgie,' he rasped.

Maybe he had. But she just wanted to be absolutely sure before giving him her answer! 'Explain it again,' she invited mildly.

Jed's gaze narrowed suspiciously. 'I'll see that L & J Group buys Gerald Lawson's land—'

'For an inflated price,' Georgie put in.

His cheeks flushed angrily at her deliberate interruption. 'At an inflated price,' he acknowledged hardly. 'Which will give him enough cash to pay all his debts. And in return—'

'Ah, this is the part I'm most interested in,' Georgie put in with dry derision.

'In return,' Jed repeated firmly, 'I'm asking you to keep up the pretence of our reconciliation until Grandie is strong enough to be told the truth.'

That was exactly what she had thought he was saying!

'What you're actually talking about, Jed, is blackmail—of the emotional kind, if nothing else,' she said bluntly, as he would have interrupted. 'Isn't it?' she prompted as his mouth thinned angrily.

His jaw tightened and his hands clenched into fists at his sides. 'I'm talking about an exchange of—'

'Blackmail, Jed,' Georgie insisted.

His eyes flashed silvery-grey. 'All right then—blackmail,' he accepted tautly. 'What's your answer going to be?'

Georgie looked at him for several long, silent minutes, deliberately keeping her expression enigmatic; although he would have hated to admit it, Jed's uncertainty was all too easy to read from the wariness of his gaze and the tension of his body!

She knew exactly what he was asking of her, exactly what price he was willing to pay for her co-operation. And, although it might not be apparent on the surface, she was furiously angry Jed thought he needed to *buy* that co-operation!

She might have only known Grandie for fifteen years, but she loved the other woman as much as Jed did. Maybe more, in her own way, because Estelle had been the first woman in her life she could confide in.

The fact that Jed was now daring to think he could *buy* her love and loyalty to Grandie was not only hurtful, but highly insulting!

In fact, she would like nothing better at this moment than to wipe that self-confident smile right off his face! But there were more ways than one of achieving that...

Georgie gave a slight inclination of her head, her expression calm. 'Okay, Jed.'

His mouth twisted. 'My offer to help bail your fiancé's

family out of trouble proved too much of an incentive for you, hmm?'

Her expression didn't change, but her eyes hardened. 'You must do what you think right concerning that situation. I'm going back to see Grandie for a few minutes now before I leave.' She opened the bedroom door.

Jed frowned darkly. 'And that's it?' He was too stunned by her complete acquiescence to be able to hide his feelings.

'That's it,' she confirmed. 'Were you expecting a fight, Jed?' She knew well that was exactly what he had been expecting.

And how he would have enjoyed bending her to his will, forcing her to accept a situation he was sure would be completely abhorrent to her! Which was a good enough reason for her not to give him that satisfaction.

There was no disputing the fact that the situation of having to come here to spend time with Grandie would be difficult, even intolerable—and not just because of Jed. She would also have to see a certain amount of her grandfather, and she knew from her brief encounter with him earlier that neither of them had yet forgiven the other for what had happened two years ago.

But, on balance, her own satisfaction at seeing Jed completely thrown off guard by her answer was enough—for the moment!—to help her get through that awkwardness!

'Not a fight, exactly…' Jed finally responded, obviously too puzzled by her behaviour to be his usual enigmatic self.

'But you did expect to have to exert a little more pressure than you actually did?' Georgie observed. 'Perhaps maturity has taught me not to waste my energy on useless battles.' And perhaps maturity had also taught her that Jed would have preferred a battle!

Because the confused expression on his face as she quietly left the bedroom to go and see Grandie was that of a man who had not only lost *this* particular battle but also wasn't sure if he hadn't lost the war as well!

And she couldn't say it didn't give her a wonderful sense of euphoria to see Jed so disconcerted, to know that she had thoroughly confused him by her answer.

Now all she had to do was try to find some way to explain this complicated situation to Andrew…!

CHAPTER SIX

'WHEN did you cut your hair?'

Georgie, having called in to see Grandie with the promise that she would be back tomorrow, had only just congratulated herself on reaching the bottom of the wide staircase without seeing any of the rest of the family when she came to an abrupt halt, before turning to face her grandfather as he stood erect and forbidding in the doorway of the family sitting room.

Her chin rose challengingly, her expression guarded. 'About six months ago,' she answered.

'Ah.' He nodded knowingly.

Georgie met his gaze unblinkingly. 'What's that supposed to mean?'

Her grandfather shrugged broad shoulders. 'I always loved your long hair. Its colour always reminded me of the leaves of a copper beech.'

His reply didn't exactly answer her question, did it? Although she didn't really need it to, and knew exactly what he had meant.

Six months ago Georgie's divorce from Jed had become final. Three weeks later she had met Andrew at a party given by a mutual friend. But in the interim Georgie had gone to the hairdresser's and asked them to cut off the long red hair she'd had as her style since she'd been a very young child.

At first the hairdresser had protested at being asked to

76

despoil such natural beauty. But much to the hair-dresser's disgust, Georgie had been adamant. The result was this boyish style that framed the oval of her face. To Georgie's relief she was no longer assailed with memories every time she looked in a mirror—of the times Jed's hands had run through her hair's long copper thickness...

Strangely, Jed had made no mention of the changed length of her hair since they'd met again yesterday evening—was it really only that short a time ago? Although Grandie had commented on it a few minutes ago. And obviously her grandfather had noticed the change too!

She quirked her mouth. 'I couldn't stay eighteen for ever.'

Her grandfather gave a humourless smile. 'You were much less trouble at that age!'

Anger coloured Georgie's cheeks now. 'You—'

'Would you like to come into the sitting-room?' her grandfather invited smoothly. 'Or are we keeping you from something?' He raised iron-grey brows.

If she said no, then she would only be adding to the constraint that already existed between them. And with several weeks in front of her of having to come here, if only to see Grandie, that was not a good idea. But, by the same token, she had no wish to be ensconced in the family sitting room with her grandfather.

'Or someone...' he added.

Georgie stiffened at the implication. 'Not at all,' she replied swiftly, sweeping down the last two stairs, across the hallway, and into the sitting room.

It looked much as it had the last time she had seen it: decorated in comfortable golds and browns, the furniture old and comfortable too, well-read books and magazines on tables beside the chairs.

Strange how for Grandie and her grandfather time didn't seem to have moved on, and yet her own life had changed considerably. She was now an independent single woman, with a successful career, and a man in her life who loved her as she loved him.

And don't let any of them make you ever forget those things, Georgie, she told herself firmly, before turning to look at her grandfather once again.

'Tea?' he offered lightly.

'No, thank you.' She roused herself to refuse the offer politely.

He nodded abruptly, as if he hadn't expected her reply to be anything else. 'What did you think? Of Estelle,' he clarified curtly as she looked puzzled.

Georgie's expression relaxed; at least they were now talking of someone they both loved. 'I understand from Jed that she's been very ill—'

'I almost lost her,' her grandfather grated emotionally, his hands clenched into fists at his sides.

She had been wrong, Georgie realised, when she'd initially thought that her grandfather hadn't changed in the last two years. He looked older—lines on his face that hadn't been there before, white hair amongst the grey now too, a certain stoop to his shoulders, as if he were weighed down with the worry of the last few weeks.

Georgie felt her heart contract in her chest, knowing in that moment that no matter what had transpired between her grandfather and herself two years ago, she still loved him and cared about him—could feel his pain now, his anxiety for his wife, as if it were her own.

'I understand that, Grandfather,' she concurred. 'But Jed tells me the prognosis is good?' she continued, almost questioningly.

'As long as we can keep her happy and worry-free for a few months,' he confirmed harshly.

Jed had said a few weeks. Her grandfather now said a few months. Georgie knew which one she was inclined to believe!

'Then that's what we have to do,' she answered determinedly.

He raised grey brows. 'And your other—commitments?'

Her mouth tightened at his hesitation over that last word. But if he refused to accept her divorce from Jed, then he could hardly acknowledge her engagement to Andrew. The engagement that had precipitated Estelle's collapse...

'They don't concern you,' she dismissed, still having no idea herself how she was going to deal with this situation as far as Andrew was concerned.

The truth would be the best option, she knew, but after the way she and Jed had behaved towards each other the evening before, as if they were complete strangers, that truth could prove a little awkward to put into practice!

'In the same way that your walking out on Jed, dragging the family name through the divorce courts after effectively having abandoned that family, didn't concern me?' her grandfather returned accusingly.

Georgie stiffened at the rebuke. 'I'm willing to come here in order to help Grandie, Grandfather,' she told him sharply. 'But don't presume to think those visits will give you any rights concerning comment on my private life!' Her eyes flashed a warning.

He drew in a sharp breath. 'Your manners certainly haven't improved in the last two years,' he bit out reprovingly.

Once upon a time such a reproof from her grandfather, given in that flinty tone of voice, would have absolutely devastated her. But not any more!

She straightened, facing him squarely. 'I'll call you concerning the convenience of time for my visits to Grandie—'

'Those visits won't be in the least convincing to Estelle if you aren't accompanied by Jed.' Her grandfather cut across her words.

'I totally disagree.' She gave a derisive snort. 'Jed and I rarely did anything together even when we were married!'

'And whose fault was that?' her grandfather came back.

'Not mine,' Georgie returned without hesitation, then instantly regretted her outburst; after all this time, raking up what had or hadn't gone wrong with her marriage to Jed wasn't going to achieve anything. 'Look, Grandfather,' she reasoned heavily, 'this situation is difficult enough as it is, without the two of us continuing with the feud that exists between us. For Grandie's sake, I suggest we put all that to one side for the moment. Agreed?'

Always a dominant man, a man who liked to have the last word in most arguments, he didn't look at all happy with this suggestion. But at the same time he knew that this time he had little choice in the matter…

Finally he subsided. 'Agreed,' he bit out tautly.

Georgie let out a relieved breath—not realising until that moment that she had been holding it in!

But this really was an intolerable situation. For all of them, she was sure. The only saving grace for any of them that Georgie could see—for Jed, her grandfather, and for her—was that they were all willing to put aside their differences for the benefit of Grandie's full recovery. In front of Grandie, at least!

How the three of them really felt towards each other wasn't relevant at this point in time, and the sooner they all accepted that, the better!

'And do you think Jed will be willing to agree to the same arrangement?' her grandfather prompted harshly.

'I—'

'I think what your grandfather really means is now that you've managed to batter him into submission, perhaps you would like to start on me?' taunted an all-too-familiar voice from close behind her.

Georgie turned quickly to face Jed as he stood in the now open doorway, realizing that she and her grandfather must have been so intent on their own conversation that they hadn't been aware of Jed entering the room. At least, Georgie hadn't been aware…

She glanced back at her grandfather, knowing by the tightness about his lips that he hadn't been so innocent of Jed's presence!

Her expression was derisive as she turned back to Jed, knowing by the challenging way he returned that stare that whatever confusion he had felt earlier, over her acquiescence, he was completely over it now. 'I wouldn't even attempt to try,' she scorned. 'I've told Grandie that I will be back to see her in the morning; I leave it up to you whether or not you will be here too.'

'Oh, I'll be here,' he responded lazily. 'Didn't I tell you? I moved back in for a while when Grandie came out of hospital.'

He knew damn well he hadn't told her that! If he had, she might have been less agreeable concerning her visits here. A fact Jed was obviously well aware of!

'That's nice,' she returned with sugary insincerity. 'Well, if you gentlemen will both excuse me?' she added pointedly before turning to leave. Only to find the doorway still blocked by Jed. She met his gaze fearlessly.

Jed met that gaze for several long, silent seconds before giving a curt nod of his head and stepping to one side. 'I'll walk to the door with you,' he murmured.

Georgie gave him a scathing glance. 'I haven't forgotten the way!'

His mouth tightened. 'I'm well aware of that.'

But he obviously still had something to say to her. Something he had no intention of saying in front of her grandfather.

Georgie shrugged before preceding him from the room. If he thought—

'Thank you, Georgina.'

She came to an abrupt halt at the husky sound of her grandfather's voice, drawing in a controlling breath before she had to turn back and face him.

It had taken much more courage than she'd realised to come here at all today—she felt a little as Daniel must have done as he stepped into the lions' den!—and now all she wanted was to get away from here. Fast!

She swallowed hard, closing her eyes briefly before glancing back at him. 'You're welcome,' she muttered abruptly, giving him no opportunity to say anything further as she strode determinedly down the hallway to the front door.

She was very aware of Jed walking behind her—was also aware that he definitely wanted to say…something. She only hoped it wasn't going to be something that provoked further argument between them—because after the fraught emotion of the last hour she didn't have a lot left in reserve to get her through another verbal battle with Jed!

'Do you have your car with you, or would you like me to call a taxi?' Jed offered as she stepped out of the house into the welcome sunshine.

'It's such a nice day, I think I'll walk for a while,' she refused, breathing in the heady freedom of being outside. Away from the domineering presence of her grandfather. Away from the physical proof of Grandie's frailty. But, most of all, in a few seconds she would be free of Jed's overpowering presence too!

Once he had said whatever it was he felt he had to say to her!

He paused while he looked down at her with intense grey eyes.

Georgie waited. And waited. But still Jed just continued to look at her in that broodingly intense way.

She moved the strap of her bag more securely on her shoulder. 'I'll be back tomorrow morning, then,' she said impatiently; she didn't have all day to stand here playing guessing games with Jed!

'I…' Jed paused, breathing heavily. 'I just wanted to say thank you too,' he finally said tersely.

Georgie's brows arched in surprise, her eyes wide. This had been the last thing she had been expecting. And, oh, how it hurt Jed to be put in a position where he had to thank her!

She gave a small smile in acknowledgement of the effort it must have cost him to show her this gratitude. 'As I told Grandfather, you're welcome,' she replied.

Jed hadn't finished. 'I realise that it's Grandie you're doing this for, that given the choice you would spit in our eyes,' he acknowledged gruffly. 'But I thank you anyway.'

He wasn't wrong about spitting in their eyes, but by the same token Georgie knew both these men well— knew that it hadn't been easy for either of them to unbend enough to thank her in the way they had.

'Don't mention it,' she responded. 'Just continue to take good care of Grandie.'

'We will. And about Lawson—'

'I told you,' she put in sharply, 'I will deal with that in my own way—'

'I was referring to Gerald Lawson, Georgie,' Jed came back. 'I accept that how you explain all this to Andrew Lawson is your own affair.'

Well, that was something, at least!

'But I want you to know that I will keep my word as regards the proposed business deal with Gerald Lawson,' Jed continued.

'I never doubted it for a moment.'

'No?' Jed seemed surprised. 'You didn't seem to have the same faith in my ability to keep the marriage vows I made to you five years ago!'

Georgie felt the colour drain from her cheeks. Her lips felt suddenly numb too, and her hands clenched so tightly into fists she could feel her nails digging into her palms. But she felt glad of the slight pain that caused—it helped to override the sudden tightness she could now feel in her chest!

'Georgie—'

'Don't touch me!' she cried as Jed tried to clasp her arm, giving him a pained look and shaking her head wordlessly before turning away and hurrying down the steps that led away from the house.

How could he talk about that now? How dared he remind her—?

Because he was Jed Lord, came the instant answer. A man who felt love for no one—with the obvious, understandable exception of his grandmother. A man who could step so uncaringly over other people's emotions. A man who—

'Georgie...!' Jed groaned her name this time, having followed her in her flight from the house, his hand light on her arm as he gently turned her to face him, clasping both her arms now. 'Georgie, I can't bear to see you like this—'

'I believe I told you not to touch me!' she bit out icily, stiff with resentment as she looked coldly up into his face. '*You* can't bear it, Jed?' she spat out. 'But you're the invincible Jeremiah Lord—you can bear anything!' she derided scathingly. 'You've certainly never had a problem with hurting me in the past—and I doubt you will have any problem with it in the future either. Now, if you wouldn't mind releasing me, the middle of a busy street is hardly the time or place for this sort of conversation. In fact, I can't think of *any* time or place I want to have this conversation with you ever again. Is that clear enough for you?'

His hands had dropped away from her arms as she spoke, his expression once again blandly enigmatic. 'Very clear,' he acknowledged tightly.

'Good,' Georgie said, the colour back in her cheeks now, even if it was due to anger. 'Not the same little Georgie you remember, am I, Jed?'

Jed continued to look at her for long, timeless seconds. 'No,' he finally conceded. 'But, personally, I preferred the old Georgie,' he added at her triumphant look.

She gave a humourless smile. 'I'm sure you did. As my grandfather has already pointed out once today, I was much less trouble when I was eighteen. For ''less trouble'', read ''more gullible'',' she finished disgustedly.

Jed gave a shrug of his shoulders, his expression quizzical. 'I don't think you're going to believe me, no matter what I say in answer to that accusation.'

'I'm not going to believe anything you say to me ever again—period,' she assured him. 'Goodbye, Jed,' she said firmly, before turning on her heel and walking away—sure that, after the things she had just said, this time he wouldn't follow her.

Her step was light and determined; she was so relieved that, outwardly at least, she had managed to suppress the emotional pain the conversation with Jed had once again brought to the surface.

But, inwardly, she knew it was another matter entirely...

CHAPTER SEVEN

'BUT I don't understand, Georgie.' Andrew frowned his puzzlement.

She gave him a reassuring smile. 'It's quite simple, Andrew. As you know, I had to come back to town this morning because I learnt my grandmother is ill. Now I need to spend some time with her. That's all there is to it.'

All there was to it! She had thought long and hard about what to tell Andrew about the next few weeks, and finally decided that a simple—if not exactly complete!—explanation would do. Except Andrew looked thoroughly confused by that explanation!

Andrew had insisted on driving her back to town this morning, after she'd told him she had received a telephone call on her mobile concerning her grandmother's illness. She'd hated telling a lie about the phone call, but she could hardly tell Andrew that she knew about her grandmother's illness because Jed Lord had paid a visit to her bedroom the night before and told her about it!

Andrew had driven her home this morning so that she could drop off her things before going on to visit her grandmother. But the two of them had arranged to meet up at a restaurant for a meal together that evening. Georgie had waited until the end of their meal to break

the news to Andrew about her proposed visits—alone—
to her grandmother…

He shook his head now. 'That isn't what I don't understand. For one thing, I thought you told me you were
brought up by your grandfather…?'

'I was,' Georgie confirmed. 'Grandie is—well, she's
my grandmother on my—er—' She could hardly say on
her husband's side! 'She's married to my grandfather,'
she concluded.

'I should hope so.' Andrew gave a teasing smile.

Georgie looked at him ruefully. He really was the
most uncomplicated of men. So kind, so warm, so—so
trusting. But why shouldn't he be? Andrew couldn't possibly guess at the complication that was her family. Or
the fact that she wasn't being exactly truthful about it.

'No, I mean Estelle married my grandfather when I
was eight.' And brought with her the man who was to
become Georgie's torment! 'But I really am very fond
of her—have always thought of her as my grandmother
too—as my grandmother,' she amended desperately.

Too! For there to be a 'too' there would have to be
another grandchild, and Georgie had no intention of telling Andrew that the man he had met the previous evening, Jed Lord, was he.

'I see.' Andrew nodded, obviously not registering that
slight slip-up on Georgie's part. 'But the other thing I
don't understand is why I can't come with you on these
visits…'

She shook her head. 'I told you, Grandie really has
been very ill. She isn't up to seeing—strangers just yet.'

Andrew reached out and clasped Georgie's hand as it
lay on the table, his fingers absently stroking her en-

gagement ring. 'But the two of us are going to be married, so I would only be a stranger to her for the very first visit,' he reminded her.

George gave a reassuring smile. 'I appreciate that. But if I could just have your understanding for a few weeks, until Grandie is a little stronger…' She grimaced. 'I realise it's asking a lot of you, Andrew—'

'Not at all,' he hastened to reassure her. 'I'm just a little disappointed that I won't be able to see as much of you over the next few weeks. Do you realise we've seen each other every day since we became engaged three weeks ago?'

Yes, she did realise that. And those three weeks, and the previous four months when she and Andrew had been dating each other, had been absolutely wonderful.

If a little artificial…?

Much as she hated to admit it, perhaps that was so. It had been all too easy to block out the past, her family, her marriage to Jed—made life so much less complicated if she didn't have to think of those things. But it wasn't the full picture, was it? The past existed, as did her family, and sooner or later she was going to have to tell Andrew that she had once been married to Jed Lord.

But just not now…!

Andrew was looking at her so concernedly, love shining brightly for her in his trusting blue eyes; she simply couldn't bear, after the awful time she had already had, to face the possibility of losing that unconditional love and trust.

'I do know, Andrew.' She squeezed his hand. 'And I shall miss not seeing you every day too. But it will only be for a short time. And there are telephones, you know.'

She knew she was probably going to need those tele-phone calls as much as Andrew!

It was going to be a very difficult few weeks anyway, trying to juggle those visits to her grandfather's house—where Jed was in residence too!—so that they didn't in any way clash with her dates with Andrew, or put any sort of strain on their relationship.

'I can see that you've already made your mind up about this.' Andrew gave a resigned sigh. 'Never mind. I'm sure that we'll survive. They do say absence makes the heart grow fonder.'

'Or alternatively, out of sight, out of mind,' Georgie reminded him. 'Strange how there's always a negative response to those old-fashioned adages.'

Andrew's hand tightened on hers. 'You're never out of my mind, Georgie,' he assured her.

'I'm glad.' She squeezed his hand in return. She knew that the next few weeks were going to be difficult for her; it would certainly help to know that Andrew was waiting for her at the end of them.

Andrew sat back as the waiter delivered coffee to their table, waiting until the other man had left before resuming their conversation. 'I have a feeling I'm going to be kept pretty busy myself over the next few weeks any-way.' He grinned. 'I had a telephone call from my father this afternoon, asking me to draw up some legal papers for him. Apparently the socialising angle works; Jed Lord has offered my father an absolutely unbelievable price for that piece of land I told you about yesterday.'

Jed hadn't wasted any time in making that offer!

Or maybe he was just sewing up that particular deal to make sure she didn't go back on their agreement...?

Not that she would. But, knowing Jed, he wasn't going to take any chances.

'I hope your father grabbed the offer with both hands!'

'Yes. And no,' Andrew added consideringly. 'Oh, I'm going to draw up the required legal documents, of course, but in the meantime my father is going to check into why Lord should be making such a large offer for a piece of land valued at only half that price.'

Why hadn't either she or Jed thought about that possibility?

Or perhaps Jed had…?

It wasn't like Jed to make mistakes, especially when it came to business; surely he would have known that Gerald Lawson would become suspicious if Jed appeared too eager to finalise the deal or offered too large a sum for the land? Of course he would have known.

Her mouth tightened. 'You think this Jed Lord is up to something?'

Andrew shrugged. 'Perhaps he knows something about that piece of land that we don't.'

'Such as?' Georgie probed.

'Maybe he knows that someone else is interested in it and he intends getting his offer in first. Or maybe the government has plans for the land and would make a good offer for it.' He laughed. 'I'm not a businessman; I really wouldn't know. But when I met Jed Lord last night he certainly didn't come over as a fool to me. So if he's willing to offer a lot of money for a relatively small piece of land that was actually valued as being worth half that amount, then there has to be something about it that we don't know.'

How shocked Andrew would be if she were to tell him that what he didn't know was that she had once been Jed Lord's wife, and that was the reason for the inflated offer on the land.

But of course she intended telling him no such thing! 'Oh, well, I'm really pleased for your father.' She busied herself picking up her evening bag so that she didn't have to look at Andrew and so risk his seeing the expression of guilt she was sure was on her face. 'Shall we go?' she suggested brightly.

Damn Jed, she brooded as Andrew drove them both back to her apartment. How could he have been so stupid as to arouse Gerald's suspicions by coming back to the other man so quickly with an offer that seemed totally out of line with the current property market? Although, like Andrew, she was inclined to think the move hadn't been a stupid one on Jed's part at all. But for different reasons…

Something she intended bringing up with Jed the next time she saw him!

'You had better come through to the sitting room.' Jed sighed wearily, having taken one look at her face after Brooke had opened the door to her ring. 'Although I should warn you I don't have a lot of time, if you expect me to accompany you up to Grandie's room. I expected you earlier than this.' He glanced pointedly at the gold watch on his wrist. The hands pointed to exactly midday. 'I have an appointment at one o'clock.'

Georgie arched derisive auburn brows. 'An appointment? At one o'clock on a Sunday?' she scorned sceptically, knowing that the 'appointment' was probably with a female—and, from the casual way Jed was dressed, in black denims and an open-necked grey shirt, it had nothing to do with business. 'And I don't expect you to do anything, Jed. Grandfather was the one who thought we ought to be together when I visit Estelle,' she pointed out. 'Personally, I would rather be with anyone else other than you!' She was still smarting from the necessity of keeping these visits separate from her life with Andrew for these few weeks.

Jed scowled darkly. 'And instead you're stuck with me!'

'Not for long,' she returned forcefully.

'Surely that depends on how long it takes Grandie to make a full recovery?'

'We'll have to see, won't we?' Georgie replied uncooperatively.

Jed sighed his impatience. 'You obviously have something on your mind, Georgie, so what is it?'

'Andrew told me last night that you've made his father an offer for the land—'

'Isn't that what you wanted me to do?' Jed interrupted exasperatedly.

Georgie's eyes narrowed. 'Not so promptly that it instantly aroused suspicion, no,' she answered slowly, watching him closely to see what his reaction was to this accusation. Being Jed, a man who closely guarded his response to most things, there wasn't any visible this time either.

'And has it aroused suspicion?'

'Of course it has,' she snapped. 'Gerald wants to know why you offered so much.'

Jed shook his head exasperatedly. 'Is there *any* pleasing you, Georgie?'

'The last six months of not seeing you have been extremely pleasant,' she assured him sweetly.

'Ha-ha,' he rasped harshly. 'Shall we go up and see Grandie now?' he suggested impatiently.

'Of course,' she taunted as she swept past him out of the room. 'You mustn't be late for your date, must you?'

Jed's hand snaked out to clasp her arm tightly, halting her in her tracks. 'And what if it *is* a date I'm going on?' He glowered down at her.

Georgie shrugged. 'Then it's of absolutely no interest to me—'

'Exactly.' He nodded his satisfaction with her answer, abruptly releasing her as they walked up the wide staircase together.

Exactly.

Except...

Except for some reason she couldn't—or wouldn't—explain, Georgie found that it *was* of interest to her that Jed was going off in a few minutes to meet some mystery woman. It shouldn't be, she acknowledged with a frown, but somehow it was.

'Okay, tell me what you want me to do about Lawson,' Jed demanded, having seen her frown—and completely misunderstood the reason for it.

Thank goodness! How awful if he were to realise she was feeling some belated—and totally unacceptable!—jealousy concerning the woman he was meeting for lunch.

But perhaps this feeling was a normal response to someone you had once been married to? After all, divorce didn't automatically cut off all the feelings once felt for an ex-partner. Even Jed had acted slightly green-eyed when he saw Andrew's ring on her finger on Friday evening—and he certainly didn't love her!

She shook her head. 'I don't see that there's anything you can do now. But I'm not at all happy with the thought of Gerald snooping around to see if there's a particular reason for your over-generous offer.'

Jed grimaced. 'You think he may eventually come across the fact that my ex-wife is about to become his daughter-in-law? In those circumstances, surely I would be more inclined to let him sink in his own debts?'

That might be one reaction—if Jed had ever loved her. Which he hadn't.

'You still haven't told Andrew Lawson the truth about me, have you?' Jed realised slowly.

Guilty colour darkened her cheeks even as she avoided meeting the directness of his gaze. 'Not yet, no,' she confirmed reluctantly.

Jed snorted derisively. 'I'm the last person to be advising you about anything—'

'You most certainly are!' she replied disgustedly.

'—concerning your behaviour towards Lawson,' Jed finished decisively. 'But surely you realise, Georgie, that you're just digging a bigger and bigger hole for yourself to fall into as regards your lack of honesty towards your fiancé.' His mouth tightened over the latter word.

Her eyes widened accusingly. 'You're the last person to be lecturing me about honesty, Jed!'

He gave an impatient shrug. 'Well, don't say I didn't try to warn you...'

'Let's just go and see Grandie, hmm?' she prompted,

knocking sharply on the bedroom door and entering at Grandie's call of welcome.

Her grandmother looked a little brighter today. There was colour in her paper-thin cheeks, blue eyes sparkling with pleasure as she watched Georgie cross the room to join her in the bay window.

Georgie's own smile wavered a little at the older woman's opening remark!

'What mischief have you two been up to?' Grandie teased. 'You're both looking terribly guilty,' she added.

'Really, Grandie.' Jed moved forward to kiss his grandmother on the cheek. 'You make Georgie and I sound like naughty children!' he admonished affectionately.

Which was just as well—because Georgie had been rendered completely speechless by Estelle's reference to them looking 'terribly guilty'!

Estelle laughed softly. 'Probably because to me that's what you'll always be! Pour the tea, would you, Georgie?' she suggested lightly, indicating a tray of tea things set on the table in front of the window. 'Actually, I was wondering if the two of you had perhaps been discussing a date for your wedding?'

Georgie considered it was just as well that no one was actually looking at her at that moment—because the milk she had been pouring into the three cups ended up on the tray instead, so great was her shock at Estelle's question!

Wedding? What wedding? Okay, so Grandie considered that Georgie and Jed were once again a couple, but surely that was no reason for her to suppose—

'We don't intend rushing things this time around,

Grandie.' Jed was the one to answer smoothly. 'I think Georgie deserves to be courted a little first,' he added huskily, his hand running familiarly down Georgie's spine as he did so.

So familiarly that, to Georgie's dismay, her back arched in instinctive response!

Her inner response to Jed's touch was no less disturbing, if less discernible to anyone but herself. Pleasure coursed through her body, there was a sudden tightness in her chest, and her back seemed to burn where his fingers had so lightly touched.

'What an absolutely wonderful idea, Jed!' His grandmother smiled her approval of this plan. 'We women like a little romancing, don't we, Georgie?' she said conspiratorially.

Not with Jed, Georgie didn't!

Although it would certainly be novel. The first time around, as Jed had put it, he had simply proposed to her on her eighteenth birthday. A proposal she had eagerly accepted, she recalled now with an inner cringe of embarrassment.

After the announcement of their engagement to their respective grandparents the wedding plans had moved along so fast, leaving them so little time for themselves, that before Georgie had known where she was, she was a married woman. Married to a man she had been able to realise even then, she barely knew.

Oh, she had known Jed as Estelle's loving but reserved grandson—known him as the respectful young man he always was to her grandfather. But the teasingly off-hand man she had come to know during the latter part of her own childhood had no longer been there, and in his place had been someone she couldn't relate to at all—a remote stranger. A man who was her husband.

Not a very auspicious beginning to any marriage!

Although they might even have surmounted that difficulty if Jed had been willing to bend a little, to be the lovingly attentive husband she had hoped he would be. But how could he have been? When he didn't love her at all, let alone wish to be attentive to her!

She put down the milk jug—before she managed to do any more damage with it! 'We do.' She was noncommittal in her agreement with Estelle concerning romance; she wasn't sure Jed even knew what the word meant!

Estelle eyed Jed's casually smart appearance. 'I hope he's taking you somewhere nice for lunch today, Georgie?' she teased.

He wasn't taking her anywhere!

She flickered an uncertain glance in Jed's direction. 'Er—'

'I have a business meeting lunchtime today, Grandie.' Jed was the one to answer lightly. 'So that I can free some time later in the week to spend with Georgie,' he added as his grandmother began to look upset.

So glib. So smooth. So untrue!

'Anyway, Grandie.' She turned back to the older woman, reaching out to lightly clasp Estelle's hand in her own. 'I thought I would have lunch with *you* today.' She smiled reassuringly.

'Well, of course that will be lovely, dear.' Estelle still seemed a little troubled. 'I just don't want your grandfather and I to intrude on the time you and Jed should be spending together.' She hesitated, then went on, 'I'm sure that was part of the problem last time you were together.'

Georgie was equally as sure it had nothing to do with the breakdown of her marriage to Jed!

Oh, the circumstances of their upbringing, of their respective grandparents being married to each other, had meant they were probably a much closer family unit of four than they would otherwise have been. But none of that would have mattered if Jed had loved her. If her grandfather hadn't deceived her!

'Not at all, Grandie,' Georgie assured the old lady with complete honesty, turning her attention back to pouring the tea. 'As Jed says, we can spend some time alone together later in the week.' And the moon was made of cheese!

Because her wanting to spend any time alone with Jed—ever!—was as much a fairy tale as that was!

'Of course we can,' Jed agreed, casually reaching out to rest his hand familiarly on Georgie's thigh.

Almost causing Georgie to pour the hot tea all over the tray this time!

'Would you like me to do that?' Jed offered dryly, dark brows raised mockingly as he looked pointedly at her shaking hand.

Georgie straightened resentfully, her fingers closing determinedly about the handle of the teapot. 'I can manage, thank you,' she snapped dismissively.

'Thank you, dear.' Estelle accepted the cup of tea Georgie had carefully poured for her. 'You may as well pour the fourth cup; your grandfather should be joining us in a moment.' She smiled warmly at the thought of her husband.

Georgie instinctively poured tea into that fourth cup, adding a dash of milk only, no sugar at all.

How familiar she was with those little everyday things about her grandfather, such as how he liked his tea. How he liked to read the newspaper over breakfast. How he liked a single glass of malt whisky when he came in from work in the evening. The food he preferred. The authors he read.

Yes, she knew all those small things about her grandfather—and yet two years ago she had realised in other ways she didn't really know him at all.

Jed gave a brief glance at his wristwatch before standing up. 'I'm afraid I have to go, Grandie,' he excused himself. 'Walk downstairs with me, Georgie?' he asked.

She had no inclination to go anywhere with him, especially as he was leaving her to the lions while he obviously went off with the latest woman he was involved with. But by the same token she realised that if she didn't go downstairs with him Jed was more than capable of just kissing her goodbye in front of his grandmother!

'Of course.' She stood up gracefully, although her composure deserted her a little as the bedroom door suddenly opened. Her grandfather stood in the doorway.

He raised iron-grey brows. 'Not leaving us already, are you, Georgina?' he observed disapprovingly.

Her cheeks coloured resentfully. 'I—'

'I'm the one that's leaving, I'm afraid, George.' Jed was the one to confess, stepping forward, his arm moving lightly about Georgie's shoulders as he looked across at the older man. 'I have an appointment I can't avoid.' He gave a rueful shrug. 'Georgie was just walking me down to my car,' he explained as the two of them left the room.

Georgie began to breathe a little easier once they were safely away from her grandfather, though she was not at all sure she was going to be able to cope with this. She had thought Jed was going to be her main problem during these visits to Estelle, but it was the confrontations with her grandfather that were proving the most difficult.

'He loves you very much, you know.' Jed cut softly into her worried thoughts.

Georgie gave him a withering glance as they walked outside. 'Then my grandfather's idea of love and mine are vastly different!'

Jed looked surprised. 'Somehow I doubt that.'

She had no intention of discussing the past with Jed— of all people, he was the one who should know exactly what her grandfather was capable of!

'Look—' Jed turned to her '—I accept that things didn't work out between the two of us, Georgie, but that doesn't mean—'

'That has to be the understatement of the year!' she scorned.

'You know, Georgie, bitterness is an extremely destructive emotion—'

'I'll thank you not to tell me what emotions are or aren't destructive—' Georgie's angry tirade came to an abrupt end as Jed reached out for her, his mouth coming down forcefully on hers.

And remaining there…

The force of Georgie's anger instantly melted, and the heat that now flowed through her veins, into every particle of her body, had nothing whatsoever to do with anger.

Jed's arms about her were warm and compelling, his mouth against hers firm and searching, the hardness of his body fierce and demanding.

Georgie was melting in that demand…!

It was as if the last two years had never been, as if she and Jed had never been apart, as if she still loved him—

She wrenched her mouth away from his. 'No!' she cried protestingly, desperately pushing him away from her, wanting to put as much distance between them as she possibly could. 'No,' she repeated vehemently, and Jed reluctantly released her to step back and look down at her searchingly. Two spots of colour were angry in the otherwise paleness of her cheeks, green eyes blazing with anger.

'Why did you do that?' she demanded coldly.

'Why not?' Jed returned, although his own face was slightly paler than usual, and a nerve pulsed in the rigidity of his tightly clenched jaw.

Why not—? 'If you ever touch me like that again, Jed, I'll—'

'You'll what?' he prompted quietly.

Her eyes flashed deeply green. 'I'll hit you with the first available object,' she assured him, glancing pointedly at one of the large plant pots that edged the driveway.

'Ouch!' Jed easily saw the direction of her gaze, his mouth quirking. 'That seems a little ungrateful on your part, when I was only trying to perpetuate the myth that the two of us are back together.'

Georgie looked perplexed. 'In what way could kissing me do that?'

Dark brows rose over mocking grey eyes. 'Someone in the house may be watching us out of the window—'

'Don't be ridiculous, Jed; I'm sure the staff are far too busy preparing lunch to bother spying on us!' she retorted.

'I was referring to my grandmother,' he replied evenly.

'Oh. Of course!' Georgie exclaimed, suddenly knowing that of course Jed hadn't really wanted to kiss her! 'I'm sorry if I—if I misunderstood your motives,' she added awkwardly, hating having to make the apology at all.

'Don't give it another thought,' Jed responded, a smile playing around the hard mockery of his lips as he obviously enjoyed her discomfort. 'Any message you want me to pass on to Sukie over lunch?' he enquired, even as he pressed the button on his keys to unlock his Jaguar and prepared to slide agilely inside.

Georgie's eyes widened, incredulous. Sukie—? Sukie *Lawson*? Andrew's sister? Jed's luncheon appointment was with Andrew's sister, Sukie?

'No?' Jed taunted her obvious speechlessness. 'I'll see you later, then,' he said, closing the car door with a slam.

Georgie stood dazedly in the driveway as he started up the Jaguar's engine, lowering a window to wave a hand at her as he drove away.

Jed was having lunch with Sukie Lawson!

The predatory Sukie. The cynical Sukie. The fun-loving Sukie. The beautiful Sukie…!

Georgie gave a groan, knowing that her emotional response to the thought of Jed going out with Sukie was too raw for her to mistake it for anything other than what it was.

Jealousy.

Complete and utter jealousy!

CHAPTER EIGHT

SOMETHING else occurred to Georgie as she slowly made her way back up the stairs. Estelle's bedroom was at the back of the house…

Which meant there was no possible way that Jed's grandmother could have been a witness to that affectionate parting he had claimed was for Grandie's benefit!

Georgie just didn't understand any of it. Not Jed's reason for kissing her. Not her response to it. Certainly not the jealousy she felt at knowing Jed was having lunch with Sukie Lawson!

To feel jealousy over Jed's date with another woman surely she would also have to feel love? And she certainly no longer loved Jed!

Then why had she allowed him to kiss her earlier? Worse—she had responded to it!

Well, it certainly wasn't because she loved him, she affirmed decidedly. Any love she had once felt towards Jed had been well and truly killed two years ago.

How could it not have been, after the things she had learnt about him…?

She remembered that Jed had been away on one of his frequent lengthy business trips, to the L & J Hotel in Hawaii that time. She had gone to stay with her grandfather and Estelle for a few days, to alleviate some of the boredom of being in their apartment on her own.

She had been absolutely stunned when she'd opened

the daily newspaper over breakfast and seen a photograph of Jed in the gossip pages, standing next to the beautiful blonde actress Mia Douglas.

'What is it, Georgina?' Her grandfather had leaned concernedly across the table when he saw the distress she hadn't been quick enough to hide from his astute gaze.

Georgie silently handed him the newspaper, feeling as if she had just had all the breath knocked out of her body. Jed and the actress Mia Douglas?

It couldn't be. Jed had telephoned her only the previous afternoon. Admittedly it had only been a brief conversation, but he had made no mention then of being in Los Angeles. Georgie had assumed he was still in Hawaii.

Assumed…

Yes. But Jed hadn't actually said that was where he was, had he? In fact he had really only said it must be a brief telephone call because he didn't have a lot of time. Because he'd been in a hurry to get back to Mia Douglas…?

She didn't understand. Admittedly, Jed had been gone almost a week now, but the night before his departure he had made love to her until dawn. In truth, after months of their not having made love at all, Georgie had been surprised at his ardour, but had assumed it to be because, despite the strain which had developed in their relationship just recently, he was actually as reluctant to be apart from her as she was from him.

Assumed.

There was that word again.

Maybe it hadn't been because he would miss her at

all; maybe it had been his guilty conscience because he'd already known he was going to be unfaithful to her…?

'I shouldn't take too much notice of this.' Her grandfather threw the newspaper down in disgust. 'Pure publicity, I expect.'

Georgie's gaze was drawn back to that damning photograph as if by a magnet. Jed stood smilingly next to the stunning, beautiful actress, his arm draped lightly across her shoulders, while Mia Douglas looked up at him with a definitely avaricious light in her glowing blue eyes.

'Publicity for whom?' Georgie asked her grandfather hollowly. If it were something to do with L & J Hotels…

'Mia Douglas, presumably,' her grandfather speculated.

Nothing to do with L & J Hotels, then.

Georgie looked back at the photograph, feeling sick just at the sight of Jed with another woman. How could he? How could he do this to her after all the pain and disappointment of recent months?

The caption beneath the photograph did nothing to alleviate her anxiety! 'Mia Douglas with her escort Jed Lord at a charity dinner hosted by director Hamish McCloud'.

'Her escort'… No chance meeting, then. No mistaken identity. Jed had openly accompanied the other woman to dinner—in aid of charity or otherwise!

She threw the newspaper down and stood up abruptly. 'I think I'll go up to my room.' She turned away blindly.

'Georgina!' Her grandfather halted her flight. 'I—I think it's time you and I had a little chat about…things, don't you?'

She blinked the tears away, looking across at him, perplexed. 'What things?'

'That photograph, for one thing.' He gestured grimly towards the newspaper she had discarded. 'Your marriage to Jed, for another...'

'My marriage to Jed?' she repeated guardedly. Surely Jed hadn't discussed their problems with her own grandfather?

Her grandfather grimaced. 'I did try to warn Jed when he asked my permission to marry you and we came to our arrangement. I thought perhaps you were too young, but I had hoped the marriage would prove a success nonetheless. From the way the two of you have been behaving towards each other just lately I can only conclude that I was wrong,' he finished regretfully.

Georgie sat down suddenly; what 'arrangement'? 'Go on,' she invited breathlessly.

Her grandfather gave a disgusted snort. 'It obviously isn't working at all, is it!'

'Isn't it?' She was still guarded.

'You know it isn't.' Her grandfather sighed. 'Do you think that I haven't noticed the way the two of you no longer spend any time together? That you're only politely civil to each other? Of course I've noticed those things, Georgina. You know I'm right—otherwise you wouldn't be here and Jed—somewhere else.'

With another woman, he could have added, but didn't—although the implication was there nonetheless.

But it was his previous statement that held Georgie's attention. What arrangement had her grandfather been talking about?

'He's away on hotel business,' she said lamely.

Her grandfather didn't seem impressed. 'He doesn't work twenty-four hours a day—'

'Obviously not,' Georgie snapped back with an angrily pointed look at the open newspaper.

Her grandfather looked across at her with raised brows. 'What did you expect, Georgina? Jed is a normal red-blooded man, with all the needs that go along with that.'

She knew exactly how physically passionate her husband could be! At least...she had. 'That doesn't excuse—'

'It's a wife's place to be with her husband,' her grandfather pointed out grimly. 'Especially when that wife doesn't have the ties of her own work.'

Georgie tried to defend herself. 'Jed has never asked me to go with him.' But even as she said it she knew that wasn't completely true.

When they'd first been married Jed had often asked her to go with him when he had to go away on business, and for a while she had done exactly that. But not recently. Not for eighteen months, to be exact.

Because it was round about then that the strain had developed in their marriage. A strain they had recently learnt was insurmountable...

'Or children that would keep her tied closer to the home,' her grandfather continued, as if she hadn't spoken.

The insurmountable problem.

Because, after months of medical checks and tests, Georgie had learned that the likelihood of her ever having a child, of giving Jed a child of his own, was extremely remote.

A fact neither Georgie or Jed had yet chosen to confide in anyone else...

She bristled resentfully at her grandfather's obvious criticism. 'I do have a life of my own to live, Grandfather—'

'Lunches and coffee with old schoolfriends,' he dismissed scathingly.

Her cheeks became flushed. 'It may not be your idea of a life, Grandfather, but—'

'It most certainly isn't.' Her grandfather stood up impatiently. 'Obviously it isn't Jed's either.'

'I don't care whether Jed—' She broke off her angry reply, breathing deeply in her agitation.

'Whether Jed...?' her grandfather prompted softly.

She shot him a resentful glance. 'Grandfather, you said a few minutes ago that you had a hand in our marriage. You mentioned some sort of arrangement,' she reminded him stiffly.

'Maybe so,' he agreed. 'But I did it with the best intentions. You and Jed seemed happy enough when you were first married. But just recently... What went wrong, Georgie?'

What went wrong?

What had gone right!

She had married Jed because she loved him. But over a period of time it had occurred to her that he had never said those words back to her. As the weeks then months passed, with Georgie trying in every way she could to find out exactly what Jed felt towards her, she had come to the conclusion that it certainly wasn't love.

But they were married, and Georgie was very much

in love with Jed—so much so that she had hoped a child might bring them emotionally closer.

But even that wasn't to be. After almost a year of trying she had persuaded Jed to visit a doctor with her to find out why she wasn't conceiving.

They had received the results from those tests to find that Georgie was the one with the problem.

If anything the strain between Jed and herself had become even worse, with the result that Georgie felt completely inadequate as a woman and, as such, unwanted by Jed. So much so that she had started to avoid being with him whenever she could.

A fact her grandfather had obviously been only too well aware of!

But there was still her grandfather's puzzling comment about his own arrangement with Jed concerning their having got married at all...

It most certainly hadn't been an arrangement on her part, but was that how Jed viewed their marriage? With Georgie as George's only heir, and Jed as Estelle's, their marriage was yet another cementing together of the Lord and Jones families—keeping the L & J Group completely within that family circle. After all, Jed had never once claimed to love her.

With a sickening jolt of her stomach Georgie realised that at last she had the answer to the puzzle of Jed's feelings towards her. Now she knew that the reason Jed had never told her he loved her was because he didn't, he never had. He had only married her at all to prevent her marrying someone outside the family.

With or without her grandfather's collusion...?

One glance at the hard determination in her grandfather's face had been enough to answer that question; her grandfather was the one who had claimed earlier that her marriage to Jed was an 'arrangement', and Georgie realised now that that was exactly what it was—a business arrangement between the two men! Obviously her own feelings in the matter hadn't been important to either of them.

Except Georgie had now foiled that arrangement by being incapable of providing the Lord-Jones heir...

All this time she had believed in her grandfather's love for her, dismissing all those people who had claimed he was a hard-headed businessman who allowed nothing and no one to stand in his way once he had made up his mind to do something.

Looking at him now, at the hard determination in his face, she realised that all this time she was the one who had totally under-estimated him...!

And Jed...

She stiffened, rising slowly to her feet, her movements measured as she forced herself to remain calm, not to give in to the scream of protest raging inside her to break free at the enormity of what these two men—two men she had loved absolutely—had tried to do to her.

'You're right, Grandfather. My marriage to Jed is a disaster,' she told him evenly. 'So much so that I've decided I don't wish to go on with it any longer.'

'You don't wish—' His cheeks became mottled with suppressed anger. 'Georgina, surely this is something you need to discuss with Jed when he—'

'I said *I've* decided, Grandfather,' she cut in forcefully. 'Which means I have no intention of discussing it with Jed—when he comes home or at any other time in the future.' Her voice hardened angrily.

'You're just over-reacting to the photograph of Jed in the newspaper with another woman,' he cajoled.

But Georgie was adamant. 'My decision has nothing to do with that photograph in the newspaper. It's something I've been thinking about for some time.'

'Look, Georgina, don't do anything when you're upset like this.' Her grandfather attempted to soothe her. 'I realise it must have been a disappointment to you to discover there will never be a child, but—'

'Jed has *told* you that I can't have children?' she gasped, feeling nauseous at the thought of Jed's complete betrayal.

'Of course,' her grandfather confirmed. 'It's something that you couldn't keep a secret for ever, Georgina,' he added placatingly as he saw how pale she had become. 'And poor Jed—'

'Yes—poor Jed,' she echoed. She had thought she couldn't be hurt any more than she already was after learning of Jed's duplicity in marrying her at all, but to learn that he had discussed her inability to conceive with her grandfather—and she could only guess at the reason he had felt the need to do that!—without even discussing it with her first was the biggest betrayal of all as far as she was concerned.

'He had to talk to someone, Georgina,' her grandfather reasoned chidingly.

'Of course he did,' she dismissed scathingly. 'I'm sorry I've proved such a disappointment to you, Grandfather. But I'm sure my decision will only make things awkward for a short time. You and Jed will soon come to some other "arrangement" that will suit you both. If it helps the situation at all, I can assure you I will be making no future claim on anyone or anything to do with L & J Hotels.'

'You—'

'I mean it, Grandfather,' she assured him hardly. 'With any luck I will have moved out before Jed gets back. But, I state again, I will be making no claims on any of you.'

'But—'

'Of any kind,' she continued determinedly. 'Financial or otherwise.'

He frowned darkly at this. 'But how will you live?'

'I have my legacy from my parents, and—well, I'm sure there must be something I'm good at. After all, I'm obviously no good at being a wife or mother,' she added emotionally.

The pain of knowing how much these two men had betrayed her, and her love for them both, she would deal with later. Much later. Once she was well away from here. And them.

'Georgina—'

'Please don't, Grandfather.' She cut him short as he would have reached out to her. 'I think it's best if I go now, don't you?' she reasoned. 'Please tell Jed when he returns that my lawyer will contact him concerning our divorce.'

'Divorce?' Her grandfather looked startled. 'Georgina, you're not giving this enough thought—'

'I've thought of nothing but the disaster my marriage is almost since its conception,' she assured him honestly.

She had known from the beginning that there was

something seriously wrong with her relationship with Jed, that all the love seemed to be on her side. As far as she was concerned, knowing the reason she had felt that way completely exonerated her from any responsibility to either of these men—emotionally or in any other way.

'I will tell Jed of my decision on his return,' she told her grandfather flatly.

'As long as you realise he isn't going to take that decision lightly,' her grandfather warned her.

'Oh, I think he'll be more than happy to agree to the divorce once he realises the freedom it will give him.' The freedom to choose a woman who could give him the children needed to continue the Lord line! 'In the meantime, I'm going upstairs to pack my things before returning to our apartment.' Where she intended packing all her other things and having them put into storage while she searched for somewhere of her own to live.

By the time Jed returned home he would probably be gratified to realise it was almost as if she had never been in his life at all...

Georgie blinked back the tears as she remembered all too clearly the pain and disillusion she had known two years ago as she returned to their apartment and packed away her marriage to Jed into several large cartons.

That day hadn't been the end of it, of course. There had been several heated scenes with Jed once he returned and finally managed to track her down to the hotel where she was staying temporarily while she looked for an apartment of her own. Not one of the L & J group, of course!

But despite Jed's anger Georgie had remained adamant about never returning to him or the marriage that she now considered a complete sham. Finally Jed had agreed to accept their separation, and the signing of their divorce papers six months ago had been a mere technicality. On Jed's part there had never been any real marriage to divorce from, and Georgie had long since made a new life for herself—one that didn't include Jed or her grandfather.

But none of those painful memories brought her any closer to understanding her feelings of jealousy today concerning Jed's date with Sukie Lawson. Or explain why Jed had just kissed her in the way that he had...

She was still in this state of confusion later that evening when she picked up the telephone and found it was Jed at the other end of the line!

'What do you want?' she questioned suspiciously as she instantly recognised his voice. 'And how did you get this telephone number?' she added accusingly.

'Obviously I want to talk to you,' Jed returned lazily. 'And I've had this telephone number for some weeks, Georgie.'

'Some weeks...!' she echoed, wondering exactly how he had obtained her ex-directory number. But of course he was Jed Lord, with the contacts to find out anything he might want to know. 'But—then why didn't you just telephone me to let me know about Estelle's illness?' Instead of going through that elaborate charade at the Lawsons' on Friday evening...?

But she already knew the answer to that question. Jed had gone through that elaborate charade for no other reason than that he wanted to—because Jed never did anything he didn't want to! The real question was, why had he wanted to meet her at the Lawsons at all…?

'Too easy,' he explained derisively. 'I'm on my way over to your apartment right now, Georgie,' he continued briskly. 'Make sure your watchdog of a doorman knows to let me in, hmm?'

'I— But—' She was babbling! 'I don't want you here, Jed,' she told him forcefully, her hand tightly gripping the telephone receiver in her agitation.

She couldn't bear to have him here in her apartment, to have the memory of him in any part of her new life; it was bad enough that she would wonder in the future, every time she went to the Lawsons', whether or not she might bump into Jed there, without having the memory of his overwhelming presence in her apartment too!

'Too bad,' he replied. 'Because I need to speak to you. And I need to do it now,' he stated harshly as she would have protested once again. 'Unless, of course, Lawson is already there…?' he added softly.

'As it happens, Andrew isn't here this evening,' Georgie informed him. She had arranged to meet Andrew tomorrow evening, unsure how she was going to feel after visiting her grandfather's home today. As it happened, bearing in mind her earlier confusion, it had been a good decision. 'But he does have a perfect right to be here if he chooses to be,' she defended.

'Unlike me, hmm?' Jed murmured appreciatively.

'Yes!' she confirmed swiftly.

'Nevertheless, I will be there in five minutes, Georgie,' Jed told her. 'I don't expect there to be any problem about my being allowed in,' he said pointedly, before ending the call.

Or else, his tone clearly implied, Georgie realised frustratedly as she slowly replaced her own handset.

Never mind that she didn't want him here. Never mind that he was intruding on her privacy. Never mind that he was totally aware of all that—Jed was on his way to her apartment and that was the end of the subject.

That was what he thought!

CHAPTER NINE

'NICE,' Jed murmured appreciatively as he stepped out of the lift straight into the outer hallway of Georgie's apartment.

Georgie knew he had to be talking about the elegance of her apartment and not her; she was looking most unelegant herself, in the faded denims and over-large rugby shirt that she wore at weekends when doing her housework! Her face was bare of make-up too, and she had just briefly run her fingers through her hair.

In truth, she had deliberately not made any effort concerning her own appearance—had no intention of letting Jed think for one moment that his visit here this evening was anything more than an inconvenience.

Jed, however, was still wearing the casual clothes he'd had on when he went out earlier to meet Sukie Lawson for lunch, posing the question: had he been home at all since lunchtime?

Probably not, Georgie decided as she looked at him coldly. 'What do you want, Jed?'

He calmly returned her hostile gaze. 'You asked me that earlier, and I seem to remember I told you I want to talk to you,' he replied tersely.

'So—talk,' she invited rudely.

Jed frowned darkly, grey eyes opaquely silver. Evidence that, no matter how coldly aloof he might seem on the outside, inside he was actually extremely angry.

Well, that was just too bad—because Georgie was angry too. And as far as she was concerned with more reason!

Jed drew in a deeply controlling breath. 'Invite me in, Georgie, and I just might do that,' he drawled.

'I—'

'You're looking good, by the way,' he observed lightly.

Georgie gave him a withering glance. 'You're talking rubbish, Jed—and we both know it!'

'No, we don't,' he rebuked mildly. 'You look—relaxed, comfortable, completely natural. Beautiful, in fact. In the past you always tried too hard,' he told her as she would have spoken.

'I'm so sorry!' she answered with complete insincerity. 'I'll have to remember in the future that the scruffy look is what appeals to you—and make sure I'm always extremely smart in your presence!' She glared at him.

Jed grinned, obviously not at all put out by her annoyance. 'Please yourself,' he said. 'I like your hair in that style too, by the way,' he added huskily.

At last he had mentioned her change of hairstyle—but not at all in the way Georgie had expected. 'You never used to be this complimentary, Jed,' she derided.

He grimaced. 'I never used to be a lot of things,' he responded. 'Are you going to ask me in or not?' he persisted.

'Not,' Georgie came back instantly, crossing her arms in front of her to look at him challengingly.

'That isn't very friendly of you, Georgie—'

'We aren't friends!' she snapped.

'I've only come here to do you a favour,' he continued firmly.

'A favour?' Georgie echoed. 'For me? Somehow I don't see that happening!'

His mouth thinned, his eyes narrowing. 'If you don't invite me in you'll never know, will you.'

Georgie glared at him frustratedly, half of her wanting to tell him to go to hell, the other half curious as to what he could possibly have to say to her that would be doing her a favour. And along with that latter curiosity she had the fact that she really didn't want to invite him further inside her apartment...

She gave a rueful smile. 'I think I can live without knowing, so if you wouldn't mind—?'

'Sukie Lawson knows I was in your bedroom on Friday evening,' Jed cut across her.

'You told her about it?' Georgie gasped accusingly; she hadn't believed that even Jed would—

'No, I didn't tell her about it,' he barked impatiently. 'Damn it, Georgie, when are you going to stop believing my greatest pleasure in life is to cause you as much discomfort as possible?'

'Maybe when you stop enjoying watching me squirm!'

Jed sighed, shaking his head. 'I have never enjoyed watching you squirm,' he rejoined tersely. 'Now, stop being so damned inhospitable and let's go and talk about this situation with Sukie Lawson,' he instructed irritably.

'You're the one who has a "situation" with Sukie,' Georgie told him.

'Will you stop letting your prejudice show where I'm concerned and actually try listening to what I'm saying to you?' Jed rasped impatiently. 'Personally, it's of no interest to me if Andrew Lawson finds out I was in your bedroom on Friday evening—but I had a feeling that it might be of interest you!'

And he was right. Of course he was right. She was just having difficulty coping with the fact that Jed was here at all. But of course she had to hear what Sukie had said to him about Friday evening—if only so that she had an answer ready for Andrew if, or when, he should ask her about it! Brother and sister weren't close and never had been, but Sukie was still an unknown quantity to Georgie—as was what she might actually do with the information concerning Jed's visit to her bedroom...

'Okay, you had better come in,' she invited ungraciously, pushing open the door behind her that led straight into the sitting room of her apartment, preceding him into the room but turning so that she could gauge his reaction to her rather Bohemian style of decor.

There were no carpets on the highly polished wood floors, just scatter rugs. Several heavy chairs and sofas were placed about the room, with colourful throws over them, and an abundance of plants and flowers cascaded down walls and furniture. One wall of the room was completely shelved, with books overflowing from those shelves onto the floor. The whole effect was one of comfort rather than style—a haven of rusticity that Georgie was sometimes very loath to leave.

'This is great, Georgie!' Jed looked about him admiringly, his response too natural to be anything other than genuine.

She gave a perplexed frown, remembering all too clearly the symmetry and minimalist style of the apartment she and Jed had shared when they were married. Jed had brought in an interior designer to transform the rooms into places of cool elegance. As a place to entertain it had been perfect; as a place where Georgie could actually live in relaxed comfort it had failed utterly, its expensive elegance only adding to her misery.

'Glad you like it,' she returned with dry scepticism.

Jed turned back to her, head tilted to one side as he looked at her dispassionately. 'You don't believe me, do you?' he guessed ruefully. 'If I were to tell you that I wish we had made a success of our marriage, would you believe that either?' He studied her from between narrowed lids.

'No,' Georgie answered unhesitantly, her expression hurt.

'Hmm.' He grimaced thoughtfully. 'Well, what if I were to tell you that—?'

'Jed, could you just get to the point?' she snapped, her nerves already stretched to breaking point. It was bad enough having him here at all, without his prolonging the occasion with these ridiculous comments.

'The point...?' He frowned. 'Oh, yes,' he realised. 'Aren't you going to offer me a sociable drink?'

She shook her head. 'This isn't a social call.'

'But—'

'Ex-husbands do not pay social calls on their ex-wives!' Georgie retorted.

'Who says they don't?' he mused.

'Jed!' she cried.

Lunch was pretty unappetising, and I've had nothing to eat or drink since that time, so I think it would be only good manners if you were to—'

'Okay!' Georgie held up defensive hands. 'One cup of coffee. And then you leave,' she advised warningly. Anything to get him to say what he had to say and then just go!

'I would prefer a whisky, if you have some,' he requested lightly as he sat down in one of the hugely comfortable armchairs. 'I don't have anywhere else to drive this evening, so—'

'You have to drive home!' Georgie reminded him forcefully, but moved to pour the whisky into a glass anyway; now that he had made himself comfortable she doubted that Jed would move until he got what he wanted. And he knew very well that she had some whisky in the apartment; the nearly full bottle was on clear view on the dresser.

'Only around the corner,' Jed replied. 'I can easily stay at my own apartment tonight. I moved out of our place a year ago,' he explained at her questioning look. 'When it became obvious you weren't coming back. It's amazing, really; we've been living almost next door to each other for the last year.'

What was she supposed to say to that? Oh, goody? Wonderful? What a marvellous coincidence?

Well, if that was what Jed expected he was going to be disappointed, because she wasn't going to say any of those things. She was more interested in the remark he had made just before that; what did he mean, when it had become obvious she wasn't coming back? After the way they had parted he couldn't possibly have believed she would ever go back to him or their marriage— could he?

'Here you are.' She handed him the glass with its half

an inch of whisky in the bottom. A fact that Jed noted with a mocking rise of dark brows. 'You still need to be sober to walk home,' she told him firmly, sitting down in the armchair that faced his.

'You're a hard woman, Georgie,' he joked, before sipping the fiery liquid. 'I almost took up drinking this as a hobby after you left me,' he continued conversationally.

Georgie felt very uncomfortable with these references to their past relationship. 'Before you realised you still had all the things you had before you married me—your work, the grandparents, your freedom,' she pointed out.

Jed looked across at her consideringly. 'But not you,' he murmured softly. 'Aren't you joining me?' He indicated the glass in his hand.

She shook her head. 'I've never liked whisky.' Although she *was* tempted to go and pour herself a glass of wine from the bottle she had open in the cooler, Jed didn't look as if he were in any sort of hurry to leave, and she was finding this conversation more and more disturbing; she and Jed had never talked together like this in the past.

'Sukie?' she reminded him.

'Hmm,' he said. 'Apparently she was on her way to her bedroom on Friday evening—'

'You're sure she was on her way to her own bedroom?' Georgie couldn't stop herself from taunting.

Jed shot her an impatient glance. 'Georgie, I have never slept with Sukie Lawson. Have no intention of ever sleeping with Sukie Lawson. Do not feel the least attraction towards Sukie Lawson. Clear enough for you?' he grated harshly.

'Very,' she replied. 'But you went out with her for lunch today—'

'At her invitation, not mine,' Jed quickly explained. 'We met at breakfast yesterday morning—something you and Andrew Lawson noticeably missed, by the way.'

Georgie tried not to rise to his bait. 'Don't you remember, Jed? I rarely eat breakfast,' she said calmly.

'And Andrew Lawson?'

'I have no idea,' she dismissed, meeting his gaze unflinchingly. 'So, you and Sukie met at breakfast yesterday morning…?' she reminded him.

He nodded tersely. 'She invited me out for lunch today.'

'But you didn't have to accept,' Georgie observed.

Jed looked serious. 'She implied she had something important she wanted to discuss with me. Besides, it would have been extremely rude to have refused, in the circumstances.'

Georgie shot him a sceptical glance. 'So, Sukie was on her way to her bedroom on Friday evening…?' she prompted—yet again. Really, Jed used to be more concise than this!

He took a leisurely sip of his whisky. 'She heard voices in the guest bedroom—your guest bedroom—'

'Wouldn't it have been natural to assume—in the circumstances—that my nocturnal visitor was Andrew, and just move on?' Georgie derided.

Jed shot her a look of dark irritation. 'Maybe,' he replied. 'But she obviously didn't think so. She saw me leaving your bedroom a few minutes later.'

'On her way to…?'

'Nowhere.' Jed's mouth twisted. 'She was honest enough to admit she hung around in the hallway waiting to see exactly who was visiting you at that time of night. A little shocked at the thought of her younger brother misbehaving right there in their parents' home, probably.'

Georgie winced with distaste at the mere thought of Sukie watching outside her bedroom in that way. 'She must have found it well worth the wait then, when it turned out to be you who left and not Andrew! What explanation did you give her today for having been in my bedroom Friday evening?'

'Ah,' he said.

'Ah, what?' Georgie exclaimed. 'Jed, you did give her an explanation?' she demanded incredulously.

'Of a sort. You have to realise, Georgie, I was thrown slightly off-balance by the question. I had no time to come up with any other answer than—'

'The truth?' Georgie said, jumping impatiently to her feet to glare down at him. 'You told Sukie Lawson that the two of us were once married to each other?' She glared at him accusingly. 'Jed, how could you—?'

'Of course I didn't tell the woman that,' he responded, sitting forward on the edge of his chair to place his empty whisky glass down on the coffee table. 'Give me credit for having a little sensitivity, okay!'

She gave a pained wince. 'But if you didn't tell Sukie the truth, what did you tell her?' Georgie had a distinct feeling she wasn't going to like the answer to this particular question.

Jed looked up, grinning, grey eyes alight with devilish

humour. 'That I was attracted to you. That I went to your bedroom to try to proposition you!'

'You—' Georgie broke off, absolutely astounded by this explanation. 'You told Sukie *what*?' she finally managed to burst out.

'That I went to your bedroom to try to proposition you,' Jed repeated vaguely, his gaze caught and held by something behind her. He stood up to walk past her in the direction of the bookcases against the far wall. 'I've been trying to get this book for weeks now.' He took a hardback book off one of the shelves, opening it up to read the fly-leaf. 'Have you read it yet?' he asked distractedly.

'As a matter of fact, yes,' she answered, a little surprised that Jed, of all people, should have been trying to get a copy of that particular book. 'Jed, you told Andrew's sister that—'

'Yes,' he confirmed impatiently. 'Is it any good?' He held up the book.

'Excellent,' she responded. 'Jed, you told Andrew's sister—'

'You already said that.' He sighed. 'And I've already said that, yes, I did. Is it as good as the rest in the series?' He held the book up.

'Yes, it is.' Georgie was becoming more and more incredulous by the minute.

The book Jed was holding was the fifth in a very popular children's series. Over a period of years it had become popular with adults too, each successive book taking the country by storm and heading the bestseller list; Georgie just hadn't expected Jed to be one of those adults who read them...

'Can I borrow it?' he enquired expectantly.

'No! Yes! I don't know,' she rejoined in complete confusion. 'What did Sukie say after you told her that?'

'Well, as I had rebuffed all *her* advances—Friday evening as well as today—she was probably relieved to know it wasn't her brother I was attracted to! Okay, okay.' Jed held up pacifying hands as Georgie's anger visibly grew. 'So, I told Sukie that—would you rather I *had* told her the truth?'

'No,' she said. But neither was she happy about her future sister-in-law thinking she had let a man other than Andrew into her bedroom on Friday evening.

After all, it was hardly the time of night for anyone to be paying a purely social call! And Jed had already told Sukie that he was attracted to her, which pretty well took care of Georgie trying to use that excuse herself when she next spoke to the other woman...

'Besides,' Jed went on, putting down the book he was holding to look at her with eyes that were suddenly opaquely grey, 'it was the truth.'

'What was?' Georgie said, not sure quite what he meant.

She was lost in thought about what she could say to Andrew if his sister chose to tell him about Jed's nocturnal visit to her bedroom; she certainly wasn't about to confirm to Andrew that it had been because Jed was attracted to her—

Georgie looked up suddenly, eyeing Jed suspiciously as his words—if not their meaning!—finally registered. 'What did you just say?' she said slowly.

'I wish you would pay attention, Georgie,' Jed drawled. 'I said it was the truth,' he told her evenly.

Georgie frowned uncomprehendingly. 'And I said, What was?' she reminded him.

'So you did,' Jed agreed, taking a step towards her. 'It's true that I find you attractive, Georgie,' he said quietly. 'In fact, I find you very attractive.'

She stared at him, sure that he couldn't have said what he just had, and that if he had he couldn't really have meant it.

Could he…?

CHAPTER TEN

GEORGIE stared up at him. 'Jed, you and I were married...'

'Yes,' he confirmed.

'To each other!' she added.

'Yes,' he acknowledged with a rueful quirk of his mouth.

Georgie's confusion deepened. 'But now we're divorced,' she reminded him.

Jed sobered. 'Unfortunately, the answer to that statement is also—yes.'

Georgie eyed him frustratedly. 'Divorce implies a little incompatibility—if not a lot!—of incompatibility!'

'You were the one who divorced me,' Jed reminded her softly.

'Exactly! Which implies, if nothing else, that—'

'It implies that you wanted to divorce me, Georgie,' Jed cut in evenly. 'It does not imply that I felt the same way about you.'

'But— But—' She broke off, realising she was starting to sound like an old engine that wouldn't start! 'You agreed to the divorce,' she recalled.

'At the time your grandfather advised that it would probably be the wisest course—'

'My grandfather?' Georgie repeated in astonishment. 'But he told me he doesn't believe in divorce!'

'Exactly,' Jed said with satisfaction.

131

'I don't understand any of this,' she said, running a trembling hand over her brow, feeling completely puzzled and befuddled—but then, when had she ever been anything else where Jed's emotions were concerned?

'You wanted a divorce, Georgie, so I agreed to let you have one,' Jed told her. 'That doesn't necessarily mean I wanted to divorce you, though, does it?'

No, it didn't. But she had thought— 'Jed, we had been living apart for eighteen months by the time I applied for our divorce.'

'Yes,' he acknowledged.

'You agreed,' she pressed.

'I've just told you why I did that,' Jed reasoned.

Georgie gave a frustrated shake of her head. 'Are you now telling me that you didn't want a divorce from me?'

'Not only am I telling you that,' he replied, 'but I'm also of the same opinion as your grandfather when it comes to divorce—I don't recognize it, Georgie!'

'But—' No, she would not sound like that stalling engine again! 'No matter whether you recognise it or not, Jed, we *are* divorced,' she assured him firmly. 'A judge said so. The law says so. *I* say so,' she added determinedly.

Jed gave a considering inclination of his head. 'I doubt you would have become engaged to another man if you didn't truly believe you were free to do so,' he responded calmly.

'Well, then—'

'Well, then nothing!' Jed suddenly came back, taking another step towards her. 'Georgie—'

'I thought Grandie seemed a little—better when I visited her today.' She desperately latched onto another subject—in an effort to give herself time to catch up with this one!

She and Jed had rowed very badly when she'd told him she wouldn't be coming back to their apartment to live with him. They had barely spoken for almost a year after that, and following that time all communication had been through their respective lawyers. Jed had signed the divorce papers, for goodness' sake—he couldn't just suddenly decide to change his mind about that now!

Although, if he were to be believed, he wasn't claiming to have changed his mind about anything—was very firmly stating that he hadn't wanted the divorce in the first place. Not only that, he was claiming he didn't recognise it!

Well, *she* recognised it—and that was all that mattered!

'Grandie?' Jed echoed now, his gaze narrowing.

'Yes,' Georgie confirmed hurriedly. 'She's still physically very frail, obviously. But I'm sure I detected a spark of her old indomitable self today as we talked together. She's not at all happy with you, by the way, for just disappearing in the way that you did,' she told him, sure Estelle would be having words with her grandson later today.

'Georgie, ordinarily I would be quite happy to discuss my grandmother's progress with you, just not now, hmm?' he prompted chidingly. 'Why did you become engaged to Lawson, Georgie?'

'Why?' she said dazedly, once again completely unprepared for this frontal attack on her personal life; so much for trying to divert Jed's attention onto something else! 'Because I love him, of course. Because I intend marrying him!'

Jed stood inches away from her now, giving her a considering look. 'Are you absolutely sure about that?' he finally pressed.

Georgie swallowed hard, knowing that she would be lying—to herself!—if she didn't inwardly acknowledge that she was deeply disturbed by Jed's close proximity.

He was so close now she could see the black flecks in the grey of his eyes, could see every pore of his skin, could smell the aftershave that she knew she would always associate with him, could feel the heat given off by his body. A body she was intimately familiar with...

Should she be this aware of Jed when she was engaged to marry another man...?

More to the point, should she be engaged to Andrew, even thinking of marrying him, when she was this aware of Jed, the man who had once been her husband?

She had a feeling that the answer to that was no...

She straightened defensively, at the same time meeting Jed's searching gaze unflinchingly. 'Yes, I'm sure about that,' she told him firmly. 'Now, if you wouldn't mind, it's very late—'

'What reason do you intend giving Lawson for my having been in your bedroom on Friday evening?' Jed put in softly.

Reminding her all too forcefully that she would probably have to give that in the very near future! Not only would she have to explain Jed's presence in her bedroom, she would also have to explain that he had once been her husband. Once she had admitted to the latter,

was Andrew going to believe any explanation she made
about the former…?

'His name is Andrew,' she returned smartly, angry
with Jed all over again for having put her in this defensive position. 'And what I choose to tell Andrew—about
anything—is my own business.'

'Your book is selling very well, I believe.' Jed
changed the subject.

'My book…?' Georgie scrabbled mentally to catch up.

'Yes,' Jed said. 'I hear sales are going very well, and
that when your second book is published early next year
there's even talk of a—'

'You hear, Jed?' Georgie exploded indignantly. How
on earth did he know these things?

'—of a book-signing tour,' Jed completed calmly.

Her cheeks became flushed. 'You hear correctly,' she
bit out resentfully. Never mind how he had found out
these things about her book. He was Jed Lord; he could
find out anything if he chose to do so!

Jed seemed unconcerned. 'No doubt there will be re-
porters present at some of those book-signings?
Nowadays the public seems to have an interest in not
only reading the books, but learning more about the personal life of—'

'Your point, Jed?' she cut in impatiently—although
she had a feeling she already knew what that point was
going to be.

Oh, why hadn't she just told Andrew the truth from
the beginning—admitted to having been married and divorced? It would have saved all the trouble she was having on the subject now. Although she wasn't sure having

to admit Jed Lord had been her husband wasn't damning enough on its own!

'I'm sure you already know what that is, Georgie,' Jed suggested gently. 'What you choose to tell Lawson about me and our marriage is probably going to be totally irrelevant after your book-signing tour next year. The press is going to be all over you once they realise exactly who author Georgie Jones is!'

'The ex-wife of Jed Lord?' she snorted.

He shook his head. 'The granddaughter of George Jones—founder and co-owner of the L & J Group.'

Her cheeks flushed even more. 'But also the ex-wife of Jed Lord, his obvious successor,' she persisted.

He gave a rueful grimace. 'Yes.'

She had always known that there was a possibility her connection to both George and Jed could come out, if her books became successful, but she had hoped by that time she and Andrew would already be married—that she would be able to explain the past calmly and dismissively.

As it deserved to be explained!

She had been eighteen years old, for goodness' sake—had loved Jed all her life, it seemed; of course she had married him when he asked her. It had taken maturity to help her realise the reason he had felt compelled to ask her in the first place.

'I'll just explain that we all make mistakes,' she stated.

Jed's expression darkened. His eyes narrowed to steely slits. 'Our marriage was not a mistake, Georgie—'

'Of course it was,' she responded.

'No,' Jed countered, 'it wasn't.'

Georgie wasn't about to give in. 'We'll just have to agree to differ about that—because I have no intention of getting into an argument about it, now or at any other time. I thank you for coming here and warning me that Sukie may decide to cause trouble because of what happened on Friday evening—'

'That isn't why I'm here,' Jed interrupted her.

She gave him a startled look, moving slightly away as she saw the intensity of his gaze fixed on her parted lips. 'I— You—' She couldn't help it—her tongue moved instinctively to moisten those lips, and Jed's gaze darkened even more as he watched the movement. 'Jed—'

'Georgie…!' he groaned, even as his hands reached out to lightly grasp the tops of Georgie's arms, his head slowly lowering towards hers.

Attack, Georgie, she instructed herself. Attack—before you lost the will to do anything more than go weak at the knees!

'Strange isn't it, Jed?' she began with deliberate self-derision. 'How I ended up writing children's books and I can't have children of my own. How lucky for you, Jed, that will never change!'

Jed froze, his expression unreadable now. 'Lucky?' he echoed slowly.

Georgie nodded. 'That I'll never have a child who could challenge your sole right to the L & J Group!'

His face twisted thunderously. 'That's a hell of an accusation to make!'

'But so true,' she taunted. 'Don't you realise, Jed? You don't need me any more to achieve your goal in life—'

'You're wrong,' he denied, his hands tightening on
her arms. 'You're exactly what I need to achieve my
lifetime ambition. In fact,' he added, 'I can't do it without you!'

Georgie had no time to question this statement, no
time to puzzle over his strange reply to her accusation—
because at that moment Jed's head lowered completely
to a level with hers, his lips claiming hers with a familiarity that took her breath away.

Yet, as Jed's mouth began to explore hers, Georgie
realised it wasn't completely as it used to be; she was
older, her self-esteem boosted by a successful career, by
Andrew's complete admiration for her achievements.
And she now met Jed's unmistakable passion as an
equal, as someone who knew her own worth—and cherished that knowledge.

The combination was completely explosive!

Her arms became entwined about Jed's neck and she
pressed closer, her body curving into the hardness of his
as desire burst into consuming flame. She literally felt
as if she were on fire!

All the time that meeting of lips continued. Deepened.
Searched. Found. Asked. Received their reply.

Only the two of them existed, their heat, their desire,
their need for each other. Georgie offered no resistance
as Jed swung her up in his arms and carried her towards
the open door of her bedroom, their fevered kisses continuing.

It was as if they couldn't get enough of each other.
As if they had been through a drought and now wanted
to drown. In each other.

It was only semi-dark as Jed placed her gently down

on top of the bed. Georgie looked up at him with complete knowledge of what she was doing. Of what she was about to do.

Jed knelt on the side of the bed, his hands reaching out to frame Georgie's face. 'You are so beautiful,' he groaned. 'So absolutely beautiful that I—'

'Please don't talk, Jed,' she begged as she reached up to pull him down to her.

She didn't want him to say anything that would spoil the perfection of this moment. Of these moments. She wanted only to belong completely to him. And for him to belong completely to her.

His lips once more claimed hers, and their clothes disappeared almost as if they had simply evaporated, until nothing divided the warmth of their naked bodies. Bodies that fitted so perfectly together they were like two halves of a whole as Jed lay down beside her.

The silver intensity of his gaze held hers as one of his hands caressed the length of her body, cupping a breast before his head lowered and moistly warm lips and tongue sipped and caressed the sensitive flesh there.

Georgie arched ecstatically against him, her fingers buried in the dark thickness of his hair as she silently pleaded for him not to stop.

She never wanted this to stop, wanted to remain like this for ever, part of Jed as he was a part of her.

He felt so good to touch, his body warm and muscled where her hands ran caressingly up and down the length of his spine, moving in butterfly movements to the hardness of his desire, touching, teasing, wanting!

'Georgie…!' Jed's head reared and he gasped weakly. 'Now, Jed,' she encouraged him, taking one of his hands and moving it so that he should know of her readiness for him. 'Please, now!' she begged.

He was like a perfect sculpture as he rose up above her, gently nudging her legs apart to slowly, oh, so very slowly, meld his body with hers.

Even that was too much for Georgie. Her body was on fire as spasms of pleasure coursed through her, enveloping them both as she clung to Jed's shoulders in heady release.

'Steady,' Jed gasped throatily as he once again looked down at her face in the half-light. 'Not yet, Georgie,' he breathed intensely. 'Not yet!'

She lost track of time, of space, of everything that wasn't Jed, completely consumed by him, by the passion between them. Only Jed existed in her universe.

Jed took her to the end of that universe time and time again, only allowing his own pleasure when he couldn't hold back any longer, the two of them reaching higher than Georgie had ever believed it possible to go.

'Wow...!' Jed murmured dazedly as he sank down beside her, his arm about her shoulders as he cradled her against him, her head resting on the dampness of his chest.

Wow, indeed.

Georgie had never known anything like this. She felt completely satiated, her whole body tingling with awareness, every nerve-ending, every pore in her skin, attuned totally to Jed.

Jed gave a husky laugh. 'I can't believe I just said anything so ridiculous,' he said self-derisively.

Neither could Georgie, but she knew it was really just

another part of the madness that had overtaken them. Both of them.

The problem was, what did they do now?

Being with Jed like this had been wonderful, magical. But at the same time completely removed from reality. From their reality. Because nothing had really changed. Jed was still—Jed. Heir to L & J Group and her ex-husband. And she was still Georgie. Completely separate from everything connected to the L & J Group and the ex-wife of Jed Lord, who could never provide an heir to the empire he headed. The fact that their incompatibility didn't go as far as the bedroom changed none of that.

'You've gone very quiet.' Jed looked down at her through the darkness of her bedroom.

Her cheeks burned with embarrassment as she remembered the way she had cried out her pleasure, again and again, during their lovemaking.

Jed turned on his side so that he could see her properly, his arm still about her bare shoulders. 'Georgie…?' he prompted uncertainly.

What Georgie most wanted to do was pull the covers up over both of them. Their nakedness was just a reminder of their uninhibited lovemaking. Although the tingling of her body told her she wasn't going to be able to forget this time in Jed's arms even if she tried!

She swallowed hard, gazing somewhere over Jed's shoulder in an effort not to look at him directly. One glance had told her that he looked almost boyish, with his dark hair falling over his forehead, his face relaxed into lines of physical satisfaction. 'I don't know what to say,' she admitted.

Jed smoothed the hair back from her brow. 'Are you

worried about how you're going to explain this to
Lawson?' he sympathised.

She hadn't given Andrew a thought the last hour or
so—how could she have done when the only person she
was aware of was Jed, his touching her, her touching
him?

She stiffened. 'I don't think now is the time to discuss
Andrew, do you?' she said; the two of them lying naked
together on the bed in the languidness after their lovemaking really wasn't the time to talk about another man.

'Possibly not,' Jed conceded gently. 'But he does have
to be told, and I wondered if you would like me to—'

'Has to be told what?' Georgie cut in, frowning up at
him now.

'About us, of course,' Jed answered quizzically.

Georgie's frown deepened. Of course she had to break
her engagement to Andrew—couldn't in all conscience
even consider marrying him after what had happened
here this evening. But surely that was completely up to
her, had nothing to do with any 'us'…?

She felt more in need than ever of the bedcovers that
unfortunately lay beneath them. 'Jed, I really don't think
now is the time to talk about this.'

'But I want to tell your grandfather and Grandie about
us as soon as possible—'

'You want to *what*?' Georgie sat up abruptly, pushing
away from Jed to swing her legs over the side of the bed
and sit up, her back towards him now.

'They're going to be so pleased, Georgie—'

'Jed!' she cried. 'I don't know what you think happened here this evening, but I can assure you it isn't

something you should tell our grandparents about; I'm sure they would be very shocked.'

She was shocked. And dismayed. Had no idea how she and Jed were going to even pretend at a relationship between them in front of Estelle in the future.

'Are you joking?' he exclaimed. 'They will be over the moon when we tell them we're back together!'

Georgie stood up abruptly, no longer concerned with her nakedness—although she picked up her robe from the chair and pulled it on anyway, tightly tying the belt about the slenderness of her waist before turning back to face Jed.

He sat up in the bed too now. 'We *are* back together, Georgie.' Jed's words were a statement, not a question.

'No,' she denied. 'No, we're not, Jed,' she added more firmly. 'What happened—just now—' She gave a dismissive wave of her hand in the direction of the rumpled bed. 'It didn't mean anything, Jed—' She broke off as he surged to his feet, his expression so fierce she instinctively took a step backwards.

His mouth twisted angrily. 'Don't worry, Georgie, I'm not going to touch you,' he said. 'I'm too angry to risk it,' he admitted harshly. 'What do you mean, our lovemaking didn't mean anything?' he rasped, grey eyes glittering silver.

She hesitated. 'I believe it often happens—like that—when two people were once married to each other. It's—it's called post-marital—'

'I don't want to hear what some so-called expert calls it!' Jed burst in coldly. 'I said it was lovemaking because that's what it was.'

Georgie gave a deep sigh. 'Perhaps,' she conceded. 'But—'

'No perhaps. No buts.' Jed gave an abrupt shake of his head. 'We made love with each other, Georgie! Doesn't that mean anything to you?'

She thrust her hands into the pockets of her robe, her shoulders hunched. 'I've already explained that I think it was regrettable, that it only serves to make this situation more difficult. But maybe in the circumstances it was inevitable,' she allowed. 'I believe it's called unfinished marital business—a need to—'

'Georgie, will you kindly stop quoting rubbish from some tacky magazine article you've obviously read on the subject?' Jed cut in scathingly, sitting down on the bed to begin pulling on his clothes.

Clothes that, like hers, were scattered haphazardly over the bedroom carpet!

Georgie bent down and picked up his shirt from where it lay at her feet, holding it out to him gingerly, careful not to get too close; she might be trying to sound calm and sensible about this whole sorry mess, but that didn't mean she was immune to the attraction of his nakedness—that she didn't feel the same yearning of an hour ago to lose herself in their desire for each other.

'Thanks,' he said shortly as he took the shirt. 'So, what you're saying, Georgie, is that our time together just now was just some—need on your part, to see if I was still attracted to you enough to go to bed with you?'

'I said no such thing!' she burst out resentfully. 'Why *did* you make love with me, Jed?' she challenged angrily.

'At this moment in time, in all honesty, I have absolutely no idea!' He stood up, fully dressed now. 'I think I should leave now, don't you? Before either of us says something the other will find completely unforgivable?' he offered heavily.

'Yes,' Georgie agreed, looking at him regretfully, desperately hoping her inner misery wasn't apparent on her face.

She didn't want him to go, didn't want them to part like this. But she knew there was nothing else they could do. There was no going back to their relationship before this evening, but there was no future for them either…

'Fine,' Jed said tersely, striding over to the doorway, pausing before leaving the bedroom. 'I—I hope this won't prevent you from visiting Grandie? She seems so much better.'

'No, of course not,' Georgie assured him distantly, once again unable to look at him, her shoulders even more hunched as she fought the need to stop him from leaving.

'I'll go, then,' he stated.

She swallowed hard. 'Yes.'

She didn't see him leave, but she was nevertheless aware that he was no longer in the bedroom with her. That awareness was confirmed a few seconds later with the arrival and then departure of the lift. Jed was on his way down to ground level.

All Georgie's strength deserted her and she sank down onto the carpeted floor, tears falling hotly down her cheeks as she felt her heart breaking for the second time.

Because no matter what she might have said to Jed, no matter how she had excused what had happened between them, she knew in her heart that she had made love with Jed for one reason and one reason only.

She was still in love with the man who had once been her husband!

And he was no more in love with her than he had been two years ago…!

CHAPTER ELEVEN

'How are things between you and Jed?'

Georgie looked up from the newspaper she had been reading so that she could read articles aloud for Estelle's benefit, to find her step-grandmother looking back at her concernedly.

'How are things between Jed and me?' she repeated, playing for time. What on earth could she truthfully reply to that?

Since that Sunday evening four weeks ago, when the two of them had made the mistake of going to bed together, Georgie couldn't honestly say she had seen much of Jed. But perhaps that was telling enough in itself to know how things were between them!

'Fine,' she answered firmly. 'Jed's very busy, of course. But then, so am I. Did I tell you my editor has just approved my second book—?'

'Georgie, I know I've been ill.' Estelle smiled gently. 'But I'm not senile!'

Georgie's eyes widened. 'Well, of course you aren't. Who on earth—?'

'You and Jed.' Estelle grimaced. 'There is no reconciliation, is there?'

It was so unexpected, so completely out of the blue, that Georgie could only stare at the older woman, wondering which one of them—her grandfather, Jed, or herself—by something they had done or said, had given the game away. No doubt Jed would claim it was her fault anyway!

Despite the awkwardness that now existed between Jed and herself, Georgie had continued to visit Estelle daily the last four weeks, spending time walking outside in the garden with her, or reading to her as she had been doing today. Jed popped in occasionally during those visits, as did her grandfather, and she had believed they were all doing a good job in convincing Estelle everything was all right between the three of them. Obviously she had been wrong!

She shook her head. 'If I've done anything to make you think that, then I—'

'Please, Georgie, don't think that I'm in any way criticising anything you've said or done these last weeks.' Grandie reached out and squeezed her hand reassuringly. 'I think you've been absolutely marvellous. And it can't have been easy for you, either, to keep up the pretence—'

'Grandie—'

'Please let me finish, dear,' Estelle interrupted gently. 'Georgie, the truth of the matter is, I'm very concerned about you; you don't look well.' She conveyed her concern.

The last four weeks had certainly been a strain, one Georgie had thought she wouldn't be able to get through at times. But Jed had helped in that by not being around too often when she visited Estelle, and her grandfather had also done his best not to be too visible.

But it had still been very hard to come here day after day, to keep up a bright and happy pose for Estelle—

when in reality her private life was falling apart. Was? It had already fallen apart!

'I've been working hard on the book—'

'You've been working hard on placating an old woman who ought to know better,' Estelle announced with her old indomitability. 'Georgie—' She broke off as the door to her sitting room was suddenly opened and Jed strode into the room, obviously having come here straight from the office, still wearing his business suit and snowy-white shirt.

Georgie literally felt her cheeks pale just at the sight of him. For one thing, no man had a right to be as attractive as Jed undoubtedly was. For another, if anything, her love for him had deepened over the last four weeks. As had her desire for him...

'Jed,' his grandmother greeted him warmly, holding out her hand for him to join the two women where they sat in chairs in the huge bay window that overlooked the garden. 'Georgie and I have just been having a little chat.'

'Well, I hope you don't mind, Grandie, but I would like to steal Georgie from you for a few minutes.' He smiled for his grandmother's benefit, but as his gaze passed over Georgie it felt as if she had been hit by a blast of icy cold air.

Was it any wonder, with Jed behaving like this, that Estelle had grown suspicious about this so-called reconciliation?

'Georgie is looking a little pale, don't you think?' Estelle prompted her grandson.

'Then a walk in the garden will do her the world of good,' Jed replied—without really replying at all.

Had he noticed the changes in Georgie the last few weeks? The fact that there were now shadows beneath her eyes, her cheeks were pale and hollow, that she had lost weight? From memory, Georgie knew that Jed hadn't looked at her enough to be aware of any of those things!

'Lovely.' She stood up, smiling brightly for Estelle's benefit—but inwardly wondering what on earth Jed had to say to her that necessitated their being alone together.

Because that was something both of them had avoided these last three weeks. Georgie, because of the embarrassed dismay she felt at the realisation of her love for him. And Jed—who knew how Jed thought or felt about anything…?

'Georgie, I want you to come back here and finish our conversation after you and Jed have finished talking,' Estelle called out to Georgie as she preceded Jed out of the room.

Jed turned to give his grandmother a chiding smile. 'Haven't you monopolised her enough for one day, Grandie?'

Estelle pouted across at him. 'You still aren't too big for me to reprimand, you know!'

'I do know.' Jed laughed softly. 'But I haven't seen Georgie all day,' he reasoned lightly.

'Take her out for dinner to make up for it,' Estelle suggested.

Jed glanced down at Georgie. 'I just might do that,' he agreed noncommittally.

Both of them knew he would make no such invitation, and that even if he did Georgie would refuse it.

Georgie turned to him in the hallway once he had

closed the door to Estelle's room. 'What is it?' she asked.

'The garden seems as good a place as any for us to talk,' Jed answered cryptically. 'Besides,' he continued as Georgie would have refused, 'Grandie might just be looking out for us there.'

Georgie turned abruptly to precede him down the hallway and stairs, her cheeks slightly pink as she remembered the last occasion he had said that Grandie might be looking at them, and Jed had kissed her.

But at least she felt as if she could breathe out in the garden; somehow any room in the house that contained Jed as well as herself was just too claustrophobic.

Jed wasted no time in coming to the point. 'I thought you would like to know that the deal with your boyfriend's father was just finalised,' he informed her disparagingly.

Georgie schooled her features to show no adverse reaction to this piece of news. Oh, she was glad that Gerald Lawson had received the money from the deal with the L & J Group that he needed to clear his debts. But Andrew was no longer her boyfriend...

There had simply been no way she could remain engaged to Andrew after she and Jed had made love together. No way she could ever think about marrying another man when she knew herself still irrevocably in love with her own ex-husband.

Her last meeting with Andrew, four weeks ago, had been painful to say the least. She had had to explain to him that she no longer intended marrying him, that their relationship was over.

Andrew had been devastated by her decision, couldn't

understand the reason for her sudden change of heart. In the circumstances—because she doubted that Sukie would keep quiet for ever where Jed's visit to Georgie's bedroom that evening was concerned!—Georgie had told Andrew as much of the truth as she felt necessary. That he had been stunned was putting it mildly.

Georgie thought Annabelle Lawson would not feel the same dismay at the broken engagement—she had probably wasted no time in producing the 'Lady-something-or-other' whom Jed had once mentioned as Annabelle's idea for Andrew's future wife!

But Georgie had hated having to hurt Andrew in the way that she undoubtedly had, and the last thing she felt in the mood for at the moment was Jed's derision where Andrew was concerned!

Her mouth quirked ruefully. 'What you're really trying to say, Jed, is that the L & J Group's deal with Gerald Lawson, for the purchase of some land he owned, has been finalised.'

'Am I?'

'Yes!' she assured him forcefully.

She had had no intention of telling Jed, or indeed anyone else, that her engagement to Andrew had been well and truly broken. Neither did she see why Gerald's deal with the L & J Group should be put in jeopardy just because she was no longer going to marry Andrew. By keeping up the pretence of a reconciliation in front of Estelle, Georgie considered she was keeping to her side of the bargain; there was no reason why Jed shouldn't be made to do the same.

Although, after the conversation she had just had with Estelle, she had the distinct feeling that one of them had definitely let the side down as regarded their supposed reconciliation!

'Whatever,' Jed said. 'The man has his money.'

'And you have your land,' she reasoned.

'The L & J Group has its land,' Jed corrected harshly. 'I don't appear to have anything!'

'Poor Jed,' Georgie derided unsympathetically.

'You—'

'You know, Jed, I think perhaps you ought to go up and have a quiet word with Estelle,' she interrupted. She knew from experience that exchanging barbed comments between the two of them was not going to achieve anything! 'She seems less than convinced by our so-called reconciliation,' she added thoughtfully.

'She doesn't?'

'Mmm,' Georgie replied. 'That's what she was talking to me about when you came in.'

'Damn,' he muttered with an irritable glance up at the window of his grandmother's room.

'No, "it's all your fault"? No, "you should have done better, Georgie"?' she taunted.

'Believe it or not, I don't consider you the fall-guy— or girl!—for everything that goes wrong in my life!' Jed's scowl deepened.

Georgie took the opportunity to note the changes in him over the last four weeks. The grey hair at his temples seemed more defined, his face thinner—and grimmer! Perhaps he had found the last four weeks a strain too?

'You surprise me,' she said with deliberate flippancy; she could not start feeling sorry for Jed. That way lay certain disaster! 'But perhaps it's time to tell Estelle the truth? She seems so much better, and—'

'And you're eager to get back to your fiancé!' Jed finished scathingly. 'No doubt the wedding plans need some working on too!'

'You—' She broke off her angry retort; if she lost her temper with him she might just say something she would later regret. And there was already enough for her to regret… 'I refuse to argue with you, Jed,' she told him calmly.

'Do you?' he responded challengingly.

'Yes,' she assured him determinedly. 'My suggestion that you tell Estelle the truth has nothing to do with— with Andrew.' She swallowed hard.

'Somehow I find that a little hard to believe,' Jed returned dryly.

'Somehow, Jed, I just don't care what you believe,' she rejoined. 'Estelle is obviously suspicious. I just think it would be better to tell her the truth now, and explain our reasons for the subterfuge, rather than let her find out later and be disappointed.'

'In me? Or you?' Jed prompted scathingly.

Georgie gave a weary sigh. 'In any of us. Grandfather was in on this too, remember?'

'So he was,' Jed agreed. 'You want me to go upstairs now and tell her? Is that it?' He looked grim at the prospect.

'Well, I think it might be better coming from you,' Georgie said slowly. 'I'll come back and see Estelle tomorrow, as usual, of course—'

'Oh, of course,' he grated.

'Look, Jed, either you can do it or I will,' she told

him. 'I just feel that the pretence has gone on long enough.'

He thrust his hands into his trouser pockets, turning away to look out over the extensive gardens, his shoulders hunched in thought.

Georgie let him think, knowing she was right about this. Estelle was a lot better, stronger, and wouldn't thank any of them for keeping up this pretence any longer than was necessary—would probably accuse them all of trying to make a fool of her if they did. In fact, if Georgie knew Estelle, the older woman would probably be thoroughly annoyed with all of them!

Finally Jed turned back to face Georgie, his expression grimmer than ever. 'Okay,' he agreed. 'I'll go up and talk to her. But I would appreciate your moral support, at least, when you visit her tomorrow.'

What he meant was that his grandmother was going to be angry with him anyway over the pretence, that he was going to need Georgie and her grandfather's support for what he had done!

'Of course,' Georgie assured him wearily, turning back towards the house.

'Oh, and Georgie…?' Jed called after her.

She turned back reluctantly. 'Yes?' she replied warily.

'Grandie is right,' he said. 'You don't look well.'

How did he expect her to look? Four weeks ago the two of them had made love. As a result of that she had broken off her engagement to Andrew. Worst of all, she had realised, despite all her attempts to bury the emotion, that she was still deeply in love with Jed!

She shrugged. 'I'm sure the last few weeks haven't been easy for any of us.'

Jed didn't look convinced by this explanation. 'How's the work going?'

She brightened slightly. 'Absolutely fine. I've just had my second book accepted.'

'That's good,' Jed agreed slowly, his gaze still focused on the paleness of her face. 'I don't suppose— No.' He stopped himself. 'Bad idea.'

'What is?' Georgie persisted.

He drew in a harsh breath. 'Grandie suggested the two of us had dinner together this evening. I just wondered— But I suppose you'll probably be out with Lawson this evening, celebrating your second literary success?'

Had she misunderstood, or was Jed really inviting her to have dinner with him tonight…?

A few minutes ago, when Grandie had made the suggestion, Georgie had thought the idea unacceptable to both of them—had been sure she would refuse even if Jed made such an offer. But now that he might actually be doing so…!

She shook her head, watching him warily. 'I have no plans to go anywhere this evening.'

Jed's eyes widened. 'You don't?'

'No,' she confirmed.

'I thought— Never mind what I thought,' he dismissed harshly. 'Georgie, would you allow me to buy you dinner this evening to celebrate the acceptance of your second book?'

Georgie stared at him, realising as she did so that this was the first time—ever!—that Jed had actually asked her out. Five years ago there had been no real courtship, just a proposal on her eighteenth birthday, and the two of them had never actually gone out together as such.

Oh, not that she thought Jed was inviting her out on a date this evening either, but it was certainly a novel experience!

She glanced across at Jed. His expression was guarded, as if he already knew what her answer was going to be—and was already prepared for her refusal!

'Dinner this evening would be lovely, thank you, Jed,' she accepted, holding back her smile as his eyes widened predictably with shocked surprise; he really had thought she was going to refuse!

His surprised expression turned to one of wary suspicion. 'You're really agreeing to go out to dinner with me…?' he pressed.

Georgie grinned at his obvious disbelief. 'If you're really asking me—yes!'

Why not? The last four weeks, apart from her visits to Grandie, had been spent mostly in her apartment; certainly she hadn't been out in the evening at all. Besides, it was worth accepting the invitation just to see Jed's uncharacteristic confusion. Although whether she would still feel that way at the end of the evening was another matter!

'Oh, I'm really asking,' he confirmed, straightening determinedly. 'I'll book a table somewhere for eight and call for you about seven-thirty, shall I?'

'Fine,' she accepted, avoiding looking at him now that the decision had been made. 'Now, I know that Estelle asked me to go up and see her again after the two of us had spoken together, but I really think it would be better if you went back alone. Tell her I will call back to see her tomorrow.' Georgie paused, then went on, 'She definitely knows something isn't right about this situation.'

And Georgie was already shaking enough from having accepted Jed's invitation to have dinner with him this evening. She didn't feel up to explaining things to Estelle as well!

Jed said, 'I'll talk to her.'

'Right, then,' Georgie agreed, not quite sure how to take her leave now that it had come to it. 'I'll see you later.' She turned away, ready to leave.

'Georgie…?'

She came to a halt as Jed called her name, turning slowly back to face him. 'Yes?' she responded uncertainly.

His eyes blazed deeply silver. 'Thank you.'

Georgie wasn't at all sure what he was thanking her for.

'Seven-thirty,' he confirmed.

'Yes…' she said.

He gave a slight smile. 'I'm looking forward to it.'

'Good,' Georgie returned, before turning and hurrying away, completely unable to return the sentiment—because she had no idea how she felt about going out to dinner with Jed!

That she loved him she didn't doubt. That she desired him she also had no doubt. That Jed definitely felt the latter, if not the former, she also had no doubt after their time together four weeks ago.

But was that enough for them to even get through an evening together, let alone anything else…?

CHAPTER TWELVE

BY THE time seven-thirty came around Georgie had worked herself up into such a state of nervous tension that she almost felt as if she was going to faint!

What on earth had she thought she was doing earlier, accepting an invitation to go out to dinner with Jed, of all people? Of all men!

She hadn't been able to resist, came the unhesitant reply.

Not that she had had too much time to reflect and berate herself in the last three hours. She had gone to the telephone half a dozen times with the intention of ringing Jed at her grandfather's, to tell him she couldn't make it after all. She'd gone through her wardrobe an equal amount of times, trying on outfit after outfit and deciding she didn't look or feel good in any of them. In short, she was a nervous wreck. A hot and bothered nervous wreck, at that.

She had lost weight during the last few weeks, and yet none of her clothes fitted her properly—too tight in some places, and too loose in others. The plain black dress she had finally settled on—having gone back to one of the first things she had tried on!—didn't feel right either. But as she had run out of time, it would just have to do.

Her face was hot and flushed, and no amount of make-up could hide the dark smudges beneath her eyes caused

159

by lack of sleep. Her lip-gloss didn't seem to want to go on straight either, and her hair—freshly washed—seemed to have a will of its own that included standing up on end in places!

But it was too late to worry about all of those things now, because Jed was already in the lift on his way up to her apartment!

'You look lovely,' Jed told her appreciatively as she met him coming out of the lift.

Georgie just couldn't help it—she burst out laughing.

'Was it something I said?' Jed gave a quizzical smile at her response, looking very handsome and self-assured in a black dinner suit and snowy white shirt.

'I'm having a bad hair day.' She gave a rueful shake of her head as she reached out to lightly clasp his arm and draw him into her apartment. 'As well as a bad make-up day and a my-clothes-don't-fit-me day,' she exclaimed. 'It must be so much easier for men—you just take a shower, put on your dinner clothes, and you're ready to go!'

'You think?' Jed grinned.

Georgie gave him a considering look. He did look absolutely wonderful in his dinner clothes, his hair slightly damp from the shower he must have taken—and he smelt gorgeous too.

'I think,' she finally confirmed. 'Would you like a drink before we go?' She indicated the bottle of white wine she had opened earlier, having drunk a glass herself in the hope that it would steady her nerves. She had obviously been wrong—she was so nervous now her hands were shaking!

'Thanks.' Jed accepted the offer, unbuttoning his

jacket before sitting down in one of the armchairs. 'In the face of your own admissions, I feel it only fair to tell you that I cut myself shaving, tried on two other shirts, also white, before settling on this one, decided I need to go up a size in a dinner suit—and sprayed shaving foam under my arms instead of deodorant!'

Georgie turned to stare at him, arrested in the action of pouring his glass of white wine. Surely Jed wasn't as nervous as she was about the two of them having dinner together…? Somehow the words 'Jed' and 'nervous' just didn't go together!

'You're just trying to make me feel better,' she said as she handed him his glass of wine.

He raised dark brows. 'I forgot to mention that originally I also put on one black sock and one brown one, only discovering my mistake when I came to put on my shoes,' he elaborated self-derisively.

Maybe he wasn't just trying to make her feel better, after all…

Although Georgie still refused to believe it would have been the thought of dinner with her that had caused this uncharacteristic behavior.

Of course it wasn't!

'Was your chat with Grandie that bad?' she prompted as she sat down in the chair opposite his.

'My chat with— Ah,' he nodded. 'Would you mind if we talked about that later?'

'Not at all.' She shrugged, sipping her wine, and almost choking on it at Jed's next words.

'I've booked a table for us at Fabio's,' he told her.

Their favourite restaurant! Well…perhaps that was too intimate a description for the Italian restaurant he had just mentioned, but they had certainly frequented that particular restaurant often during their marriage—had celebrated their wedding anniversaries there too. All three of them!

'Are you okay?' Jed queried, sitting forward to look at Georgie concernedly as she coughed slightly, some of her wine having gone down the wrong way.

'Fine,' she told him shakily, putting down her wine glass before standing up. 'Perhaps we had better be on our way.'

'There's no rush,' Jed assured her as he stood up to hold her red jacket for her to put on. 'Fabio was so pleased to hear from us that he told me he's going to keep our usual table for us.'

To hear from 'us'... Their 'usual table'...

Georgie was taken aback. 'But surely you've been back there in the two years since—since—?'

'Since the two of us parted?' Jed finished softly. 'No. As I just said, it's our restaurant. It wouldn't have been right to take anyone else there. Besides—'

'Besides...?' Georgie pressed, looking at him from beneath lowered lashes as the two of them descended in the lift.

He looked at the elevator's ceiling. 'Something else we can talk about later.'

There seemed to be an awful lot of things they were going to discuss later: his earlier conversation with Grandie, and now this.

Oh, well, at least they would have something to talk about rather than just sitting looking at each other all evening!

* * *

'I feel a complete fraud,' Georgie said, glancing uncomfortably around the restaurant after Fabio himself had escorted them to their table, personally seeing her seated opposite Jed before snapping his fingers imperiously for the waiter to come and take their drinks order.

None of the other diners appeared to be taking any undue interest in them, but, as Georgie knew from visits here in the past, it wasn't the done thing to appear interested in your fellow eaters.

She turned back to Jed. 'Fabio is obviously under the impression we're once again a couple,' she observed awkwardly.

Jed looked at her. 'It doesn't matter what he may or may not think—does it?'

No, not really. She just wasn't comfortable with it.

'Thank you.' She smiled up at the waiter as he poured some wine into a glass for her.

'You know, Georgie,' Jed said slowly once they were alone again, sitting forward in his seat to look across the table at her, 'you really aren't looking well. Perhaps you should see a doctor?'

She raised auburn brows. 'I thought you said earlier that I look lovely,' she reminded him dryly.

'You do,' he confirmed impatiently. 'It's just—'

'Jed, I just need to eat,' she assured him, deliberately burying her nose in the menu so that she didn't have to look at him.

She was determined to enjoy this evening. She knew that very soon her visits to Estelle would have to come to an end, which meant that her occasional meetings with Jed would be over. This evening might be all she would see of him for some time...

'I'm going to have the avocado vinaigrette and Dover sole,' she decided, before closing the menu. 'How about you?' she questioned conversationally.

Jed closed his own menu. 'I'll have the same as you. Georgie—'

'Shall we drink a toast to Estelle's full recovery?' She held up her wine glass.

Jed looked irritated by her interruption. 'Very well,' he agreed, lightly touching his glass against hers.

The wine barely touched Georgie's lips before she replaced her glass down on the table. 'She is so much better, isn't she?' she said thankfully.

Jed's expression hardened. 'Eager to get back to your fiancé, Georgie?'

She met his gaze unblinkingly. 'About as eager as you must be to get back to your own life,' she returned non-committally.

'I—' He broke off as the waiter arrived at their table to take their order, giving the other man a hard stare. 'Two avocado vinaigrettes, and two Dover—'

'I've changed my mind about the main course,' Georgie cut in lightly. 'I think I'll have the lamb noisettes instead of the Dover sole.' She smiled up at the waiter in apology. 'A woman's prerogative,' she told Jed humorously as he looked at her once the waiter had made a discreet exit.

'So I believe,' Jed acknowledged. 'Does Lawson know that you're having dinner with me this evening?' His voice had hardened noticeably.

'No,' Georgie answered without hesitation.

Once Andrew had calmed down, after she'd broken their engagement, the two of them had talked more rationally and had agreed that they would remain friends. But Georgie already knew that the friendship would consist of them being polite to each other if they should happen to meet by chance. It was very sad, and she really was sorry to lose Andrew's warmth and kindness from her life, but she also knew she had had no other choice.

Jed was watching her from between narrowed lids. 'Do you intend telling him?'

'No,' Georgie stated flatly.

'Why not?'

'Because it has no bearing on our relationship.' Their now non-existent-relationship…

'Georgie—'

'Jed, couldn't we just enjoy this evening? There's really no need to complicate things by talking about Andrew or—or anyone else you may have in your own life at the moment.'

Despite having had lunch with Sukie Lawson, Jed obviously wasn't too taken with the other woman. But that didn't mean there wasn't some other woman in his life…

Unpleasant though that thought might be!

'Unlike you, I don't have anyone else in my life,' Jed bit out harshly. 'At the moment, or at any other time!'

Georgie's eyes widened. His tone was too vehement for it to be anything other than the truth. But in that case *why* didn't Jed have someone in his life…?

'Georgie, you just don't get it, do you?' he continued, sitting forward in his chair as he did so.

Didn't get what? She—

She sat back in her seat as their first course was placed in front of them. 'This looks delicious,' she approved as she began to eat, and the moment—whatever it might have been!—passed. Jed picked up his knife and fork and also began to eat, albeit uninterestedly.

'This is very good,' Georgie murmured after several minutes' silence—a silence that was becoming more and more awkward while Jed only picked at his food rather than eating it. Her own appetite was rapidly waning too, in the face of Jed's brooding distraction. 'I wonder why it is that food always tastes better in a restaurant than when you've prepared it at home? Probably for that very reason.' She gave the answer herself seconds later, as none seemed to be forthcoming from Jed. 'After shopping for the food, and then spending time preparing and cooking it, I've usually lost interest by the time it comes to—'

'Georgie—stop it!' Jed cut in forcefully, grey eyes opaquely silver as he glared across the table at her. 'Just stop it!' he ordered, putting down his knife and fork and pushing his plate away as he gave up any pretence of eating his food. 'We aren't strangers out on a first date together! You don't have to make to make meaningless conversation to fill in any awkward silences!'

Making meaningless conversation…? Was that what she was doing? Probably. But the silence between them *had* been awkward!

'I'm sorry,' she apologised, pushing away her own plate, with most of the avocado uneaten. 'Maybe this wasn't such a good idea after all—'

'Of course it was a good idea!' Jed rasped. 'I just—' He reached across the table and clasped one of her hands between both of his. 'Georgie, do you have any idea how much I've longed to spend time with you like this? How much I—?'

'Jed, stop it!' She was the one to cry out now, staring at him with shocked eyes as she pulled her hand away from his, ignoring the tingling sensation she felt just from his touch. 'There's no audience—at least none that matters,' she amended, for the restaurant was packed with people. 'You don't have anyone to put on an act for now—certainly not me!—so—'

'I'm not putting on an act,' he grated, a nerve pulsing in his jaw. 'Damn it, Georgie, don't you know—have you never realised—just how much I—?'

'Is everything all right for you, Mr Lord?'

Georgie felt quite sorry for Fabio when his polite enquiry received a fiercely angry glare from Jed. The restaurant proprietor took an involuntary step back as Jed's gaze narrowed on him furiously.

'You—'

'Everything is wonderful.' Georgie cut in on what she was sure was going to be Jed's impolite reply. 'Thank you, Fabio.' She smiled again, to take the sting out of her own obvious dismissal of the restaurateur. 'How much you what, Jed?' She reminded them of their interrupted conversation once they were alone again, not sure she wanted to hear the answer to that question, but knowing she had to ask it nonetheless.

He closed his eyes briefly, at the same time drawing in a harshly controlling breath. 'You were right in your suspicions earlier concerning Grandie,' he said starkly. 'In fact, I would go one step further and say that you were more than right. Grandie admitted to me earlier this evening that she has always known that there was no reconciliation between us, that it was all a pretence!'

Georgie stared at him uncomprehendingly. 'I don't understand.'

'She was seriously ill when I told her the two of us had reconciled,' Jed explained, his expression grim. 'And that certainly was a factor in her initial recovery. But apparently she has known since seeing the two of us together again that there really was no reconciliation, that it was all an act.'

'I— You— But it's been weeks now!' Georgie gasped incredulous. 'And if she's known all this time why didn't she just say so and put an end to all this subterfuge?'

Jed pursed his lips. 'For the same reason I told her the lie in the first place. For the same reason I didn't just telephone you and tell you Grandie wanted to see you, but sought you out at the Lawsons' home instead. For the same reason I've wanted to hit Andrew Lawson every time I've seen the two of you together. For the same reason I had lunch with Sukie Lawson—'

'You aren't making any sense, Jed!' Georgie burst in emotionally. 'None of those things are related to each other—'

'Of course they're related!' he protested impatiently. 'No—'

'Yes!' Jed hissed fiercely, the nerve in his jaw beating a wild tattoo now. 'They are completely, one hundred per cent related—when you take into account the fact that I love you! That I have *always* loved you!'

Georgie could only stare at him.

And continue to stare...

CHAPTER THIRTEEN

FINALLY—when it seemed Jed was going to add nothing to that ludicrous statement!—Georgie drew in a deep breath before she answered him. 'Have you been drinking, Jed?' she asked suspiciously. 'Oh, I don't mean now,' she said, as his gaze flickered to his almost untouched glass of wine. 'Before. Maybe that was the reason you were so confused earlier when dressing—'

'I have not been drinking. Either now or earlier,' he stated firmly.

'But—'

'Georgie, is it really so difficult to believe that I love you?' he pleaded.

'Difficult?' she echoed. 'The very idea is ridiculous!'

His gaze remained unwavering on her face. 'Why is it?'

'Because—' She drew in a deeply controlling breath. 'Jed, even if it were true—'

'It is,' he assured her sincerely.

'Even if it were true,' she repeated firmly, 'how can you possibly equate such a claim with taking Sukie Lawson out to lunch?'

Let's see him get himself out of that one! Jed might claim he hadn't been drinking earlier this evening, but there was certainly something very wrong with him. How could he possibly claim to love her. It just didn't make sense!

In fact, this whole evening was starting to take on a dream-like quality—or did she mean nightmarish?

'I had hoped to make you jealous,' Jed admitted.

He had succeeded! Georgie could still clearly remember her feelings that day when she'd learnt that Jed was going out with Sukie, and it wasn't a pleasant memory. She had wanted to hit Sukie, and scream and shout at Jed!

'The same jealousy I feel towards Andrew Lawson,' he continued harshly. 'Every time his name is so much as mentioned I want to hit something! And as for thinking of the two of you together—'

'Jed, Andrew and I don't have that sort of relationship,' Georgie shot in. She wanted no misunderstandings on that point; this situation was already complicated enough!

She still couldn't accept anything of what Jed was saying to her. They had been married for three years, for goodness' sake, and not once during that time had Jed ever told her that he loved her. Unless he had discovered these feelings since the two of them had parted? But, no, hadn't he just claimed to have *always* loved her...?

'Jed—'

'Are you telling me that you and Lawson aren't— physically involved?' Jed cut across what she had been about to say.

Her cheeks coloured hotly. 'I don't have to tell you anything about my relationship with Andrew—'

'But you just did,' Jed reasoned determinedly.

Yes, she had. And she wished that she hadn't. 'Jed, I'm not sure we should be having this conversation at all—let alone in the middle of a busy restaurant.'

'I disagree. Oh, not about the location,' he conceded dryly as the waiter discreetly removed their used plates. 'But I think the conversation itself is long overdue. Five years overdue, to be exact.'

Five years... They had married each other five years ago...

But they had parted again three years later, she reminded herself. Because Jed hadn't loved her. Because he'd been involved with another woman. She might have been naïve two years ago, but even she had known that wasn't the behaviour of a man in love with his wife!

She shook her head sadly. 'Jed, nothing has changed in the last two years—'

'I disagree,' he rejoined. '*You've* changed. Your grandfather warned me that you were too young when we married, that you needed a few more years to grow up, to enjoy your freedom. But I wasn't willing to wait—'

'I may have been young, Jed, but even I knew that there had to be something seriously wrong with your marriage when your husband was publicly having an affair with another woman!' she burst out.

'When I *what*!' Jed exclaimed.

'Mia Douglas,' she reminded.

'Mia Douglas...?' he repeated, his expression blank.

Georgie felt the sting of tears in her eyes. Had Jed's relationship with the other woman been so unimportant to him that he even had trouble remembering it now? That same relationship that had blown her own world apart?

Or was it just that he had never realised she had known about his affair with the actress?

When Jed had returned from his so-called business trip two years ago it had been to find Georgie, and her belongings, removed from their apartment. When he'd finally tracked her down to the hotel where she was staying she had refused to discuss anything with him, except to tell him that she had made a mistake, that their marriage was over. Oh, he had argued, and cajoled, but to no avail. Georgie had remained adamant in her decision.

That had been when Jed had really lost it—demanding to know if there were someone else in her life, if she were seeing another man!

Georgie had then thrown his own motive back in his face by telling him she had only married him at all to please her grandfather, but that her inability to have children now made that arrangement null and void, and their marriage was well and truly over.

How dared he now pretend he didn't even remember his affair with Mia Douglas?

'Mia Douglas, Jed,' she said tightly. 'Surely you remember her? Tall. Blonde. Beautiful. A charity dinner you attended with her in Los Angeles?'

'I've never been to Los Angeles,' he responded. 'And to my knowledge I've only ever met Mia Douglas once. She was attending some dinner or other being given at our hotel in Hawaii one time when I was there, and a damned nuisance the whole thing was too, with photographers all over the place disturbing the other guests—' He broke off, his gaze narrowed as he looked at Georgie suspiciously. 'Georgie, you aren't telling me that you left me two years ago because of some damned publicity photograph of Mia Douglas and myself that somehow found its way into the English newspapers?'

Georgie could barely breathe. A pain in her chest seemed to constrict her airway.

Was she saying that? Had she been mistaken all this time? Had there been no reason for her to leave Jed after all?

But of course there had been a reason, she instantly berated herself. Jed hadn't married her because he loved her, but because it had been yet another business merger on behalf of the Lord and Jones families. That was the real truth of the matter. Jed's supposed involvement with another woman was merely a side issue—a side issue! At the time she had thought she might die from the pain of seeing Jed with another woman…!

But she hadn't died, and in the last two years she had grown much stronger as a person. She was successful in her own right, completely independent financially. Nothing Jed said now could change any of that.

She straightened. 'I left you two years ago, Jed, because our marriage was over. If it ever really began!' she added scathingly, before picking up her evening bag and standing up. 'Just as I am leaving now. If you'll excuse me?' she told him pleasantly, and turned away.

The first she knew of Jed following her was when she emerged out onto the street and found him standing beside her. She wished he hadn't—because she wasn't sure how much longer she could hold back her tears!

'I'm driving you home, Georgie,' he told her firmly, before she could utter a word.

She glanced back at the brightly lit restaurant. 'Fabio—'

'I've made our apologies and settled the bill,' Jed explained grimly. 'Being the romantic that he is, Fabio probably thinks I'm whisking you away early so that the two of us can spend the rest of the evening making love together.'

'That only increased our problems the last time we did that!' Georgie returned waspishly.

Jed shot her a sharp look. 'What do you mean?'

Georgie avoided that searching gaze. 'Nothing,' she said. 'I really don't need you to drive me home, Jed—'

'*I* need to drive you home,' he decided. 'Let me at least have the peace of mind of knowing you got there safely, hmm?' he encouraged hardly, before reaching into his pocket for his keys and unlocking the car.

'I've managed to achieve that for the last two years without any help from you,' she told him.

His mouth tightened at her deliberate barb, but he made no reply, simply opened the passenger door pointedly for her to get inside the car.

Georgie just wanted to get away, to be on her own. But at the same time she didn't feel like continuing this stand up verbal fight with Jed to achieve it…

'Oh, okay!' she accepted, before getting into the car, her face averted from his when he got in beside her seconds later.

But he didn't start the engine, instead turned to her in the semi-darkness of the interior of the car. 'Georgie, for me, making love with you four weeks ago was like dying and going to heaven,' he said.

She trembled, not sure how much longer she would be able to hold on to her emotions.

This was hard, so much harder than she could ever have imagined.

How could she go on fighting him if he said things like that to her?

But she had to! There was no going back now, only forwards. And that future didn't—couldn't!—include Jed.

'I love you, Georgie.'

No…! Not now! All that time, all those years she had yearned— She couldn't—

'I've loved you since the moment I first saw you,' he continued huskily. 'You were like the little sister I had never had. Eight years old, all arms, legs and eyes, weighed down by a long mane of copper-coloured hair,' he recalled affectionately.

'And I worshipped the ground you walked on!' Georgie remembered self-disgustedly.

Jed smiled. 'If by that you mean that you accepted me unconditionally, then, yes, I suppose that's true. You were the first person who ever had.'

'Estelle—'

'Loved me,' he acknowledged. 'But not unconditionally. I was the son of the daughter who had so let her down—'

'She let you down too!' Georgie defended, only able to guess at what it must have felt like to be abandoned by your own mother in the way that Jed had been.

'Yes.' He sighed. 'But don't you see? Estelle was always looking for signs of that emotional instability in me, was never sure that I would still be around once I was an adult. Whereas you—' he smiled again '—you always expected me to keep my promises. I honestly don't think it ever occurred to you to doubt that I would. Heady stuff, Georgie. By the time you were eighteen I was completely under your spell, totally and utterly in love with you.'

She swallowed hard. 'But you never said those words to me…!' she remembered achingly.

'I didn't dare,' Jed confessed. 'My mother walked out on me when I was four years old. My grandmother, although she loved me, kept me slightly at arm's length, always waiting for the day I would just disappear.' He sighed shakily. 'I didn't dare tell you how much I love you, Georgie! I—I was frightened to tell you—thought the hurt would be less if you ever left me. I was wrong,' he added heavily.

She could see how it might appear that way to Jed, how much his mother walking out on him as a child must have damaged his trust in any other woman who claimed to love him. But at the same time she was afraid herself—so afraid—to believe what he was telling her. Because if she did—

'And I suppose this declaration of love has absolutely nothing to do with your ''arrangement'' with my grandfather?' she reminded him accusingly.

'You mentioned that two years ago… I had no idea what you were talking about then, and even less so now! The only agreement I had with your grandfather five years ago was that I wouldn't swamp you with the love I felt for you, that I would give you time to grow up, to reach your full potential, in whatever direction that might lie. Of course, I hoped it would still be as my wife, but…' He sighed. 'You've obviously achieved your ambition these last two years without me.'

Yes, she had, but— 'I could still have done that as your wife,' she told him softly. 'I—my grandfather seemed to think our marriage was a business arrangement?' But she was less forceful in the accusation now, less sure of herself, and wondered if she could possibly—just possibly—have misunderstood what her grandfather had said two years ago.

'Definitely not,' Jed denied. 'Damn it, Georgie, if you really believe that I'll give up all claim on the Lord & Jones Group—branch out on my own!'

'You would really do that?'

He nodded. 'I'm not saying it would be easy, but— yes. If it means that you would believe me once and for all when I tell you I love you, that's exactly what I'll do! Without you, Georgie—' his voice broke slightly '—my life has no meaning anyway.'

Georgie couldn't believe he was saying these things. And meaning them! Because she could tell by the grim determination of his expression that he *did* mean them.

'My lifetime ambition is to be with you, Georgie.' He reminded her of the accusation she had thrown at him four weeks ago. 'To just love you and be with you,' he emphasised clearly.

She needed time—not too much time!—but some time to fully take in the things Jed had said to her this evening. Most of all she needed time to accept that he really did love her, that he always had!

'Could you drive me home now, please, Jed?' she requested evenly.

'I—'

'Please?' she requested again intensely.

He looked at her for a long time, and then he nodded abruptly. 'Of course,' he acceded tautly, switching on the car engine at last to begin the journey back to her apartment.

Georgie leant back in her seat, her eyes closed, desperately trying to make sense of the things Jed had said to her this evening and finally concluding that the only thing that did make sense was that he loved her! And the 'arrangement' between her grandfather and Jed had only been made at all because the older man had been aware of just how deeply Jed loved her. He had feared for her own personality in the face of such intense love, and it was her grandfather's own love for her that had prompted him to ask Jed to proceed with caution where she was concerned.

Jed loved her...!

Had always loved her.

Would always love her.

Did she really need to know anything else? The answer to that was a definite no!

But there were some confessions of her own she still had to make. She wondered what Jed's response would be to at least one of them...

CHAPTER FOURTEEN

'WOULD you like to come in for coffee?' Georgie offered shyly once Jed had parked his car outside her apartment building.

'I would love to come in,' he confirmed. 'But I never drink coffee at this time of night.'

'That's okay,' she assured him as she got out of the car. 'Neither do I!'

And her invitation had nothing to do with offering Jed a cup of coffee. They still had so many things to talk about. But all of them were based on her accepting the possibility that Jed might really have been in love with her all this time. Something she still found a little hard to believe.

'Georgie—'

'Let's just go upstairs, hmm, Jed?' she suggested, waiting for him to get out of the car and accompany her.

They didn't speak on their way through the reception area, or as they went up in the lift together. But Georgie could feel the tension between them, knew that Jed was as nervous about the outcome of the next few minutes as she was.

She kicked off her shoes the moment they entered the apartment, turning to raise questioning brows at Jed as she heard him make a sound behind her.

'It's been years since I've seen you do that,' he told her gruffly. 'You always used to kick off your shoes the moment we came home from an evening out,' he explained at her puzzled look.

'Oh, dear.' Georgie grimaced, could feel the warmth of embarrassment in her cheeks. It wasn't a habit she had ever been aware of. But obviously Jed had… 'How irritating for you,' she said.

Jed looked at her unblinkingly. 'Georgie, nothing you do has ever irritated me. Or ever could,' he added softly.

Georgie turned away from the intensity of that silver gaze. 'As you don't want coffee, can I offer you a glass of whisky?'

'No, thanks.' He sat down in one of the armchairs. 'I would rather be stone-cold sober when I receive the executioner's sentence.'

'The—? Don't be silly, Jed,' she responded. 'You mentioned earlier that Grandie had deliberately kept up the subterfuge about our reconciliation? Does she know that you—that you—'

'That I love you?' Jed finished dryly. 'Of course. The only one who has never been aware of it seems to be you, Georgie.'

Because she had been very young when they'd married five years ago. And very immature. An older woman might possibly have seen Jed's reticence concerning actually saying the words 'I love you' for exactly what it was—the only self-protection he had left!

'I see,' she said. 'I've been extremely stupid, haven't I, Jed?'

She closed her eyes briefly. 'Stupid and selfish. I was so confused by the time my grandfather mentioned some sort of an arrangement between the two of you two years ago that I completely misunderstood and thought I had merely been part of a business deal. And I've refused to speak to Grandfather for the last two years because of that misunderstanding.

'I'm sure if you explain—'

'I'm going to do more than that,' she assured him, tears shimmering in her eyes. 'All this time he was only trying to protect me—as he always had! When I see him tomorrow I will offer him my most humble apologies for ever doubting him.'

Jed gave her a sympathetic smile. 'I'm sure he will appreciate that.'

Which brought them back—inevitably—to the situation between Jed and herself...

'Jed, you asked me earlier what I was going to tell Andrew about having had dinner with you this evening—'

'And you, very rightly, told me to mind my own business,' he drawled ruefully.

'I'm not under any obligation to tell Andrew anything any more,' she confessed uncomfortably. 'Jed, I—I broke my engagement to Andrew four weeks ago!'

'Four weeks ago—!' He straightened in the chair, his expression watchful now. 'But—'

'The day after the two of us had made love.' She confirmed the conclusion she could see dawning in his expression.

'Why?' he prompted.

'Well, for one thing it would have been very wrong not to. For another...' She hesitated, a small part of past hurts still lingering. But Jed had bared his soul to her this evening, the least she could do was to be truthful about her own feelings towards him. 'Jed, when we married five years ago I was deeply in love with you—'

'I know that,' he groaned achingly. 'I was just always so frightened of losing you that I didn't dare tell you I felt the same way. I had hoped that I showed you how I felt when we made love—'

'You did,' she assured him undoubtingly; maturity had helped her to see that was exactly what he had done. As he had four weeks ago when they made love together again… 'You said earlier that I've changed the last two years.'

'You have,' he responded admiringly.

'One thing about me has—has never changed, Jed,' she continued more assuredly. 'I loved you five years ago and I love you now. If anything, I love you more now than I did then!' The words just burst out of her, as if she had to say them before she lost her nerve. 'I didn't just break my engagement to Andrew because the two of us had made love together. I also broke it because I could never marry one man while being deeply in love with another.'

'Me…?' Jed's voice was so low it was barely discernible. A nerve pulsed erratically in the hardness of his cheek.

'You,' she went on warmly. 'Oh, Jed, I love you so much,' she told him, going down on her knees beside his chair to take one of his hands in hers. 'I love you,' she said again, that emotion shining in the brightness of her eyes.

Jed gathered her up into his arms, gazing at her wonderingly for several seconds before his mouth moved to gently claim hers.

Love. It had been there all the time. In Jed's every touch. Every kiss. The difference between now and five years ago was that she knew it with every fibre of her being.

'Will you marry me?' Jed breathed when at last he raised his head to look at her with dark eyes.

'Oh, yes,' she accepted without hesitation. 'And let's make it soon, hmm?' she encouraged throatily.

Jed's arms tightened about her. 'I want it to be different this time, Georgie. I want to give you an old-fashioned courtship—take you out, send you flowers, leave you in no doubt as to how I feel about you—'

'I think I could stand a week or two of that.' She nodded, eyes sparkling mischievously. 'But no longer, hmm?'

He smoothed the hair at her temples, his hand shaking slightly. 'I don't want to rush you into anything, Georgie,' he explained. 'This time you have to be very sure—because once you're my wife again I will never let you go! I only let you go last time because your grandfather advised me that by letting you go you might one day come back.'

Georgie could see the logic in that—even if it hadn't exactly worked out that way! What a shock the announcement of her engagement to Andrew must have been for all of them...

'I don't ever want to leave you again,' she assured Jed with certainty. 'I love you, Jed. I always will. But I also think it might be nice for our son or daughter if we are actually remarried before they're born. Don't you?' she encouraged.

'Our son or daughter…?' Jed repeated, looking at her uncomprehendingly.

'You told me earlier today that I don't look well, that I ought to see a doctor,' she reminded him happily. 'I've already seen one. Two days ago. He confirmed that I am going to have a baby. Our baby, Jed,' she told him emotionally. 'Our million to one chance is a fact—and due to be born in eight months!'

'But— I— You—'

She laughed happily at his totally dazed expression. 'It's true, Jed,' she assured him lovingly. 'We're pregnant!'

Emotions flitted rapidly across his usually guarded face: disbelief, doubt, hope, and finally, as Georgie continued to smile at him with ecstatic certainty, complete wonder.

'I can't believe it!' he gasped at last.

'Neither could I to start with,' she admitted, unable to stop smiling, it seemed. 'But the doctor has assured me that there is no mistake.'

She had gone to the doctor initially because she really hadn't been feeling well: nauseous, dizzy occasionally, with her appetite extremely erratic. When the doctor had calmly announced she had all those symptoms because she was pregnant, Georgie had almost fallen off her chair, asking him if he was sure. A simple test had only confirmed his diagnosis.

Georgie had been walking around in a seventh heaven for the last two days, torn between euphoria that she was at last to have Jed's baby and despair because she couldn't share it with him. But now she could!

'It really is true, Jed,' she told him. 'My sudden

change to lamb for dinner this evening?' she reminded him. 'That was because the thought of fish suddenly made me feel ill. I'm pregnant, Jed, and I couldn't be happier!' Her smile was radiant.

Jed still looked totally dazed, staring at her as if he couldn't believe she were quite real.

Georgie snuggled against him reassuringly; after all, she had had forty-eight hours longer than he had to get used to the idea, and she still pinched herself occasionally to see if she wasn't dreaming.

'I can't wait to see Grandfather's face when we tell him we're going to make him a great-grandfather!' she said mischievously; perhaps the news might help alleviate, in part, some of the hurt she must have caused him when she wouldn't even see him these last two years…! 'Would you like a boy or a girl, Jed?' She looked up at him quizzically.

He swallowed hard, his eyes glistening. 'I really don't care which it is—as long as you're both healthy,' he finally managed. 'But if it's a boy it certainly won't be called Jeremiah!'

Georgie giggled happily. 'I'm sorry I teased you about your name that evening.' She grinned. 'But I'm sure we'll be able to think of something a little more attractive than both our names. After all, we have eight months to think of it!'

Jed's arms tightened about her. 'And a lifetime together to enjoy! I really do love you very much, Georgie. And I intend saying that often in the future.'

Strange, now that she knew Jed loved her, the words no longer seemed necessary…

But at the same time there was a certain joy in the freedom of at last saying those words to each other.

A joy that Georgie had no doubts would last for a lifetime. Their lifetime together.

BLACKMAILED BY THE BOSS

by

Kathryn Ross

Kathryn Ross was born in Zambia where her parents happened to live at that time. Educated in Ireland and England, she now lives in a village near Blackpool, Lancashire. Kathryn is a professional beauty therapist, but writing is her first love. As a child she wrote adventure stories and at thirteen was editor of her school magazine. Happily, ten writing years later, DESIGNED WITH LOVE was accepted by Mills & Boon. A romantic Sagittarian, she loves travelling to exotic locations.

CHAPTER ONE

THERE was no excuse, it was probably one of the most stupid things she had ever done in her life—apart from getting involved with David of course, that went without saying, but this… Her thoughts trailed off. This was incomprehensible it was so stupid.

She turned her head slightly on the pillow and looked across to the other side of the bed. They had left the bed-side lamp on last night, so she could see him quite clearly—it hadn't been a dream, he was still there and fast asleep. Charlotte felt panic rising like a spring inside her, gushing like iced water through her veins. Jordan was her father's business partner, for heaven's sake; and more than that he was her boss. How could she have let this happen?

Her eyes drifted over his features; he looked different asleep, less formidably handsome…more vulnerable. It was an absurd thought; Jordan Lynch was anything but vulnerable; in fact he was one tough cookie, a dynamic businessman with a never-ending stream of glamorous girl-friends who just seemed to fall at his feet. Charlotte had watched them come and go and she had sworn she would never be one of his conquests. So what had happened? It wasn't even as if she could blame it on drink—two glasses of sparkling water was hardly mind-altering.

She cast her mind back to yesterday. She remembered her eyes had connected with his through the glass partition of the office. And she remembered thinking that he had the sexiest eyes on earth, before hurriedly looking away again. But that wasn't so unusual; she was a red-blooded woman after all, and very often she'd glance at Jordan and admire the sheer male perfection of him. But it didn't mean anything, it was a transitory thought that probably went through every woman's head at least once when they looked at him.

She had applied herself back to her work, reminding herself that he may be thirty-eight, single, wealthy and gorgeous, but his latest girlfriend was a twenty-three-year-old sultry Latin-American model. And anyway he wasn't her type—he was too arrogantly sure of himself; good-looking but knew it.

In fact Charlotte had quite enjoyed pretending she didn't notice him. Being coolly dismissive when everyone else was fawning around him appealed to her rebellious side. She hadn't particularly agreed with her father taking him on as a partner last year. They had been doing fine without him, then along he'd come with his newfangled ideas and his haughty manner. The first couple of months the air had been a bit frosty between them. But since then things had thawed slightly. To be honest, she'd had to get on with him because her father was rarely here these days and Jordan was running the show.

Then the phone on her desk had rung...

She'd ignored it, thinking her assistant, Frank, would pick it up in the main office. But it had continued to ring until in desperation she'd snatched it up. 'Charlotte McCann speaking; how may I help?'

'Hi, Charlie, it's Melanie. Just thought I'd touch base with you, see how you are. Bearing up, I hope?'

'Oh…hi, Melanie.' Charlotte's heart sank as she heard the sympathetic tones radiating from the other end of the line. Everyone was talking to her like that these days. She knew people meant well but she hated it. 'I take it you've heard?'

'Yes, Erica told me. I couldn't believe it; David always seemed such a solid, dependable type.'

Something twisted inside Charlotte. 'Yes, well, obviously appearances can be deceptive.'

'I'm really sorry, Charlie. You must be devastated.'

'Not really. Actually I'm feeling pretty positive about the situation; it's probably for the best.' Charlotte scribbled her pen rather violently through a memo Frank had left on her desk. 'Things had been cooling between us for some time now.'

'Even so, it's tough when a relationship ends,' Melanie purred. 'Listen, why don't you come for supper tomorrow? I'm having a lot of the girls over and it would be lovely to see you.'

And talk about the entire story in gory detail, Charlotte finished for her silently. She didn't want that—she'd rather forget it. 'It's a bit short notice, Mel… I'm pretty tied up—'

'Now, listen, it would do you good. Cindy Smith will be here and Janice Pike, and you haven't seen them for ages.' Melanie cut across her in a no-nonsense tone.

Janice Pike! Biggest gossip in London! Charlotte shuddered as she imagined what the evening would be like. They might as well bring along a bright light and a pair of thumbscrews to make it complete.

'It's not that…' She paused as Jordan came into the office and she mouthed to him that she wouldn't be a minute.

He perched on the edge of her desk, looking very suave in a dark suit with a pristine white shirt beneath. She probably should have taken that as a signal to hang up, but she ignored him, telling herself that she could take a few minutes to chat to a friend when she was always in the office half an hour earlier and half an hour later than anybody else.

'So what is it?' Mel persisted, never one to give in easily.

Charlotte took a deep breath and improvised wildly. 'The fact is, I'm seeing someone and it's early days…you know what it's like when you're in the "getting to know someone" stage.'

'Well, yes…' Melanie sounded stunned.

She noticed that even Jordan looked surprised—his dark eyebrows rose slightly.

'Gosh, that was quick, Charlie!' Mel drawled. 'I must say, you don't hang about.'

'Well, it is four and a half weeks since David and I split up.' As soon as she said the words she knew they were a mistake. When you were still counting the days, did it mean you weren't over someone? 'Anyway, I'm going to have to go, Mel.' She tried to wind up the conversation before she made things worse. 'Jordan has just walked into my office and I mustn't delay him.' That, at least, was the truth.

'Sorry about that,' she said as she put the phone down. 'Now, I've got those details ready about the latest designs, and I'm happy to say it's all coming on really well.' As she spoke she was running an eye over the drawings that lay before her on the desk.

'I didn't know you were dating someone new.' Jordan ignored her words and instead zoomed in on the very thing she wanted to gloss over.

She hesitated and for a moment contemplated lying to him as well, and then shrugged. What was the point in pretending?

'I'm not.' She didn't glance up; instead she shuffled the papers in front of her, trying to get back to the work. 'I want to talk to you about the budget for the new scheme—'

But Jordan wouldn't let the subject go. 'So why did you tell someone you were dating?' he persisted, stopping her in her tracks.

'Because…' she leaned back in her chair, running a flustered hand through her long blonde hair. 'Well, I suppose I didn't want Melanie to know that the most exciting thing I've done recently is watch a rerun of *Dallas* and order a take-away pizza.' The truth just popped out and she was surprised by his reaction because he seemed to relax somewhat, as if he found it terribly amusing.

'Oh, I see.'

'Not that I haven't had offers, of course,' she continued swiftly, feeling cross with herself for telling *him* that. 'But I've just been too bogged down with all of this.' She flicked the work in front of her derisively.

'Yeah, I know you've been working very hard,' he replied seriously.

Something about the way he looked at her set off a prickle of awareness inside that was deeply disturbing.

'Anyway, I know I'm nearly over budget on the curtaining for these apartments.' She returned the conversation very firmly to work. It wasn't the first time he'd had that effect on her and she supposed it wouldn't be the last. But it didn't mean anything; it was because he was a predatory male, and she read the danger signals loud and clear.

'But I want to use the more expensive sheer muslin for the front windows. I mean, what's the point of building somewhere with fabulous views and then spoiling it with the window dressing? It's like buying a fantastically expensive dress and teaming it with horrid shoes. Spoils the whole image.' She looked up and fixed him with wide, fervent green eyes. 'So can I up the budget?'

'Again?' His voice was dry. 'What are you doing, gold-plating the whole apartment block?'

'The windows will sell the place,' Charlotte said firmly. 'Women will walk into those apartments and fall in love with them at first sight.'

'That's what it takes, is it—good window dressing?'

Jordan grinned. 'OK,' he shrugged, 'you're the interior designer. I'll go with your recommendation and I'll up the budget.'

'Great—'

'On one condition.' He cut across her.

'What?'

'Have dinner with me tonight.'

The invitation took her aback. She looked up into his hazel eyes and all sorts of warning bells rang. 'I can't, Jordan. I'm sorry, but I've far too much on.'

'One evening won't make much difference on the work schedule. And anyway, there are a few things I think we should talk about.'

She had been left unsure as to whether he was asking her out to discuss business or asking her out on a date.

Charlotte freeze-framed the memory now as she lay in bed. She was still unsure about that.

She stared at the ceiling and analysed that invitation. They'd eaten together a few times over the last year, usually business lunches, sometimes with her father, sometimes alone. They'd never ended up naked in bed together the next morning!

Jordan moved in the bed, rolling over onto his side so that he was facing her. For a moment she thought he was waking up and her nerves jangled alarmingly, her heart pumping as if she'd been running on the treadmill at the gym. He settled down and continued to sleep. She noticed how dark his hair was against the white of the pillow, and how the sheets had slipped from his shoulders, revealing a tanned torso that was enticingly muscled. Remembering how tenderly those strong arms had held her last night, she felt her stomach dip in another pang of alarm.

This was terrible. She didn't want to think about what had actually transpired. She was going to have to get out of here, and fast, before he woke up. Because she couldn't face him. The whole thing was mortifyingly embarrassing.

Slipping a foot out of the bed, she sidled across from beneath the covers, trying to ease herself out so as not to create a sound or a draught. She ended up on her hands and knees on his floor and there she crouched for a few moments, trying to get her breath back, casting her eyes frantically around for her clothes.

Even as she was kneeling there she registered the ridiculousness of the situation. She was a thirty-two-year-old businesswoman, for heaven's sake—in fact, thirty-three in a few months' time—and here she was, almost hiding under a man's bed! She needed to be adult about this, she reasoned with herself. People had sex these days and they didn't agonise about it, they just enjoyed it.

But the logical words didn't cut much ice with her. Trouble was, she had never got with the modern programme—had never done the casual-sex bit. She needed to be in love with a man before she slept with him. All right, it was old-fashioned, but that was just how she was. So what had happened to change that last night?

She heard the bed creak as Jordan moved again. Her head shot up as she saw his hand dangling over the side, almost touching the top of her blonde curls. Any moment now he was going to lean over and ask her what she was doing crouching on his floor.

She waited for it, prepared to lie that she was looking for her contact lenses. But she didn't wear contact lenses, and he probably knew that.

Taking a deep breath, she forced herself to stand up. She needn't have worried—he was still asleep, this time sprawled over onto her side of the bed. Not that it was her bed, or her apartment. Darting a look around the room for her clothes, she could only see his shirt on a chair, so she picked it up and held it in front of her. At the same time

Jordan's hand seemed to be searching in the small space beside him, then he opened his eyes.

'Hi.' He smiled at her sleepily, then sat up slightly, his eyes moving over the long length of her legs to the shirt she held in front of her.

She, on the other hand, found her eyes drawn to his chest, which was broad and hairy and brought memories from last night trickling through her consciousness like red-hot lava.

'Are you OK?' he asked huskily.

She transferred her gaze quickly to his face to find his eyes resting on her with a kind of tender concern.

'Of course I'm OK.'

He raked a hand through the thick darkness of his hair. 'It's just…well, I thought you were on the floor for a moment.'

'I always start the day with a good crawl around on the bedroom floor.' She hadn't planned the sarcasm—it just slipped out. 'It helps to tone the body.'

He smiled. 'Your body doesn't need much toning,' he murmured, looking admiringly at the shapely long legs and the curves that were now hidden behind his shirt.

'I was looking for my clothes, actually.' Her voice seemed to have risen two octaves.

'I think you'll find them in the lounge, but what's the hurry?' He glanced at the illuminated numbers on his bed-side clock. 'It's only early.'

How could he be so relaxed? As if this was nothing? Wasn't he even the slightest bit embarrassed? OK, maybe he was used to waking up with different women in the morning, but they had to work together, for heaven's sake!

Before she could reply the telephone on the other side of the bed rang. As he rolled over to answer it Charlotte glanced through the open bedroom door and caught sight of her clothes lying in a heap on the lounge floor. Thank heavens for phones, she thought as she hurriedly launched herself out through the door before he could turn around. Firmly she closed it behind her.

Never had she dressed as quickly in her whole life. Pants, stockings, skirt were all put on with record-breaking speed. Then, just as things were going so well, she couldn't find her bra. She looked along the cream leather settee and lifted a few cushions, but still couldn't find it. Hearing the phone go down in the other room, she gave up and instead threw her blouse on, buttoning it up with scant regard for anything other than the need to escape. Her bag was on the coffee-table, and the only thing hanging up was her coat out on a stand in the hallway. She practically flew to it, then out through the front door. Not waiting for the lifts, she ran down the stairs of the luxury apartment block as if being pursued by the devil himself.

It was only when she was outside in the cool darkness of the early-morning air that she realised she had no car. She had taken a taxi to meet Jordan at the restaurant last night and then they had walked back to his place.

She put her head down as it started to rain and turned towards the nearest underground station.

It was rush hour. Charlotte stood well to the right on an escalator that trundled slowly down into the bowels of the earth; a never-ending stream of people hurried past her, their shoulders brushing against hers, but she was barely aware of them. There was a constant thundering sound as trains sped through the passages below and a warm vortex of air spiralled upwards, blow-drying the rain from her blonde hair. Charlotte felt numb, as if she wasn't really there.

How could she have done that? she kept asking herself. How could she?

A busker stood in one of the tunnels, his voice echoing eerily as he sang about how much love hurt. The sound was accompanied by the silvery clinking of the coins that people threw on the way past. Maybe, like her, they agreed with his sentiment. Charlotte dug deep in her pockets and added her coins to his collection.

She had found out from David just how much love could hurt.

Maybe that was the reason some people…like Jordan…abandoned the idea of love completely and chose to just concentrate on the physical side of things. She had never really agreed with that way of thinking before, but now…now she wasn't sure how she felt about anything. Because buried away in the deepest recess of her mind was the knowledge that last night had been extremely pleasurable.

There was a train waiting on her platform and she raced towards it, just squeezing in before the automatic doors closed. She stood, hemmed in by the sheer volume of people, and grabbed at a handrail to steady herself as the train left the station. Then she closed her eyes and thought again back to last night.

She had insisted on meeting him at the restaurant. Somehow arriving under her own steam had made her feel more in control of the situation. It meant she would be able to leave when she wanted instead of having to wait for him. Charlotte liked to be independent.

They had started off talking about work. Jordan had made her laugh; he had a very dry, very witty sense of humour. She remembered a few women had cast envious eyes over towards their table and she had felt almost proud to be the one who was getting his undivided attention.

She realised now, that should have been her first warning signal.

'So where is your girlfriend tonight?' she had asked him when there was a pause in the conversation.

'Benita and I split up a couple of weeks ago.'

'Oh! I'm sorry.'

He shrugged. 'These things happen—as you know. Have you seen anything of David recently?'

She shook her head. 'I think he's still in the States on business.'

'Do you still have feelings for him?'

The intensely personal question took her aback and she hesitated, not knowing what to say.

'According to your father, he was never right for you.' Jordan filled the gap drily.

'Has my father been discussing my private life with you?' She was instantly annoyed.

'Only in passing.' He shrugged easily. 'You went out with David for a long time, didn't you.'

'Two years. How long were you with Benita?' Swiftly she changed the subject back in his direction.

Jordan frowned. 'I don't know; I'm not one for counting much any more.'

'Any more?'

'When I was married to Nadine I used to count anniversaries, important dates—you know, the usual kind of thing.'

His statement intrigued her. She had heard he had been divorced, but that was all, because Jordan was extremely aloof when it came to talking about his past. Charlotte had assumed, because he seemed such a womaniser, that he had ended the marriage. 'It sounds as if you loved her very much.'

'I did.' His voice was heavy. 'But it didn't do me a lot of good. Sometimes loving someone isn't enough.'

'Well, she was obviously just the wrong person for you.'

He smiled at that. 'You're not going to go all Pollyanna-like on me, are you?'

'No.' She felt herself blushing and he smiled.

'I've enjoyed tonight, Charlie; thank you.'

'I've enjoyed it too.' She was aware that she didn't really want the evening to end.

Jordan took out his wallet to pay the bill and she fumbled for her handbag.

'We'll go Dutch,' she said firmly.

'Dutch?' He stared at her as if she was speaking that language.

'Yes. I like to pay my own way, thank you.'

His lips twisted in a wry curve. 'Well you can pay next time,' he said dismissively, putting his credit card on the silver salver. 'How's that?'

Before she could make a reply to that he had switched the subject. 'Have you heard anything from your father recently?'

'Not since Ruth rang to tell me they wouldn't be coming home from France at the appointed time. Dad must really love it out there because it's not like him to want to take extra time off work. You know what he's like, a complete workaholic.'

'And she didn't say anything else?'

'No. It was a very brief conversation, but then it always is with my stepmother. She's usually in a hurry.' Charlotte frowned. 'Why?'

'I just wondered.' The waiter brought the counterfoil for him to sign. 'You get on all right with Ruth, don't you?' he asked casually as he handed the piece of paper and the pen back.

'Yes. She seems to make Dad happy.' She paused and frowned. 'Everything is all right with Dad, isn't it? You have spoken to him since he's been away?'

'Of course.' Jordan rose smoothly to his feet. 'He is my business partner; he couldn't be away for seven weeks without being in contact.'

He had put his hand at her back as they had walked out

of the restaurant. It had just been a light touch but Charlotte had been extremely conscious of it.

The train jerked to a halt and her eyes flew open. It was her station; she struggled to step out, battling amongst the hordes getting in.

The April rain was cold against her skin as she emerged again onto the streets above. But her mind was still tuned into the night before. They had walked back towards his apartment and he had invited her in for coffee. 'You may as well wait for a taxi in the comfort of my place,' he had said easily.

So she had followed him up to the stylish penthouse apartment. She had never been to his home before, and it had felt different being somewhere with him that wasn't work-related at all. It had made her suddenly self-conscious. And when he had reached to take her coat, she had felt more acutely aware of him than she had ever done.

As he disappeared through to the kitchen to make the coffee she had wandered around the lounge, admiring the décor. 'Who did the interior design to this apartment?' She called out the question to him through the open door.

'I don't know. I wasn't particularly interested in interior designers until I met you.'

She smiled at the compliment. Then noticed a photograph of a little girl, about three years of age, with dark shiny hair and a mischievous grin.

'Who is this?' she asked as Jordan came back through to the lounge.

'That's my daughter, Natasha.'

'I didn't know you had a child! She looks adorable.'

'Yes.' He put the tray of coffee down on the table and then went over towards her. 'She was adorable.' He reached out a hand and took the photograph from her.

'Was?' Charlotte had a cold feeling inside as she heard

the ominous tone in his voice and saw for a moment raw emotion in the darkness of his eyes.

'She died almost two years ago.'

'I'm so sorry, Jordan.'

She watched as he carefully put the photograph back where it had been. And in that instant she wanted to reach out to him, soothe the shadows from his face. Jordan was always so controlled, so confident; she had never seen that rawness of expression on his face before. Instinctively she reached up and touched him, trailing her fingers in a soft caress along the side of his cheek.

He caught her hand in his and then, as their eyes met, the unguarded emotion changed into something else, and he turned the hand to kiss the inside of her wrist. The gesture was totally unexpected and there was something extremely provocative and yet sensitive about it…something that made her insides turn over.

'You look beautiful tonight,' he murmured, and his eyes moved over her body in the softly flattering blue suit. 'But then, you always look beautiful.'

She raised questioning eyes to his. There had always been some kind of turbulent chemistry between them; maybe subconsciously that was why she had always kept a distance from him. Because she knew he spelt danger. But now that feeling of danger was teamed with something else, something much more powerful. She felt it spiralling inside her like a spinning top, whipping around and around in her insides. And she wondered what it would be like to kiss him.

He had reached out and touched her face the way she had his and the touch had been like a spark to a can of petrol because the next thing she remembered she had stood on tiptoe to kiss him.

She had made the first move.

Remembering that made her heart stand still.

After the initial moment of surprise he had kissed her back. And what a kiss that had been! Just thinking about it now made her insides clench with desire again. Jordan Lynch knew exactly the right way to kiss a woman. His lips had travelled over hers with a slow, seductive warmth that had been so deliriously wonderful it had made her toes curl.

As passion exploded quickly out of control, there had been a moment when Jordan had pulled back. 'Are you sure about this?' he had asked seriously.

She had smiled and reached to kiss him again.

Remembering that now made Charlotte's skin burn.

Hurriedly she let herself into her flat and leaned back against the door. She was faced with her familiar, modern, perfectly designed home, but it felt different to her now. It was as if the person who had left here last night was not the same person who had returned. It was as if she didn't know herself any more.

The phone rang on the hall table and her nerves jumped. Would that be Jordan? She didn't answer it and after a few moments the answering machine clicked in.

'Hi, sweetheart, it's David. I hoped I'd catch you before you left for work. Look, I just wanted to tell you again how sorry I am. It was one night, honey, and it didn't mean anything, not compared with my love for you. It was a mistake, a terrible mistake, a moment of insanity. Anyway…' His voice trailed off, became more hopeless than eager. 'I'm flying back to England tomorrow. I'll call you then.'

The earnest, pleading voice touched the far recesses of her mind. Yesterday she wouldn't have understood a moment of insanity, but yesterday she had been a sensible person and now…now she didn't know what the hell she was doing any more.

CHAPTER TWO

His timing was wrong. Jordan knew that, he'd known it last night but he hadn't been able to stop himself. He disliked himself intensely for the weakness. Yet perversely he didn't regret it. Charlotte had been everything he'd dreamed she'd be; passionate, warm…it had been intensely pleasurable. How could he regret that?

He reached for his briefcase and climbed out of his car. When should he tell her? he wondered. Today wouldn't be right, not now. He was grimly aware that he was putting off the inevitable again. Charlotte was going to find out, and sooner rather than later, whether he told her or not. It was better that she heard it directly from him and not through a third party. But not today.

The sky was a heavily leaden grey. It was reflected in the choppy waters of the River Thames and the modern glass building that was the central administrative centre for McCann Developments.

Charlotte's grandfather, George McCann, had started the business years before. He was a builder who had worked his way up from small beginnings to create a successful development firm of good repute. Charlotte's father, Simon, had taken over the running of the place twenty-five years ago and things had ticked along fairly well until they had hit the recession five years ago, leading to dwindling profits and eventually the necessity of taking on Jordan as a partner.

Being the newcomer on the block hadn't been as easy as Jordan had anticipated. But he was a talented architect and an experienced businessman with a nose for a good deal. He'd been here for just over a year and already the profits were up. Along the way he'd had to make a few changes to streamline the running of the place, and he knew that even more changes were necessary if the business was to thrive.

His thoughts went to Simon McCann. He admired him and the business was sound. That was the reason he had invested in it in the first place, but just recently he had noticed a change in Simon. He had become reluctant to look at new designs that were essential for them to keep ahead of the opposition. It was almost as if he had lost his enthusiasm. And it was becoming more apparent that if Jordan was to make any real inroads into the success of the business he would need to have the casting vote.

It was coming to crunch time, when he might be forced to get Simon to sell his share of the business to give him overall control, and he didn't think Charlotte would be too happy about that.

Added to all of that there was the matter of the missing money.

'Morning, Jordan.' His secretary paused to wait for him by the lifts in the front lobby.

'Morning, Laura.' He smiled back at the attractive brunette, but in truth his mind was skipping ahead to his meeting with Charlotte. Wondering how he should play things after last night.

His eyes were drawn to the brass plaque in the lift, with the name McCann Developments. He wondered how Charlotte would feel if the business ceased to be a family affair. Somehow, he thought she wouldn't be too pleased.

Charlotte had started work here six years ago and was in charge of the interior-design side of the business. When Jordan first met her he had found her a bit prickly—had thought that she was probably a spoilt little rich girl who had got a job here purely through nepotism.

In reality he couldn't have been further from the truth. He had discovered she was an exceptionally talented designer who worked extremely hard and had once owned her own successful interior-design business. Her father had persuaded her to join the family company by promising her much bigger and more lucrative projects. As well as designing the interior of their show houses she ran an after-sales service for customers who wanted their homes bringing up to the same high standards. This was proving so successful that they'd had to expand the company's design section.

No, somehow he couldn't see Charlotte being pleased if her father was to leave the business.

As soon as he stepped out onto the top floor of the office he saw that she was already seated at her desk. He'd half wondered if she would be late this morning. Then he smiled to himself. He should have known better. Charlotte was always in her office bright and early, no matter what. She was a dedicated career girl.

He took a moment to study her now. She seemed completely engrossed in the papers in front of her. Her long blonde hair was piled up on top of her head, exposing the creamy length of her neck. As usual she was dressed in a smart, businesslike black trouser suit, with a white blouse open at the neck. She had a great figure—he allowed himself to remember her soft curves and the long, shapely legs and found himself wanting her all over again. Not a good start, he warned himself with annoyance. He was going to have to play this very carefully.

She glanced up and their eyes collided briefly. Only the pallor of her skin and the faint shadows under her green eyes gave away the fact that she wasn't entirely at ease. She gave him a brief smile then returned her attention to her work.

Charlotte cursed herself as she fixed her eyes on her

papers. Maybe she shouldn't have smiled? She had been telling herself all morning that she should just act like normal—but what was normal? She couldn't seem to remember how she usually behaved around Jordan. It was all muddled up in her mind now with memories of red-hot passion last night. Concentrate on work, she told herself fiercely.

At least her designs were taking good shape, she thought, running a critical eye over them. Sometimes it seemed as if she did her best work when she was under duress—maybe because she used work like an escape valve. When she entered her world of interior design she could shut the door on everything and everyone else. Jordan was a bit like that as well; they had remarked long ago that when it came to work they were remarkably similar, both totally dedicated. Which was probably the reason they had worked so well together lately.

Had she jeopardised that last night? Right at this moment Charlotte doubted very much that she could even pretend to be relaxed around him again.

The door of her office opened and she was aware of his dark eyes raking over her even before she glanced up. She held herself very straight, as if she was completely at ease and in control of the situation, and gave him a brief smile. 'Hi, Jordan. You're late—the accountant will be in soon and we have those figures to sort out.' She was pleased at how confident she sounded.

'Of course I'm late.' He put down his briefcase and came around to perch on the edge of her desk.

Couldn't he just use the seat opposite like any other normal person? Charlotte wondered nervously. She felt at enough of a disadvantage this morning without him looming over her like some kind of bird of prey.

'Some feisty young woman kept me very busy last night.' His voice was softly teasing.

She felt her skin glow with vivid colour.

There was a moment's silence, a moment where he waited for her to say something. When she didn't his eyes moved with thorough gentleness over her upturned face, taking in the colour on her high cheekbones, the softness of her lips. 'Why did you rush off like that this morning?' he asked.

She leaned further back in her chair, trying to feign an indifference that she just didn't feel. 'Last night was… pleasant, Jordan—'

'Yes, it was,' Jordan agreed, a wry gleam in his eyes. 'Very pleasant.'

'But we've got to work together and I don't think we should complicate things.'

'Who said anything about complicating things?' Jordan shrugged. 'I'm all for keeping things simple.'

She nodded. 'Of course.' She had never for one moment thought that he would read anything serious into last night. 'Look, I'll be honest with you, I'm feeling a bit awkward.' She tried desperately to hold his gaze but failed miserably and had to look away. 'I'm hoping we can put this…incident behind us and forget about it, go back to the way things used to be.'

Jordan reached out a hand and tipped her chin upwards so that she was forced to meet his eyes. 'Do you feel guilty about last night because you are still in love with David?' He asked the question quietly.

The question and the touch of his hand against her skin brought a very heated response coursing through her veins. 'I don't think that's any of your business, Jordan,' she snapped, pulling away from him.

He shrugged. 'Well, if you are still holding a torch for David, you're making a big mistake. The guy is a loser.'

'And I really don't need your analysis of David, thank

you. You're hardly a model of perfection where women are concerned yourself.'

Jordan smiled at that. 'You weren't complaining last night,' he said teasingly and watched the even brighter flare of colour in her cheeks.

'You see! This is exactly why last night was such a mistake,' she spluttered indignantly. 'I can't have you reminding me about it every two minutes we have to work together.'

'I'm not reminding you about it every two minutes; we were discussing the implications of last night before moving on to the day's work, like a couple of grown-ups—remember?'

'Don't get smart with me, Jordan. There are no implications from last night; it was just two people enjoying a bit of light-hearted fun. So let's just forget about it and move on. OK?'

'Fine with me.' Jordan shrugged.

'Good.' She picked up some papers that were sitting beside her. 'Those are for you; they are the estimates for the soft furnishings.'

'Great, thanks.' His voice was dry. 'I'll look through them and get back to you.'

'Good idea.'

'And I've got something for you.' He opened his briefcase. She thought he was going to pass her some papers that he wanted her to look at. Instead he took out a folded black lacy bra and put it on her desk. 'It was on the floor in the lounge.'

Mortified beyond belief, Charlotte grabbed it and stuck it in the top drawer of her desk. 'What are you thinking of?' she said shakily, glancing around through the glass walls to see if any of her co-workers had noticed. Her office made her feel a bit like she worked in a goldfish bowl—everyone could see what she was doing.

'Well, I was thinking that you might just be missing your bra,' he said with a smile.

'I've got to work here, Jordan! I don't want everyone knowing that I've had a moment's insanity with the boss.'

'Charlotte, they'd have to have bionic vision to see what that tiny scrap of material is,' he said with a shake of his head. 'Relax, for heaven's sake.' Before she realised his intention he reached out and tipped her chin up so that she was forced to meet his eyes.

'And as moments of insanity go it was very, very pleasant,' he murmured huskily, his eyes moving towards her lips.

Then he released her and walked out of her office. Her heart was thumping. She felt sick inside with the knowledge that she had just handled that situation appallingly. Maybe she should just have laughed the whole thing off instead of acting so uptight?

Breathing deeply to release the tension inside, Charlotte tried very hard to think straight. But her mind was a jumbled mess of words and feelings she couldn't get a handle on. In desperation she reached for the phone and dialled her sister's number.

The answering machine came on and she was just about to hang up in complete frustration when Jennifer answered, sounding a bit breathless.

'Oh, hi, sis. Sorry, I was just attending to Matilda here. She won't stop crying.'

In the background Charlotte could hear her four-week-old niece giving full vent to her lungs. 'Sorry, I've obviously caught you at a bad time. I'll ring back later.'

'No, no, it's OK,' Jennifer assured her hastily. 'What's the matter?'

Charlotte smiled to herself. Jennifer was her younger sister by five years but they were very close. 'You know me so well,' she murmured.

'I know that tone in your voice, if that's what you mean.' Jennifer was shushing her baby and Charlotte could hear her picking her up, could imagine the scene as she wedged a phone on one shoulder whilst holding a wriggling infant on the other.

'I don't know what's the matter with me. I'm not coping with anything at the moment, and my emotions are all over the place.'

'Well, I think that's pretty normal given the circumstances with you and David. You have been dating him for a long time; you're bound to be upset. You should have taken time off work—'

'Jen, I did something terrible last night.' She cut across her sister, swiftly needing to unburden herself. 'I slept with Jordan.'

There was a deathly silence at the other end of the phone. Even Matilda had gone quiet.

'Crikey, Charlie!'

'I know!' Charlotte flicked a glance through the glass partition and saw Jordan's secretary laughing with him. He looked incredibly relaxed and for some reason that made Charlotte feel even more on edge. 'I don't know what happened! One moment I was going to have coffee with him and the next we were in bed.'

Jennifer laughed.

'It's not funny.'

'No, but it's not that terrible either! To be honest, I've always secretly thought that Jordan would be perfect for you. Dad thinks so too. In fact he was saying not so long ago how well you two work together now and what a blessing he has you both at the business. And Jordan is so nice and so good-looking—'

'Oh, come on!' Charlotte cut in drily. 'Don't start taking artistic licence. The only thing Dad would say is that

Jordan makes lots of money for the company. Dad is a businessman first and foremost.'

'No, he's not. He's a big softie really, and he'll be pleased you're having a relationship with Jordan.'

'We're not having a relationship—it was sex!'

'Well, a relationship has to start somewhere. Why not in bed? At least you've sampled the goods and found them in working order.' Jennifer giggled. 'I'm so pleased. If nothing else, you needed someone to take your mind off David.'

Jordan had certainly done that, Charlotte thought wryly.

'Listen, why don't the two of you come for Sunday dinner?' Jennifer said excitedly.

'I don't think you've been listening to me, Jen. We're not dating. In fact, we're barely being civil to each other this morning. And besides, you know what he's like where women are concerned—I'll be just another notch on his bedpost.'

'Not necessarily; you could be special.'

'And the world could be flat,' Charlotte drawled. 'Anyway, it's too close for comfort. I've got to work with the guy and I don't want the complications; I've enough problems. I don't know what the hell possessed me.'

'I do—he's gorgeous!' Jennifer giggled again. 'All right, well, you just come for dinner then. I'd better go. Madam here has just been sick down my blouse. See you Sunday.'

'See you Sunday.' Charlotte was speaking to a dead phone line now. She supposed she shouldn't be surprised that Jennifer would be pro-Jordan. She'd been singing his praises since he had joined the company, and her husband, Steve, had got very friendly with him. Even though they lived just outside London in quite a rural area, Jordan was often over at their house. In fact it was through her sister that Charlotte got to hear snippets of information about Jordan's girlfriends.

It was a wonder Jennifer didn't know about the fact he had once had a daughter. But she definitely didn't, otherwise Charlotte would have heard about it. Obviously it was just too painful a subject for Jordan to talk about, which was understandable.

She glanced down at the designs in front of her, but her mind was flicking over Jennifer's words.

I've always secretly thought that Jordan would be perfect for you. Dad thinks so too.

Where had that come from? Jennifer had never said that to her before. And as for her father, he would think anyone was good for her as long as it wasn't David. He really disliked David, and that was before he had heard of their break-up.

But Jen was wrong. Romantically speaking, Jordan wasn't her type. He was too sure of himself, arrogant even. But then she remembered last night and the way he had made her laugh at dinner…the way he had looked so raw when he had spoken of his little girl…the way he had kissed the inside of her wrist… Why had that kiss been so erotic? she wondered. She had never thought of the wrist being an erogenous zone before.

She frowned. All right, maybe last night Jordan had sort of grown on her a bit. But not romantically, definitely not romantically; Jennifer was wrong about that. The sex had been wonderful though.

Charlotte scored a line through the piece of paper in front of her. She had to work with the guy, she told herself fiercely. Remembering things like that wasn't helpful.

She looked over at him again; he was signing something now and he gave Laura a boyish smile that for some reason had a funny effect on Charlotte's loins. He *was* basically a nice man. Obviously he had loved his wife, and his little girl. Whatever was going on in his life now, he'd certainly been through a tough time in the past.

Maybe she should apologise for being a bit sharp this morning. They had both enjoyed last night. She should have acted in a more mature way about it all.

She watched as Laura left his office. He was talking to someone on the phone now. If she was going to apologise, now was probably the time to go over, whilst his secretary was out. She didn't want the whole building knowing that she was Jordan's latest conquest. That would be too humiliating.

Before her courage could desert her she got up and went across to his office. They never knocked on each other's doors, so Charlotte didn't think twice about just walking in on him. He was sitting with his back to her, having swivelled around in his leather chair, and he was still talking on the phone.

'We went out for dinner,' he was saying. 'Then I invited her back to my place for coffee.' He laughed, a deep, husky, teasing kind of laugh. 'OK, what can I say? I'm weak, yeah…that's right, I got sidetracked. Not one of my better moves. But it was very enjoyable.'

Charlotte's blood started to freeze in her veins as she realised he was talking about her.

Her first instinct was to get out of the room before he saw that she was there. She certainly wasn't going to apologise to him now. Hurriedly she started to back away, closing the door behind her with a quiet click. How dared he? she thought as she stormed back to her office. Not one of his better moves, indeed! He could say that again!

She sat back down at her desk and glared at the back of his head through the plate glass. How dared he discuss her like that…and who had he been talking to? She hoped it wasn't someone they worked with—if this got out in the office everyone would be gossiping about her.

She burned with the indignity of it all. She had always been an intensely private person. And she had always prided herself on being in control of her emotions. Now her personal life was being bandied around for all and sundry to know, and she certainly wasn't in control of her emotions because at this moment she really thought she hated Jordan Lynch.

His chair swivelled around suddenly and their eyes locked through the glass. Hers simmered with intense anger, his were coolly unperturbed.

Swiftly she lowered her head and returned her attention to her work. That was it; she would have nothing more to do with Jordan Lynch, she told herself fiercely.

CHAPTER THREE

IT WAS Sunday afternoon, the sky was a clear blue but the breeze that stirred the trees, sending showers of cherry blossom fluttering onto the front lawns, was ice-cold. It felt more like March than the first day of May, Charlotte thought as she pulled up outside the tall Victorian detached house where Jennifer and Steven lived.

She parked her car on the road and walked into the driveway past her sister's people carrier, Steve's convertible and Harriet's bicycle, which had been abandoned at right angles by the front door in a strategically placed booby trap.

Smiling to herself, Charlotte stepped over it and in through the front door, which had been left ajar.

The first thing that hit her was the smell of roast beef wafting through from the kitchen; the second was the discordant sound of Harriet practising her scales on the piano in the lounge.

'Hello,' Charlotte called out. Immediately the playing stopped and her six-year-old niece came flying out, feet thundering on the polished wooden floors, blonde pigtails bouncing as she flung herself at Charlotte like a whirling dervish.

'Auntie Charlie!' she screeched with delight as Charlotte picked her up and whirled her around. 'Guess what…guess what?'

'What?' Charlotte hugged her tight and then put her down.

'Uncle Jordan is here as well.'

'Oh.' The moment of happiness inside Charlotte faded

as she looked up and saw Jordan framed in the kitchen doorway, watching the welcome she had received. Charlotte was used to seeing Jordan dressed in suits but today he was wearing jeans and an open-necked blue shirt. The casual look suited him, made him look younger than his thirty-eight years, and even sexier than usual, if that was possible. She dragged her gaze away from him, annoyed for thinking along those lines.

'Hello, Jordan.' She was aware that her voice was very cool, but she couldn't help it. She had been looking forward to a relaxing dinner with her family, away from her problems, especially the problem of Jordan. 'What are you doing here?' Even as she asked the question she knew the answer.

'Jennifer invited me over for lunch.'

She hoped to high heaven he didn't think she'd put Jen up to it! Jordan Lynch didn't need his ego boosting any further—it was already off the scale.

'That was nice of her.' There was a definite edge to Charlotte's tone now.

He smiled, totally unperturbed. 'Yes, I thought so too.'

Charlotte took off her beige suede jacket and slung it over the end of the banisters. She was going to kill her sister.

'Where is Jen?'

'On the phone, trying to dig Steve out of the golf club. He went for a quick game and apparently should have been home over an hour ago.'

Charlotte smiled. That sounded like Steve. 'I'm surprised you didn't join him.'

Jordan shrugged. 'I had to go into the office today to sort out some paperwork.'

For the first time Charlotte realised just how much extra work Jordan had on his desk with her father staying on in France all this time. 'If you need some help with paper-

work I don't mind giving you a hand,' she offered impul-
sively. 'I know I'm more on the design side than office
management, but I can do both. I did run my own business
once.'

'Yes, I know.' He smiled at her. 'Thanks, I'll bear that
in mind.'

Something about the way he smiled at her made her go
hot inside. Hurriedly she glanced away. Then, catching her
niece's eye, she remembered she had some sweets for her
in her jacket pocket. She took them out and passed them
to the little girl.

'Thanks!' Harriet's eyes lit up. 'These are my favourites.
And look what Uncle Jordan brought.' She raced into the
lounge and came back with a rag doll in one hand and a
teddy in the other. 'This is for me, and this…' she bran-
dished the teddy '…is for Matilda.'

'How lovely.' Charlotte smiled. 'I hope you said a big
thank-you to Uncle Jordan.'

Harriet nodded. 'He's a lovely uncle.' She said the
words with a seriousness that sounded very grown-up for
a six-year-old.

Charlotte laughed and glanced over at Jordan with
amusement.

'It's official, I'm a lovely uncle.' He nodded, humour
also sparkling in his dark eyes. 'Even if it is only an hon-
orary title.'

Maybe he was a bit of a rat when it came to love, but
you couldn't help but like the guy, Charlotte thought.
'Well, it was very kind of you.'

As she made to follow him into the kitchen she noticed
the gleam of male interest that took in her close-fitting
beige leather trousers and cream jumper. It was as if he
could see straight through to the scanty underwear beneath
and, shockingly, it made her body leap in a response that

was purely sexual as she remembered the wild passion they had shared on Thursday night.

Instantly she was annoyed with herself, and annoyed with him for looking at her like that. Would their night together never be forgotten? She had the horrible feeling that it was going to haunt the rest of their working relationship. Remembering the way he had talked about her on the phone, she cringed inwardly. She'd been such a fool.

Matilda was in her carry-cot by the French doors, and, glad of the diversion, Charlotte went across to peep into the lacy crib. She expected the baby to be asleep, she was so quiet, and got quite a surprise when Matilda turned big blue eyes up at her and seemed to smile.

'Hello, darling,' Charlotte cooed and touched one of the tiny hands that rested on the counterpane. 'Hello.'

Jennifer was so lucky, Charlotte thought, so incredibly lucky to have two such gorgeous children.

'Would you like a glass of wine?' Jordan asked from the other end of the kitchen. 'I opened a bottle of Chablis a little while ago.'

'Thanks.' Charlotte glanced down the modern white kitchen. He seemed very much at home here, she thought as she watched him open up the fridge and pour her the wine.

'Won't be a minute, Charlotte,' Jennifer called down the stairs. 'They are sending search parties out to find Steve at the golf club—he's going to be dead meat when he gets home.'

Charlotte laughed. 'Leave him alone, you bully,' she called back.

'No chance. Harriet, I can't hear you practising your scales.'

The little girl pulled a face at her mother's words but

dutifully disappeared back towards the lounge to resume her discordant serenade.

'Married bliss, eh?' Jordan smiled as he brought her drink over and put it down on the table next to her. She almost smiled back at him, and then stopped herself. She really was going to have to keep a cool distance from Jordan. OK, he had notched her up on his bedpost, but he needn't think she was a pushover.

'I hope you don't think that I asked Jen to invite you here today,' she told him bluntly as she sat down. 'Because I didn't.'

'The thought hadn't occurred to me. I'm often here.'

'So I believe.'

He took out one of the wrought-iron chairs from the kitchen table and put it down to sit facing her.

'Can we go back to being friends, Charlie?' he asked quietly.

She noticed how his knees were almost touching hers. Her eyes rested on his hands, which were large and capable-looking. She remembered how they had felt against her body, caressing her to a fever pitch of desire. Remembered how she had writhed and moaned and kissed him with a hunger that she had never known before.

'Charlie?' he prompted.

'Of course,' she replied quickly.

She looked at him and her eyes shimmered intensely green. But had they ever been just friends? she wondered suddenly. She had always been so acutely aware of him, always intensely careful to keep a distance. And with good reason, she realised now.

Charlotte's words didn't convince Jordan. It was as if she had just rolled down steel shutters on herself.

'You could have fooled me,' he said steadily. 'Since our evening together there's an occasional chill coming off you that feels as if it could be rolling in from Antarctica.'

'Is there?' She frowned. 'Well, I'm sorry if that's the case. I really don't want to jeopardise our working relationship.'

She noticed how his lips twisted drily at those words. 'No, neither do I.' He leaned back in his chair. 'We need to stick together, Charlie, because we have a lot of…stuff to get through over the next few weeks.'

'You mean with Dad being away and it being so busy in the office?'

'Sort of…' Jordan hesitated. 'I think you should know that I offered to buy your father's share of the business from him a while ago.'

Instantly Charlotte felt apprehensive. Her father was her only safety barrier between herself and Jordan. And after their night together she needed that protection more than ever.

He watched her reaction carefully as he spoke and saw the concern in her eyes. 'He turned down my offer.'

'Oh…' There was relief in her look now. 'Well, you can't blame him, Jordan. The business has been in our family for two generations.'

'And family is very important to the McCanns.'

'Yes.' She shrugged. 'There's nothing wrong with that, is there?'

'No, and I can understand your sentiments. Obviously you want to take over a share of the running of the company one day, and so you should. You've worked very hard to make the interior-design division a success.'

'Why do I sense that the word "but" is going to creep into this?' Charlotte reached for her glass of wine.

'I don't think your father can afford to turn down my offer,' Jordan said bluntly.

'Why ever not?' She laughed at the absurdity of that remark. 'He's a wealthy man. He can afford to do whatever he likes.'

Jordan looked thoughtful. 'But it isn't only down to money. He has become forgetful and his business judgement isn't as sharp as it has been in the past. I know he lost a lot of money on shares last year and...' He hesitated and lowered his voice. 'I really haven't wanted to tell you this, Charlotte, but I feel I must. The auditors did a spot check and there is a substantial amount of money missing from the company accounts.'

It took a moment for what he was saying to sink in. 'Are you saying my father is stealing from the company?' Her words trembled alarmingly.

'I didn't say that.'

'You might as well have!' She cut across him. 'My father is an honourable man—how can you suggest such a thing?' She glared at him.

'I'm just being honest with you, so there's no point being angry.' Jordan's voice was calm. 'If it makes you feel any better, I think your father is innocent and that Ruth is the culprit. I have a feeling she has taken the money without your father's knowledge.'

'This is preposterous.' Charlotte shook her head. 'Why would Ruth take money from the company?'

'I don't know. But I got a phone call from her last week and she was very agitated. At first I couldn't make out what she was talking about. She was babbling on about the accounts and money but before she could explain she got cut off.'

Charlotte stared at him in distress. And a prickle of unease crept in to disturb her certainty. Her father had only been married to Ruth for two years and Charlotte had worried about the match at first, but her only concern had been their age difference. Her father was nearly sixty; Ruth was forty-six. However, they seemed so ideally happy together that Charlotte had stopped thinking about age as an issue at all. And she had grown extremely fond of Ruth. 'I can't imagine for one moment that Ruth would dip into company funds.'

'Well, I've given the matter serious thought since the phone call,' Jordan said. 'And Ruth used to work in the accounts department, didn't she?'

Charlotte nodded.

'So she knows her way around the systems very well.'

'I still can't believe she would do such a thing,' Charlotte said firmly. 'Apart from anything else, Dad is a wealthy man. She wouldn't need to do it.'

'Well, the money is definitely missing. And, reading between the lines, that's how it looks to me—'

'There must be something more to this, something we don't know.' Charlotte's voice was emphatic.

'Don't you think it speaks volumes that they haven't come back from France?' he asked quietly. 'And since discovering the money has gone, I haven't been able to make contact with them.'

Charlotte had to admit that was a bit odd. Her father was such a workaholic; he loved the office. But she had thought that Ruth was making him take an extra-long break. In fact she had even secretly applauded Ruth for the action, because her father had looked so tired before he left. But now...

'How much money are we talking about?' she asked curiously.

'It's not the amount of money that's the problem, it's the implication. These are serious charges; if they were to be made public the scandal could ruin the good reputation of the business. I'm sorry, Charlie...really I am.' He reached to touch her but she flinched away.

Then, unable to bear his close proximity a moment longer, she got up from her chair to stand with her back to him, staring out of the windows.

'Look, the situation can be salvaged, but it will have to

be done fast. If your father can't afford to pay the money back, then we can come to an agreement. I can afford to pay the debt and in return your father can transfer the equivalent shares in the business over to me, giving me overall control of the company.'

The calm, businesslike words made a wave of anger rise in Charlotte. He had it all sorted out in his mind by the sound of it. 'How convenient for you,' she murmured. 'You've wanted control of the business from the moment you walked in, haven't you?'

'That's not fair, Charlie.'

'But it's true.' She stared sightlessly at the tulips that danced in the breeze at the end of the garden. 'You're ambitious…and you like power.'

When he didn't answer she turned around to look at him. He got up from his chair and came towards her. 'There is nothing wrong with being ambitious,' he said softly. 'You are too, otherwise you wouldn't be so good at your job.'

When she didn't reply he stepped closer. 'You are not so different from me, Charlotte McCann.'

'I think we are very different,' she replied steadily. 'I'm worried about my father. Whilst you are worrying about getting control of the business.'

'I'm worried about the future of the business and that's a different thing. I told you this affects us all and it could be serious.' He looked very cold now and very hard. 'And I'll have to be honest with you, Charlotte. Your father hasn't been his usual self these last six months. And I can't have a business partner that I can't rely on.'

She flinched at that. Jordan Lynch was a businessman first and foremost, she thought. The business side of her could see exactly where he was coming from. But the emotional side, the side that remembered that he had been her father's friend, was having severe difficulty in accepting those words.

'But you will allow time to sort this out, Jordan—if Ruth has taken the money you will give them time to pay it back?'

Jordan didn't answer her straight away and the serious look in his eyes made her heart jump. 'I don't think I can. I need control of the company now.'

She felt sick suddenly.

'And I'll need your help.' Jordan's voice was decisive. 'I can't contact your father on his mobile phone and I don't know exactly where he is in France. You are going to have to help me track him down, perhaps speak to him for me. Because we can't go on like this.'

Charlotte felt her heart thumping against her breast so forcefully that it was painful. 'I'm sure this is all just some terrible mistake,' she murmured brokenly.

Jordan came closer to her. 'But you'll help me to sort it out?'

She hesitated for a second and then nodded.

'Thanks. Try not to worry too much about it.' The softness of his voice and the closeness of his body were sending very conflicting signals through her now. He had been so cold and businesslike when he had spoken about her father, and that made her angry, but weaving its way insidiously through that anger was the memory of how tenderly and passionately he had held her the other night and it made her want to fold into his arms. She despised herself for the momentary weakness and yet perversely the feeling lingered.

There was the sound of footsteps on the stairs and Jordan reached out a hand and took hold of her arm. 'Don't mention any of this to Jennifer,' he told her. 'I know you tell each other everything, but this is one thing you need to keep to yourself. She's just had a baby, and Steve is already a bit worried about her.'

'I know that.' Charlotte frowned. She was well aware of the fact that Jen had enough to cope with. She was just surprised that Jordan had the sensitivity to realise it.

When Jennifer came through the doorway Charlotte could tell instantly that she flew to all the wrong conclusions when she saw them standing so closely together. Her face lit up in a brilliant smile that shone from her gentle blue eyes.

'Hi, sis; did you find Steve eventually?' Charlotte moved hastily away from Jordan and went to kiss her sister on the cheek.

Jennifer and Charlotte were not unalike; they both had the same blonde hair that was inclined to curliness, only Jennifer's was cut in a short style that suited her delicate features. She'd lost a bit of weight, Charlotte noticed, because she was already back in the jeans she had been wearing before becoming pregnant. That wasn't so good. They had to keep an eye on Jennifer because she had suffered from anorexia as a teenager and she was still prone to bouts of worrying about her weight. But they never talked too much about that—she had recovered and they wanted to keep it that way.

'Yes, he's on his way home in a taxi.' Jennifer's eyes darted from her to Jordan speculatively. 'You two seemed very deep in conversation. Everything all right?'

'Oh, yes, fine.' Charlotte lied airily.

'Great.' Jennifer gave a satisfied smile and suddenly Charlotte had the distinct impression that Steve's disappearance to the golf club and her non-appearance for so long had all been an elaborate charade to throw them together. And obviously Jen believed it had worked.

'Right, well, I'll see to dinner. Steve will be here in a minute and he'll be starving.'

'I'll give you a hand,' Charlotte said, following her sister to the other end of the kitchen.

'So how are things at the office?' Jen asked conversationally as she took an enormous roast of beef out of the oven.

'Busy as usual.' Jordan was the one to answer.

'I'm surprised Dad has stayed away so long. I reckon Ruth must be good for him. Usually he'd be frothing at the mouth to get back to his desk.'

Half an hour ago Charlotte would have laughed and agreed. Now her eyes met with Jordan's and she felt the weight of what he had just told her press down on her.

They were saved from having to reply to that because Matilda started to cry.

As Jennifer was busy seeing to the vegetables and Charlotte was making the gravy, Jordan stood up. 'Would you like me to see to her?' he asked.

'If you wouldn't mind?' Jen nodded.

'I'll come through in a minute,' Charlotte told him, wondering if he could cope, but she needn't have worried. When she glanced down the room she saw that he was cradling the child on his shoulder, gently rubbing her back.

'There, there, honey, that's a big noise for a little girl, isn't it?' he murmured.

And this was the same man who had been so cold and businesslike just a few moments ago? Charlotte thought. He seemed so warmly at ease now and he was so good with the baby. Considering Matilda was so tiny and fragile against the large hands that held her, he didn't seem the slightest bit awkward. After a moment she gave a little hiccup and the crying stopped.

'That's better,' Jordan soothed, and went to put her back down again. A few minutes later they could hear him talking to Harriet as she banged away on the keyboard.

'Isn't he wonderful?' Jen grinned at Charlotte.

She wouldn't think he was so wonderful if she knew what he had just been saying about their dad, Charlotte thought grimly. 'I think you can leave the matchmaking bit out, Jen,' she said.

But Jennifer was undeterred. 'Bet you're glad I invited him now, aren't you?' she said smugly. 'I can see how things are between you two. If I'd waited a couple more seconds you'd have been in a passionate clinch. Wait until Dad hears—he'll be thrilled.'

Charlotte wanted to say that it wasn't how it looked, but refrained in case Jen started to question her too deeply. 'Have you heard anything from Dad?' she asked casually instead.

'No. I really miss him, Charlie. I can't even reach him on his cell-phone because it's switched off.' She pulled a face. 'I hate not being able to talk to him; ridiculous, isn't it…?' She trailed off and smiled.

They heard the slam of the front door and Steve's voice shouting that he was home.

'About time too,' Jen called back and then grinned at Charlotte.

'You're not cross with him at all,' Charlotte said, glad that the subject was changed. 'And if you are thinking of starting a career in matchmaking I'd give it a miss, if I were you. You're lousy at it. For the record, Jordan and I are just good friends.'

'That's what I used to say about Steve.'

There wasn't much time to talk after that. Charlotte busied herself assisting with the dinner, glad to have something to help take her mind off her father. But once they were seated at the dining table she started to think about him again. And, delicious as the food was, it seemed to stick in her throat.

She kept remembering other happy occasions when they had sat at this table with her father.

Steve was talking about his engineering business, but Charlotte was thinking that they had been sitting here when their father had announced he was getting married again.

'I've met the woman I want to spend the rest of my life with,' he had announced. It had been such an emotional and happy moment and they had all really wanted this marriage to work out for him.

Jordan had to be wrong about Ruth, he just had to be, she thought fiercely.

As if he could read her thoughts Jordan's eyes locked with hers across the table. He seemed to be watching her very intently.

Suddenly she remembered the way he had questioned her about her father when they were out for dinner. Was that why he had asked her out in the first place? If so, it made what had happened later even more excruciatingly hard to think about without breaking into a cold sweat.

'You're very quiet, Charlie,' Jennifer remarked suddenly.

'Am I?' Conscious of everyone's eyes suddenly on her, Charlotte felt herself colouring guiltily. 'Sorry, I was just relaxing.'

'Charlotte's been working far too hard,' Jordan cut in. 'You're probably tired, aren't you, Charlie.'

'Probably.' Charlotte glared at him; she could speak for herself.

Jennifer shook her head. 'Honestly, sis, you're just like Dad where that business is concerned. I know it's very important to you, but you need to let up—take advantage of the fact you've got Jordan at the helm now and relax a bit.'

Charlotte studiously avoided Jordan's eyes. 'Yes, you're right,' she murmured.

Steve lifted the wine bottle and made to refill her glass.

'Oh, I can't have another drink, Steve, I'm driving.' She hurriedly put her hand over the glass.

'I'll drive you home, Charlotte.' Jordan's voice was firm, making more like a command than an offer.

After a moment's hesitation she lifted her hand. She needed to talk some more to Jordan about the situation anyway, so she might as well let him drop her home, she thought resignedly.

The light was fading outside and Jennifer lit the candles on the table.

'Anyone want coffee?' Steve asked, standing up.

'Not for me, thanks.' Jordan smiled. 'But I'll give you a hand to stack the dishwasher.' He waved away Jennifer's objections as he got to his feet. 'It's the least I can do after such a lovely meal.'

'You OK?' Jennifer asked Charlotte as soon as they were left alone.

'Yes, fine.' Charlotte smiled and then hastily got to her feet. She had to get away before her sister started probing further. Jennifer knew her too well not to realise something was wrong.

'Excuse me a moment,' she said.

Escaping into the downstairs bathroom, she flicked on the overhead light and leaned back against the door. Her reflection stared back at her from three walls, her eyes looked too big for the delicate, heart-shaped face and her skin was very pale. She realised that the shock of what Jordan had told her was only just starting to sink in fully. Splashing her face with cold water, she reapplied her lipstick and tried to gather herself together. There would be a reasonable explanation for why the money was missing from the business, and her father would be fine. But she would like to speak to him before Jordan did. It might be easier.

The best thing she could do now was to make an excuse

and leave before her sister realised something was wrong. Having come to that decision, she felt a bit better.

She could hear voices coming from the kitchen as she walked back out into the hall. Jordan was asking Jennifer if she'd heard from her father recently.

'No. I was saying earlier to Charlotte, I miss him, but at least he must be having a great time.'

'The south of France is very beautiful. I used to live there, you know, and I still have a place not far from St Tropez. As a matter of fact, I was the one who recommended them to that area. I actually offered my villa to Simon, but Ruth said they were just going to do a bit of touring, that she had already booked all the accommodation.'

'Yes, I think Ruth had a fair idea of where she wanted to go. When they were down there late last year she just fell in love with the place.'

Charlotte stood in the doorway and took in the scene. It all looked very cosy. Jordan and Steve were doing the dishes. Jennifer was sitting at the table with Matilda on her knee.

'So where do you think Ruth and your father will have gravitated to?'

The question was asked with expert ease. If she hadn't known better she would have thought that Jordan was just a lovely person making polite conversation. But she did know better, and the white heat of panic flooded through her.

'Well, the last thing Dad said to me was—'

'I'm sorry to break up the party,' Charlotte cut across her sister swiftly, 'but Jordan and I are going to have to leave now.'

They all looked around at her.

'But it's still only early!' Jennifer said.

'I'm sorry, Jen, but I've got work to do before to-morrow.'

'Work again.' Jennifer rolled her eyes. 'It's Sunday evening!' She turned back to Jordan. 'Tell Charlotte she has to have the night off, Jordan,' she said with a smile. 'Remind her who is the boss, for heaven's sake.'

Jordan looked over Jennifer's head and met Charlotte's steady cool gaze. 'I'm the boss—no work tonight, Charlie,' he complied, his voice authoritative. Then he grinned, and lowered his voice huskily. 'What you need is an early night.'

The implied innuendo hung heavily and embarrassingly in the air.

'Oh, I see,' Jennifer giggled. 'You should have said so before! In that case I'll let you two lovebirds go home.'

Charlotte felt angry at how Jordan had turned that around, but somehow she managed to smile tightly. Luckily her sister just seemed to think she was self-conscious.

'Anyway, we won't detain you,' Jen said, standing up and following her out to the hallway as she turned away.

As Charlotte reached for her jacket on the banister Jordan took it from her and helped her into it. The touch of his hands brushing against her body made her temperature rise even more. She wanted to push him away but couldn't because both her sister and Steve were standing watching them.

'Oh, I keep forgetting to tell you, Charlie,' Jennifer said suddenly. 'Steve and I have asked Jordan to be Matilda's godfather and he's agreed. So you'll both be godparents— isn't that lovely? And sort of romantic in a way with you two…getting on so well.'

'Lovely.' Charlotte could hardly find her breath. 'But we're not—'

'Sure what to buy as a christening gift,' Jordan cut in

firmly and the hand that was resting on her shoulder tightened imperceptibly.

'Oh, we've got loads of time to talk about that,' Jennifer said happily. 'It's not until the beginning of June. Hopefully Dad and Ruth will be back by then. You do think they will be, don't you?'

'Oh, yes,' Jordan said briskly. 'It's ages away.'

'It's to be hoped we have loads of time,' Steve said with a grin as he put an arm around his wife. 'We still haven't agreed on a real name for Matilda here.'

'I'd stick with Matilda if I were you. It's kind of grown on me,' Jordan said easily.

'Oh, no.' Steve shook his head. 'Matilda was just a stopgap so we weren't calling her ''the baby'' all the time. She's going to be Estelle, after my mother.'

'I think not.' Jennifer grinned.

Charlotte tried to pull away from Jordan but the hand on her shoulder was too strong.

'Well, thanks again for a lovely dinner.' He smiled and reached to kiss Jennifer on the cheek. Then looked down at the sleeping baby in her arms. 'Whatever you call her, she's a beautiful baby.'

The front door opened, letting in a blast of unseasonably cold night air.

'Goodnight, Steve…Jen.' Charlotte kissed them. 'Thank you for a lovely evening.'

She walked out of the door with Jordan's hand still on her shoulder.

'Bye, Uncle Jordan…bye, Auntie Charlie.' Harriet's small voice drifted to them and they turned to wave to her.

For a moment the family were silhouetted against the warmth of the hall. Then the door closed and they were alone.

CHAPTER FOUR

'WAS that remark really necessary?' Charlotte's voice was as cold as the weather.

'What remark?' Jordan asked with a grin as he moved to walk around to the driver's side of his sports car.

'I'm going to take my own car home,' she said, glaring at him across the machine's roof. 'I didn't touch that glass of wine Steve gave me, so I'm perfectly OK to drive. And I don't think we should talk until I've had time to think about things.'

'Just get in, Charlotte,' he said curtly. 'It's too damn cold for histrionics.'

'Histrionics?' Charlotte wanted to throw something at him. She had never felt a need to vent her anger physically before but it was boiling up inside her now.

He unlocked his car and got in and she was left standing on the pavement with enough heat coming off her to roast the night air.

The engine of the car started with a powerful purr, then the electric window wound down. 'Are you going to stand there freezing, or are you getting in? Harriet is watching you from an upstairs window.'

Charlotte glanced around and saw the little girl framed in her bedroom window. She was still waving. Charlotte waved back and then, gritting her teeth, got into the car.

It was already warm inside and it smelt of leather and Jordan's cologne, a strange, clean, cool kind of mixture that for some reason made her feel even more on edge.

As soon as her seat belt clicked into place he pulled out into the road.

'Are you going to tell me why there is steam coming out of your ears?' he enquired with maddening equanimity.

'I think you are a bit of a charlatan.' She glared across at him. 'You told me not to worry Jen with this business about Dad, and then I hear you quizzing her in the kitchen.'

'I wasn't quizzing her.'

'You could have fooled me,' she said derisively. 'Heard anything from your father yet, Jen?' She mimicked his friendly, bantering question. 'Know where he is so I can send the fraud squad around? Very friendly.'

He flicked an amused glance over at her. 'I was just making conversation.'

'You should have been a politician, Jordan Lynch,' she muttered. 'They are good at kissing babies and pretending to have a heart too.'

'Have you quite finished?'

'And you were filling Jen's head full of nonsense about us,' she continued heatedly. 'That was an outrageously suggestive remark about us having an early night, totally over the top.'

'It got us out of there, didn't it? And as excuses go I thought it was quite believable,' he said with a grin and glanced over at her. 'Well, it's not as if we haven't spent the night together before, is it?'

'Will you just forget about that?' She glared at him. 'That was a mistake.'

'Lighten up, Charlie; we both enjoyed the other night and you know it.'

The light-hearted arrogance fuelled the temper inside her even further. 'Let me tell you,' she blustered, 'I'd rather sleep with…with…with the devil himself than sleep with you again. I wouldn't want you to touch me.'

Jordan glanced over at her with a wry expression in his eyes, but he said nothing.

As soon as Charlotte made that remark she knew she had just gone a step too far. The rage that had suddenly gripped her was now fading as fast as it had appeared. And she realised that a lot of what was wrong with her was shock. She was upset about her father, and she was angry at Jordan's arrogant attitude.

But she should never have made that last remark. It had been downright insulting. She opened up her mouth to apologise but the words just wouldn't come out.

Silence stretched and deepened and she felt even more uncomfortable.

She looked over at Jordan. His features seemed closed and very formidable in the half-light of the car. She wondered what he was thinking.

Probably that he wouldn't take a gold clock and sleep with her again either. At least he was gentlemanly enough not to say it.

She looked away from him again. They were in her road now and he was slowing down as they came to her apartment block. Charlotte searched for something to say, something that would lighten things between them again. After all, she had to face him at work tomorrow.

'Look, Jordan, you can't blame me for being upset. You have cast terrible aspersions on my father's character tonight—'

'I believe I said more about Ruth than your father,' Jordan cut across her calmly. 'I know you are angry, and worried about things. But just for the record I am not the villain of this piece. I'm the victim,' he said quietly.

She glanced over at him with a frown. Try as she did it was very hard to see Jordan Lynch in the role of victim: he was too self-assured, too arrogantly cool. And he did stand to come out of the whole sorry mess smelling of roses. He wanted control of her father's company and he was probably going to get what he wanted.

She looked away from him again back at her hands. That didn't mean what her father or Ruth had done—if indeed they had done anything, she reminded herself fiercely—was right.

'I realise I was probably out of order with the remarks I made about you being a charlatan,' she conceded in a low tone.

'Not probably, you *were* out of order.'

'Sorry.' She muttered the word almost under her breath.

'What did you say?'

'I think you heard me.' She glanced over at him sharply. 'I'm sorry, OK?'

'You don't like admitting that you're wrong, do you?' he said with sudden amusement.

She took a deep breath. 'Look, this might all be very amusing to you—'

'I can assure you I'm not that amused,' he cut across her heavily. 'Not with the position my company is in.'

'Oh, so it's *your* company already, is it?'

He pulled the car to a standstill. 'We will have to wait and see about that.'

'Yes, we'll have to wait and see.' Trying to make a dignified exit, she reached for the door handle. 'Thank you for the lift home,' she said with stiff politeness.

She got out of the car and headed for the front door, thinking he'd just drive away. But disconcertingly he turned off the engine and also got out of the car, following her towards her front door.

'We shouldn't argue,' he said gently. 'It's not going to solve anything.'

He watched the way her hand shook as she tried to put the key into her front door and then reached to take it from her. The touch of his hand against hers made her shiver deep inside. But it wasn't with anger—this was an emotion totally at the other end of the scale. She stepped away from him sharply. How could she feel passion for him after the words that had just passed between them?

Not only had he made love to her the other night and then bragged about it to someone at the other end of a phone, but he was also ruthlessly going to pursue her father for his shares. This was not a man to fantasise over.

If Jordan noticed how quickly she moved away from his touch, he said nothing. He simply pushed open the door and stood back to allow her to enter first.

He glanced around the apartment as he stepped inside, noting the beauty of the décor. Unlike his flat, which had a minimalist style, this was warm and feminine; there was a clever use of colour and lots of books and flowers.

'My father isn't hiding here,' she told him. 'If that's why you've come inside with me.'

'I never for one moment thought that he was.' Jordan took his coat off and threw it over a chair. 'After Ruth phoned me I checked and found the call was international.'

'I'll just call you Inspector Clouseau, shall I?' She couldn't help the sarcastic remark.

'If it makes you feel better, call me anything you like.' His voice was equally sardonic.

She watched as he walked into the lounge. 'Nice flowers,' he commented as his eyes lit on the crystal vase of red roses.

They had arrived from David the day before; absurdly, her first thought had been that Jordan had sent them…now, how crazy was that? Not quite as crazy as the pang of disappointment when she had discovered they were from David.

OK, David had cheated on her, but he suddenly seemed like a pretty safe alternative to the man roaming around her apartment.

'Are you going to make a coffee?' Jordan asked her

suddenly. 'Or are you going to just hover there looking nervous all night?'

'I'm not nervous!'

'Good.' He smiled at her. It was a particularly warm smile and it made little flutters of apprehension turn in her stomach. 'Black, no sugar.'

She turned away and went through to the kitchen. 'Man's a damn nightmare,' she muttered to herself.

'You know, talking to yourself is the first sign of madness,' Jordan called through from the other room.

She banged the coffee jar down from a cupboard. He could have instant and like it, she thought. Why had he come inside with her anyway?

She suddenly remembered the other night and how he'd been the one in the kitchen making coffee and she had been wandering around his lounge. More memories followed...how he'd kissed her and the heat of their passion had totally blown her away.

She remembered how she hadn't been able to get enough of him, how she had welcomed the feeling of his hands slipping beneath her blouse, unfastening her bra, finding the warmth of her skin and teasing and caressing her into complete arousal.

Her hand slipped as she picked up a china cup and it smashed on the floor.

'Need some help?'

Jordan's voice close behind her in the small confines of her kitchen made her nerves scream. 'No! I can manage, thank you.'

She bent down to pick the pieces up and promptly cut her wrist on a jagged edge. It was surprisingly deep and blood oozed from the gash.

Jordan was beside her in an instant. 'You need to bathe that,' he said, turning to run the tap on the kitchen sink.

She didn't protest as he put her hand under the running water.

'Have you got some antiseptic and a plaster?'

'Yes, there's a first-aid kit in the top cupboard.' She nodded towards the place she meant, and watched as he went straight to the box.

'I'll manage now, thanks,' she said as he took out the antiseptic and cotton wool.

'Don't be silly, it's your right hand. I'll do it for you.' Without waiting for her approval, he soaked the cotton wool in the antiseptic and then, taking her hand, dabbed it gently across the wound. It stung, and she winced and tried to pull away from him.

'Hold still,' he rebuked. 'It's a deep cut and it needs cleaning.'

Gently and thoroughly he rinsed the wound again before applying more antiseptic.

The stinging was fading but what was really bothering her now was this close contact. The touch of his hand against her skin was too familiar; it was making her feel hot and awkward.

'I'll take over now.' She tried to pull away from him but he wouldn't let her.

'Don't be such a baby. Just hold still,' he said firmly.

Charlotte glared at the top of his dark hair. This was pure, unmitigated torture. She felt clumsy and stupid…no, more than that, completely idiotic, because the way he was holding her wrist now made her remember how he had kissed it the other night, sending a flame of fire shooting straight through her heart.

She was fidgeting from foot to foot now, willing him to release her. It seemed an eternity before he finally stuck a plaster over the wound.

'You are such a baby.' He smiled up at her, his dark hazel eyes warmly teasing. She remembered how he had called her 'baby' when they were making love, but then it had been a husky endearment whispered close against her ear, as he took full possession of her body.

The memory made her feel as though someone had scalded her, and as he loosened his hold she wrenched away from him.

'Thanks,' she muttered. Self-consciously, she couldn't look him in the eye, but pretended to be examining the plaster.

'You're welcome.' His voice was sardonic. 'I wasn't going to eat you for supper, you know. There's no need to be so nervous.'

'I'm not nervous!' It was the second time she had said that to him tonight, and it was a downright lie. 'I'll make you that coffee.' She turned away from him and got another cup down from the cupboard.

Behind her she was aware of Jordan clearing up the broken crockery. She wanted to tell him to leave it, the kitchen was too small for them to be in together, but then so was the lounge—so was the whole damn apartment. If he were at the other end of a football pitch it would be too close for comfort.

As she turned to get milk from the fridge she almost walked into him. Awkwardly she sidestepped him. She'd never felt so acutely conscious of a man before. It was as if she had suddenly regressed to being a very young teenager again, hormones racing out of all control.

As she turned back to the coffee she found him barring her way. 'Are we going to call a truce, Charlotte?'

'A truce?' She looked up at him uncertainly.

'Well, we can't go on like this, can we?'

'I don't know what you mean.'

'I think you do.' He took the milk from her and put it down on the counter behind him.

'I'm sorry about what's happened, OK?'

Which particular thing was he sorry about? she wondered. Notching her up on his bedpost or accusing her stepmother of fraud?

She tried to step past him but he wouldn't let her. He put one hand behind her, resting on the fridge, so that she felt hemmed in.

She looked up into his eyes. It wasn't that he was too big for this kitchen: he was too big for her life.

'So are we going to work together to sort out this problem with your father?'

'I already told you I'd help you.'

'So why did you object so much to my questioning Jen?'

'There was no point to it and I was upset.'

'So are we on the same side in this business with your father, Charlie? I need to know.' He took hold of her chin, forcing her to look at him.

The touch of his hand made her tremble inside. She flinched away from him.

'Sorry.' He dropped his hand. 'I forgot that you don't like me to touch you.' The humour had a dry edge to it.

She looked up and met his eyes and tried to concentrate on her father, not that last remark. 'I find it hard to believe that Dad or Ruth would have taken that money. But if they have…I definitely don't think it's right.' She hesitated and her voice lowered. 'But he's still my father, Jordan. No matter what he's done, I still love him.' Her eyes pleaded with him to understand. 'So I can't be on your side. Unless…'

'Unless what?'

'You allow him some extra time to pay back the money that's missing.'

He dropped his hands.

'Please, Jordan.' Her voice was soft.

He looked deep into her green eyes; they looked wide and innocent, gently vulnerable. With a sigh he raked a hand through the darkness of his hair. 'All right…just for you.' The words lingered softly between them. 'But only an extra few days, OK? Don't be thinking I'm a pushover because I'm not.'

'OK.' She smiled at him. There was no way she would ever think Jordan Lynch was a pushover.

It was the first real smile she had given him all evening, Jordan thought. And it had probably just cost him dearly, because he did want control of the business and it needed to be sorted out sooner rather than later.

His eyes lingered for a moment on the softness of her lips, then moved down over the V-neck jumper she was wearing, its silky lines clinging to her curves. He wanted to take her into his arms, make love to her again; the need burnt inside and he could feel his body gearing up for it.

The phone in the lounge rang and it seemed to release them both from the sudden trance that had held them.

'I…I'd better get that.'

After quite a few bleeps, the answering machine cut in. 'Hi, Charlie, it's David again.'

The deep voice drifted clearly through to them. 'I hope you liked the flowers.'

Charlotte started to move hurriedly through to the lounge to pick up the receiver so that Jordan couldn't listen to this.

'Please forgive me and have dinner with me. We need to talk.'

He'd hung up before she got to the phone.

'Didn't give you much chance to answer, did he?' Jordan said drily from behind her.

'He probably didn't expect me to be in.'

'Maybe he's just a wimp and it's easier talking to the machine.' Jordan gave her a wry look. 'He sounded very contrite. What is he apologising for?'

'I don't want to talk about David if you don't mind.'

She moved past him back into the kitchen and brought their coffees through. When she returned he was looking at the answering machine. 'You've got six messages on here.'

'Have I?' She handed him his coffee.

'Maybe you should listen to them. There might be one from your father.'

'I'll listen to them later.'

'Why?'

'Because there might be something personal on there.'

'You can fast-forward the personal stuff.'

He was looking at her with the light of challenge in his eyes. 'I'm only interested in where your father is so we can talk to him. I thought we had an agreement, Charlie.'

She glared at him and then with a sigh pushed the play button on the machine.

'Hi, darling, it's me—' She snapped David's voice off very quickly. The tape wound on to the next call.

'It was a one-night stand! I love you—' David again. She snapped the tape off, feeling herself going red with embarrassment. The third one couldn't be David again, surely? Gingerly she pressed the play button once more.

'I know when we talked about marriage once…' She was in such a frantic scrabble to turn that particular piece of conversation off that she missed the button and it played too long. 'We could still make a go of things; I've had a change of—' The machine snapped off.

'That was just getting interesting,' Jordan said wryly. 'What do you think he's had a change of? Underpants?'

Charlotte glared at him. 'My telephone conversations are none of your business and I'm not playing this game any more.'

'You've only got a few more to go, and we know the last one is David again. They can't all be him. Surely he's fed up talking to a machine by now?'

Charlotte wasn't too sure. Her hand hovered over the machine. This was like playing Russian roulette.

Taking a deep breath, she pressed 'play' again. This time it was Ruth's voice that filled the room. 'Charlie, are you there?' There was a pause while she waited to see if the phone would be lifted. 'Charlie, I'm in desperate trouble…' Her voice cracked slightly as she continued. 'I borrowed some money from the business account. It's not what it seems but I'll explain that later. It was only supposed to be a temporary measure but things have gone horribly wrong and I don't know what to do. Can you come over here immediately because I really need your help? Take the address down. I'm in Port Grimaud…' Charlotte sprang up to scribble the address on the pad next to the phone. 'See you soon, I hope.' The phone went dead.

Tears sprang to Charlotte's eyes. So it was Ruth! Even now she couldn't believe it. She was so upset that she didn't turn the machine off and it went on to play the next message. It was David again. 'Charlotte, ring me immediately.'

Charlotte switched him off in full flow. She had more to worry about than David.

'That guy is a prat,' Jordan said in disgust.

Charlotte made no reply. She kept her head down so that Jordan couldn't see the tears in her eyes.

'Are you OK?' he asked softly.

She nodded, but still didn't look up. 'I just hated hearing Ruth so upset. Whatever possessed her to do it?'

Jordan made no reply. Then, all of a sudden, he put his coffee down on the table and reached for the phone.

'What are you doing?' Her head jerked up, her eyes wide. 'Jordan, what are you doing?'

Her heart started to thump in fear as he began to dial. 'You're not phoning the police, are you? I thought we had a deal! Please, Jordan! Don't!' She reached out to him, catching hold of his arm. 'I'll do anything…but please don't get the police.'

His eyes locked with hers. 'Anything?'

Her eyes were wide with anguish.

'Anything?' He shook his head and for a second his eyes moved over the sweetness of her curves. 'Let's see…' He reached out and touched the side of her face in a butterfly-soft caress. And despite everything she felt desire stir quite forcefully to life inside her.

'Pity I'm not really your type though. What was it you said—you'd rather make love with the devil than make love with me again?' he said laconically.

She felt her face flare with colour.

Then he pulled away from her as whoever was at the other end of the line answered. 'Hi, yes, I'm ringing to see when I can get two seats on the first available flight to Nice.'

Charlotte felt her skin colour change dramatically as the full horror of her mistake dawned on her. He hadn't been ringing the police at all.

'Tomorrow afternoon is fine,' Jordan continued calmly.

Why hadn't he just answered her when she'd questioned him? She wanted to curl up and die of embarrassment. She had thought that waking up in his bed had been mortifying but this…this was almost worse.

Jordan watched her as he spoke, noted the scalded colour of her cheeks.

'Yes, Jordan Lynch, Charlotte McCann.' He reached into his back pocket and brought out a wallet to find his credit card.

'Yes, OK, thanks.' The phone went down again. And there was the most awkward silence Charlotte had ever lived through.

'I thought you were ringing the police,' she said numbly.

'So I gathered.' His lips twisted in dry humour. 'I almost wish I had been now. That was a very interesting offer—tempting too.' His eyes flicked down over her body again and she felt them as if they were physically touching her. 'Trouble is, I like my women a little more willing. It would take the edge off things, knowing it was just payment in kind…so to speak.'

She averted her eyes from him awkwardly. 'Very funny, Jordan,' she said angrily. 'And when I said anything…I didn't mean *that*.'

'Really? Sounded like you meant *that* to me. Perhaps I could take a rain check and think about the idea,' he murmured, coming closer towards her.

He reached out, tipping her chin up and forcing her to look at him again. 'And for now I'll just take a kiss on account,' he said huskily.

She didn't say anything, just continued to stare up at him, her heart thumping so heavily against her chest she was sure he could hear it.

Jordan lowered his head and his mouth found hers. The kiss was gently persuasive and it made her insides turn to fire. His thumb stroked along the side of her jaw, holding her face up towards his, but he had no need to hold her still. When the kiss deepened she kissed him back hungrily, meeting the pressure of his lips with a desire that was raw with need. In those few minutes she forgot everything apart from the thrill of being in his arms.

He pulled back from her, his eyes raking over her upturned face, noting the softness of her lips, the dazed expression in her misty eyes.

'Not bad for a woman who said she didn't want me to touch her again,' he murmured. 'Can we leave my credit account open…because I'm going to have to leave now?'

She didn't answer him. Maybe this was funny to him, but she couldn't laugh. Her emotions were all over the place.

He turned away from her and picked up his coat from the chair. 'You had better throw a few things into a bag for tomorrow. We'll leave for the airport straight from the office. That way at least we'll get a chance to organise things at work before we go.'

How could he talk so coolly about work after the emotions that had just ricocheted through them? Charlotte wondered fiercely. But she already knew the answer: he could switch his mind to work because he hadn't felt the same depth of desire. Lovemaking was just a game to him. All Jordan really cared about was getting her father's business.

The front door closed quietly behind him and she pressed her hand against her lips. They felt as if they were still throbbing and her body was alive with an aching need for him to come back and finish what he'd started. It was mortifying that a man who felt so little for her could turn her on so much.

CHAPTER FIVE

'How come you're suddenly rushing off to the south of France?' Frank looked at the overnight case that was sitting by her office door.

'There's some land ripe for development that Jordan wants to look at.' The lie tripped off her tongue: this was the second time she had issued it this morning and it was getting easier. 'Also, there are some documents I need Dad to look at.'

Jennifer had laughed when she had told her this. 'I've heard everything now, sis,' she had said. 'But you can't kid me. You're off on a romantic few days to the sun.'

Charlotte had pretended to laugh as well, glad that her sister had no inkling of what was going on.

Her assistant, Frank, wasn't laughing though. He just looked concerned. 'The business isn't going under, is it?' he asked abruptly.

'Going under?' Charlotte stopped what she was doing and looked up at him. 'No! Whatever makes you think that?'

Frank Simmons, a good-looking man in his late twenties, shrugged and looked slightly uncomfortable. 'There have been rumours flying around because of your father failing to come back to work.'

'Have there?' Charlotte was genuinely surprised. She hadn't heard any rumours, but then she spent the majority of her time either buried in here under a weight of paper or downstairs in the workshop.

'Well, tell everyone that the business is perfectly OK.

Dad is just taking a well-earned rest. He deserves it, you know.'

Frank nodded and put some papers down on her desk. 'You had better take these with you. It's the spec for the new apartments over in Richmond; there's an artist's impression of the building and the measurements for the interior. You need to get in contact with the suppliers as well—I said you'd phone tomorrow because—'

'Yes, OK. I'll take all this with me and phone them from my mobile.'

So much for Jen's impression that she was going to have a few days' rest, she thought as she put the paperwork on the growing pile beside her ready to go into her briefcase. She was taking enough work to last a week: hopefully they would return tomorrow, but there was no knowing for sure when they would be back.

Charlotte glanced across towards Jordan's office. She had dreaded facing him this morning but they had both been so busy that it had been all right. There had been a few moments first thing when he had come into her office and her blood pressure had risen dramatically but he had been completely laid-back, as if the phone call from Ruth had never taken place—or the kiss that followed.

'The official line is that we are going to France to look at some land and to get your father to sign some papers, OK?' he had said easily as he put some memos down on her desk.

'Fine.'

He had turned to leave the office almost immediately and she had been the one to detain him. 'Jordan, should I get Frank to sort us out a hotel?'

'No need,' he had said, closing the door behind him.

Why wouldn't he let her get a hotel? she wondered now. They were definitely going to need one. By her reckoning the flight would land in Nice about five-thirty local time, and it was another few hours down to Port Grimaud. As they had no return flight booked, it surely would be to-morrow at the earliest before they were able to come back.

Suddenly she remembered something Jordan had said to Jen about owning a piece of property over there. Was he thinking that they could stay there? Charlotte wasn't so sure she liked the thought of that. A hotel would be better, less intimate than them being alone together in some apart-ment.

'I'll be back as soon as possible,' she told Frank, drag-ging her attention from Jordan. 'Will you be able to deal with things in here?'

'Of course,' Frank said easily. 'Oh, and by the way, Ruth was on the phone earlier. You were on the other line so I asked if she could leave a message or phone back.'

'What did she say?' Charlotte asked, instantly alert.

'She said she'd phone back.'

Charlotte stared at him in complete frustration. 'Did she at least leave a new number that I could contact her on?'

Frank shook his head.

'Well, if she rings again, I want you to give her priority. Put her straight through to me.'

'Fine! Don't worry,' he drawled with a grin.

'No, I mean it, Frank. It's important.' She stared at him earnestly.

'I'll put her straight through.' He held up his hands. 'Promise.'

'Thanks.' She took a deep breath.

'You need a break, Charlie,' he said, shaking his head as he went out of the door. 'You're working too hard.'

A good night's sleep would do, Charlotte thought grimly. She had hardly slept a wink last night, her mind had been so filled with worries about Ruth and her father, and disturbing thoughts of Jordan.

The strange thing was that the one person who had been

missing from her thoughts recently was David—the person that, up to a few short weeks ago, she had thought she was going to spend the rest of her life with. Life could be very unexpected sometimes.

As the plane levelled out Charlotte started to relax. She hated take-offs: in fact her heart had been pumping in her chest almost as hard as when Jordan had kissed her. Immediately the thought crossed her mind she wished it hadn't. She was trying to forget Jordan's kisses.

Charlotte glanced sideways at him. He was reading a business report, had been immersed in it from the moment they had got into the taxi outside the office until now. Her eyes moved over the lightweight grey suit he was wearing—it was very classy, and looked just right teamed with his silver-blue shirt. In fact, he looked altogether too attractive for her peace of mind.

The air stewardess obviously thought so too. She smiled very provocatively at Jordan as she came down the aisle with the drinks trolley.

'Drinks from the bar, sir?'

Jordan looked over at Charlotte and she weakened to a glass of wine. Jordan just had a cola.

'Do you ever drink alcohol?' she asked him before he returned his attention to his report.

'Occasionally, but never when I drive.'

Now she came to think about it, she had hardly ever seen him with a glass of alcohol in his hand. Even when they'd had dinner together he'd had a soft drink.

The pilot interrupted their conversation to tell them what altitude they were flying at and that the weather in Nice was a favourable twenty-eight degrees.

'Not a bad temperature for this time of the year,' Jordan remarked.

'Better than London, that's for sure.' Suddenly Charlotte

found herself wishing that Jen had been right in her assumptions and that this was just a romantic pleasure trip, just her and Jordan and nothing else to worry about. The thought seemed like heaven.

She was obviously going mad, she thought sardonically. Maybe Frank was right and she was more in need of a holiday than she'd thought. Having a romantic liaison with Jordan would be asking for trouble. And she was still fretting about the way he had wound her up with that telephone call last night.

She glanced over at him again. Trouble was, it was hard to stay cross with him for very long. He was giving her father more time and he was reasonable enough to want to come out here and speak to him face to face. He didn't have to do that. Especially as they were so busy in the office.

Was he going to spend the whole flight with his head in that report? she wondered. She should be pleased—at least when he was working he wasn't teasing her unmercifully, something he seemed exceptionally good at. How was it that Jordan Lynch was such an enigma to her? She felt she couldn't really get a handle on knowing him. OK, they had slept together, but she still didn't really know him, not properly. The fact made her uncomfortable.

She had known David for ages before she had slept with him. They had met at a business fair on interior design and had struck up a friendship. But it was only within the last two years that their relationship had become intimate. At one time, if someone had asked her to sum David up in three words she would have said solid, dependable and level-headed. But if he had been any of those things he wouldn't have jumped into bed with one of her best friends. She switched her mind abruptly away from that.

'So why didn't you let me ask Frank to book us into a hotel for tonight?' she asked Jordan.

'Because we may as well stay at my place; it's just across the bay from Port Grimaud.' He hardly glanced up from his paperwork.

'Wouldn't a hotel be better?'

'Why?'

She had his attention now.

'Well, for one thing it would be less trouble for one night. No making up beds.' Deliberately she used the plural. She didn't want him getting any wrong ideas after last night's little fiasco.

His eyes roved over her face. He looked amused for a second and she could feel herself growing warm. 'Don't worry; you won't have to make up any *beds*. I have an arrangement with a woman who comes in and sees to all of that for me.'

She watched him as he returned his attention to his papers.

There was a few minutes' silence between them. Charlotte fidgeted in her seat and looked out of the window. She told herself that she should get some of her own work done. But her mind wouldn't settle. She didn't want to work, she wanted to talk to Jordan. 'So how come you own a place over in France anyway?' she asked, finally giving in to her curiosity.

'My ex-wife is French. After the divorce Nadine got our house in Paris and I got the place in the south, which was our holiday home.'

'Did you argue about who was keeping what?' She didn't know why she asked that, or why she was so curious about his past life.

He put down his papers. 'No, we didn't argue at all. It was remarkably civil. And neither of us wanted the holiday home...in fact, I haven't been out here since the divorce just over a year ago.'

'A year is a long time to have a property and not use it.'

'I suppose it is.' He was reading his papers again and she had the distinct impression he really didn't want to talk about this any further.

But Charlotte wanted to ask him more. It was only the memory of that picture of his little girl that stopped her. She knew Jordan didn't like to talk about the past; maybe some things were just too painful to talk about, especially on a plane at thirty-two thousand feet when he was trying to concentrate on work.

'I'm really worried about Ruth,' she told him, switching the subject. 'She phoned me again this morning, at the office this time.'

'What did she say?' He looked over at her with a frown.

'I never got to speak to her. I was on the other line to the fabric warehouse at the time and Frank didn't realise it was important. She said she'd ring back. I tried Dad's mobile again but it's still switched off. Maybe it's just as well because if he had answered I wouldn't have known what to say.' She sighed. 'I wish Ruth had been more forthright with her explanations.'

'Well, we'll find out soon enough what it's all about.'

'Yes.' The words made her apprehension about the situation increase. She took a sip of her wine and looked out of the window at the clear blue sky.

Charlotte wondered how this whole sorry mess was going to affect her father's marriage. She hated to think of him being in such a vulnerable position; he'd always been so strong, so kind and wise. Well, she was just going to have to be there for him now and help him through whatever mess needed to be cleared up.

She remembered suddenly how he had drawn her to one side, before he had made Jennifer the wedding gift of her house. 'I want you to know, Charlie that the business will be yours one day,' he had said gently. 'Just in case you are thinking that these gifts are a bit one-sided.'

She had told him she didn't want or expect anything from him, that she was quite happy with the way things were.

'Yes, but my hopes for the future of the business rest with you,' he had said solemnly.

The words rang in her head.

She had really meant it when she had told her father she didn't expect anything from him. And she still didn't; she was well able to stand on her own.

'I hope this won't be the end of Dad and Ruth's marriage.' She blurted out her fears, unable to keep them to herself a moment longer.

'I hope not.' Jordan paused before asking cautiously, 'How did you feel about your father marrying Ruth?'

She looked at him with some surprise. 'I was delighted. Both Jennifer and I felt so happy for him. He deserved to find happiness after all he'd been through. And he had been on his own for so long.'

His eyes were gentle on her face. 'What happened to your mother?' he asked.

'She died of cancer when I was sixteen.'

She looked away from him out of the window so that he couldn't see the emotion in her eyes.

Jordan's hand covered hers on the seat rest between them; the warm touch made her heart miss a beat.

'Do you know there is a rumour going around the office that we are in trouble and might be folding?' She tried to change the subject.

'Yes, I heard. I've just been waiting to sort things out with your father before I scotch it,' he said gently. 'It's because he's stayed away for so long. People aren't stupid; they know Simon lives, eats and breathes the company. So they know something is up.'

The seatbelt sign came on and the pilot told them they were about to make their final descent into Nice Airport. Jordan released her hand to pack up his papers and fold away the tables in front of them.

'Don't worry any more, Charlotte,' he said. 'We'll sort things out together.'

Charlotte could feel her stomach dipping as the altitude dropped...or was that simply caused by the gentle way Jordan had spoken?

It was hot as they walked out of the terminal and Charlotte wished she'd had time to change out of her black business suit before travelling. It felt very inappropriate for this climate. She took off her jacket and pushed up the sleeves of her white blouse as she stood waiting for Jordan, who was talking to the car-hire people. Then she searched in her handbag and found a tie for her hair so that she could pull it up off the back of her neck.

'Feeling the heat?' Jordan asked with a grin as he strolled back over to her and noted the change of hairstyle and attire.

'I should have worn something cooler. It's hard to believe it can be so much warmer after such a short flight,' she said.

'You'll feel better when we get in the car and I turn on the air-conditioning.' He picked up her bag and her briefcase.

'It's OK, I can manage those,' she said. But he was already striding ahead with them.

They located their hire car and Jordan threw everything into the boot. 'What on earth have you got in that briefcase?' he asked with amusement as they turned to get into the vehicle. 'It's almost heavier than your overnight bag.'

'My workload for tomorrow. I suppose I should have

been like you and done some of it on the plane, but somehow I couldn't settle to concentrate.'

'You must be worried,' Jordan murmured sardonically. 'One thing I've noticed about you over this last year is that you always seem to put work first.'

'Do I?' She glanced over at him as he started the car engine. Somehow it bothered her that this was what stood out about her. 'Are you trying to tell me that I'm boringly sensible?'

'Are you fishing for compliments?' he countered, grinning teasingly at her.

'No.' She felt her skin burn and was glad when the air-conditioning came on and the vents blasted her with cool air. 'I was just curious as to how you perceive me.'

'I think I could be in a lot of hot water if I answer that,' he said with a definite glint of humour in his voice.

Now, what did he mean by that? 'Well, I hope you're not judging me on last night,' she ventured, feeling her pulses start to race. 'Because I wasn't offering you my body, you know. You just jumped to the wrong conclusion.'

'Did I?' Jordan smiled. 'Why would I have done that?'

'Because you've got a one-track mind, of course.'

Jordan laughed, but didn't say anything. He was busy manoeuvring his way through the traffic.

They travelled in silence for a while. Jordan seemed to know the roads well, and he was a good driver, she noticed. His reactions were fast and he handled the powerful car well.

Surreptitiously she watched his face. He looked so very much in control of everything around him. It made her feel very safe and protected. David had never made her feel like this.

'Thanks for doing this, Jordan,' she said suddenly.

'Doing what?' He glanced at her.

'Taking the time out from the office to sort this matter out with Dad. And giving him more time…you know…' She shrugged.

'You've already thanked me for that.' He grinned. 'One kiss on account, wasn't that how it went?'

'Something like that.' She tried to make light of the subject the way he did, but she could feel her senses clamouring as she remembered that kiss. Maybe she needed to put him straight on a few things, she thought suddenly. Maybe she needed to be truthful and tell him she didn't view sex in the same casual way he did. Then maybe he would stop winding her up about it.

They lapsed into silence. They were on the motorway now, sailing along at top speed.

She looked over at him again and took a deep breath. 'Jordan, I want to tell you something.' She cleared her throat nervously.

'This sounds serious.' He glanced at her.

'You know the other night when we…made love…?'

'Yes.'

'Well, I've never done anything like that before.'

'David is even more stupid than I first thought, then,' Jordan murmured drily.

'I don't mean I haven't been to bed with a man before!' She glared at him. 'I mean I've never had a one-night stand before.'

'If this is your ham-fisted way of telling me that you were on the rebound from David the other night, I wouldn't bother, Charlotte,' he said acerbically. 'I think I've already figured that out for myself.'

She frowned and opened her mouth to tell him she wasn't on the rebound from David, that in the last few days she'd hardly given David a second thought. Then she closed her mouth again. Maybe being on the rebound was as good an excuse as any for that night of madness.

She looked away from him and thought that she probably shouldn't have said anything, but something perversely made her carry on. 'Anyway,' she muttered, 'I just thought I'd tell you because really I'm quite old-fashioned when it comes to affairs of the heart.'

'Nothing wrong with that,' Jordan said lightly.

'Any minute now you are going to tell me in a very patronising tone that you believed in love once upon a time as well.'

'Yes, I did.' He glanced over and their eyes locked for a second before he looked back at the road in front. 'Once upon a time.'

Charlotte supposed he was talking about his ex-wife. She wondered what Nadine had been like. Probably extremely stylish; all French women were stylish. If she closed her eyes she could almost picture her: petite, with dark hair, ultra-feminine.

'But now you like to love them and leave them and concentrate on your business ventures?' she said lightly.

'Is that how you perceive me?'

'You do have a lot of glamorous women in your life.'

'Not all at once though,' he laughed. 'You make me sound like a woman-eating monster.'

'I don't think you're a monster,' she said quickly. 'In fact, in a lot of ways you seem to be a pretty decent bloke.'

'Well, thanks…' He slanted a wry glance over at her. 'I think.'

She looked away from him. She hadn't told him that when she relaxed and allowed him to be in control it made her feel safe, or that her insides turned to liquid jelly when he smiled at her in a certain way. Or that she liked the way he kissed her. Or that he made her laugh…or that he was very, very good in bed. He was big-headed enough. Besides, she didn't want him bragging about her on the phone again!

They travelled on in silence. Charlotte noticed how quickly the daylight faded into night. The powerful gleam of headlights on the road ahead was almost mesmerising and she felt sleepy for a while.

But as the road signs for Port Grimaud came into sight she was instantly wide awake. 'Are we going straight to find Dad?' she asked, her attention moving to what lay ahead.

'Yes, I think it's best we get things sorted out as quickly as possible, don't you?'

'Yes, of course,' she agreed with him and felt the prickle of anxiety and unease about this situation return in full force.

The determination in his tone reminded her clearly that behind the charming façade that Jordan was able to project when it suited him, his first priority was the business.

They drove from the main road down towards huge gates that were manned by security guards.

'What kind of place is this?' Charlotte said in surprise.

'The kind of place where millionaires and movie stars hang out.' Jordan smiled. 'Sit tight for a moment, while I go and talk to the guard, tell him who we are here to see and reassure him that we are not members of the paparazzi out to cause trouble.'

Charlotte watched as he got out of the car and walked over to the security guard. He was back within a few minutes and they drove on past the guards and into the tree-lined streets beyond.

It was too dark to clearly see the village they had entered. But Charlotte had the impression of a yachting community: there were waterways and inlets at every turn and by the light of the street lamps it had a mystical stillness.

'This is the address,' Jordan said, slowing the car.

'Are you sure?' Charlotte followed his gaze up towards

a large private house that was in complete darkness. 'I thought they would be in a hotel.'

'This is the address that Ruth left on your machine.' Jordan switched off the car engine. 'Stay here and I'll investigate.'

Charlotte wasn't about to be left behind. This was her father and she wanted to be there to help in any way she could when Jordan confronted him.

'I thought I told you to stay in the car,' Jordan muttered with irritation as she caught up with him by the front gate.

'You are not my keeper, Jordan,' she said, moving swiftly ahead of him to walk down the path towards the front door. There was no bell so Charlotte rapped several times with the wrought-iron knocker. The sound vibrated on the wooden door and they stood and listened for any movement within.

There was silence except for the whistling of the rigging on nearby yachts as the breeze playfully caught them.

'There doesn't seem to be anyone in,' Charlotte murmured, reaching to knock again. Impatiently Jordan moved away from her, following the path around the side of the house.

'Where are you going?' she called after him.

'Doing a little investigating of my own,' he said without breaking his stride.

'Jordan!' Nervously she hurried after him. 'You can't go snooping around like this.'

'Watch me,' he said grimly. As if to prove the point he climbed agilely over a wrought-iron gate that barred his way.

'Jordan.' she called after him but he didn't turn back and, after a few moments' hesitation, Charlotte kicked off her high heels and followed him. It wasn't hard to get over the gate because it wasn't too high, but she had to leave her shoes behind. It was pitch black around the side of the house, forcing her to slow her steps and proceed cautiously in her bare feet. The scent of jasmine and bougainvillea mingled with the salt of the sea and as she turned the corner she could see the Mediterranean bathed in the soft glow of moonlight, and realised that what she had thought was the front of the house was in fact the back. The house faced out over the bay, the waters of the Med lapping directly in front of it. A huge white cabin cruiser was moored alongside a private jetty and there was an enormous patio area with wooden decking and a barbecue area.

'Well, they're definitely out.' Jordan distracted her attention from the beauty of their surroundings as he strolled over to stand by her side. 'There is no car in the garage.'

'Obviously they're out,' Charlotte murmured. 'We hardly needed to come skulking around here to discover that. If they had been in, they would have answered the door.'

'Not necessarily.' Jordan walked onto the patio and peered through the sliding glass doors into the darkened rooms beyond.

Charlotte glared at him. He was really starting to annoy her now. 'My father wouldn't hide from me, Jordan, if that's what you're trying to insinuate.'

'I'm not trying to insinuate anything.' Jordan moved to look through one of the other windows. 'I'm just checking all the possibilities.'

His calm, matter-of-fact manner didn't do anything to improve Charlotte's mood. 'Perhaps I should start raking through the undergrowth at the side of the house?' she suggested sarcastically. 'Just in case they are hiding under a gooseberry bush?'

He glanced over at her then and grinned. 'By all means. Don't let me detain you from the task.'

'This isn't funny, Jordan,' she said angrily.

'You're the one cracking the jokes.'

'You're the one dragging my father's reputation through the mud.' She put one hand on her hip.

'Not without provocation.'

'My father wouldn't hide from me. If he was here, he'd open the door.' For a second her voice trembled precariously, revealing the extent of her anxiety, and then she swung away to go and stand at the end of the patio, staring out across the sea at the lights that glittered on the other side of the bay, trying desperately to pull herself together.

'Well, you're right about one thing. There's no one in.' Jordan came to stand behind her and she noticed how his voice had softened. 'I suggest we go home and forget about this for tonight.'

Charlotte wished she could forget about it. But the worry about her father just seemed to be increasing inside her.

'Charlotte?' He put a gentle hand on her shoulder. 'Come on, I didn't mean to upset you. It's late and we're both tired.'

'This might not even be the right address.' She pulled away from the touch of his hand and turned to look at him. 'You could have made a mistake.'

'I haven't made a mistake,' Jordan said calmly.

'No, sorry, silly me. Jordan Lynch doesn't make mistakes, does he? Not like the rest of the human race.'

'Believe it or not, I have made my fair share of them,' Jordan replied impassively, taking hold of her arm. 'Now, come on, let's go home.'

'Home is hundreds of miles away, Jordan,' she muttered, trying to shrug off his hand as he started to propel her towards the side of the house. 'And I think I'd prefer just to wait here and see if Dad arrives.'

'Home for tonight is my place, which is a few more miles down the coast.' He didn't release her until they reached the side gate. 'And anyway, it's infinitely more sensible for us to face your father after a decent night's rest, when we are both thinking more clearly.'

The words dispelled the red heat of anger clouding her mind and brought a chilling clarity. He was right, she thought as she watched him climb over the gate. It would be in all their interests if Jordan was in a good frame of mind in the morning.

Suddenly it struck her forcibly all over again just how vulnerable they were. It was obvious Ruth had done something wrong, otherwise she would never have made that phone call. And if Jordan decided to prosecute they would be in a terrible mess. That the future happiness of her family could rest on something as flimsy as Jordan Lynch's goodwill was extremely sobering.

Jordan reached out a hand to help her as she started to climb over the gate to join him.

'I can manage, thank you,' she said.

'OK, Miss Independent,' Jordan murmured.

She bit back a sarcastic reply and then promptly lost her balance as one foot connected with firm ground and the other with a stray shoe. Jordan caught her as she stumbled and for a second she found herself in the warm circle of his arms.

It was the strangest sensation being so close to him. The familiar scent of his aftershave and the gentleness of his arms assailed her senses, stirring up a weakness and longing for him that was deeply disturbing, whilst at the same time strong, sensible voices inside were telling her in no uncertain terms that this man wanted control of the family business, that he was therefore her father's enemy and she must beware.

'Are you OK?' he asked softly.

'Yes, of course.' She pulled away from him sharply and busied herself finding her shoes and slipping them on. 'You're right, we should go back to your place and have an early night. We'll need a clear mind for tomorrow.'

CHAPTER SIX

'CHARLOTTE, we're here.'

As the car pulled to a standstill, her eyes flew open. 'Sorry,' she murmured sleepily. 'I closed my eyes for a moment and I shouldn't have done.'

'That's OK; it's been a long day.'

'I wasn't asleep, I was thinking about this situation with Dad. If that was the right address, I wonder—'

'Charlotte, you've worried enough about that today. Just leave it now,' he cut across her firmly.

'Easy for you to say,' she murmured. 'I can't just switch off—'

'I know.' Jordan cut across her again, but this time his voice was gentle. 'If it is any consolation, I do understand how you must be feeling.'

'Do you?'

His eyes moved over the pallor of her skin, the bright glitter of her eyes. 'Yes.' His voice was huskily soft. 'And I hate to see you so upset, Charlie.'

She couldn't find her voice to reply to that because suddenly from nowhere a lump had appeared in her throat. How was it that Jordan could be so damn irritating one moment and then so warm and understanding the next?

He switched off the car headlights, plunging them into complete darkness. She could just make out the shadowy outline of a large house against the night sky.

'Have you got an apartment here?' she asked as he reached for the door handle.

'No. It's just a house. Come on, let's get inside and I'll put some lights on so we can see what we're doing.'

The first thing that hit Charlotte as she stepped out of the car was the tropically strident sound of cicadas. Obviously Jordan's house was in the countryside. A warm breeze rustled through the palm trees—she could see their tall, dark silhouettes moving against the moonlit sky—and as her eyes became accustomed to the darkness it soon became apparent that this wasn't *just* a house, as Jordan had nonchalantly stated. It was a very beautiful villa with graceful lines that seemed straight out of a book on the best of French architecture—a high-pitched roof and square classical lines, enormous long windows covered by wooden shutters and elegant steps up to the front door.

She watched as Jordan found the keys and opened the door. 'You go on inside; I'll get the luggage,' he said as he switched on some lights.

Charlotte stepped inside. The hallway had black stone flags and white walls. It led through to an enormous lounge with large windows looking out towards the sea. As if in keeping with the nautical theme, the settees were blue against plain white walls. A large stone fireplace filled one wall and plain rugs covered a wooden floor that gleamed under the crystal lights like the deck of a ship.

Wandering over towards the windows, Charlotte looked down at the gardens. A pool was illuminated a brilliant turquoise against the darkness of the lawns.

'This is some place,' she murmured in admiration as Jordan came into the room behind her.

'Yes, it's OK.' He sounded coolly indifferent. 'Would you like something to eat and maybe a coffee?'

'I think just the coffee would be lovely; it's a bit late for eating. I'd like to take a shower first. Would you mind?' She looked around at him.

'No, of course not; go right ahead. I've put your bag in your room—it's the second on the right at the top of the stairs.'

As she moved past him she noticed he was looking at the room as if deep in thought—as if she wasn't even there.

She wondered what he was thinking about as she went out and up the stairs. Maybe the last time he had been here had been with his wife?

She walked along the corridor, noticing all the doors were closed except for that of the room Jordan had directed her to. It was as lovely as the rest of the house—plain white walls and an enormous double bed dressed in pure white linen. The only colour was the black wrought-iron bedstead and the pictures of tropical gardens on the walls. There was an *en suite* bathroom in the same cool white.

Charlotte lost no time stripping off and climbing into a warm shower. It was bliss to stand under the forceful jet of water, allowing the journey and the stresses of the day to wash away. She felt a hundred times better when she got out and wrapped herself in one of the white fluffy bath sheets. Wrapping her hair turban-style in another towel, she padded back through to the bedroom and opened her case.

Charlotte hadn't brought much in the way of clothes, just a dress, a pair of jeans and a few tops. She didn't relish the thought of putting on any of them. Her hand lingered over her blue silk nightdress and matching dressing gown. As it was after eleven o'clock, maybe it would be OK to put them on—she'd have a cup of coffee and turn in for the night.

Quickly she dressed in the nightwear and then gave her hair a blast with her hairdryer. She'd almost finished drying it when she heard Jordan's voice calling her. Tying the belt firmly around the waist on her dressing gown, she went downstairs to see what he wanted.

There was no one in the lounge. She wandered through to the kitchen, her eyes flicking over the modern eggshell-blue cupboards and beech counters. There was a very nice smell of food in here that, despite her earlier comments, made her feel quite hungry.

'There you are.' Jordan came in from the other door. 'I know you said you didn't want anything, but I've made us some supper.' His eyes took in the slender lines of her body in the blue silk.

'Oh! Sorry, I'd have got dressed if I'd known.' She felt suddenly awkward. 'I was just going to turn in.'

'You look fine the way you are,' he said. 'And you really should eat something, Charlotte.'

'Yes, I suppose you're right… Thanks, I will.'

He smiled.

'Would you like a glass of wine? There's a bottle in the fridge.'

'No, I'll just stick with coffee, thanks.' She went over to put the kettle on. Then leaned back against the counter as she waited for it to boil, watching Jordan as he moved around the kitchen. She noticed that he had changed into jeans and a T-shirt and that his hair was still damp from a shower. 'You're a fast worker. You've showered, changed and now you're making supper!'

'It's just an omelette.' He smiled. 'I thought it best to stick to something light at this time of night.'

She watched as he put a dressing on a salad and tossed it. He seemed quite at home in a kitchen, she thought. Watching him, it was almost hard to believe that he was the same high-powered businessman that she worked with, the same man who had told her with cold determination that he wanted complete control of the business. But he was and she needed to remember that at all times, she told herself as her thoughts started to veer towards how attractive he was.

She turned away from him to make the coffee. 'Jordan, how much money is actually missing from the company?'

She tried to make her voice light as she asked the question for the second time. 'You never told me the exact amount.'

The query met with silence and she looked back over at him.

'Let's not go there, Charlotte.' His dark eyes met hers steadily and very seriously. 'Let's just relax tonight, pretend the business doesn't exist.'

'I've never been one for burying my head in the sand,' she said with quiet dignity.

Jordan noticed how ramrod straight she held herself. She had given a lot towards the business and this couldn't be easy for her.

As he named the sum of money involved he watched the colour drain away from her skin. 'As I said to you in London, if your father can't afford to pay it back then we'll come to an agreement with regards to the shares of the business.'

Although Jordan's voice was nonchalant there was a steely undertone that she heard very clearly.

'And that's what you really want, the shares in the company.'

'You know it is.' His eyes narrowed on her face. 'This won't affect your job, Charlotte. I'll be relying on you more than ever to run the design department when I take over.'

She noticed how he spoke as if this was already a done deal and felt a spurt of anger. 'I think you mean *if* you take over,' she reminded him, then flashed him a bright smile to accompany the tough tone.

'You've got guts, Charlotte, I'll give you that,' he said quietly. 'I have a feeling that you would fight to your last breath to protect someone you love and believe in.'

'You're right, I would.' She met his eyes steadily. 'I just hope it won't come to that.'

'So do I.' He nodded. 'The last thing I want is to be on opposite sides from you.'

That was the last thing Charlotte wanted as well, and it wasn't just because she knew Jordan would make a formidable adversary. There was something that drew her to him, some weakness that stirred within her when he looked at her in a certain way; she couldn't exactly say what it was…and she wished it would go away because the situation she was trapped in was complicated enough.

'But getting back to what I was saying about your job. No matter what happens, I will want you to stay on.' His voice was firm.

'We'll have to wait and see how things go.' She kept her voice deliberately vague.

Jordan wasn't happy about that. In fact the idea of not having Charlotte around in the office was quite horrifying.

'Now, do you want any help with that omelette?' she asked brightly. 'Because I'm suddenly starving.'

He hesitated then allowed the subject of work to drop. There would be plenty of time to discuss the situation later. They both needed to relax now.

'No, you go and sit down. The table is laid outside. I won't be long.'

Charlotte picked up the coffee-pot and headed outside. She paused in the doorway as she saw the table out on the terrace. It was laid perfectly with a white tablecloth and candles. 'You seem to have gone to a lot of trouble,' she murmured, looking back at him.

'Well, I think after the day we've had we owe ourselves a little respite, don't you?'

Maybe he was right, she thought as she sat at the table and sipped her coffee. It had been a really long day and it was soothing sitting out here. The night was beautiful, not a cloud in the star-studded sky, and the air felt heavy and drowsy with the scent of flowers. The only sounds were those of the cicadas and the gentle whisper of the breeze. She put her cup down and stretched her hands upwards, rolling her head around to release the tension in her neck.

She stopped abruptly as she looked up and saw Jordan standing beside her at the table. 'Is this another one of your toning exercises?' he asked with a smile. 'Like crawling around on the floor first thing in the morning?'

She tried very hard not to lose her composure at the blatant reminder of their night together. She gave a small laugh. 'I was just unwinding that's all. Everything feels as if it needs stretching out.'

'Well, don't stop on my account.' Jordan put her meal in front of her and then sat down opposite. 'In fact, maybe you'd like a hand?' he asked, his eyes dipping to where her dressing gown had parted slightly and he could see the creamy curve of her skin.

'No, thank you.' She smiled at him. 'And if you're trying to embarrass me it won't work. I'm through getting hot and bothered around you.'

Jordan laughed at that. 'Now, that is a pity,' he drawled teasingly.

Carefully she ignored him and concentrated on the food instead. 'This is good,' she said, tucking into the omelette. 'Who did all the shopping for you?'

'Madeline. She's the woman I was telling you about on the plane.'

'Ah, yes, the woman you have the arrangement with.'

'She's a neighbour, a very good one as well. She organised a cleaner to come in for me and generally keeps an eye on everything. I don't know what I would have done without her over the last year.'

Charlotte glanced over at the pool shimmering in the artificial lights that lit it from beneath. 'How could you bear not to come here for so long?' she asked him suddenly. 'It's so beautiful.'

When he didn't answer straight away she looked over at him. The handsome features were serious now and there was no hint of the light-hearted man of a moment ago.

'Jordan?' she prompted him softly.

He shrugged. 'To be honest with you, I never wanted to come back here again. There are too many memories.'

'Of your ex-wife?'

'And of Natasha. Of the night we lost her.'

'It happened here?' Charlotte stared at him in consternation. No wonder he had looked strained when he walked into this house.

'It was a car crash while we were here on holiday.'

'I'm so sorry, Jordan.' Her voice was a mere whisper on the gentleness of the warm breeze. 'Maybe we should have booked into a hotel. It must be very painful for you coming back here.'

'I did think about a hotel. But what's the point when this place is sitting here?' He glanced back at the house. 'And anyway, I don't have to be here for the memories to pack their punches—that can happen anywhere.' He looked over at her. 'In the middle of a conversation or at work…or when I look at a child.' He shrugged. 'Even seeing Harriet. Natasha would have been about her age now.'

Charlotte desperately wanted to get up and go and put her arms around him. 'Losing a child must be the worst thing in the world,' she said softly. 'And to lose her in an accident…' She trailed off, words failing her. 'Were you driving?'

He shook his head. 'I was finishing up some paperwork that I had brought with me.' His words were resigned and flat. 'Nadine had taken Natasha down to the village to buy some milk. They were only supposed to be fifteen minutes. I often think, if only we'd done the shopping the night before, or if only I hadn't been doing that damn paper-work.'

'You can't blame yourself.' Charlotte frowned. 'Or your ex-wife. Accidents happen; life isn't always fair.'

Jordan's lips twisted wryly. 'I know that.'

Looking across at him, Charlotte wondered if it had been the strain of losing their child that had torn his marriage apart. Something like that would be hard to deal with.

'I wish there was something I could say to make you feel better,' she said quietly.

He smiled over at her. 'Just having you here when I walked through the front door helped,' he said.

She felt her heart miss several beats as she looked over into his eyes.

'I don't think I realised just how much I didn't want to face this place on my own until today.'

The shrill ring of the telephone coming from the house broke the mood, and Jordan pushed his chair away from the table. 'Won't be a minute,' he said.

Charlotte watched a moth fluttering too close to the flame of the candle as she waited for him to come back. She thought over the tragedy that had torn his life apart. He seemed so strong, so indomitable most of the time, the tough businessman who got his own way in most things. And yet beneath that tough surface there was another man, a different man, who really wasn't as formidable or as cavalier as he liked to pretend. She liked that Jordan Lynch, she thought suddenly. Liked him more than she could say.

Impatient with herself, she got up from her chair and started to clear away the empty dishes from the table. When she went into the villa she heard a foreign voice drifting towards her down the hallway, and for a moment she thought there was someone else in the house. Then she realised it was Jordan speaking fluent French on the phone.

She wondered to whom he was speaking at this hour of the night as she put the dishes into the dishwasher. For a moment she paused, listening to the deep, melodic flow of his conversation. She could only pick out the odd word, as her schoolgirl French wasn't that good. But it sounded wonderfully sexy. Impatient and annoyed with herself, she returned outside and poured herself the last of the coffee. She was like that moth, she thought as she watched it fly around and around the flame, occasionally making little darts towards it. Fascinated by him, yet terrified by the heat.

She blew the flame out and then, picking up her coffee-cup, walked down towards the pool. It looked very inviting; idly she dipped a toe in, and found the water silkily warm.

As Jordan returned outside he saw her beside the pool and stopped to watch her for a few moments. She probably didn't realise it but the lights from the water were shimmering behind her nightclothes so that he could see the outline of her body beneath. Unable to help himself, he ran his eyes up over her long legs and shapely curves and thought how beautiful she was. Like some Pre-Raphaelite painting with her long blonde hair flowing over her shoulders in glossy curls.

She dipped her toe into the water again and swirled it around.

'Go for a swim if you want,' he offered. 'The water is perfect. I have it regularly maintained.'

She spun around, surprised to find him standing on the patio, watching her. 'I didn't bring a swimming costume.'

'It doesn't matter. We're not overlooked out here.'

He watched her shrug awkwardly.

'If I were alone, maybe,' she murmured.

'Oh, I see.' He grinned. 'Well, if you're worried about me, don't be. I can already see everything there is to see.'

His eyes slipped down over her body again in a leisurely perusal. 'That night attire is completely see-through when you stand against the light.'

'I hope you're joking!' She moved very quickly away from the pool and he laughed at her consternation.

'I thought you were through getting embarrassed around me?' he asked mischievously.

'Yes, well, you continually sink to new lows,' she muttered, putting her empty coffee-cup down on the table. 'How long have you been standing there watching me?'

'Long enough.' He grinned. 'I don't know why you are so embarrassed. It's not as if I haven't seen everything you have anyway.'

She glared at him. 'If you were any kind of a gentleman you wouldn't bring that subject up, and you wouldn't have stood there watching me like…like some peeping Tom.'

'I'm only human, Charlie, and you have got a gorgeous body,' he said with a smile. 'And anyway, I never laid claim to being a gentleman.'

'You got something right anyway.'

She made to swing away from him but he reached out and caught her arm before she could move. 'Come and have a swim with me,' he invited huskily. 'I haven't got a swimming costume either.'

Dark hazel eyes held hers in a brazen challenge and suddenly her annoyance and embarrassment left her.

For a moment the thought of gliding through the water next to him, naked skin pressed against naked skin in the warm, silky heat, made her body burn with raw desire.

She wanted very much to throw caution away but, remembering how that moth had fluttered around the flame, she pulled away from him determinedly. 'That isn't a good idea, Jordan,' she murmured.

'Why not?'

'Because we are both tired and it's getting late…' She

broke off in panic as he reached out and flicked a light switch behind him, plunging the whole of the pool area into inky blackness. 'And we need to keep a clear head for tomorrow—'

'Are you always so sensible?'

The slightly mocking tone made her bristle inside. 'When I have to be.' She raised her eyes to his.

'You know I want you, don't you?' The whispered words set her blood on fire, as did the touch of his hand as he reached and brushed a stray strand of her hair away from her face.

She felt every nerve in her body tighten and tingle with awareness. Yes, she knew he wanted her, could see it in the predatory light in his eyes. She wanted him too; her heart was beating out of control against her chest and the longing to melt into his arms was so acute it was a deep ache.

'I…meant what I said earlier today, Jordan. I don't want to have a casual fling with you.' Her voice was unsteady as she fought against the traitorous weakness inside her.

'Because you're an old-fashioned girl?' His voice was husky and playful, and it set alarm bells ringing deep inside.

'Apart from all of that, we are on opposite sides of a divide.'

'We don't have to be on opposite sides, though, do we?' he murmured.

His eyes moved to her lips, and then slowly he lowered his head and kissed her. After a moment's hesitation she kissed him back. The sensation that flared between them was one of pure arousal, and suddenly she couldn't think straight any more; all she could do was wind her arms up and around his neck and hold on to him, give herself up to the hedonistic bliss of being so close to him.

He lowered his head and kissed her neck, then his fingers found the ties of her dressing gown and moved beneath to the warmth of her breasts, caressing the hardened nipples, making her catch her breath with ecstasy.

'You're so very beautiful,' he whispered.

'And you are very practised in the art of seduction.' Her voice held a tinge of grounded good sense and yet at the same time her lips were searching for his again.

His hands stroked down over her back and the dressing gown was pulled lower until she was freed from it. Then his hands curved around her narrow waist and his mouth trailed heated kisses over her naked shoulders.

'I thought you only wanted to go for a swim,' she reminded him huskily, rolling her head back as he kissed the sensitive hollow of her neck.

No one had ever kissed her the way Jordan did. The softness and the passion of his lips seemed to steal all rational thought away from her.

'To hell with the swim, let's just go upstairs.' His voice was laced with need and it echoed inside her, making her feel dizzy, as if she had been drinking.

She ran her fingers through his hair, loving the texture of it against her skin. Pressing herself closer, she reached to kiss him again. 'Yes, let's go upstairs,' she agreed huskily.

It was a shock when he suddenly swept her off her feet to carry her inside the house. There was something wildly exciting about being carried like this. She curved her arms around his neck and buried her face against his shirt, breathing in the scent of his cologne, loving the feeling of power about him. Her body felt alive with anticipation, with need, and with an excitement that only seemed heightened by her attempts to stem the flow of passion with words of caution. The knowledge that all she was doing tonight was playing with fire didn't stem her ardour—instead it seemed to be feeding it in some bizarre way. The danger and the excitement and the need were all entangled deep within her, making her want him more than ever.

They didn't turn the lights on in her bedroom; just a single shaft of moonlight fell softly from the window over the bed. It lent everything a strange, cool, silvery shade of unreality. As Charlotte leaned back against the pillows and watched Jordan undress she felt as if she wasn't really here at all, that it was all some wildly exhilarating dream.

She watched as his shirt was discarded, admiring the muscled perfection of his shoulders, the broad, powerful chest. As he sat on the edge of the bed beside her and began to unbuckle the belt of his jeans she felt the excitement inside suddenly turn to a kind of acute nervous apprehension. He had such a fabulous body and she remembered with vivid intensity how well he was able to use it.

'Jordan.' She reached out a hand and touched his arm.

He turned to look at her then and saw the apprehension clearly in her eyes. Leaving his jeans on, he moved to join her on the bed.

The flimsy silk of her nightdress might as well not have been there for all the difference it made. She was aware of every part of him in that moment, the strength of his body pressed close against hers.

He stroked her hair away from her face and looked deeply into her eyes. 'What's going through that mind of yours?' he asked softly.

'All the reasons why this isn't a good idea,' she whispered honestly.

'Sometimes it's a mistake to analyse things too deeply.'

'I should just relax and enjoy the moment, you mean.' Her voice was light. 'Not think about relationships at all.'

'There's nothing wrong with enjoying the moment you're in.'

They were so close that she could feel the vibrations of his voice against her chest.

He kissed her lips softly. It was passionate and compelling and it tore at something deep inside her. There was a sensation in the pit of her stomach as if someone had just pushed her off a cliff edge on a bungee rope.

Trouble was, she wanted more than just a moment in time with Jordan Lynch. She wanted much, much more.

I'm in love with this man, she thought hazily. Then, as the thought cleared and took a deeper hold on her consciousness, she felt herself freeze inside with fear.

'Jordan, this really isn't a good idea.' Her voice was breathless as if she had suddenly been running a race. She pushed him away from her but she needn't have tried to use force. He instantly moved back, allowing her the freedom to swing away from him and sit on the other side of the bed with her back to him.

'Why not?' His voice was very calm.

'Because...' She looked over at him. Jordan Lynch wasn't the kind of man to fall in love with, she told herself fiercely. Not unless you enjoyed having your heart broken. He was fickle when it came to women, enjoyed the chase and the thrill of lovemaking but didn't want the commitment. The only allegiance Jordan wanted was to the business.

'Because?' Jordan prompted her.

'It's just not a good idea, that's all.' Her voice was flat as she tried to close out the emotions that he stirred in her. 'And I'm worried about what's going to happen tomorrow with Dad and this money business.' Desperately, she tried to concentrate on the realities of their situation. 'I know you said you'd give him a few days to sort the problem out. But a few days might not be enough.'

'Oh, I see.'

She noticed the change in his tone from gently reasonable to cold and incisive.

'What do you see?' Her blonde hair swung around as she turned to look at him again.

'You are still in love with David, but you are not above using that beautiful body of yours as a bargaining chip after all.'

She flinched at the coldness of the words. And suddenly the implications of the way she had behaved struck her forcibly—her heat and passion one moment and now this. 'That's not true, Jordan.' Earnestly, she strove to set things straight. 'I told you this morning I wasn't like that and—'

'And you're just an old-fashioned girl?' His lips twisted wryly. 'You know, I believed that once, Charlie. But I don't think it's going to wash a second time.'

'Jordan!'

'Tell me, which is it that concerns you most—your father's fate? Or the shares you would like in the company?' He watched the colour flare under her skin. 'Just how much help are you hoping for?'

'I think you'd better leave,' she said tightly.

'Hit a nerve, have I?' He shook his head. 'You know, the really strange thing is that I still want you.' His eyes raked over her body before coming to rest on her face with a kind of deep intensity that made her body burn. 'Maybe because I recognise a kindred spirit, a person who knows what she wants and is not afraid to use whatever means she has at her disposal to get it.'

He reached out a hand and touched her face in a caress that was strangely at odds with the coolness of his words. His touch made her body heat up instantly and, to her humiliation, desire still stirred forcefully inside her. She flinched away from him, hating herself for the weakness. How he'd laugh if he knew the emotions that had really been driving her.

'OK, you're right.' She said the words shakily. 'I do want my rightful share of the family business and I do want you to go easy on my father.' She raised her eyes to his with a determination she was in reality far from feeling. 'And maybe I'm prepared to do anything it takes if you'll help.'

There was silence for a moment as Jordan studied her, dissected the words and then fitted them with the look of anguish in her eyes, the sudden pallor of her skin.

The anger that had driven him a second ago had been motivated by pure frustration. He wanted her…wanted her with a need he hadn't known in years. But he didn't want to hurt her and he was hurting her now. There was something about her demeanour that reminded him of a trapped animal, wounded but still determined to fight and protect what she loved.

'Your father is a lucky man to have you in his corner, Charlotte.' He said the words softly and then stood up.

She watched as he walked around the bed to stand with his back to her, looking out of the window.

For a long moment there was nothing said between them and Charlotte felt her nerves twisting with apprehension. She wished now that she hadn't tried to be clever, that she had never said those words. She wasn't in a strong enough bargaining position anyway; Jordan could have any woman he wanted. All this could do was make things worse. Charlotte opened her mouth to tell him she hadn't meant what she'd said, that she was tired…that she was frightened…anything that would extract her from the mess. But before she could speak he turned and looked at her again.

'OK, this is the deal.' He spoke coolly and decisively. 'If your father can't pay up but hands over the necessary amount of shares to me I won't prosecute—on two conditions.'

'And what are they?' Her heart was thumping painfully against her chest and her voice sounded as strained and as tense as she felt.

'One is that you stay working in the business for at least twelve months. We have a lot of contracts to finish, and tight deadlines. The last thing I need is you walking out right now.'

Her lips twisted wryly. She might have known that Jordan's main priority would be the business. 'And the second condition?' She angled her head up, wishing that the full force of the moonlight wasn't shining on her face, leaving him in darkness. She felt at enough of a disadvantage as it was and she really would have liked to be able to see his expression.

'That you make yourself available to me when I want you.' The words had a hard, uncompromising edge.

She felt her heart miss several beats. 'What do you mean by make myself available?'

'Just what I said. I think we need to work in closer unison, both in office hours and out of them.'

'You mean you want me to grace your bed whenever you feel like it?' She forced herself to ask the question.

'Why are you sounding so outraged, Charlotte?' Jordan's tone was quiet. 'Isn't that just what you were offering me a moment ago?'

'Jordan—I didn't mean to say that.' She stood up and moved a few steps closer to him. 'I'm under a lot of stress at the moment and—'

'And you really should think before you speak,' he cut across her firmly. He reached to touch her, smoothing her hair back from her face and studying her with quiet intensity. 'I have no intention of forcing you into my bed... that's not how I get my kicks, I can assure you.'

The touch of his hands made her senses cry out for him. Little did he realise that he wouldn't have to do that much forcing—she would willingly have gone into his arms even now.

OK, she wanted him; she admitted the truth to herself savagely—but she would never, ever tell him that. She had her pride. It was better to be branded cold-blooded than branded a fool, she told herself firmly. And she had enough sense to know that loving Jordan was a road to nowhere. He would respect her for wanting a share of the company, for wanting to help her father—but not for wanting him. He was a hard-headed businessman, not a sentimentalist.

'The deal is, you stay working for me and offer me as much of your time as I feel I need.' He moved away from her slightly so that they weren't touching. 'We can leave what happens between us in the bedroom as an optional extra.'

The coolness of his tone cut through her.

'Anyway, I don't expect an answer tonight. It's late and I suggest we both get some sleep. We'll talk tomorrow.'

Then he was gone, closing the door behind him with a quiet finality.

Charlotte sat back down on the bed and tried to get her head around what had just happened. It seemed she had brokered some kind of deal for her father and she felt relief at that…but at what personal cost to herself?

CHAPTER SEVEN

JORDAN knocked on her bedroom door. 'Charlotte, are you awake?'

There was no sound from inside the room. He knocked again and then pushed the door open.

Sunlight filtered through the windows, slanting over the bed where she was curled up, fast asleep. The white sheets were low, showing the flawless, creamy perfection of her skin, the soft curve of her breast. Her lashes were dark against her face, her lips softly parted. Her hair lay in golden curls over the pillows, framing her face. She looked warm and seductively inviting.

'Charlotte?' He trailed a finger down the smoothness of her cheek and then stroked a silky strand of hair from her face so that he could see her more clearly.

She looked vulnerable and fragile and it brought out an answering surge of protectiveness inside him that he hadn't felt in a long, long time. That was quite an act she had put on last night, he thought. How far would she really go to protect the people she loved?

He put the drink he had brought her down on the bed-side table. 'Charlotte, you need to wake up,' he said softly.

She smiled in her sleep and stretched luxuriously. The movement showed the firm, creamy curve of her breast and suddenly he wanted to lie down beside her and take her into his arms, drown once again in the sweetness of her body. But then he had wanted to do that last night as well. It had taken all his self-control to leave this room.

Afterwards he had gone back outside and had swum as

many laps of the pool as possible in an effort to exhaust himself and get her out of his head. But it hadn't worked.

'Charlotte.' He raised his voice slightly.

The familiar voice trickled deliciously through her consciousness. For a moment she couldn't think where she was. Her eyes flicked open and met with Jordan's.

It took a moment for realisation to dawn on her and then she hastily pulled the sheet over herself.

'I've been trying to wake you for ages.'

'Have you? What time is it anyway?' She felt flustered and embarrassed as the full memory of last night flooded through her.

She remembered her ludicrous statement that she had only wanted to sleep with him to save her father and the business. Had he really believed that? She hoped he had, prayed that he didn't guess that somehow somewhere along the way she had fallen in love with him. That would be too humiliating to bear.

She flicked a nervous glance up at him and noticed he was fully dressed in lightweight fawn trousers and a cream polo shirt.

'It's seven forty-five.' He picked up the china mug from the table and handed it over to her. 'I wasn't sure if you were a tea person in the morning or a coffee. I took a guess at tea.'

'Thanks.' Self-consciously she sat up, struggling to keep the covers in place over her body before taking the cup from him. How could he talk about something as mundane as tea after what had transpired between them in here last night?

As she glanced nervously up at him he smiled and she wondered if that was a gleam of amusement playing around the sensual curve of his lips. He probably found this whole situation extremely entertaining. Even if he didn't prosecute her father, he was still in a very strong position to oust him from the company, and he was powerful enough and ruthless enough in business to do it.

Add to that the fact that he was probably congratulating himself on tying her into the business for a year, and all in all he had himself a nice little coup.

The thought was galling.

'So was I right or wrong?' he asked.

She looked up at him blankly, and then remembered what he had been saying. 'Oh, about the tea—yes, you were right. I drink tea in the morning.'

He nodded. 'You're not fully awake yet, are you? I'll leave you to come around in peace. Then we'll go and have breakfast in town.'

As the door closed behind him she put her tea down on the bedside table with a thump and rested her head back against the pillows. Breakfast! That was the last thing she wanted with the weight of anxiety that was hanging over her. All she wanted was to get today over with, find her father, face whatever problems had to be faced and forget those feelings for Jordan Lynch. Because he didn't deserve her love—he was cold-blooded and calculating.

She flung back the covers and got out of bed to head into the bathroom. Maybe she didn't really love Jordan at all, she told herself sharply as she stood under the full force of the shower jet. Maybe it was just a passing moment of insanity.

Maybe Jordan was right and she was on the rebound from David? She closed her eyes and thought about her feelings for David, but they seemed pale and insipid now next to the weight of feeling for Jordan.

Surely she wasn't so shallow that she imagined herself in love with him because they'd had great sex? She cast her mind back to that first night together, how close they had stood next to each other in his lounge, how he'd reached to touch her…the sensational, erotic, shivery feelings that had flowed through her when they'd kissed. The chemistry had been there between them even before they'd made love, she realised. But she'd been too blind to see it. Too blind—or too frightened by the intensity of feeling he seemed to stir up in her.

She remembered the first time she had ever met Jordan, when her father had brought him into her office to introduce them. She remembered looking up at him and how he'd smiled at her. That smile had seemed to ignite inside her into a million butterflies and she had immediately put up defensive barriers. She had watched from the safety of her relationship with David as a succession of beautiful women went through his life and she had told herself that she was doing the right thing keeping a distance from him. He was an unknown quantity…a dangerous entity…a heartache waiting to happen.

She had been right about all that, she told herself as she stepped out of the shower and dried herself briskly. Jordan was definitely dangerous: powerful, ambitious and sensually explosive.

Her hands trembled for a moment as she remembered the way he had kissed her by the pool last night, and the way he had made her feel so out of control.

Angrily she tried to shut the memory away. She couldn't deal with her feelings for Jordan right now. One thing at a time, and today she would face the problem of her father and the business.

Dressing in a bright pink sundress, she pinned her hair up and paid careful attention to her make-up. She felt quite satisfied with the results as she stepped back from the mirror and surveyed her reflection. At least she had managed to disguise the fact that it had taken hours before she finally slept last night and she looked her usual cool and capable self. Pity it was all a charade, she thought as she picked up her bag and headed out.

There was an open door along the corridor and her attention was caught and held by the view it afforded across lush greenery towards the bright azure blue of the Mediterranean. A few yachts were skipping over the waves, white sails fluttering in the breeze. The scenery was so captivating that she didn't realise for a moment that the room she was looking into had once been a child's bedroom. It was only as she turned to move on that she noticed the teddy bears on the bed, and the sight of them sent a shiver of sadness through her. This had obviously been Jordan's daughter's room.

She noticed the framed photographs on the dressing table—one of Natasha on her own, the other a family portrait: Natasha between her mother and father. Even from this distance she could see that Jordan's ex-wife was as beautiful as she had imagined. Her short dark hair was immaculately groomed and she had the chic look of a Parisian, high cheekbones, almond eyes and a wide, attractive smile.

A sound behind her in the corridor made her turn. Jordan was walking towards her. His eyes flicked from her to the open doorway she was standing in and she felt a pang of guilt as if she had been caught intruding on something intensely personal.

'I was just admiring the view,' she murmured as he reached her side.

He stretched past her and without a word closed the door. She noticed the shuttered expression in his eyes as he looked back at her. 'If you're ready, we should go.'

'Yes, of course.' Despite the coolness of his tone she had the impression that just glancing into that room was an unspeakable ordeal for him, and it made her heart go out to him. But before she could murmur any gentle words he moved away from her abruptly, leaving her feeling foolish for daring to think he might need her compassion.

'I rang the airline earlier; there's a flight back to London available at four-thirty this afternoon. I've booked us on it.'

She felt a pang of unease at the brisk, businesslike words. 'But what if Dad isn't there when we return to the house? It might take longer than just today to sort things out.'

'Charlotte, I have a business to run. The problem with your father will have to be sorted out today, one way or another.'

The decisive words made the knot of tension inside Charlotte tighten even further. Had Jordan changed his mind about the deal he had put to her last night? It seemed likely he had, otherwise surely he would have mentioned it again this morning. She followed him silently downstairs and out of the front door, trying desperately to gather the courage to bring the subject up.

The silence between them continued as they drove along the coast. The heat in the car was intense; Charlotte could feel it burning her through the fine cotton material of her dress, yet inside she was cold with fear.

If her father wasn't at the house this morning, would Jordan just call the police and be done with the problem?

She flicked an anxious look over at him, but his features seemed closed and guarded. It was impossible to tell what was going on in his mind.

As if sensing her eyes on him he spoke suddenly. 'I thought we'd have breakfast in St Tropez.'

'Jordan, I can't eat breakfast. I'm too wound up to eat anything.' Her voice came out in an agitated rush.

'Starving yourself isn't going to help anyone.' His voice was irritatingly calm. 'But, OK, we'll go straight to Port Grimaud.'

'Thanks.' She stared down at hands that were tightly

clenched in her lap. 'You will go easy on Dad, won't you?' she asked in a low tone.

He didn't answer her immediately and she glanced up as he slowed the car and then pulled it into the side of the road.

'Did you think about my proposition last night?'

'Yes, of course I did!' She looked into the depths of his hazel eyes and felt something inside her twist painfully at the remoteness of his tone and his manner.

'And?'

'And if the offer is still open then I accept your conditions.' She looked away from him out of the car window. 'I'll stay working in the business for a year.'

'Even if your father is no longer a part of the business?'

The calmly asked question made her anger return. 'I don't see why Dad should have to completely leave the company. OK, there is a lot of money outstanding from the business, but not that much!'

'The deal is that I don't prosecute and you stay on in the business, lending me your full co-operation, support and time in whatever capacity I feel I need it.' He cut across her with a dangerous quietness. 'That's the offer on the table, Charlotte—take it or leave it.'

She clenched her hands into tight fists of frustration. 'And you'll go easy on Dad.' She refused to back down completely. 'You'll treat him with deference.'

'Yes,' he nodded, 'of course I will. I've always liked your father—this isn't personal.'

She looked back at him, meeting his eyes steadily.

'Just business,' she said frigidly, hating the way he was able to dismiss all feelings, all sentiment when it came to the company.

'Just business,' he agreed.

'OK, then.' With the greatest of difficulty she kept her

voice light, tried to pretend that this agreement wasn't sticking in her throat. 'You've got yourself a deal.'

Charlotte noticed the gleam of satisfaction in his eyes and it aggravated her intensely, but she said nothing more. What else was there to say? The simple fact was that Jordan Lynch held all the cards in this game, and he knew it.

He put the car into gear and moved slowly back out into the road. 'Let's go and get this over with, then,' he said smoothly. 'The sooner we get back to normal, the better.'

Amen to that, Charlotte thought as she gazed out over the rows of vines in the fields and the wild poppies that decorated the roadsides.

Viewed in the daylight, Port Grimaud was every bit as select and beautiful as Charlotte had suspected. It was like a miniature Venice with canals and charming little hump-back bridges, each glimpsed view a true artist's delight. The houses were painted in ice-cream colours and they glinted fresh in the sunlight, their shutters open to the heat of the day. Most of them seemed to have their own private moorings, with yachts and small pleasure craft tied up alongside.

Despite the fact that Charlotte had intended not to speak to Jordan until she had to, she found herself remarking on how beautiful the surroundings were.

'Yes. It was the brainchild of an architect called Francois Spoerry and it's built on land reclaimed from the sea.'

'So it's relatively new, then? It looks as if it has always been here.'

'It's a designer's dream, isn't it? Everything about it is practically perfect. I think it was one of the projects that inspired me towards becoming an architect.' He slowed the car as they approached the house where they had called last night.

'Looks as if someone is at home anyway,' Jordan remarked, and she followed his gaze past the huge house with its pale pink walls and blue shutters towards the garage, noting that the doors were open and a blue car was parked inside.

Charlotte could hardly wait for the car to come to a standstill so that she could jump out.

As she hurried down the path someone else was coming around the other side of the house. She looked over and to her delight saw that it was her father.

'Dad!' she called to him and he turned and looked around at her, surprise clearly etched in his eyes.

'Charlotte! What on earth are you doing here?'

'Come to see you, of course.' As she walked over to him Charlotte noticed that he didn't look well. Simon McCann had always been a good-looking man who wore his age well, but now his face was gaunt and pale and he had lost a lot of weight in the weeks since she had seen him.

'Dad, are you OK?' Her voice catching with concern, she put her arms around him and gave him a hug.

'Well, I'm all the better for seeing you, sweetheart.' He hugged her back. Then over her shoulder his eyes connected with Jordan's.

'I'm glad to see you, too,' he said with quiet dignity. 'We have things to sort out.'

Jordan acknowledged the words with a nod.

As Charlotte moved back from her father Ruth walked around the side of the house. Her eyes widened as she saw Charlotte. 'I've been trying to ring you for days!'

'Well, I'm here now,' Charlotte said and noticed how the other woman looked over at Jordan with apprehension.

'Let's get inside.' Swiftly Ruth turned to lead them around the house towards the front door.

Her stepmother looked as immaculate as ever, Charlotte

noted. She was very slender and always perfectly groomed, her short blonde hair sat in its usual tidy style, and she was wearing casual white trousers and a white top that had a designer cut to them. It was only when Charlotte got close to her as she stepped inside the house that she could see there was something wrong. Despite the fact that Ruth had been in the sun for some weeks, her skin was white, and her eyes were heavy with anxiety.

'So how about a drink?' Ruth asked, her tone bright.

A drink was the last thing on Charlotte's list of requirements. She glanced around the house. It was like a Hollywood set, its huge rooms furnished with elegant style, and offering a view out across the bay of St Tropez that was truly spectacular.

'So what's been going on?' Charlotte cut directly to the point as she looked from her father to Ruth. It was the least probing of a number of questions running through her mind. But neither answered her.

'I'm sure you'd like a cool drink,' Ruth continued determinedly, giving a silent signal to Charlotte to follow her through to the kitchen.

Charlotte frowned and glanced again at her father. There was a frailty about him that she had never noticed before. 'Go and help Ruth with the drinks,' he said gently. 'I want a quiet word with Jordan.'

Charlotte's eyes darted to Jordan as she speculated about what the two men were going to say to each other. Whatever it was, she hoped Jordan was going to go easy on him; her father didn't look strong enough to take much in the way of confrontation.

As if he could read her thoughts, Jordan said soothingly, 'It's OK, Charlotte.'

'I hope so,' she murmured, turning to leave them.

Ruth was waiting for her in the kitchen. She was leaning against the blue kitchen counter, her arms tightly crossed in front of her, her whole body language screaming defence. 'Are you angry with me over this business?' she asked as soon as Charlotte stepped through the door.

Charlotte's eyes flicked over her stepmother and noticed that behind that wary expression she looked tired.

'No, I'm not angry,' Charlotte said quietly. 'Just puzzled.'

'Oh!' Ruth unfolded her arms and the look of relief in her blue eyes was immense. 'Thank God for that. I don't think I could have dealt with any more anger. I've had enough from your father.'

'So what's all this about?' Charlotte asked crisply. 'Why is there money missing from the company accounts?'

Ruth looked miserable. 'It's all a terrible mistake, Charlotte, and I'm so sorry... I can't tell you how sorry I am.' She turned and opened a cupboard and took out a bottle of Scotch. 'I could do with something stronger than a soft drink. What about you?'

'No, I don't want anything.' Charlotte sat down on one of the stools at the breakfast bar and tried to be patient, even though curiosity was eating her away.

'Is Jordan furious about the money?' Ruth asked in a strained whisper.

'I don't think he's too happy,' Charlotte said. 'But he's a businessman, Ruth; what can you expect? It was a lot of money. And it wasn't even so much that as the way it was done.'

Ruth nodded and poured herself a generous measure from the bottle of whisky. 'I hope he isn't too hard on your father, Charlie,' she said anxiously. 'This was all my fault, not his.'

Charlotte glanced around towards the lounge and saw that the two men had stepped outside onto the deck.

They didn't seem to be talking at all at the moment, she noticed. Her father was leaning on the rail, staring down into the sea as if deep in thought. Jordan was standing next to him, glancing out across the bay as if he was just admiring the view.

Charlotte turned her attention back to Ruth. 'So are you going to tell me what all this is about?'

Ruth took a deep swallow of her drink. 'He told me not to tell you this,' she murmured. 'Made me swear to it. But I can't carry this worry all on my own, Charlotte. I've tried, and look at the mess I've got into.'

'What worry? What is it you aren't supposed to tell me?'

'Your father has a heart condition.' Ruth said the words softly. 'The doctors have told him that if he doesn't give work up he could be dead within the year.' She watched Charlotte's face drain of colour. 'That was seven months ago,' she stated grimly. 'Since then I've begged and pleaded with him to retire. But he wouldn't listen. Then I managed to get him out here for this holiday after Jordan had mentioned casually how beautiful the Côte d'Azur was.

'We rented this place and then discovered it was up for sale. Simon loved it, and toyed with the idea of buying it. Said that, just for me, he would give work up as the specialist had advised and we'd live out here and enjoy his early retirement.' Her voice cracked. 'And then at the last minute he changed his mind. Said that leaving the business would be letting everybody down. I begged him and pleaded with him…' Her eyes filled with tears suddenly. 'But he wouldn't listen.' Fiercely Ruth rubbed the tears away from her eyes.

'So?' Charlotte prompted softly.

'Other buyers came on the scene, and I was panicking, Charlotte. Your father wouldn't budge. So in desperation I used the money from the business account. I had the access code and I knew what to do.'

'I can't believe you did that,' Charlotte said in a hushed tone.

'It was only supposed to be an interim measure! I thought your father would have the funds to cover the money I took. After all, he was thinking of buying the place up to a few weeks ago.' Ruth ran her hand through her blonde hair in agitation. 'How was I to know that the reason he was suddenly against the purchase was the fact that he'd have to sell some shares in the company to afford it? He never told me that…but of course he wouldn't dare because he knows I want him to give the business up completely, never mind just a small part. The place is killing him, Charlotte!'

Charlotte was stunned into silence.

Ruth caught her eye. 'I was desperate,' she said firmly. 'Please don't look at me like that! There has been a marked improvement in your father's health since he has been out here. He even agreed to stay longer than we'd originally planned. I thought, if I could ease him over here with the purchase of the house, he'd finally let go of the business and realise how much he has to lose by ignoring the doctor's orders.' Ruth glared at her through a mist of tears. 'Under the circumstances, were my actions really so wrong? Simon is older than me anyway. I knew when I married him that we might not have as long together as some couples…and I want time with him… I love him.'

'I know.' Charlotte heard the real anguish in the other woman's tone and got up off the stool to go and put her arms around her. 'I know you love him.'

For a while the two women just stood there together, holding each other. Charlotte couldn't bear to think of her father being so ill. That he might die. It put all the worries about money and business very firmly into perspective.

'I've put everything in his name, you know, Charlotte.

I haven't done anything that wasn't in your father's best interests.'

'I don't doubt your intentions, Ruth,' Charlotte said as she pulled away. 'I just wish you had told me about this sooner. I'd have helped to try and talk him into retiring.'

Ruth shook her head. 'You know what he's like...so damn stubborn. The more you try to talk him around, the more likely he is to go completely the other way. That's why I ended up taking things into my own hands. I realise now what a mistake it was.

'When I told him a few days ago what I had done, he nearly had apoplexy. Told me that I was a bloody fool and he couldn't put the money back because he didn't have it! I can't tell you how shocked I was, Charlotte. I thought it would just be a simple matter of transferring funds from one account to another. And I thought it could be done within a matter of minutes with the electronic banking system that we have in place. But apparently Simon has made bad investments in shares...lost a considerable amount of his savings. Unfortunately he didn't deign to tell me about it.' Her voice hardened as she turned to take another drink from her glass.

'But the situation is salvageable.' Ruth talked with her back to Charlotte now. 'I rang Jordan a few days ago and asked him in a round-about way if he would be willing and able to buy some of your father's shares in the business. Jordan said categorically that he would, that in fact he'd like to buy Simon out completely.'

'But Dad doesn't want to sell?'

Ruth turned then and her eyes were heavy with regret. 'No, he doesn't. He's been running around for the last three...no, four days, trying to raise the money to pay the debt off so that he doesn't have to touch his shares and he doesn't have to leave the business. Last night he went to see the people who were bidding against us for this house, offered it to them for fractionally less than I paid. Now, how crazy is that?' For a second her voice wobbled precariously and she looked close to tears again. 'I feel such a fool, Charlotte, but worse, I feel that your father doesn't love me at all. Because if he did he wouldn't want to go back to work. He'd want to take things easier, if not for himself then for me.'

'You've got to understand, Ruth, that Dad is a very proud man,' Charlotte said softly. 'For one thing, he won't want to lose face in front of Jordan—'

'Oh, you're right there. We both thought that we'd have a few more days before Jordan found out about this. The audits were due in next week, not last week. Simon was hell-bent on having the money back by then.'

'Yeah, well, you reckoned without Jordan's eagle eye. Nothing escapes his attention in that office. Actually, he's like Dad in a lot of ways, now I think about it.'

'Probably why the two of them get on so well.' Ruth sniffed loudly and reached for a tissue. 'What am I going to do, Charlotte? Do you think Jordan will bail us out?'

'If Dad is prepared to compromise, I think he might.' Charlotte thought about the deal she had cut with Jordan last night. 'In fact, I know he will.'

Tears of relief streamed down Ruth's face. 'I always liked Jordan, he's a pretty good bloke really.'

'He has his moments,' Charlotte muttered. She glanced outside again; the two men were deep in conversation now. Nervously she hoped that Jordan was keeping his end of their deal, and was playing everything gently down.

'I hope he's calming Simon down a bit…' Ruth said as she followed Charlotte's gaze. 'We are barely on speaking terms at the moment.'

'Yes, I hope he is too,' Charlotte murmured. 'Dad really doesn't look well.'

'Which is why he needs to retire,' Ruth said firmly. 'He

should be selling our apartment in London, not this house. He needs to get completely away from the office.'

'I agree.' Charlotte looked back around at the other woman. 'But we can't force him into leaving the business. At the end of the day, it's going to have to be his decision. You've got to understand, Ruth, the business has been everything to him for years. After Mum died he buried himself in it completely. That's one of the reasons Jen and I were so delighted when he married you—he actually does take time off now, which is more than he ever did before. But it will be very difficult for him to let go entirely, especially as it's been a family concern for so long. We're going to have to handle this very carefully.'

'Actually, the problem has been solved.' Jordan appeared in the doorway behind them and they both turned around in surprise.

'Simon wants to know if you'll bring out the bottle of champagne from the fridge, and four glasses.'

'Champagne?' Ruth sounded bewildered. 'Are we celebrating something?'

'Yes. The fact that you have acquired a full-time husband and I have acquired a business.'

The decisive words made consternation flood through Charlotte. 'What do you mean? What's happened?'

'I mean that we've talked the matter through and, in view of Simon's health, we have decided that it's best that I buy him out. This way your father can enjoy a comfortable and well-deserved retirement.'

There was a stunned silence for a few moments.

Charlotte frowned. 'Ruth told me he was determined to go back to the business.'

'Well, he's changed his mind.'

Charlotte met the dark strength of Jordan's eyes and felt a wave of fury at the nonchalant way he said those words. She didn't believe for one moment that her father had changed his mind so easily and so quickly of his own free will.

'Well, this is good news for me,' Ruth said with a sigh of relief. 'Anything that means Simon won't be going into that office is a good thing.'

Simon came into the room behind Jordan. He gave his wife a shaky smile. 'Well, you've got your wish—you're going to have me under your feet for twenty-four hours a day, Ruth. I just hope you're not going to regret it.'

'So my neck isn't to be put on a chopping block after all,' Ruth commented wryly.

'Not this week anyway,' Simon grinned, in a shadowy attempt at his once robust humour.

'Hold on a minute, Dad.' Charlotte cut across the conversation swiftly. 'Everything is moving just a little too quickly here. Are you happy about this?'

'The business will always be of interest to me...but...' Simon glanced over at Ruth. 'Maybe Jordan and Ruth are right. Some things in life are more important than work. I'm sorry, Ruth, I know I've put you under a lot of strain these last few months. And you're right, my health and our relationship should come first. I intend to put things right.'

Charlotte watched as he moved to take Ruth into his arms. Then she turned and stepped past Jordan to head outside and give them some privacy.

It was hot on the deck; even the breeze that swept across the bay did little to reduce the temperature. Charlotte leaned against the rail and looked out to sea. The town of St Tropez shimmered in the distance, a terracotta blaze of colour between the green of the mountains and the blue of the Med.

Jordan came to stand next to her and suddenly the heat around them was nothing to the heat of the temper inside her.

'Well, you've got control of the business at last.' She practically hissed the words. 'Congratulations.'

'I'd like to say thanks, but your tone of voice doesn't seem to lend itself to the word.'

His lazy indifference was the last straw. 'You really are a bastard, Jordan Lynch.' She swung to face him, her eyes blazing into his. 'A complete bastard.'

'That's not a very nice way to speak to your boss, Charlotte,' he said drolly.

'I don't give a toss how I speak to you. I think you're contemptible. You've strong-armed him into this, haven't you?' she continued furiously. 'Blackmailed him into selling out to you completely, just as you've blackmailed me into staying on at the business.'

'I haven't blackmailed Simon into anything.'

'You must think I'm totally naïve if you imagine I'd believe that.' She shook her head. 'I know how you operate, Jordan. I've seen you in action. And you disgust me.'

'Really? Am I to take it, then, that our deal is off?'

The quietly spoken words caused a ripple of cool in the heat of her anger. 'If I say our deal is off you'll call the police in.'

Jordan shrugged. 'So the ball is in your court.'

Charlotte's eyes shimmered like cool chips of green malachite in the heat of the day.

'If it makes you feel any better your father is retaining ten per cent of his shares, so you will have something of the family business one day.'

'Gosh! You've allowed him to keep ten per cent. How big of you!' she grated derisively. 'How magnanimous. Shall I kiss your feet now or later?'

'Later will do.' Humour danced in Jordan's eyes for a second. 'I like a bit of privacy when people are kissing my feet.'

'Laugh all you like, Jordan. But you can't exploit people the way you do and get away with it.'

'I can assure you I haven't got away with anything. Unravelling the mess your father was in and buying out the majority of his shares has not come cheap.' Jordan looked over towards the doorway as her father and Ruth came out onto the deck to join them, bringing a tray with the champagne.

'And I suggest if you don't want all the good work that has been done today to go to waste, you paste a smile on your face and wish your father well in his retirement.'

CHAPTER EIGHT

IT WAS early evening as they got into a taxi outside
Heathrow Airport.

'Would you mind dropping me off at Jennifer's house
first?' Charlotte asked Jordan as they settled themselves
back in the seats.

'No problem,' Jordan agreed and gave the instructions
to the driver.

Then he closed the glass partition and sat back beside
her. The same tense silence that had accompanied them
since leaving her father and Ruth enveloped them again.

Charlotte stared out at the grey and gloomy London
weather and told herself that if she never spoke to Jordan
Lynch again, it wouldn't be a moment too soon. And the
notion that she might be in love with him seemed absurd
now; in fact she was starting to believe that in reality she
might actually hate him.

How she had managed to keep up a cheerful front for
her father and Ruth she didn't know, because inside she
had been seething. And her father's graceful acceptance of
the situation had just made her feel worse. He had behaved
like a real gentleman towards Jordan, but inside he must
have been devastated. After all those years of building up
the business it must have been heartbreaking to have it
taken forcibly away from him with the threat of prosecution.

Jordan picked up his briefcase from the floor now and
his sleeve brushed against hers. She moved further away
from him across the seat as if his touch might contami-
nate her.

120

They hadn't stayed very long with her father because Jordan had said he'd some business to take care of in St Tropez. What that business was she had no idea; he hadn't told her and she hadn't asked. She'd wandered around the crowded streets alone, looking into the windows of the smart boutiques and admiring the luxury yachts lined up along the harbour, trying to calm down before meeting him back at the designated café. There was no point arguing with him, she had told herself firmly. She couldn't win.

They had ordered lunch at the café. Charlotte could still see the colourful blaze of the day as the heat shimmered over the smart, sophisticated crowds, the artists on the quay, the boats in the bay. She had studied it all quite intently, determined not even to glance over at Jordan.

It had been the same on the aircraft on the way home. She had totally ignored him and concentrated instead on the work she had brought with her.

Of course, Jordan didn't care. He had actually had the audacity to say he was glad they had got off to such a good start with her demonstrating her commitment to work.

She watched now out of the corner of her eye as he took out his mobile phone and started to make a few calls. They were all work-related, checking appointments with builders and other contractors and finally ringing his secretary Laura to tell her he'd be into the office in the morning.

Charlotte listened to the friendly banter and it just irritated her further. Strange how he could sound like such a nice guy when in reality he was a barracuda.

'Everything seems to be in order in the office,' he remarked as he ended the call. 'In fact they've had a very productive day by the sounds of it.'

'More money in the coffers. You must be overjoyed,' Charlotte replied drily. 'I know how important that is to you.'

'How long are you going to keep this up?' he asked suddenly.

'I don't know what you are talking about.' She kept her face averted from him.

'I'm talking about the stony silences broken only by the occasional barbed remark, as well you know.'

She looked around at him then. 'We had a deal. You said you'd go easy on Dad; you said you'd treat him with deference.'

'And I did. The matter is resolved, Charlotte, so just leave it.'

'The matter isn't resolved as far as I'm concerned. My father is a gravely ill man and you took advantage of that.'

'Yes, your father is gravely ill and he needs to retire. You need to face facts, Charlie—it was that or a premature death. Maybe you should think about that before criticising me.'

She bit down on the softness of her lips and looked away from him again. The truth was she couldn't bear to think too deeply about that at all.

'The right outcome has been reached for all concerned today,' Jordan continued in a more gentle tone.

'Now it just remains for me to break the news to Jen,' Charlotte said quietly.

'Tell Jen what exactly?'

'What's the matter, frightened I might tell her how you ruthlessly grabbed the family business?' For a moment her voice was scathing again, then she dropped the tone. 'Well, you needn't worry. I was referring to the fact that I'm going to have to tell her something about Dad's health.'

'He was quite adamant that you shouldn't say anything to her,' Jordan reminded her.

'I know, but it's not really fair, is it? If something should happen to him—and, God willing, it won't and he'll be fine now—but if the worst should happen it would be a

terrible shock for Jen. I need to say something to pre-
pare her.'

The taxi turned into the street where her sister lived and
started to slow down. 'Anywhere along here is fine,' she
called to the driver and started to collect her belongings.

Jordan reached to help her with her bag and their hands
connected on the handle. The contact sent a dart of awareness rushing through Charlotte's body and she swiftly
pulled away. 'I can manage, thank you,' she said stiffly.

But he didn't release the bag and, as the taxi stopped
and she alighted, he still didn't hand it over to her, but got
out on the pavement beside her.

'Well, goodbye, Jordan; I'll see you in the office tomorrow.' Her voice was coolly dismissive.

'Your car is still here from Sunday, isn't it?' he said,
totally ignoring her words and glancing down the road to
where it was parked.

'Yes…'

'Good. You can give me a lift home.'

His arrogance really grated on her but there seemed little
she could do because he was already getting his overnight
case from the taxi and paying the driver.

'You must be really worried about what I'm going to
tell Jen,' she muttered as he walked with her up to the
front door.

'I'm not worried at all.' Jordan stated with cool confidence.

'It would be a bit of a blow to your ego if I was to dent
your ''Mr Nice Guy'' image, though, wouldn't it?'

'Go ahead, be my guest.'

She really wanted to ruffle that smug confidence of his,
itched to march in to Jennifer's and tell her exactly what
had been going on.

But, as the door opened and Harriet flung herself out to
greet them, she knew that doing such a thing wasn't really

an option. Jordan was too cold-blooded to care what she said and it would only upset Jennifer.

'Uncle Jordan's here! And Auntie Charlie!' Harriet called out to her mother in loud, excited tones, hardly able to wait for Jordan to put down the bags in the hallway before she pulled at his sleeve and he swung her up into his arms, making her giggle helplessly.

'Gosh, you're back already!' Jen appeared in the kitchen doorway and came over to greet them with a kiss. 'We didn't expect you for at least another four days.'

'Call of the office,' Jordan said with a grin. 'Otherwise we might have been tempted to stay.'

'Come on through—I've just put the kettle on.' Jennifer led the way into the kitchen. It was warm and smelt of coffee.

Was it really only two days since she'd last been here? Charlotte thought as she glanced across the kitchen table at Jordan. So much had happened in the interim that it felt like a month ago.

'Did you have a nice time?' Jen asked as she placed two china mugs of coffee before them.

Charlotte carefully avoided Jordan's gaze. 'It wasn't really a pleasure trip—we went to see Dad. There are a few things I need to tell you.'

Harriet was skipping around the table. 'I was painting at school today, Uncle Jordan,' she said happily. 'I painted a picture for you.'

'For me?' Jordan said with a grin.

Harriet nodded. 'I'll go and get it.'

In the ensuing silence as Harriet left the room Charlotte started to tell Jennifer about their father's health. Jordan noticed how carefully she chose her words, playing down the situation enough so that it didn't come as such a terrible shock and answering Jennifer's questions with a quiet calm.

There was only the slightest edge to her tone as she went on to tell her sister that Jordan would now be running the company while their father took things easy in France.

Jordan smiled at her as their eyes connected briefly across the table and for a second her composure slipped and he saw the gleam of fury in her green eyes.

Harriet came running back into the kitchen at that moment, breaking the silent communication between them across the table.

'Here, Uncle Jordan, here's my picture.' She shoved the piece of paper in front of him proudly.

'My goodness, your daughter has hidden talents, Jen,' he said with a grin. 'She could go and take a pitch on the quay at St Tropez.'

Jennifer laughed.

'Show Auntie Charlie,' Harriet urged him excitedly.

Jordan made the sound of a roll of drums with one hand on the table and then turned the masterpiece for Charlotte's inspection.

It was a jazzy impression of blue sea and waving palm trees with two matchstick people, arms entwined, faces close together, wearing heavy black sunglasses and manic grins.

'That's you, Auntie Charlie,' Harriet said, pointing to the figure with wild yellow hair.

Charlotte had to smile. 'It's wonderful, darling.'

'Hasn't she captured the mood perfectly?' Jordan said with a gleam of amusement in his dark eyes. 'And she tells me she has never been to France.'

'That's true, isn't it, Mummy? I've never been to France.'

'No, darling, but maybe it won't be long before you do go because Grandad and Granny Ruth have bought a beautiful house out there.'

'Wow! What colour is it?'

'Pink,' Jordan said. 'And the sea is just outside the windows.'

'Great! I'll go and draw a picture.'

As Harriet hurried off her mother called after her, 'Try not to wake the baby, please, darling.'

Jennifer smiled over at Jordan. 'So, congratulations about the business.'

'Thanks. It's a shame I'll be taking over under such trying circumstances for your father. He did a good job over the years building up the company.' Jordan spoke to Jen but his eyes were on Charlotte. 'I have always respected Simon.'

Hypocrite, Charlotte thought angrily.

'Well, you've got Charlotte.' Jennifer grinned.

'For the time being.' Charlotte couldn't resist muttering the words in an undertone and she knew Jordan had heard her by the way his eyes narrowed slightly with displeasure.

'Dad always used to say she was his right-hand man,' Jennifer continued, her attention distracted by the cries from the baby monitor that was plugged in beside them. 'I had better go and see to her. Why don't you two stay for supper? Steve will be home soon.'

As Charlotte opened her mouth to refuse Jordan spoke for her. 'Thanks for the offer, but we've got to get off. Charlie and I still have things we need to discuss before going into the office tomorrow.'

Was there no end to the man's arrogance? Charlotte thought. He seemed to be taking her over and she hated it. What did he want to discuss with her anyway? she wondered. Or was that just an excuse to get her out of the front door before she said anything else about his so-called 'respect' for their father?

'Thanks for the coffee, Jen.'

'You're welcome. I'll just go and pick Nicole up; I won't be a moment.'

'Nicole?' Charlotte looked across at her sister and smiled as they walked out into the hallway. 'You've had a breakthrough with choosing a name, then?'

'Yes, we've compromised,' Jennifer said happily. 'We'll give her Estelle as a second name, after Steve's mother.'

'That's really pretty.'

'Yes, I think so.' Jennifer started to hurry up the stairs. 'Hold on a moment—I'll just lift her up…won't be long.'

'Are you going home?' Harriet asked dolefully as she popped her head out from the lounge. 'I haven't finished my picture yet.'

'We'll see it next time,' Jordan smiled. 'And there's a little something here for you from France.' He opened the side flap of his briefcase and brought out a small gift-wrapped present with a gold sticker saying St Tropez on it. 'Now, be careful how you open it, there is a little pet inside so you don't want him to escape.'

Harriet's eyes lit up with excitement. 'Thank you,' she said, tearing open the paper.

Charlotte watched with interest as she lifted out a small box covered in yellow and green traditional Provence fabric.

'What is it, Uncle Jordan?' she asked in anticipation.

'Open it up and see.'

Gingerly she opened the lid, her eyes widening in surprise at the sound that issued forth immediately. It was the singing hum of a cicada and inside a little black insect was bobbing up and down in a little dance.

Harriet slapped the lid back down. 'Is it real?' she asked, her face a picture of animation.

'No, it's just pretend. But it will sing for you every time you open up the lid.'

She opened it again to peep inside and once more the sweet sound filled the air.

'That's cool! Wait until I show my friends at school.'

Jen laughed as she returned down the stairs with Nicole in her arms. 'We can all listen to that and pretend we're in the tropics.'

For Charlotte the sound brought back the vivid memory of Jordan's villa, and the way Jordan had held her in his arms that night on the terrace before going upstairs. The memory was so disturbingly intense that she felt her whole body heating up from it.

'He's such a nice guy, isn't he?' Jen said in a low tone as he walked ahead of them to put the luggage in the boot of Charlotte's car. 'I'm so glad that you're hitting it off so well.'

Charlotte made no reply. There was a part of her that was touched that Jordan had remembered to bring Harriet a present…it confused her, threw all the brutal words she had been silently aiming at him all day into muddled disarray.

He was a ruthless, blackmailing swine, she tried to remind herself, but, as she watched him grin in a good-natured way at Harriet as she jumped up and down beside him, the words lacked the fire that they should have had.

'Right. I'll speak to you tomorrow, Jen.' Charlotte busied herself opening the boot for Jordan. She couldn't allow herself to be taken in by him, she told herself fiercely, not when she knew the truth. 'And Dad said he'd phone you, and not to worry, he'll be back in plenty of time for the christening.'

'Do you want me to drive?' Jordan offered as he put the bags into the car.

'No, thank you.' She moved away from him and slipped behind the wheel of her car. At least if she was driving she felt as if she had some control over the situation, however flimsy that might be.

'That went all right,' Jordan murmured as they waved goodbye to Jennifer and pulled away down the road.

'Yes, your "Mr Nice Guy" image is still intact,' Charlotte murmured.

'But not with you,' Jordan said sardonically.

'I know the real Jordan Lynch, remember.'

'You know, I'm starting to think that you quite like telling yourself that I'm a heartless bastard. It's like a convenient safety barrier that you can hide behind, isn't it? Saves you facing up to the fact that there is a very strong sexual chemistry between us.'

'There is no such thing!' That remark sent her blood pressure shooting up. 'The only feelings I have for you are ones of…of distaste.'

'You're lying, Charlotte, you know it, and so do I.'

The calm words made heat frizzle inside her. 'All I know is that you are arrogant and cold-blooded.'

'You didn't think I was cold-blooded the night we made love. In fact, as I remember it you were very enthusiastic…very responsive.'

'That night was a mistake.' Charlotte's hands gripped the steering wheel so tightly that her knuckles gleamed white.

'And when we were at the villa you kissed me with equal passion…you came on to me as much as I came on to you.'

'You know why I did that.' She glared at him furiously. 'I was worried about my father and…and…'

'And you made me an offer. Yes, I remember.' He smiled. 'And we agreed terms.'

The words caused extreme consternation inside her. What did he mean by that? Was he telling her that he intended taking her up on that offer? Would he be calling in payment in kind?

A silence fell between them again but it wasn't the cool one that had been there all day. This seemed to be laced with a raw, intense heat.

She tried to pretend that she wasn't conscious of the way he was watching her now. Tried not to think about that offer, or their kisses, or the disconcerting memory of how much she had really wanted him last night.

'Anyway, emotionally I'm still smarting over David.' She drew her ex's name like a sword to protect herself, but even as she said the words she knew they weren't true.

'Even though he slept with your best friend?'

'She wasn't my best friend…she was just *a* friend.' The cool words caused havoc inside Charlotte. 'And how the hell do you know that?' She swung her eyes away from the road to glare at him.

'It's common knowledge around the office.' Jordan shrugged. 'And do you think you could keep your eyes on the road? I know it's quiet out here but I want to arrive back in London in one piece.'

Charlotte glowered at the road ahead. 'So when you asked me at my apartment what David was apologising for, you already knew?'

'Yes, but I was interested in your side of the story. I just wondered how you felt about him now,' he said softly. 'Obviously the subject is still very raw. But he's not worth being upset over.'

'I'm not upset with him. I'm upset with you for gossiping about me in the office.'

'I overheard it, that's all,' he said coolly. 'I haven't got time for gossip in the office.'

The offhand remark made her even more annoyed. 'You've got time to gossip when it suits you.' She couldn't resist the sideways swipe. 'I heard you telling someone on the phone about how you'd slept with me.'

He frowned at that. 'I have never discussed my private affairs with anyone.' His voice sounded ominously cold now.

'I heard you,' Charlotte insisted firmly. 'It was the

morning after we slept together and you were laughing and saying how you'd invited me in for coffee and got carried away…'

She began to wish she hadn't started this subject now. It was far too embarrassing and the way Jordan was watching her through those narrowed dark eyes was very disconcerting.

'I was talking to your sister,' he said coolly.

She frowned. 'My sister?'

'She phoned to invite me for Sunday lunch. And strangely she already seemed to know what had happened between us because she was teasing me quite unmercifully.'

He watched the consternation in her expression and grinned suddenly. 'So if we're apportioning blame for gossiping here, it seems that you are the guilty one, not me.'

'But I thought—'

'Yes, it's clear what you thought,' Jordan cut across her flatly. 'But I can assure you, Charlotte, I have never got my kicks in that way.'

She flinched. 'Yes, well, you can't really blame me for thinking what I did,' she mumbled. 'You do have a bit of a reputation where women are concerned.'

'Maybe.' He shrugged and conceded the point. 'I decided the day my divorce came through that I wasn't going to fall in love again. And a lot of women have passed through my life. But that doesn't mean I haven't treated them with respect.'

She wanted to make some kind of sarcastic reply to that, but found she couldn't. Jordan must have been hurt badly by the divorce. Maybe he still had feelings for his ex-wife even now? Not that she cared, she told herself fiercely. She couldn't give one fig about Jordan's love life.

'Can you really forgive David for the affair?' Jordan said into the silence. 'And forget about it totally?'

'It wasn't an affair, it was one night.' Her eyes shimmered emphatically as she glanced back over at him. 'You and I of all people should know that doesn't mean anything.'

'Doesn't lessen the pain of betrayal, though, does it?' Jordan said calmly.

'No.' She looked away from him.

But the strange thing was that she was more upset about her friend Linda's betrayal than David's.

They were heading away from the countryside now and the sun was trying to get out behind the greyness of the clouds in a final burst of colour before it set for the evening.

Charlotte paused at a crossroads, wondering which way would be the quickest. She needed to dump Jordan outside his apartment as speedily as possible. She couldn't think straight with him around.

'The road to the left would be best,' Jordan suggested.

'I'm not sure that's the quickest way for you.'

'No, but it's the quickest route back to your place.'

She looked over and met his eyes and the consternation inside her seemed to increase a hundredfold.

'There's a taxi rank around the corner from your place,' he said calmly. 'I'll take one from there; it will save you having to drive across the city.'

Charlotte hesitated for a moment. What he'd suggested made sense. With a bit of luck, and if she put her foot down, she might be free of Jordan Lynch very soon. She turned the car left with a feeling almost of relief. As soon as she was away from his close proximity she would be able to clear her head, think about things objectively— something she seemed incapable of doing around him.

However if she had thought that losing Jordan would be a straightforward and easy manoeuvre she was wrong.

When they finally pulled up outside her apartment he insisted on carrying her bags inside for her.

'OK, thank you very much.' She stood by the open front door as he put the bags down, tried to pretend that she was busy flicking through the mail she had lifted from the floor. But in reality she was trying to make it clear to him that she was waiting for him to leave.

As he walked back over towards her she hoped he was just going to say goodbye and walk out, but to her annoyance he took hold of the door and closed it.

'I thought you were leaving.'

'We've got unfinished business.'

'What kind of unfinished business?' She felt her nerves spiralling as he reached and took the envelopes from her hand, placing them down on the hall table beside them. He was standing very close to her...too close for comfort, and she took a step back, but there was nowhere for her to go. She was pressed against the wall.

'Well, for one thing we need to talk about where we go from here.'

'You go home and I give a big sigh of relief.' She met his eyes and tried to pretend that she was completely impervious to him.

'You see, this is the problem; this attitude of yours isn't very helpful, Charlie. We've got to work together tomorrow and I don't see that it's going to be a very successful union with you glaring at me all the time as if I'm public enemy number one.'

'In my eyes you *are* public enemy number one. You might have bought the business, Jordan, but I'm not part of the fixtures and fittings. I might have to work for you, but I don't have to like you.'

'Such tough words.' He leaned one hand on the wall next to her and bent closer. 'So why is it, do you think, that your lips tell me quite a different story?' She noticed the way his eyes were lingering on her lips and the look made her tremble inside, but not with fear, or distaste or any of the emotions that should have been shaking her; this was desire, pure and powerful.

'I don't know what you are talking about.' Her voice was huskily unsteady now.

'I think you do.' He leaned even closer and his lips were a whisper from hers now. 'I think you are well aware of what I'm talking about.'

She was aware of the familiar scent of his aftershave, delicious and provocative, the powerful body was just inches from hers and weakly she felt drawn to it as if by some magnetising force.

She clenched her hands into tight fists at her sides, determined to fight the traitorous feelings. 'All I'm aware of is how much I hate you,' she maintained stubbornly.

'Hate is such a strong emotion.' He leaned down and stroked a finger over her cheek in a sensual caress. 'Shall we put those words to the test?'

'Jordan, I—' Anything else she might have said was cut off abruptly as his lips moved to cover hers.

He kissed her forcefully, and with such passion that she felt the need for him exploding inside her like a firecracker. But she was determined not to respond to him; she held herself rigidly still, her hands immobile, clenched by her sides.

Then the kisses softened, became seductively slower, compellingly fervent, and without thinking she reached up to rest her hands on his shoulders. Then she kissed him back. She couldn't help herself; the feeling of need inside her was suddenly too great to ignore, the urgent desire he conjured up too powerful.

'That's better.' His tone was husky and filled with a lazy satisfaction, and even as she registered it and told herself not to feed his ego any further but to pull away she found she couldn't. Instead she leaned closer, matching his kisses passionately, loving the thrill of his body pressed against hers.

She felt his hands moving with possessive ease over her and she welcomed them, wanted to feel them more intimately.

Her jacket dropped to the ground and then he was unbuttoning the front fasteners of her dress.

Even as she was telling herself that this was a mistake her body was welcoming him, betraying her again, taking her over so that her mind was clouded and confused, divorced from all rational thought.

Jordan's hands found the lacy material of her bra and pushed it to one side, then his fingers connected with her naked breast, stroking and caressing her until she was incoherent with need, her body screaming for him.

His lips captured hers again in a drugging kiss then moved lower to her neck, his fingers caressing the tight, hard bud of her nipple.

'You see, you don't hate me at all, Charlotte,' he whispered as his mouth travelled upwards to find hers again. 'Shall we go somewhere more comfortable and finish this?' As he pulled back and looked deep into her eyes, all she could do was nod weakly.

She didn't want to feel like this, out of control and needy. All her life she'd been so independent. Letting Jordan affect her like this was risking getting hurt, especially as she knew how ruthless he was. But she couldn't help it. She just wasn't strong enough to pull back.

CHAPTER NINE

THE air was dry and hot in the boardroom and the meeting seemed to be stretching on forever.

Charlotte watched Jordan as he sat in the chair that not so long ago would have been occupied by her father. Strong and resolute, filled with enthusiasm and dynamic new ideas, he was easily generating a feeling of support and fervour in the people who sat around the long, polished table.

The essence of what he was saying at the moment was that he expected everyone to put his or her weight behind him.

Would anybody dare not to? Charlotte thought wryly. Her eyes drifted thoughtfully over him. He looked extremely attractive in the dark suit with a pristine white shirt and silver-grey tie, every inch the successful businessman. Jordan picked up a pen and played with it as he talked, and her eyes moved to his hand, watching him, and suddenly her mind was drifting away from the boardroom towards what had transpired between them in her bedroom last night.

Jordan's hands roaming over her body arousing her more and more, finding the warm core of her womanhood and tantalising her with promises of much more pleasurable delights.

When he entered her she had been gasping with need, her hands raking and scratching over his back, her eyes closed as she tried to concentrate on keeping the exquisite ecstasy alive for as long as possible.

'You're so gorgeous...' he had murmured huskily

against her ear, moving slowly at first, pacing himself and increasing her need for him to such a pitch that she hadn't thought it was possible to feel so much pleasure.

She remembered how she had cried out for him, and together they had capitulated to the wild, blissful feeling of complete satisfaction.

Then she remembered the feeling of shame afterwards as she'd lain cradled against him, her head resting on his chest. She had been ashamed of wanting him so much, of loving him so much, despite the fact that she knew what kind of man he was and that for him this was just sex.

Lying there in the afterglow of love, their bodies hot and tightly entwined, she had thought that she couldn't despise herself enough for this. Yet when he had reached to kiss her again she had kissed him back, and the wild need for him had risen inside her all over again.

She had pretended to be asleep when he had left her bed in the early hours of this morning. Had kept her eyes tightly closed as he moved around getting dressed and gathering his belongings.

He had reached to kiss her on the cheek and she had been filled with a bittersweet sadness, a longing for him to whisper just one word of love, even if he hadn't meant it, just one sweet word. But of course he hadn't and to have hoped for it was totally naïve. She wanted him to feel the same depth of feeling that burnt inside her, because she was in love with him, but the reality was he never would.

Jordan glanced down the table and their eyes met suddenly. The gleam in his eye made her feel flustered and self-conscious. It also brought an answering surge of adrenalin, as desire seemed to appear from nowhere.

'Right, well, that seems to be everything; we'll close the meeting and get on with the day's work,' Jordan said decisively.

Charlotte let her breath out in a shaky sigh as she gathered the papers in front of her and got up to follow everyone out of the room.

This power Jordan had over her emotions was truly scary, she thought. Just one look, one smile and she wanted him with a fierceness that was astounding. She was going to have to take great care at keeping her guard up around him, because if he guessed she was really in love with him it would be mortifying. She would lose the last vestige of her pride and he'd be terribly amused.

'Charlotte, if you have a minute, I'd like a word.' Jordan's firm tone halted her before she could escape with the rest of the staff.

She wanted to ignore him and keep walking but she knew it would serve no purpose. He'd just follow her into her office. And anyway it was best to play this cool, keep up outward appearances.

'Yes, Jordan?' She was delighted at how aloof she sounded, no hint of the turbulent emotion within.

'Sit down.' He pulled out the chair next to him, but she pretended she hadn't noticed and returned instead to the place she had been occupying previously at the other end of the table.

The door closed behind Jordan's secretary and they were left alone.

For a long moment Jordan said nothing, just watched her intently. Her hair was a mass of shiny curls that she had tied back from her face, her skin was pale and yet there was a blush along her cheeks that told him she was not as cool and controlled as she looked.

His eyes drifted lower towards the white blouse, where the lacy outline of her bra was just visible.

'What do you want?' She spoke abruptly, unable to bear the tension between them a moment longer. The way he was looking at her was making her senses reel.

He smiled calmly and walked down the length of the table to perch next to her against the shiny wood surface.

'How do you think the meeting went?'

'You're not seeking my approval, are you?' She couldn't restrain the sarcasm in her tone. 'Because after the way you've gained control here, you are never going to get it, Jordan.'

'I was simply seeking your opinion.' He reached out a hand and tipped her chin so that she was forced to look him in the eye. 'What's the matter with you? I thought we had overcome the problems between us last night.'

'Heavens, Jordan, it will take more than a pleasant roll in the sack to overcome my aversion for the way you've behaved regarding the business.' She jerked away from his hand. 'And please don't touch me—people can see every movement through these glass walls. We don't want to start tongues wagging.'

'Perish the thought,' Jordan said drily.

'Now, if that's all you wanted…' Charlotte scraped her chair back and stood up. 'I've got lots of work waiting for me in my office.'

He drummed his fingers impatiently against the polished table as the door closed behind her. Then watched her moving gracefully through the office with a feeling of complete and utter frustration.

Even though they had made love a number of times last night he still wanted her. Wanted her more than he could ever remember wanting a woman, wanted to tame that fire in her spirit, bring her under his control completely and yet…at the same time when she looked at him there was an expression of such vulnerability that he fiercely wanted to protect her, throw up his hands and tell her she could have anything she wanted, anything.

Charlotte sat back down at her desk. Had that just gone very badly? She wasn't sure at all. All she knew was that she needed to treat the emotions that flowed between them with the same casual ease Jordan did, and that didn't come easy to her. Maybe she had been a bit too cool, especially about last night. Pride was a difficult emotion to balance.

Frank came in and put the plans for the new apartments down on her desk. 'That meeting was interesting, wasn't it?' he said. 'Jordan is a very astute businessman.'

'Yes, he is.' Charlotte couldn't argue with that.

'We are all going to miss Simon, though,' Frank added softly. 'He's been the backbone of this company for as long as I can remember. And he's a good man.'

'Yes.' Charlotte looked up at him. 'Thanks, Frank.'

'What for? I'm only speaking the truth.' He smiled. 'I know this transition period can't be easy for you.'

'No, it's not.' Charlotte glanced over as Jordan left the boardroom, watched as he stopped to talk to one of the secretaries in the hallway. 'But in fairness I don't think it's an easy time for Jordan either,' she reflected softly. 'It will take a few months before we all settle down into the new way of things and in the meantime he will need all our help.' As she said the words, Charlotte realised she truly meant them. All right, she would never admit to Jordan's face that she would support him and work as part of the team wholeheartedly, because to do so felt like disloyalty to her father. But privately she had to grudgingly admit he was good for the company. And if she had to be really honest she knew her father's mind hadn't been centred wholly on work for a while now. In fact, if it hadn't been for him taking Jordan on as a partner, they might all be in a terrible mess.

The acknowledgement turned painfully in her mind. It was something she really didn't want to face up to.

'Well, he's the type of person who inspires confidence, isn't he? I think everyone is with him one hundred per cent.' Frank smiled.

'Yes…' Charlotte reached for the papers in front of her and tried to close everything out bar work.

'When does Jordan want those final figures for last month's sales?' she asked as Frank turned for the door.

'They aren't needed until tomorrow. But he said if you could have them on his desk this afternoon he'd be grateful.'

'OK. I'm seeing a rep in ten minutes and I still have to give my OK on these colour swatches, but I'll do it at lunch time.'

'Fair enough.'

Charlotte glanced across at Jordan's office. A man from the planning department was sitting opposite him now and they were deep in conversation. Jordan had taken off the jacket of his suit and rolled his shirtsleeves up, a sure sign that things were hotting up in there.

She reapplied her attention to the work in hand. The phone rang on her desk and she picked it up impatiently.

'Charlotte McCann here,' she said, balancing the phone under her chin so that she could continue to arrange the swatches on the cards in front of her.

'Charlotte, it's David. Please don't hang up.'

She was so surprised to hear his voice that she almost dropped the phone. 'David, this isn't a good time,' she said, putting down the swatches and pushing a few tendrils of her hair back from her face in agitation.

'I've been trying to get hold of you for days. Did you get any of the messages I left for you?'

He sounded cross, which irritated her, After all, he was the one in the wrong…he was the one who had behaved badly. 'Things are very busy, David, and I don't have time for this.'

'I just need a few minutes to speak to you.' His voice was suddenly pleading. 'For old times' sake, won't you at least give me that?'

Charlotte sighed. She had been meaning to phone him and end things on a civil note anyway, not that he really deserved it. But she realised now that their relationship had just run its course and would have died a natural death anyhow, even without her friend Linda's intervention.

As she hesitated David cut in. 'Look, this won't take long. I'm downstairs in the foyer.'

Charlotte's eyebrows rose in surprise. 'What, here in this building?'

'Yes,' he said quietly. 'And if you don't come down, I'll come up. Because I mean to see you today one way or another.'

Charlotte glanced nervously over towards Jordan; he was still deeply engrossed in conversation. She couldn't face David coming up here, making a scene. What the heck? she thought. She might as well go down and sort this out once and for all. 'OK, I'll be down in a minute.'

She smoothed her hair back and straightened the neck of her white blouse as she moved through to the hallway. Frank stuck his head up from his desk as he saw her walking towards the lifts.

'Where are you going?' he asked.

'I've a visitor in the foyer. I won't be long.'

As the lift descended to the ground floor Charlotte marvelled at how little the prospect of seeing David again mattered to her. But now that she thought about it he had never managed to raise her temperature...except when he'd told her about Linda.

The lift door opened and there he was. Charlotte had always thought David was quite a handsome guy, dark hair, very tall and well built. He was also artistically trendy—the pinstripe suit, mauve shirt and matching satin tie were testament to that. She had always thought he was a strong character too and yet now, as she looked at him, she noticed for the first time that there was an insipid quality about him. Maybe it was the way his dark hair flopped onto his forehead in a style that was slightly too long to suit him. Or maybe it was the smile, or the way his eyes couldn't quite meet hers.

He stepped towards her eagerly. For an awful moment she thought he was going to kiss her and she stepped back.

'Hello, David.'

'Hi. You look good.' His eyes slipped down over her in warm appreciation. 'I've missed you so much, Charlie.'

'I don't really have time for this—'

'Look, I know I hurt you—'

'And this really isn't the time or place,' Charlotte continued firmly.

'But you never seem to be at home these days, and there is so much we need to say to each other.'

Charlotte shook her head. 'We don't have anything to say to each other. Listen, David, I'm not angry…I know now that we were never suited. The glue that held us together as a couple was just our similar line of work.'

'Don't say that, Charlie—'

'But it's true.' Charlotte glanced at her watch. 'Anyway, I'll have to get back to work. No hard feelings, and I wish you well for the future, but please don't contact me again.'

As she made to turn away he caught hold of her wrist. 'I believe your father is retiring from the company.'

'How do you know that?' Charlotte was so surprised that she allowed herself to be drawn closer towards him. 'The staff were only told this morning.'

'You know what this business is like. There have been rumours for a while, so is it true?'

She nodded and then found herself pulled to one side of the foyer.

'Please, David, don't cause a scene,' she whispered, very conscious that they were now the subjects of scrutiny from the women on the reception desk.

'I've got something to ask you.' His voice became low and conspiratorial. 'And don't worry, it's just to do with business, nothing else. A marvellous opportunity has come up with a multinational firm. They have offered me a contract to redesign the interiors of all their hotels. It will mean I'll have to take on lots of new staff. It's the Sheldon group and you know they are worldwide.'

'I'm impressed, but why are you telling me?'

'Well, if your father has retired I thought that would leave the way clear for you to come in on the deal with me. We'd be a great team, and I'd make it well worth your while.'

Charlotte shook her head. 'We couldn't work together,' she said firmly. 'And anyway I'm happy here.'

'Did you ever get those shares that your father talked about?' He watched the colour flood into her face. 'No, I didn't think so.'

'I'll get some shares one day, but I've never been bothered about it, you know that.'

'Yes, I know.' David nodded. 'But I'm offering you a great deal...and mega money. And if you are worried about this getting personal, then don't. It's purely business. I accept that things are over between us. Please, just think about this.' He lowered his voice even more and leaned even closer. 'It's too good an opportunity to miss and I could really do with your talent.'

Before Charlotte could answer the lift doors opened and to her dismay Jordan strode out. He took in the situation at a glance and she saw his jaw hardening, his eyes narrowing. 'What the heck is going on here?' he demanded. 'I've been waiting for those figures, Charlotte—didn't Frank tell you I needed them straight away?'

She frowned. Frank hadn't told her any such thing. 'Those figures aren't due until tomorrow, but I said I'd have them on your desk this afternoon,' she answered calmly. 'I've been busy.'

'I can see that.' Jordan glanced over at David, who gave him a strained smile.

'Nice to see you again, Jordan,' he said brightly.

'I'd like to say the same, David, but these are business hours. Haven't you got any work to go to?'

'I'm on very important business actually.' David smiled. He looked over at Charlotte. 'So what about dinner this evening and we can talk properly about this?'

'Charlotte is busy this evening,' Jordan answered for her. 'Now, if you don't mind, we have got work to do even if you haven't.'

David looked for a moment as if he was going to put up an argument. But one glance at Jordan and he changed his mind. 'OK, I'm going. I'll ring you later, Charlotte.' With a weak smile in her direction David turned and headed through the revolving glass door out into the sunshine.

Charlotte glanced up at Jordan, her eyes shimmering with fury. How dared he answer for her, how dared he march down here as if he owned her? Conscious of how avidly the receptionists were watching, she turned and walked back into the lift with Jordan following. But as soon as the doors had snapped closed her cool vanished. 'What the hell do you think you are playing at, marching down here and ordering me around, and in front of David of all people?' She angled her chin up defiantly and met his eyes. 'You are not my keeper, Jordan.'

'No, but I'm your boss.'

Something about the way he said that made Charlotte flinch.

'What did he want anyway?' Jordan asked coolly.

'He wanted to talk to me over dinner tonight and you had no right to answer for me like that.'

'Oh, come on, you didn't really want to go out with him, did you?' Jordan reached over and to her disquiet pressed the button on the lift, stopping them between floors.

'I think that is my business, not yours.'

'The guy is bad news, Charlie. He's the creep who slept with your best friend, for heaven's sake.'

'She wasn't my best friend,' Charlotte reminded him edgily.

Jordan shrugged. 'I thought you'd be pleased that I came down and got rid of him for you.'

'Well, I'm not pleased.'

'There's an old saying that goes "once bitten, twice shy"; maybe you should reflect on that.'

The arrogant statement fuelled her temper even more.

'Just because we have slept together, Jordan, it doesn't give you the right to tell me what to do in my love life. And for your information the main reason David came around here was to offer me a job, a damn good one at that, working for the Sheldon group, redesigning the interiors of their hotels...worldwide.'

Jordan's eyes narrowed on her face. 'I don't care if he has offered you work redesigning hotels for the entire galaxy. We have an agreement, Charlie. You are committed to staying here, working for me for one year.' His voice hardened. 'Or are you reneging on our deal?'

'I'm not reneging on anything,' she said quickly, the tone of his voice making her instantly regret telling him anything about David's offer.

'So you've told David you don't want the job?'

'Yes...yes, I've told him,' she admitted angrily.

'Good.' For a second Jordan's eyes moved to her lips. 'Because I don't want you seeing David again...in any capacity whatsoever.' The husky admission made her heart miss a beat painfully.

'I want you exclusively, Charlotte.' Then he put his hand on the wall next to her and bent to kiss her. She tried to make herself turn her head away, but it was the same old problem—as soon as Jordan got within a few inches of her she couldn't find the strength to move.

His lips were deliciously seductive and the hand that held her face was tenderly gentle. She felt her emotions swirl and mist with confusion. And then she was kissing him back.

He smiled as he pulled away, his eyes lazily taking in her flushed countenance and the softness of her lips. 'I don't want David coming around here to see you again. Do I make myself clear?' The words were laced with an undertone completely at odds with the words. 'And you will be having dinner with me tonight.'

The arrogance of that request struck the rawness inside Charlotte, stirring it viciously. 'Oh, I see...you mean I should make myself available for you...as per our agreement.' Her voice trembled alarmingly.

She was gratified by the dark look of anger in Jordan's eyes. But the feeling of triumph was short-lived.

'Yes, that's exactly what I mean,' Jordan said coolly.

He pulled away from her and pushed the lift button so that it started to glide smoothly on to the top floor.

'After dinner we will be attending a drinks party. It's an important business occasion, there'll be a lot of our associates present and it will be a good opportunity for us to network with them.'

She might have known that when he had stated he wanted her, he had been talking in the business sense. How stupid—for the tiniest fraction of a second she had hoped he was jealous and annoyed simply because he wanted her, not because of business.

'I'll pick you up at seven-thirty.' The steely look in his

eye and the reminder of his ruthless hold over her made her seethe inside, but she held herself ramrod straight and kept her dignity.

'Fine, I'll be ready.'

CHAPTER TEN

CHARLOTTE was sitting at her dressing table putting the finishing touches to her make-up. She looked a bit pale, she thought, reaching to put a brighter lipstick on. But then she hadn't been feeling well for a few days now.

It was seven weeks since Jordan had taken over the company. Seven dizzying weeks of hard work in the office followed by numerous PR engagements in the evening, each designed to boost the profile of the company.

Charlotte had to admit she had enjoyed the challenges, and she had very much enjoyed being by Jordan's side. Not that she would ever have admitted it to him, of course.

The first night she had accompanied him to dinner and a drinks party she had felt awkwardly unsure of exactly what he expected of her. Their argument earlier that day had simmered beneath the surface of their conversation but as the evening wore on she had found herself forgetting all about it. And Jordan had been a perfect gentleman—in fact maybe too much of a gentleman, because when he had brought her home he had kissed her only once, briefly, and then left her aching for so much more.

That first outing had set the precedent. Each time they had gone out it had been pleasant, but he had made no attempt to move on her sexually.

Of course they had been on business-related trips, and he did have a lot on at the moment. Things were manic at the office; she had never known it so busy. But even as she was telling herself these things she knew she was making excuses. If Jordan had wanted to stay and make love

149

to her when he'd brought her home, he could have. He knew how he affected her, knew she was his for the taking.

Anyway, she should be delighted that he was backing off. He spelled danger; he was callous and calculating. She was better off without him. The words echoed hollowly inside her.

The problem was that, no matter how many times she told herself those things, the words still seemed to fade to cardboard as soon as she saw him. She still wanted him, still loved him. There was something about Jordan that fired her blood, excited her and turned her on in a way she had never been turned on before.

He was bringing her to a promotional party to celebrate the completion of the Richmond apartments this evening. It promised to be an impressive affair, as they were holding it at one of London's hottest nightclubs and various people in the advertising and media world would be attending. Maybe, when tonight was over, Jordan would be feeling a little more relaxed, and when he brought her home this evening he would make a move on her.

Or maybe she should make a move on him?

She stared at her reflection in the mirror. Inviting Jordan to make love to her would be a huge climb-down and she didn't know if her pride would allow it. Even if she did want him so much that it hurt.

If only Jordan hadn't got control of the company by blackmailing her father…if only she could forget what kind of man he really was. He was so lovely in so many other ways, charming, funny, clever, sexy…

But the fact remained that she did know the truth, so it was either accept him for what he was or put him out of her mind forever.

The doorbell rang and she glanced at her watch. That would be Jordan; he was always punctual. Taking a deep breath, she went to let him in.

'Hi.' He smiled at her as the door swung open and his eyes slipped approvingly down over her figure in the blue silk dress, making apprehension and longing twist together inside her in a powerful play on her emotions. 'You look lovely.'

'Thank you.' She smiled back at him. He looked good as well. The suit he wore was well cut and a deep midnight-blue, and beneath it he wore a lighter blue shirt and matching tie. The colours seemed to emphasise the darkness of his hair, giving him an almost Mediterranean look.

Forgetting about Jordan Lynch would be no easy task, she thought unhappily. In fact, she didn't think she would ever be able to get him out of her system.

'Would you like to come in for a drink before we leave?' she asked politely.

'No, better not.' Jordan glanced at his watch. 'I think we should go.'

'Of course.' She reached to get her wrap and her purse and followed him outside onto the street.

'So everything is in place for tonight,' she said brightly as he unlocked the car and she slipped into the passenger side. 'Everyone coming who should be coming?'

'I think so. We've had a pretty good response from our advertisers and we should get a few photos and mentions in some of the top property magazines.' Jordan pulled the car out smoothly into the traffic. 'Tomorrow will be the real test though when the show apartments open for public viewing. Tonight is more about generating a high profile, and entertaining the staff into the bargain.'

'Yes, everyone is thrilled that the venue is The Tank.'

'It's a pretty good club. Have you been?' He took his attention off the road for a moment.

'No,' she smiled. 'I have to admit I haven't been to a club in ages.'

Charlotte looked out at the sunny evening. The trees in

the avenue were cloaked with the heavy fullness of their summer greenery, and flowers tumbled in profusion from window boxes and hanging baskets. People were strolling towards the park in short-sleeved T-shirts and summer dresses. 'I'm probably getting old and boring, but to be honest I'd be just as happy with a drive out to a country pub on an evening like this as with a visit to the top club.' She shrugged and grinned. 'That's very sad, isn't it?'

Jordan looked over at her and laughed. 'Not really. I was thinking the same thing earlier. And if tonight wasn't solely for work, I'd steal you away immediately.'

Charlotte liked the sound of that. 'Maybe we can do that another day,' she suggested lightly.

'Day after tomorrow?' Jordan looked over at her and then smiled when she didn't answer him immediately. 'Sunday…it's your niece's christening. You haven't forgotten, have you?'

'No, of course not.' She shook her head. She hadn't forgotten the christening but she had been hoping he might ask her out tomorrow night. Everything workwise would be completed, well for the time being at any rate, and it would be a Saturday night. It would have been nice to go out with him on a Saturday just for the hell of it—no work excuses, no family excuses for them to be together, just them on their own.

'I believe they've booked a room at a very picturesque coaching house for the party afterwards.'

'Yes.' Charlotte looked across at Jordan. 'You've been talking to Steve recently, I take it?'

'We played golf last Sunday.'

Charlotte glanced down at her hands. Would her family life always be so intertwined with him? she wondered, and suddenly she had a vision of arriving at Jennifer's at some point in the future and finding Jordan there with a girl-friend.

The thought was so horrifying that she felt it slam into her like a fist. Hurriedly she put the image away.

'Steve said your father is doing very well in France, that his health is much improved,' Jordan said as he swung the car into a parking space next to the wine bar where they had arranged to meet some of their co-workers from the office before going on to the party.

'Yes, he's not doing badly at all.' Charlotte smiled. 'He hates to admit it but I think he really is enjoying retirement.'

'Now I know where you get that stubborn streak from.' Jordan smiled back at her.

'You think I'm stubborn?'

Jordan's grin stretched wider. 'Only the most stubborn woman I've ever met. But then your birthday is in August, isn't it, which makes you a Leo? Very obstinate star sign.'

'What rubbish. You've just made that up.' She grinned at him. 'How do you know that my birthday is in August anyway?'

'I looked up your file at work, soon after I joined the company. Found out a few things about you.' He gave her a teasing look. 'First law of the jungle, find out all there is to know about your adversaries, so you can keep one step ahead.'

'So that's where I've been going wrong!' She laughed. 'Obviously I should have pulled your file months ago.'

He nodded. 'Big mistake.'

'So if I had pulled your file, what would it have told me?'

'Let's see: Capricorn, ambitious, tenacious—'

'Ah, but I already know all that. Would it have told me any of your weaknesses?'

'I think you need a private consultation to find that out.' Jordan smiled.

For a moment there was a warmth between them that

sent shivers of awareness racing through her. Then Jordan turned away. 'I suppose we should go in; we don't want to keep everyone waiting.'

Although Charlotte agreed and also turned to get out of the car she couldn't help wishing that they weren't meeting other people tonight. She just wanted to be alone with Jordan. And suddenly she didn't even care if she was playing with fire or not.

The wine bar was doing a brisk trade and at first Charlotte couldn't see any of the people from the office. Then she spotted a few of them behind a pillar.

'Over here,' Frank called. 'And you're late. We were almost off to the club without you.'

'It won't even be open yet,' Charlotte said with a grin.

'Ten-thirty is the time the party is due to kick off,' Jordan said from behind her. 'So can I get anyone a drink?'

As Jordan headed for the bar with the drinks order, Charlotte chatted with Frank's wife, Donna, an attractive woman in her late twenties. 'I can't believe we are going to The Tank for this party,' she said in excitement. 'I've wanted to go there for ages but it's really hard to get in. They say it's *the* place to be seen. Apparently the décor is fantastic; you go down in a lift to the basement and the walls surrounding you are full of tropical fish.'

'Well, I'm looking forward to having a peek at the décor.' Charlotte laughed.

'For heaven's sake, Charlie, you are under strict instructions to switch off from work. No measuring up the windows,' Frank laughed. 'We've done enough of that all day at the office.'

Jordan brought back the drinks and Charlotte reached to take her glass of white wine. As she raised the glass to her lips the smell of the alcohol made her stomach suddenly churn and she couldn't drink it.

'You OK?' Jordan looked across the table at her.

She nodded and smiled and was glad that the conversation carried on around them in a light-hearted way because she didn't want to create a fuss. But in reality she wasn't feeling at all well. She felt a bit dizzy and the nauseous feeling that had struck persisted.

As the men launched into a deep conversation about cricket, Charlotte glanced over at Frank's wife and saw that she was also drinking white wine.

'Is your wine all right, Donna?' she asked the other woman quietly.

'Fine. Why?'

'Mine seems a bit overpowering.'

She watched as the other woman picked up her glass and sniffed at it then took a sip. 'It's fine,' she pronounced, then looked at Charlotte in concern. 'You don't look very well.'

'I'll be fine in a minute.'

Even so, for the rest of the time in the bar Charlotte sat very still, hoping the feeling would pass and not get worse. And she couldn't bring herself to touch the glass of wine again.

Frank swigged back the rest of his beer. 'Hurry up, Charlotte, we should be moving on to the club in a few minutes. Jordan wants us to be there before the photographers arrive.'

'I'm ready when you are,' Charlotte said, hastily moving the glass further away.

'Are you sure you are OK?' Jordan asked her quietly once they had stepped back outside into the air. 'You looked very pale in there.'

'Too many late nights recently.' Charlotte smiled.

'It has been pretty hectic. You've either been working late every night or you've been out with me.'

'At least it's the weekend and we can relax tomorrow and unwind.'

'Well, I'll have to go down to the apartments in the morning as it's the first opening,' he said lightly. 'But you should take it easy.'

They only had to walk around the corner to the club and it was a beautiful evening. Everyone was laughing and joking and Charlotte joined in, trying not to think about the fact that she had felt a bit nauseous this morning as well, and yesterday at lunch time the smell of coffee had really set her on edge.

It was nothing, she told herself briskly. A bit of sensitivity…or perhaps she really was overtired.

A little while later they were amongst a heaving throng of people in a club that was like being in an aquarium, sharks and tropical fish circling around the glass walls in a neon glow of colour. The lighting was incredible: pillars of illumination lit the room, leaving the dance floor and most of the seating in a blue half-light as if they were in a tank under the sea.

As Jordan was caught up with members of the Press Charlotte excused herself and went into the bathroom to check her make-up.

As she walked over to the vanity basins and saw her reflection she got a bit of a shock. Her skin was deathly white and her eyes seemed to dominate her small, delicate face.

'Are you feeling any better?' Donna came and stood beside her and immediately Charlotte busied herself finding a lipstick in her bag.

'Yes, I'm fine; it seems silly really but it was just the smell of the wine.' Charlotte applied more lipstick and gave a sweep of blusher over her cheeks, determined not to give in to the feeling of weakness inside.

'That reminds me of when I was pregnant with Josh.' Donna leaned forward to put on some mascara. 'But with me it was the smell of tea—hell, that was awful. I was sick for weeks.'

Charlotte was glad she had left her hair loose tonight; at least it hid her face a little. Fluffing it up, she tried to pretend that she was concentrating on her looks, not suddenly homing in on the possibility that she could be pregnant.

She was late, now she thought of it, but that could just be stress after the worry of her father and everything. Couldn't it? Charlotte felt a sharp pang of complete panic for a moment.

Luckily Donna was the talkative type and she carried on, blithely unaware that Charlotte was hardly listening. 'I remember a New Year's Eve party as well; I spent nearly the whole night in the bathroom. But that was food poisoning…'

She wasn't pregnant, Charlotte told herself firmly. OK, she was, what, two weeks late at the most? Or was it more? When *had* she last…?

Aware that Donna had said something that required an answer, Charlotte hastily pulled herself together. 'I think I've just got a bug but it's a bit of bad timing to be feeling under the weather.' She smiled. 'What with all these photographers waiting to snap our pictures for the publicity shots.'

'Yes…' Donna agreed. 'I had my hair done at a top salon especially for the occasion.'

'I'll have to hide at the back.' Charlotte grinned as they turned to head outside. 'It's as good an excuse as any—I hate having my photograph taken.'

They stood at the bar for a while and Charlotte started to feel a bit better as she sipped a mineral water. She wasn't pregnant, she told herself firmly.

'Who is that woman?' she asked Frank as she saw an attractive brunette talking to Jordan across the room.

'That's Benita.' It was Jordan's secretary, Laura, who answered the question. 'You know, the model.'

'You mean Jordan's ex-girlfriend?' Charlotte did a double take on the other woman. Now that she looked at her she could see it was Benita. She looked stunning in a long white dress that curved with her slender body and glowed under the neon lights.

'I don't think she likes to class herself as an ex.' Laura laughed. 'She's never off the phone to him.'

Charlotte was very taken aback by that news. 'They are still good friends, then?'

'Oh, yes, very much so. But then you know what Jordan is like—a real charmer.' Laura grinned. 'She agreed to come tonight for some promotional photos to boost the level of interest in the occasion and apparently she's going to do the same at the apartments tomorrow. If you ask me, there might be a reconciliation on the cards.'

Charlotte sipped at her mineral water and tried to tell herself she didn't care, but she was lying, because when she turned around and saw the two of them posing for a photographer, Jordan's arm resting around Benita's waist, she felt a stab of jealousy unlike anything she had ever known.

The music was cranked up even louder and Laura and her husband left them to go out onto the dance floor.

'It's a great place, isn't it?' Frank said. 'I bet those glass tanks around the walls cost a fortune.'

'Yes, I bet they did.' But the truth was that Charlotte was hardly listening now. She shot a glance over at Benita again. There was still a crowd of people around her, but she couldn't see Jordan now.

'Hello, Charlie.' A man tapped Charlotte on the shoulder and, turning, she was surprised to find herself face to face with David.

'What are you doing here?' she asked in surprise.

'I thought everyone in the know would be here tonight.'
He grinned. 'After all the publicity and hype about this
launch party I didn't want to miss it.' His eyes swept down
over her figure. 'You look great, by the way.'

'Thanks.' Charlotte felt a bit embarrassed by the compliment.

'When I didn't hear anything from you I took it you
weren't interested in my job offer,' David said smoothly.

'I'm pretty settled where I am.'

'Shame.' David looked disappointed. 'Well, you know
where I am if you ever change your mind.'

'Yes…'

'I'd better get back; I'm on a date.' David looked over
his shoulder towards one of the tables. 'But I don't think
it's going to last very long; she's not really my type.'

'No one I know, then?' Charlotte grinned.

'No…no one you know.' He smiled at her sadly and
then reached to kiss her on the cheek. 'See you around,
Charlie.'

'Yes, see you around.'

As Charlotte turned back to the bar she was surprised
to find Jordan standing behind her. He smiled at her, a
tinge of irony in his dark eyes. 'At least he succeeded in
bringing some colour to your cheeks.'

'He was just being polite. He's here with a date actually.'

'Yes, I saw her earlier, a pretty brunette.'

'And you've got a good eye for a brunette, haven't you,
Jordan?' Charlotte couldn't resist the quip.

'I'm more into blondes these days.' The quiet remark
and the way he was looking at her made Charlotte's temperature increase dramatically.

He really was a smooth talker, she thought wryly. She
shouldn't fall for it, should have more sense. Yet as he put

a hand at her back, the touch of his skin against hers made feelings of desire instantly surface.

'Come on, let's go and have a few photographs taken together.'

'What's the matter, has Benita had to rush off to another venue?' she asked slightly breathlessly as he steered her over to where he had been standing earlier.

'I think she has.' Jordan smiled at her. 'But not to worry, she'll be back to pose decoratively around the apartments tomorrow.'

'Quite a coup getting your ex to give her time like that.'

'I can be very persuasive when I need to be.'

'Don't I know it?' Charlotte said drily.

She was glad that the photographers joined them at that moment, curtailing that particular line of conversation.

For a while were under the scrutiny of several different cameras, but as soon as possible Charlotte escaped from the limelight, content to watch from the sidelines as more of the office staff joined in.

'Going well, isn't it?' Frank said happily as he came to stand beside her.

'Yes, I'm sure Jordan is pleased.'

'Especially as Benita came. Everywhere she goes she's followed by the paparazzi. So we'll be in a few more newspapers tomorrow.'

'Yes…very fortunate.' Charlotte tried to keep her voice light. 'Where has she gone now, do you know?'

'She's opening a new club somewhere else tonight. Apparently she only popped in here between gigs as a special favour.'

'Lucky Jordan.'

'Yes, lucky Jordan indeed,' Frank drawled. 'Apparently he's taking her out for dinner tomorrow night as well.'

'How do you know that?' Charlotte frowned.

'I was standing next to her when she reminded him of their date. Seven o'clock at La Fortuna.'

Charlotte felt her heart starting to speed up painfully against her chest. So now she knew why Jordan hadn't asked her out tomorrow night. And very possibly why he hadn't been interested in making love to her for so long.

'Maybe Laura is right and they are getting back together again. Fancy that.' It was a tremendous effort to sound so relaxed. 'Our boss is a real dark horse, isn't he?'

'You could say that,' Frank laughed.

Charlotte followed his gaze back towards Jordan, who was now talking to a very attractive female photographer.

Who was she kidding? Charlotte thought angrily. Jordan was no dark horse: he changed his girlfriends with the weather and he had never bothered to deny it.

The stark fact hit her with brutal clarity.

'You know, Frank, I think I'll make tracks for home now.'

'Really? Well, if you hang on Donna and I will give you a lift; we have to be back for the babysitter anyway.'

'No, it's out of your way and I'm fine taking a taxi.' Charlotte glanced back over towards Jordan. 'Will you make my excuses to Jordan for me?'

'Sure.' Frank nodded.

If there was an award going for best acting performance tonight, I should receive it, Charlotte thought as she left the club and climbed into a taxi outside.

And to think it had actually crossed her mind that she should seduce Jordan this evening… Really, she had lost her senses where that man was concerned.

But then, she had always known deep down that this was how an involvement with Jordan would end. If he wasn't seeing Benita it would just be someone else. Jordan didn't believe in long-term relationships, or love. He had told her that very clearly.

So what would she do if she was pregnant?

The question crept in, taking her unawares. And suddenly her mind was flicking forward along a path of vivid imaginings. She saw herself pregnant and forced to work for him, knowing he didn't want her, knowing he didn't love her, and it was an unbearable picture.

As panic mounted inside her she tried to damp it down. She didn't know for sure and it could just be stress. First thing tomorrow she would buy one of those testing kits.

The taxi pulled up outside her flat and she hurried out. As she took her front-door key out of her handbag the sound of a car door slamming and footsteps behind her made her look around nervously.

'Jordan! What are you doing here?'

He glared at her angrily. 'Call me old-fashioned, Charlie, but when I take a woman out for the evening I generally expect to drop her home as well.'

'Well, you were busy and I didn't like to drag you away from the party. I asked Frank to explain.' She felt suddenly breathless as he came closer. She didn't want him to touch her or come anywhere near her because she didn't know how she would react. Her emotions were all over the place.

'Well, Frank didn't explain very much. What's the matter? Are you feeling ill?'

Charlotte opened her mouth to tell him she was fine and then changed her mind. She didn't feel fine at all, she felt terrible. 'Yes, I do feel ill,' she admitted shakily. 'But I'll be OK after a good night's rest. I'm sorry you've left your party because of me and thanks for your concern but you should really go back there now—'

'Don't be ridiculous. I'm not going back to the party. I have no interest in going back.' He took the key from her hand and put it in the lock. 'The media circus is pretty much wrapped up there anyway. I'm coming inside with you.'

'Jordan, this isn't a good idea and I really…' Her protests were overruled as he opened the door and steered her firmly inside.

'So what do you think is wrong with you?' he asked, snapping on the light, his eyes raking over her in a close scrutiny that made her cringe.

'I…I don't know. I'm just not feeling well, that's all…' His forceful manner was really starting to unnerve her. She pulled away from him and put her wrap and her bag down on the hall table. 'I think if you just go I'll be OK in the morning.'

'Shall I make you a cup of tea?' He looked at her with a raised eyebrow. 'How about some chicken soup?' The teasing offer made her suddenly want to cry. She didn't want him to be nice to her; it just made it harder to keep away from him.

'I don't need chicken soup or looking after. I'm fine on my own, but thank you anyway.'

'Are you sure?' He stepped closer and raised her chin so that he could look at her again, but this time his manner had lost that bossy edge and seemed filled only with concern. That and the touch of his hands against her skin made the tears rise. Fiercely she blinked them away.

'Look, you don't need to pretend to be a nice guy around me. I know the truth…I know the real Jordan Lynch.'

'Do you?' He stroked the side of her face with one finger and the gentle touch fired her blood even more.

Suddenly she was remembering what had happened the last time they had stood so closely together in this hallway. And she couldn't let that happen again. As much as she wanted him, as much as all her senses cried out to just melt into his arms, she knew that it was a mistake and that she had to break away.

'Jordan, this situation is killing me, can't you see?' Her

voice broke on a sob and she pulled fiercely away from him. 'I can't go on like this, pretending everything is fine, having to work with you day in and day out, feeling the way I do… I can't be tied to you like this, I just can't!'

Jordan took a step back from her and watched her silently for a moment. Noted the ashen colour of her skin and the tears that spilled silently from her eyes.

For a long moment she thought he wasn't going to answer her. Then he shrugged.

'I'll have to think about the situation,' he said calmly.

'You mean you might be prepared to release me from our agreement?' She brushed the tears away, her heart slamming against her chest as she asked the question.

'I said I'd think about it.'

Then he turned and walked out of the apartment, closing the door quietly behind him.

at her make-up and stared at her blotchy reflection before the mirror and vainly tried once more to put that smile on her well-rehearsed face.

She had never felt so helpless in her life, so unsure of how she could possibly get through the next few hours.

CHAPTER ELEVEN

ESCAPING to Jennifer's house the next morning seemed a good idea on Saturday. She couldn't stand being in her empty flat, and having time on her hands to think definitely wasn't helping. So when her sister rang and asked if she wouldn't mind arriving early for the christening in order to give her a hand with the children, Charlotte jumped in with both feet and told her she'd come straight away and stay overnight.

However, if she had hoped the change of scene would help put Jordan out of her mind, she had reckoned without Jennifer. Because from the moment she arrived her sister asked ceaseless questions about how their relationship was progressing. Questions Charlotte wasn't ready to answer. And her prevarications only invited more questions.

Add to that a violent bout of sickness on Saturday evening and Charlotte started to wish she'd just stayed at home.

But somehow she got through it without having to tell Jen anything. In fact she coped magnificently. Helping to bathe the children this morning, she was laughing and joking with Harriet and even surprised herself at how well she was hiding her unhappiness.

But now, as the time approached for Jordan to arrive, she found herself wishing after all that she had opened up to her sister. She needed to talk to someone, she was confused and upset...and more scared than she had ever been in her life.

It was strange how you could still feel lonely in a house full of people, she thought as she put the finishing touches to her make-up and then stood back to inspect her reflection in the full-length mirror. Her hair was in a soft chignon, a few curling tendrils around her face.

She had lost weight, she noticed suddenly; the pale pink dress that had fitted her so well a few weeks ago now hung loosely on her slender frame. Probably due to the amount of times she had been sick over the last few days. But considering she felt so wretched she looked remarkably well; in fact her skin was glowing.

She heard a car pulling up outside and went to the bedroom window. It was Jordan, and Charlotte's heart started to bounce unsteadily just at the sight of his car. She watched as he stepped out into the sunshine. He looked handsome in a dark suit and a blue shirt and tie, and her heart seemed to twist inside her even more.

There was a part of her that wanted to run down the stairs and throw herself into his arms with the same lack of inhibition as Harriet. But of course she could never do that. She gave herself one final nervous check in the mirror. She would act as if she hadn't a care in the world, as if everything between them was fine, she reminded herself firmly. For one thing she had her pride and for another she couldn't let a whisper of any unpleasantness spoil the christening. Taking a deep breath, she went downstairs to let him in.

Harriet had beaten her to it and was outside on the driveway already, dancing around him in dizzying circles. Then she skipped in past Charlotte. 'Uncle Jordan is here,' she called like the town crier.

Jordan gave an amused smile, but she noticed when his eyes moved towards her how his expression cooled.

'Steve told you I was here last night, didn't he?' she checked. She had got Steve to ring him early this morning in case he had planned to pick her up on the way out here.

'Oh, yes, I got your message,' he said.

'Good. I wasn't sure if you had planned to give me a lift out here and I didn't want you to have a wasted journey.'

Did she sound as nervous as she felt? she wondered.

He didn't say anything to that, but his eyes took in everything about her appearance in one comprehensive sweep as he stepped into the hall.

'You look good,' he murmured.

For a brief moment he seemed too close to her and just the familiar pleasant scent of his aftershave brought a bittersweet surge of emotion inside her.

She stepped back and forced herself to smile politely. 'Thank you.' There was a moment of awkward silence and she was very grateful when Steven stepped out from the lounge and the two men shook hands. After that it seemed everything happened at once as her father and Ruth arrived in a taxi and Jennifer came downstairs with the baby, resplendent in a white christening robe.

Charlotte was glad to see that her father looked very well. He had acquired a healthy tan and the gaunt lines of worry from his face seemed to have faded. Ruth was also more relaxed than Charlotte could ever remember and she looked very attractive in a pale lemon suit with a wide-brimmed hat.

It was a happy family reunion and if things had been different between herself and Jordan it would have been absolutely perfect.

'I hate to break up the frivolity but I think it's time we went to the church,' Steve said, glancing at the clock on the mantelpiece. 'Jordan, will you take Simon and Ruth in your car with Charlotte?'

'Certainly,' Jordan agreed easily.

Charlotte felt relieved that she wasn't going to be left

alone with Jordan. Now, if she could just get through today without feeling sick, she would be eternally grateful, she thought.

There was a hushed silence as they all stood around the font. Charlotte held the baby in her arms, with Jordan by her side, as they each gave their solemn promise to watch over the child.

Then the vicar took the baby from her.

'I name this child Nicole Estelle,' he said.

As the cool water ran over the baby's forehead she gave a little whimper of protest but she didn't cry.

Charlotte's eyes met with Jordan's and they both smiled. If only things were different, she thought sadly, and felt a huge wave of emotion rise up inside her.

Knowing Jordan, she felt sure he would honour that pledge for his goddaughter. She knew he wasn't the type of man to make promises lightly. And he was so good around children...

Trying not to think too deeply about that, she concentrated instead on taking hold of Harriet's hand as she fidgeted beside her mother.

The service was short and then they headed out of the old church with its colourful stained-glass windows into the full force of the summer sunshine.

'That went well, didn't it?' Jordan smiled at her as they lined up outside for a few photographs. 'And I like the name they chose for the baby. Nicole is very pretty.'

'Let's have a picture just with the godparents now,' Steve said, coming over and placing Nicole in Charlotte's arms. Jordan placed an arm around her and pulled her close as they smiled for the photographer.

Steve's mother, a large lady in a pink outfit, waved over at Charlotte. 'You look good with a baby in your arms, Charlotte. Better get a move-on, now.'

Charlotte managed a weak smile in return. She really could have done without that remark.

What would Jordan say if she told him she was pregnant? The question burnt inside her.

She didn't dare look at him and couldn't wait to pull away from him once the photo was taken.

'Right, see everyone back at the hotel,' Steve said as he took Nicole from her arms. 'Your father and Ruth are coming back with us, by the way, Charlie.'

Charlotte felt an immediate burst of consternation. She didn't want to be left alone with Jordan, not now; she wasn't feeling emotionally strong enough for any kind of contact with him.

But she couldn't protest because it would have looked odd, so she swallowed down her misgivings and forced herself to go along with the arrangements. She was being ridiculous anyway, she told herself sternly. It was only a short drive to the hotel; surely she could get through fifteen minutes on her own with Jordan.

The sensible words soothed her until she was sitting next to him in his car and then one glance across at him and she wasn't too sure if she could get through five minutes, never mind fifteen. There were so many emotions racing around inside her.

What would he say if she suddenly blurted out the truth? she wondered. She imagined it in her mind, her voice clear and steady: I'm pregnant, Jordan. I did a test yesterday and it was positive.

She glanced over at him. He looked stern and withdrawn. How could she possibly tell him that? She knew very well he didn't want any serious involvements in his life and you could hardly get a more serious commitment than having a baby.

Hurriedly she glanced away again. The thing was, she really wanted this baby. She would be thirty-three in a few weeks. She wasn't getting any younger and she had always wanted a family. The question was, could she cope on her own…?

And what if Jordan didn't release her from their agreement? As the months passed he was going to know she was pregnant whether she told him or not.

'You're very quiet.' Jordan's voice made her nerves jump.

'Am I?' She gave him a weak smile. 'Sorry, I was miles away. How did things go at the apartments yesterday? Did many people turn up?' With extreme difficulty she steered the conversation away from anything emotive. They still had a party to get through and deeper topics could wait.

'Yes, there was a lot of interest and a few of the apartments have buyers lined up already.'

'That's good.'

'Yes, I'm quite satisfied,' he said. 'We can go on to the second phase of the development now with confidence.'

The words caused a tremor of unease inside her. 'Jordan, I meant it when I asked if you would release me from our agreement.' She spoke very quietly, but her eyes were filled with earnest appeal. 'I know we had an agreement and I really am sorry.'

'Sorry doesn't cut it, Charlotte,' he answered coldly as he turned the car up a narrow country lane leading to the old black and white Tudor coaching house. 'You gave me your word.'

'I know.' Her eyes shimmered emphatically now. 'But you don't really need me at the business—you could function perfectly well without me. There are plenty of good designers out there.'

'Maybe so, but now isn't a good time to be changing the head of the department.' Jordan pulled into the car park and found a space by the front entrance. 'Maybe in another six months we'll talk.'

'Six months!' Charlotte climbed out into the sunshine and stared at him in complete frustration. 'Please, Jordan...please reconsider.'

'We'll talk about this later,' he said with cool dismissal. 'I've got a christening party to attend and I don't want to stand out here arguing about something that has already been settled. I thought you were a woman of your word.'

'I am!' She walked hurriedly after him.

'You could have fooled me.'

The derisive words tore into her. But she could see where he was coming from—she *had* promised. Only things had changed; she was pregnant. How could she stay working for him now?

'I suppose this has something to do with that job David offered you?' he muttered as they walked through the red-carpeted foyer.

'No! As a matter of fact, it hasn't.'

Jordan sent her a look of complete disbelief. 'I'm not a complete idiot, Charlotte. But I must say, I thought after the way he behaved you'd have had more sense than to want to work for him. It just goes to show how women can be totally irrational.'

'Well, that's a sexist remark if ever I heard one. You're not exactly the most judicious person in the world when it comes to the opposite sex.'

'Where you're concerned, maybe,' he conceded drily. He flicked a glance over at her and watched the colour flare under her skin with a kind of lazy complacency. 'I have been more than understanding about some of your family problems.'

'My family problems have suited your purposes very well, Jordan,' she reminded him and then lowered her voice to a furious whisper as they passed some other people. 'You wanted control of the company and you got it.'

'Yes, I did.' He shrugged.

'And a viper would be more understanding. You treated my father appallingly—'

'The fact remains that we had a deal, Charlie,' he cut across her firmly. 'And I'm not in the mood to compromise.'

She would have made some kind of rejoinder to that except for the fact that they had reached the entrance to the wood-panelled dining room where the christening party was in full swing.

A waiter standing inside the doorway offered a glass of champagne to them, and then they made their way across to join her father and Ruth, who were standing next to the buffet table.

Simon beamed happily at them both. 'Tell me, how are things in the business, Jordan?' he asked. 'We haven't had time to talk about it.'

'Everything is just fine,' Jordan answered. 'The Richmond show apartments opened yesterday.'

'I must go over and have a look. We're here for a few days so I thought I might pop into the office to say hello to everyone as well.'

'They'd all like that,' Jordan said easily.

Despite the cheerful conversation around them, Jordan's eyes were dark and serious as they met with Charlotte's a few minutes later.

'I wonder how your father will feel if he knows you want to leave the business?' he enquired in a low undertone.

'He will understand,' she muttered angrily. 'And don't try to pretend you give a damn about how my father might feel.'

She walked away from him to talk to Steve's mother and then carefully avoided him for the next hour or so.

'Everything OK with you and Jordan?' Jennifer asked

once she had mingled with most of her guests around the room.

Charlotte nodded and changed the subject. 'I enjoyed the service; it was really lovely…brought a lump to my throat.'

'Yes, everyone said that.' Jennifer looked proudly down at her baby. 'Nicole was so good; she always is. So what's with you and Jordan?'

The swift change back to Jordan took her by surprise.

'We are not getting on very well,' she admitted.

Her sister laughed. 'Sparks fly whenever you two look at each other, but then they always have. I guess it's what's known as passion.'

'It's what's known as a clash of personalities.'

Jennifer laughed again. 'I can hear wedding bells. That church we've just come from would be perfect.'

Their father came over to join them. 'What are you two laughing about?' he asked, putting an arm around each of them.

'Jennifer is matchmaking again and she's not very good at it,' Charlotte murmured.

'How are things between you and Jordan?' her father asked immediately.

'The business is doing fine. He's very competent, as you know—'

'For once I wasn't talking about the business.' Simon winked. 'He's a good man, Charlie,' he said huskily. 'I always hoped you would settle down with someone like him.'

Charlotte was taken aback by that remark, but Jennifer grinned. 'There you go. I told you so,' she said, happily moving away to talk to one of her other guests.

'You like Jordan, then?' Charlotte asked her father carefully.

'Of course I like him; I've always liked him,' Simon said with a shake of his head.

'But…but what about the way he treated you?'

'What way?'

'Well…he made you sell the business out to him almost completely and you didn't want to.' Charlotte was very confused by her father's total lack of resentment at this. Back in France she had thought he was just putting on a brave face, acting like a gentleman, but now she wasn't so sure. 'I know you needed to retire, Dad, but he was a bit brutal,' she reminded him.

'Brutal? Jordan?' Simon shook his head. 'You've lost me, Charlie. Jordan didn't force me to do anything. I decided I needed to sell up. To be honest, I felt really ill and I didn't want to be at loggerheads with Ruth for a moment longer, so I jumped at his offer when he said he'd buy me out. It was a very generous offer as well, I can tell you.'

'I see.' Charlotte felt shell-shocked by the words. She glanced over at Jordan, who was chatting easily with Ruth now. And she remembered all the accusations she had thrown at him, all the times she had said he was cold and ruthless, and she felt a huge wave of remorse.

'I will give you my remaining shares in the company one day, Charlotte,' her father added softly. 'And I'm sorry I didn't hold on to more for you, but times were just a bit tight.'

'Heavens, Dad, that's the last thing on my mind.' Charlotte looked back at him swiftly. 'I'm just glad that you are happy and you are enjoying your retirement.'

He patted her back and moved away.

She looked over at Jordan again, knowing that she would have to apologise to him, and sooner rather than later. She recalled now how he'd told her he had treated her father fairly. But in her anger she hadn't listened. And because he had forced her into staying on with the company she had assumed he'd used similar tactics on her father—wrongly, as it turned out.

People were starting to leave. She noticed Jordan glancing at his watch. She'd have to go over now and apologise. She took a deep breath and walked over.

'Jordan, I—'

'I'm going to head back to London now, Charlie.'

'Are you?' She felt inordinately tongue-tied.

'Yes.' His eyes met hers directly. 'Do you want to come back with me so we can talk?'

'I…'

He raked a hand through the darkness of his hair. 'Look, if you want to leave the company then you can.'

The sudden words took her completely by surprise.

'You're right, I probably can find some other talented designer to take over the running of the department. If you want that job with David then take it.'

'Oh!' She felt her eyes glistening with tears. 'Well, thank you… I—'

'That's settled, then.' He nodded. 'Look, under the circumstances maybe you'd better not come back to London with me. We'll sort out details in the office tomorrow.'

As he turned to walk away Charlotte felt her heart thundering against her chest.

'Jordan, I'm sorry.' She called the words after him softly but he didn't seem to have heard her, because he kept on walking.

'Jordan.' After a few moments' trying to gather herself together she hurried after him. But he must have been walking very fast because there was no sign of him in the hallway. She was practically running now through the corridors and down to the foyer. There was a group of businessmen by the front door and she got slowed down trying to avoid bumping into them. And she was really afraid that when she got outside Jordan would be gone.

But as she stepped outside into the sunshine she saw him striding towards his car.

'Jordan, wait for me,' she called and raced down the steps.

He stopped and turned around with a look of surprise. 'What's wrong?'

'Everything.' She stopped beside him and looked up into his eyes. 'Jordan, I'm so sorry about everything, about accusing you of blackmailing Dad...' Her lips twisted in bitter disdain. 'That was a dreadful thing to say and I was so...so wrong.'

'He's told you, then?' Jordan asked steadily.

She nodded. 'I really am sorry. I was just so convinced because...'

'Because I blackmailed you into staying with the company.' He finished the sentence for her wryly. 'I know. And I'm sorry for that. You were right in some of the things you said to me. It wasn't a very honourable way of behaving...but I just didn't want to lose you.'

Charlotte felt her throat closing up with a fog of tears. If only he meant that in the way she wanted him to.

She took a step closer to him. 'And I'm sorry for the things I said earlier...about you being a viper and all... I am grateful for the way you acted towards Dad.'

'Don't go overboard, Charlie.' Jordan's tone hardened slightly. 'I don't want your gratitude. I never have.'

She bit down on her lip.

'Look, I'd better go.' He turned away from her to unlock his car.

'Back to London and Benita?' The question slipped out softly.

'London, yes, but not Benita.' He turned and looked at her then. 'What made you ask that?'

'I heard you had dinner with her last night at La Fortuna.'

'Who told you that?' Jordan frowned.

'Does it matter?'

'Well, yes, it matters, because it's not true. I didn't have dinner with Benita. I did, however, agree to meet her and her fiancé at the restaurant to give them the benefit of my opinion as an architect. They are thinking of buying it and wanted to know how big a job it would be to extend the premises.'

'Benita is getting married?'

Jordan nodded. 'Yes, to her childhood sweetheart. It's all over the papers today, but I guess you haven't read them.'

'No.' She swallowed hard. 'Are you upset?'

'Upset? What, that she's getting married?' Jordan smiled and shook his head. 'No, of course not. Why should I be?'

Why should he indeed? Jordan didn't lose his heart, he just moved on to the next conquest.

She shrugged. 'I just thought you might care for her, that's all.'

'You weren't jealous, were you?' He took a step closer to her.

'No!' Pride reared fiercely to her defence. 'No, of course not.'

'So that wasn't the reason you suddenly told me you wanted to leave the company on Friday night?'

She shook her head.

'Sure?' He reached out a hand and tipped her chin up so that she was forced to look at him. 'It's just that I did think we had been getting along together very well recently...and work has been running very smoothly.'

'Yes...we had and it was... I just...'

'Just miss David?' he finished for her.

'Not exactly.' Her eyes filled with sudden tears and she blinked them away furiously, cursing her hormones. Everything seemed to make her cry these days, and she wasn't used to feeling like this.

Steve's parents came out of the hotel and called good-bye to them. Jordan waved over cheerily and then opened the passenger door of his car for Charlotte. 'Come on, get in,' he said. 'I'll take you home.'

'Thanks.' She smiled shakily and got in. 'Just drop me at Jen's house; my things are still there.'

Jordan drove quickly down the narrow lanes and suddenly she realised with a start that they were on the wrong road. 'This isn't the way to Jen's house,' she said.

'I know that.'

'So where are we going?'

'Back to my place.'

She looked over at him with a frown.

'We need to talk properly, Charlie, and if we go back to your sister's place we'll be surrounded by people. We need some time alone.'

She fell silent, and suddenly felt nervous. If Jordan was just going to try and persuade her to stay on at the business he was wasting his time. She couldn't stay, not under the circumstances.

As the miles flicked by she tried to compose herself. Whatever happened she couldn't lose her cool, couldn't blurt out the truth. If he knew she was pregnant it would change everything. Maybe he would feel morally obliged to support her, but she didn't want someone in her life who just felt obligated towards her...who didn't love her.

So she would stay calm and remain firm about leaving the company.

'I have a buyer for my house in France,' Jordan told her suddenly.

She looked across at him in surprise. 'I didn't know you wanted to sell it.'

He nodded. 'I put it on the market when we were over

there. That was what I was doing in St Tropez before we left.'

'Oh, I see.' Suddenly she was remembering his daughter's bedroom, the teddy bears on the counterpane, the pictures on the dressing table…the look of pain in Jordan's eyes when he allowed himself to talk of her. And it added another painful dimension to the fact that she was pregnant with his child.

'So why have you decided to sell?' She hastily gathered herself together, trying to push the memory of that pretty little girl from her mind.

'I just decided it was time I moved on, forgot the past. It's held me back for long enough.'

'In what way?'

He shrugged. 'Since Natasha died and Nadine and I divorced, I haven't wanted anything serious in my life. I've had one meaningless fling after another. I've put business first at every juncture, and relationships firmly second. It's no way to live.'

'What's brought you to this conclusion?' Charlotte tried to keep her voice light.

'I thought that I wanted control of the business more than anything.' His voice softened as he glanced across at her. 'But the achievement feels empty at the moment. And I realise that success and business mean very little to me after all.

'You see, I've fallen in love, Charlotte,' he told her huskily.

It started to rain as Jordan pulled the car up outside his apartment. Large spots hit the windscreen in a sudden summer squall that seemed to echo the mood inside Charlotte perfectly.

'Who with?' She looked at him in dazed astonishment, her mind running through all the women he had so much as smiled at in the last few weeks. 'I thought you said you didn't mind about Benita getting married?'

'I don't.' He turned the engine of the car off and turned to look at her steadily. 'I'm not in love with Benita.'

The drumming of the rain on the roof of the car seemed to reach a wild crescendo that filled Charlotte's senses.

'So are you going to tell me who the lucky woman is?' she asked, her voice almost a whisper.

'I thought it was obvious.' His eyes drifted over her and then lingered softly on her lips. 'I'm in love with you, Charlotte. I think I have been from the first moment I set eyes on you. I was just too stupid, too blind to realise it.'

The husky words took a moment to register with her. She wondered if she had heard him properly. Maybe this was a dream and she was going to wake up at any moment?

'Look, I realise you are in love with David. I suppose I've known that from day one. And I shouldn't have tried to keep you the way I did...that business about making you stay on in the company for twelve months...' He shrugged awkwardly. 'It was a desperate attempt on my part not to lose you to him; I thought that if we were together every day you would get over him...'

'But I am over him,' she said softly. 'I was over David the day you took me out for dinner that first time...the night you took me to bed.'

'But I thought...' He frowned. 'I thought David was the reason you were leaving the business. Especially as you saw him on Friday night—the night you told me you wanted to leave.'

Charlotte shook her head. 'I never loved David. Not really, not madly and passionately and deeply. Not the way I love you.'

The words hung between them for a few moments and

then suddenly she was in his arms and he was holding her so close, so tightly that she could hardly breathe.

Then his lips found hers and he was kissing her with such passion that she felt alive with wonder and happiness.

'I keep thinking this is a dream,' she said shakily as he released her slightly. 'I thought you didn't believe in love any more. I thought that the only person you had ever loved was your ex-wife. And if it hadn't been for the death of your child...well, I suppose you'd be with her now...'

'Natasha's death did put an unbearable strain on our marriage. And soon after, I discovered that Nadine was seeing another man. I thought the affair was a result of her grief; she blamed herself such a lot. Natasha wasn't wearing her seat belt, you see.' He broke off abruptly. 'Anyway, I wanted to try and work through our grief, but it turned out she'd been seeing this guy even before the accident, so I suppose a divorce was looming regardless of what happened to Natasha.'

'I'm so sorry, Jordan.' Charlotte's eyes filled with tears.

'Hey, don't cry; it's in the past and we have the future to look forward to now.' He brushed the tears from her eyes and looked down at her with such tenderness that it made her want to cry all the more. 'Tell me again that you love me,' he demanded huskily.

'I love you so much it hurts,' she said breathlessly.

'And you don't have any feelings left for David at all?'

She shook her head. 'Not one.'

'God, and to think I've been trying to keep my distance from you for weeks to give you a chance to get over him! It's been sheer hell taking you out and bringing you home and not touching you... I've wanted you so much that it's been driving me almost insane with frustration and desire. I tell you, I never realised I had such strong will-power before.'

Charlotte laughed through a haze of tears. 'It's been the same for me. I've wanted you like crazy as well.'

Jordan bent and kissed her and for a long time they didn't speak. There was just the warmth of their kisses, and the bliss of being in each other's arms.

'We've wasted a lot of time, haven't we?' Jordan reflected as he pulled away from her. 'I wanted to ask you out from the moment I joined the company. But you were dating David and I told myself it was best that way—I sensed even back then that you had the word ''serious'' stamped all over you.'

Charlotte smiled tremulously.

'When I heard your relationship with David had finished I could hardly keep away from you. That day when I walked into your office and you were telling someone that there was a new man in your life, I was shattered and I knew without any doubt that I wanted you and had to try to get you.'

'I thought you'd only asked me out to find out if I knew anything about Dad's whereabouts,' she whispered unsteadily.

Jordan shook his head. 'I couldn't believe the bad luck of the timing of all that. You were so angry with me and all I wanted to do was take you into my arms.'

'I didn't mean to be angry with you. I guess I was fighting my growing feelings for you and I was just so desperately worried about Dad.'

He looked into her eyes. 'I know you were…and your fierce loyalty for people you care about is one of the reasons I love you so much.' He said the words with deep feeling.

'So you've forgiven me for all those awful things I said?'

'Absolutely. You will have to pay a few forfeits, of course…extra kisses, that kind of thing.' He grinned at her playfully. 'Shall we go inside and start making up for all that time we've wasted?' he added huskily.

Desire escalated inside her, she wanted him so much. But she needed to tell him that she was pregnant before they went any further.

She hesitated, trying to find the right words, suddenly feeling very shy.

'Come on, let's get inside while this rain has abated a little.'

Before she could stop him Jordan reached for the door handle and stepped out of the car.

There was nothing for it but to follow him. She'd tell him immediately they were inside, she told herself as they ran hand in hand through the rain. But once they were in the privacy of the lift Jordan started to kiss her with such a forceful, hungry passion that she was powerless to do anything but kiss him back.

When the doors opened he led her across the corridor and in through the door of his apartment with an impatience that made them both laugh breathlessly.

'Now, where was I?' he asked as soon as the door closed behind him. 'Somewhere about here, wasn't it?' He reached and found the sensitive area of her neck that he had been kissing in the lift. 'Or was it here?' he murmured, kissing her cheeks, her eyelids, her lips.

Instinctively she put her arms up around his shoulders, leaning closer, matching the kisses and loving the thrill of his body pressed close against hers. Then he picked her up and carried her through to his bedroom.

'Jordan, there is something I need to say,' she said nervously as he put her down on the bed.

'There's something I need to say as well,' he murmured, his hands moving with possessive ease over her body. She welcomed them, wanted to feel them more intimately. Her jacket was thrown to the floor and she felt his fingers brushing against her bare flesh as he drew the zip at the back of her dress down.

She quivered helplessly as his mouth left her lips to trail a string of kisses down her throat.

'This is really important,' she whispered, although a part of her wanted to just forget words and continue like this with seduction and warmth and sensations of love. But she had to tell him the truth and she had to tell him now.

'Jordan.' She pulled back from him. 'Jordan, I'm going to have your baby.' She blurted the words out before she lost her courage and she felt him go still beside her.

'I'm pregnant,' she whispered, looking into his eyes with apprehension.

To say he looked shocked was an understatement.

'It was a shock for me as well,' she murmured unsteadily. 'It was the reason I asked you to release me from our agreement. I was so scared and I didn't want you to feel trapped or obligated in any way. I still don't... Jordan, say something,' she whispered in anguish. 'I should have told you this downstairs in the car, shouldn't I?'

'You should have told me straight away,' he said gruffly.

'I only found out yesterday myself. But I'm really pleased about it...' Her eyes filled with tears. 'I really want to have your baby.'

'Oh, God, Charlotte.' He gripped her to him, holding her so tightly she could barely breathe.

'Does this change the way you feel about me?' she whispered tremulously.

'No! Why should it?' He pulled back from her then and she saw that his eyes were fervent with emotion. 'I love you, Charlotte, and having a baby together will be the most wonderful joy in the world to me.'

Suddenly they were kissing passionately, holding each other as if they would never let go. Charlotte was so relieved and her heart was so full of happiness she felt it was going to explode.

'I love you so much,' she whispered unsteadily. 'More than words can say. Will you make love to me?'

He stroked her face with one teasing, delicate finger. 'Only on one condition.'

She pulled away from him and looked at him with puzzlement.

'Say you'll marry me,' he said softly. 'Say you'll marry me as soon as we can possibly arrange it.'

She swallowed hard on a tight knot of emotion in her throat. 'Are you asking me this because I'm pregnant?' she whispered. 'Because—'

'I'm asking you because I love you, Charlotte.' He cut across her firmly. 'I love you and I want to spend the rest of my life with you.'

She brushed away the tears from her face. 'In that case the answer is yes, Jordan, let's get married.'

Jordan pulled her down with him so that they were lying on the bed. 'Now, where were we?' he murmured playfully, reaching to kiss her again.

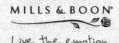

MILLS & BOON®

Live the emotion

Modern
romance™

THE CHRISTMAS BRIDE *by Penny Jordan*

Silas Stanway is furious! How did he end up playing escort to a woman called Tilly at a Christmas wedding in Spain? Silas thinks Tilly will be scheming, and a little desperate. He finds he's wrong — but he's still convinced that if she needs to hire a man, well, she…needs a man…

RELUCTANT MISTRESS, BLACKMAILED WIFE
by Lynne Graham

Katie didn't want Greek billionaire Alexandros Christakos back in her life. But the choice between her pride or the gutter pushed her to ask for his help. Her baby sons came first, and introducing them to their father didn't mean she had to fall back into Alexandros's arms…

AT THE GREEK TYCOON'S PLEASURE
by Cathy Williams

An accident has confined Greek tycoon Theo Andreou to a stay in Cornwall. Initially reluctant, he changes his mind after meeting feisty Sophie Scott. If Theo seduces her — an art in which he is very experienced — his recovery will at least be pleasurable!

THE VIRGIN'S PRICE *by Melanie Milburne*

Bryn Dwyer needed a wife — temporarily. Bryn was offering a lot of money, which hot-headed Mia Forrester seemed happy to accept. But he was unaware of why she needed to accept his proposal and cash — or that he had employed a virgin as his bride!

On sale 1st December 2006

Available at WHSmith, Tesco, ASDA, Borders, Eason, Sainsbury's and most bookshops

www.millsandboon.co.uk

All you could want for Christmas!

Meet handsome and seductive men under the mistletoe, escape to the world of Regency romance or simply relax by the fire with a heartwarming tale by one of our bestselling authors. These special stories will fill your holiday with Christmas sparkle!

On sale 6th October 2006

On sale 20th October 2006

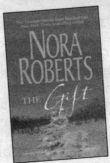

Unwrap three gorgeous men this holiday season!

For three women, the Christmas holidays bring more than just festive cheer – even as they try to escape the holiday celebrations and forget about absent partners or failed relationships.

What they don't realise is that you can't escape love, especially at Christmas time…

On sale 17th November 2006

www.millsandboon.co.uk